With Liberty & Justice

Books in the Taylor Family Saga

Historical Fiction:
Grace Falling Like Rain
Mercy's Face
Torn Asunder
The Last Key
With Liberty & Justice

Contemporary Fiction:
Anchor Point

With Liberty & Justice

Donna Van Cleve

Two Story Publishing House
Taylor, Texas

With Liberty & Justice

Published by
Two Story Publishing House
Taylor, Texas

Copyright ©2015 by Donna Van Cleve
Published February 2016
www.donnavancleve.com
Email: donna@donnavancleve.com

This book is a work of fiction. Names, characters, places and incidents are the products of the author's imagination **or** are used fictitiously.

Publisher's Cataloging-in-Publication Data

Van Cleve, Donna C.
    With Liberty & Justice / Donna Van Cleve
    336p. cm.
    ISBN 978-1-936816-06-4 (pb)
        1. Politics – Texas – History – Fiction. 2. Racism –Texas –
Fiction. 3. Romance – Fiction.

                    2015914184

Cover Photo by *Nessa Dee*
https://www.behance.net/nessadeeart

Back Cover Photo (PD) Credit:
Austin Public Library
Texas Historical Society

Acknowledgments

Our Creator

Nessa Dee
for the cover photo

Finn Roeder
for being such a trooper

Mary Jan Jenkins
for your sharp eyes & insight

Jack Van Cleve III
for giving me the gift of time to write

Lisa Bogan
for your sharp eyes

&
Francis Bellamy
I borrowed his words for this book's title

Thank you, all.

For the original Sisterhood of the Comfy Socks:
Vanessa
Audrie
Christy
Susan

my real sister Joy

& my traveling pants (I'm talking respiratory) sisters:
Mary Jan Jenkins
Janet Crain
Cindy Dromgoole
& Amy Koenning

Thank you for supporting me in so many ways.
You are all so loved.

Austin, Texas... January 1902

Jack climbed up on the shoeshine stand and propped his boots on the footrests. He pried his finger inside the stiff collar to relieve some of the chokehold as he casually glanced from right to left.

The older man began wiping the dust off Jack's boots.

"She ain't come by yet."

Jack's olive skin flushed a shade darker. "What?"

"I used to see you once a week, but you showed up every mornin' this week like clockwork whether your boots needed polishin' or not."

"Then you ought to charge me half," Jack countered with a grin.

"How you doin', Mr. Jack?" the older man asked, chuckling.

"I'm doing all right, Justus; how 'bout you?"

"I got my health; I got my family; I got my faith; life is good."

"You're the happiest man I know. And you're content shining shoes for a living?"

Justus smiled as he reached in the drawer for the blacking can. "It's all in the way you look at it, sir. I'd rather be doin' this than choppin' and pickin' cotton, and I've done plenty of that in my lifetime."

"Well, you're smart enough to be doing more than this."

Justus's smile faded. "I hope my kids have more opportunities than I had."

Jack nodded, but felt a prick of discomfort at that statement.

"Hey, when you go to the House, don't forget us, all right?" He started smearing the blacking onto the boot leather. "And I'm not complainin' for myself. I did the best I could with what I had. I just want better for my kids."

"I'll try to remember that. Where'd you get your name, by the way? My uncle's name is Justin, but I've never heard of *Justus* used as a name before."

"Momma heard it somewhere. She always said a name should mean somethin'. I named my daughter *Liberty*. And I've given my boys honorable names—names that's connected with somethin' good."

"I never thought about that." Jack looked across the street at the Driskill Hotel and checked his pocket watch. "Do you know her name?"

Justus shook his head. "She's just the paper lady to me."

"She buys newspapers from the paperboys and gives them to you."

Justus nodded.

"She doesn't even bother to read them?"

Justus shook his head. "I think she's just helpin' 'em out."

"Do you read?"

Justus glanced around before nodding his head.

"From school?"

"Nah, I've worked for as long as I can remember, but my mother's mistress taught her, and Momma taught me. My kids know how to read, too," he said proudly, wiping the excess polish off the boots. "The Freedman's School closed down before my kids were old enough to attend, but we had our own school, and one of my sons went on to Tillotson College."

"You must be proud of them. My grandmother constantly put books in my hands. She told me I could get a whole other education just from reading."

"We have a few books, but the kids read them so much they've fallen apart."

"There she is," said Jack, grabbing a worn page of the *Democratic Statesman* from below. He stared at it intently for a moment, but couldn't help cut his eyes to the side to watch the young woman walking towards them.

Her sturdy beige jacket and skirt were unadorned; her waist slender. Her straw hat seemed more practical than stylish, and she carried a sturdy, black satchel that matched the color of her shoes. Her raven hair twisted into a simple bun at the nape of her neck. Her skin looked tanned in contrast to her light-colored clothing.

Jack wasn't sure why she fascinated him so. She looked nothing like the socialites who flocked the political and charitable fundraisers around town.

The young woman stopped and spoke to a paperboy and placed something in his hand in exchange for a newspaper. She turned and walked toward the shoeshine stand.

Jack folded the paper and turned his attention to Justus's rhythmic movements with his buffing cloth, popping a beat to a song he was humming. By the time the woman came near, Justus added words to his song. She stopped and listened, along with several other passersby.

Jack's eyes traveled to her face, pleasantly lost in Justus's deep voice resonating off the building front. After a moment, she looked up at Jack, startling him with the color of her eyes— gray, maybe? She smiled before looking back at Justus, who'd added some quick turns and foot movements to his performance. At the end of the song, everyone applauded.

The woman stepped up to Justus and handed him the newspaper. "That was wonderful!"

"Thank you, ma'am. I 'preciate that."

Jack liked the sound of her voice, low and sure of herself.

"I didn't know your talents were so diverse… may I ask your name?"

"Yes, ma'am. It's Justus, ma'am… Justus Johnson."

"I'd tell you my name, but you probably can't pronounce

3

it, and I'm sure you won't remember it. But it's nice to make your acquaintance, Mr. Johnson," she said, starting to leave.

Justus glanced up at Jack sitting there with his feet still perched on the footrests. "Oh, and this is Mr. Jack Taylor."

Hearing his name triggered movement. Jack almost tripped trying to climb down and remove his hat at the same time.

"Pleasure to meet you, ma'am."

"Actually, it's *Miss.*"

"Tell me your name—I'm good with names."

"Synatzske."

"Excuse me?"

"Synatzske," she repeated, giggling a bit.

Jack thought her name sounded something like a sneeze, but her laughter tickled his ears like a wind chime.

"I must be going," she said, glancing at his feet. "Shiny boots." She smiled again before walking away.

Jack stood there frozen like a lamppost, watching her until she stepped through a doorway in a building on the next block.

Justus popped him lightly with his rag. "You gonna be late to work, sir."

Jack turned and grinned as he donned his hat. "She's beautiful, isn't she?"

"Yeah, but I think she noticed you're about to wear the leather through with your daily shines."

"You really think she noticed me before now?"

Justus laughed. "How can she hep' it? You sat here saggy-jawed every mornin' this week watchin' her walk by."

Jack looked back down the street. "What's that building she goes into every day?"

"I think it's Dr. Gilbert's office."

Jack turned and looked wide-eyed at the older man. "My cousin knows the Gilberts—especially his wife! They're coming through Austin in a couple of weeks—maybe they can…" He paused in mid-thought. "You don't think she's sick, do you? She didn't look sick."

"Maybe she's one of those people who think they're always sick, but it's all in their mind."

4

Jack frowned. "Nah, I don't think so. Now what was her name? Snoutski, no, it was more like Sintosksi, wasn't it?"

"Heck if I know. But you'd better hold off getting' your shoes shined for a couple of days, or she's gonna figure you're trackin' her."

Jack looked insulted. "I've never chased a girl in my life—never had to."

Justus chuckled. "I can understand that, Mr. Jack—you're a comely young man. But take my advice, son. Slow down and see if she makes the effort to look for you; then you'll know she's interested."

A man walked up and climbed into the chair, grabbing the fresh newspaper out of Justus's hand.

"Good morning, sir!" Justus said. "How 'bout the best shine on Brazos Street! I'll see you later, Mr. Jack."

Jack nodded and walked across the street, avoiding a wagon and a couple of carriages as he thought about what Justus said. When he reached the entrance to the Driskill, he turned and looked down the street again, trying to think of a reason to visit Dr. Gilbert. He took a quick inventory of himself, but nothing hurt other than the faint discomfort of a bruised ego when it finally dawned on him that Justus was right.

He *had* been tracking that woman.

J ack took off his hat, straightened his shoulders, and started
to walk into through the door of the Driskill when a young
man plowed into him.

"Excuse me?" Jack said, frowning.

The distracted man mumbled an apology and stepped
back, allowing Jack to walk in first.

Jack nodded, but couldn't help but notice the man's eyes--
red-rimmed and anguished.

"Are you all right?"

The man looked surprised, then averted his eyes. When
Jack paused, the man turned around and walked away.

Jack stepped into the lobby and turned his focus on
meeting his employer for their usual Thursday morning
breakfast. He reminded himself of his responsibilities to Jarvis
Baldwin, and chided himself about the lack of self-control
when it came to that woman. A future statesman for the great
state of Texas had to exhibit discipline and restraint, to be
above reproach.

He didn't even know who she was. His mind started racing
with ideas of how he could see Miss Snutski in a proper
fashion—a fundraiser, a social event—one of the inaugural
balls coming up? No, Mr. Baldwin would keep him too busy
politicking at those functions. What else was going on this
month? The Opera House! Somebody was bound to be

performing some vibrato-laden something or other, and Mr. Baldwin had box seats. Jack could procure tickets for his cousins and the Gilberts and Miss Snoski. He didn't much care for the opera, but no matter; his attention would be elsewhere.

Jack was through the lobby and at his boss's table before he realized it. The smile slid off his face when he noticed Jarvis Baldwin wasn't alone. His lead lawyer Link sat across from him.

"Good morning, sirs."

"What are you walking in here all happy about this nice, cool morning?" Jarvis asked.

"Nothing—life is good; that's all," he said as Justus's words echoed in his mind. He pulled out a chair and sat down.

Link spoke up. "It wouldn't have anything to do with a certain lady I saw you talking to a few minutes ago on the street, would it?"

Jack could feel the heat climbing up his face again. "Of course not!"

Link snorted. "You'd never make it as a trial lawyer, Jack. You can't lie worth a damn."

"I don't think lying ought to be a skill any lawyer should have to learn."

Link groaned. "Have you forgotten everything you learned in law school? Has he learned nothing from us, JB?"

Jarvis merely smiled. "It's going to be refreshing to put an honest man in the House. But first you must really know yourself, Jack, know where you stand on every issue, and then go after it with everything you've got."

"And if you're convinced you're on the right side," added Link, "sometimes the end justifies the means."

Jack frowned. "I have a problem with that, too."

Link frowned back. "Good grief, Taylor, this is basic trial advocacy. What if you're representing a guilty person? Are you going to forfeit the case?"

"I don't think I could represent a guilty person."

"Everyone has a right to a fair trial, so pre-judging your client isn't the issue. A lawyer represents his client's side—right or wrong has nothing to do with it. Abe Lincoln was a master at this; he could win either side of a case, no matter what he believed."

"Good point," said Jarvis. He looked at Jack. "Think of it as a debate to be won, not a matter of right or wrong."

Jack shook his head. "I can't help it—I have to believe in who and—"

"Whom," Link corrected him.

Jack glared at him. "—in WHOM and what I'm defending."

Link looked at Jarvis. "Then maybe Jack's not our man."

"Of course he is! Look at him. He's a natural politician--people love him. And he comes from good stock."

"He's an idealist, and he needs a lot more experience, JB. Politics is a nasty business, and his opponents are going to eat him alive."

"We'll let him find out what it's like to skin his knuckles before his first campaign."

Jack hated it when they started talking like he wasn't even there. Link played the devil's advocate, usually against him. But Mr. Baldwin always took his side, and he wasn't sure why. He knew the man had moved to Austin only five years ago and was considered one of the most powerful men in the city today, although his name wasn't on any buildings, and he never held an elected position. He preferred to keep a low profile—*the power behind the throne,* he commented jokingly one time.

Jack had never heard of Jarvis Baldwin until several years ago when he received a letter offering him a scholarship to earn his law degree from the University of Texas. Jack jumped at the chance to move to the capital city. His parents, Jimmy and Mercy Taylor, raised horses and cattle in Grace, Texas. He enjoyed growing up in their small hometown outside of Waco, but he knew he wanted more than that in life. He was twenty-four now, and his future looked very bright.

Soon after Jack arrived in Austin he met his benefactor, who offered him a part-time job in his law firm while Jack worked on his law degree. Jack asked Mr. Baldwin how he learned about him and why he chose to honor him this way.

Mr. Baldwin told him he had his ways and his reasons and *to never look a gift horse in the mouth.* Jack had heard that quote all of his life, so he just accepted his good fortune and regularly thanked God that Mr. Baldwin plucked him out of obscurity and began grooming him to run for public office. The idea of making a difference in people's lives proved a very appealing carrot hanging in front of his future. Mr. Baldwin showed him that a career in government service could do just that, and on a larger scale than he could ever imagine.

Baldwin owned a home near the upscale Bremond Block, but he kept a corner room in the Driskill Hotel where he spent most weeknights after working late into the evenings. Jack knew little about Baldwin's past; he never saw any photographs of the man's family at his home. He felt comfortable around Baldwin, but not comfortable enough to ask him about his life before Austin. He seemed to be well traveled and well read, though, and could hold his own with most any subject. His personal library at home was impressive, and he generously allowed Jack to borrow any of the books and encouraged him to read every chance he could.

Jack caught the waiter's eye and held up his empty coffee cup. "You two can debate all you want over this piece of meat called *me*, but I'm ordering breakfast."

Link guffawed at that statement. "I have to admit the boy has potential, JB."

Jarvis smiled at Jack. "I'd say we'll have him in office by '04."

"Less than three years—we have our work cut out for us."

The waiter walked up and filled Jack's cup with coffee. When he stepped away, another man stepped forward.

Jack recognized the same young man who had run into him in front of the Driskill.

"Hello, Ashton. Do you know who I am?"

Jack noticed he was speaking to Mr. Baldwin.

Jarvis Baldwin calmly wiped his mouth before answering. "I haven't the slightest idea who you are or to whom you are referring."

"Then let me refresh your memory," the man said, barely containing his anger. "You destroyed my family eight years ago when you cheated my father out of the company it took him a lifetime to build. He hung himself three days before we were evicted from the house I grew up in. I was only fifteen years old when I found him swinging from the rafters in the attic."

"Enough!" Jarvis said. "I'm sorry for your loss, but I don't have to sit here and listen to your false accusations."

"It was two days before we found him," the man said bitterly. "The smell finally led us to him."

Jack could see the young man trembling, but it wasn't from fear.

Jarvis turned to Jack. "Escort this stranger outside before Link gets the law over here." He turned back to the young man. "And you don't want to mess with the law around here, boy."

"I know exactly who you are, Ashton," the man continued, "whether you remember me or not."

Jack started to stand, but the man shoved him back in his seat as he reached in his pocket and pulled out a pistol, aiming point-blank at Jarvis Baldwin.

Jack lunged as the pistol exploded.

J ack tackled the man and grabbed for the pistol. They both fell hard as the gun fired again. Jack was oblivious to the chaos of people screaming and knocking over chairs trying to get out of the restaurant.

The man was shorter than Jack, but it felt like he was wrestling an angry bull thrashing around on the floor. Two more shots were fired, and Jack felt a searing pain in his left arm.

That made him mad, so he butted the man in his face, which bloodied his nose and addled him long enough for Jack to jerk the pistol out of his hand. When the young man grabbed for it again, Jack held it out of his reach and yelled in his face.

"Stop! It's over!"

Their eyes met as the gun went off again, opening a dark hole in the young man's temple. His eyes dulled to unseeing, and his body stilled beneath Jack.

Jack looked at the pistol in his right hand. His finger wasn't even on the trigger. He tried to push himself away, but his left arm refused to do his bidding.

Suddenly Jarvis dragged him off of the dead man. When Jack cried out in pain, Jarvis stopped and took the pistol out of his hand and set it on the table before opening Jack's suit coat.

"You're bleeding!" He looked around and yelled for someone to fetch the doctor. "Link's gone to get the marshal."

Jack sat on the floor staring at the lifeless body. He had seen dead people in coffins at funerals, but never this close, and never this violent. He scooted back across the floor until he could go no farther, butting up against the wainscoting.

Jarvis followed him. "Let's take your coat off and get a look at your arm."

Jarvis quickly pulled the sleeve off Jack's right arm and then carefully pulled the coat off the left. The arm hung loose by his side and his white shirt quickly absorbed the spreading red stain. Jarvis started ripping the buttons off, and Jack reached with his right hand to stop him.

"This is my best shirt," he said numbly.

"I'll buy you another damn shirt." Jarvis pulled it off Jack's shoulder to find the bullet wound. Blood ran from a hole in his upper arm.

"Bring me a towel or something!" he shouted to some men standing over the body.

Jack watched someone hand Jarvis several cloth napkins from a nearby table. He pressed a folded one against the wound and shook one open to tie it around his arm. Jarvis tightened the knot and Jack cried out again, but then he turned back to stare at the body.

"Don't look over there." Jarvis leaned in to block his view. He gently touched Jack's good shoulder. "I think your arm's broke, Jack. The doctor ought to be here any minute."

A crowd began to gather. Jack couldn't tell if minutes or hours had passed, but Justus suddenly appeared in front of him. Justus and Miss Snetsky.

What was she doing here? Does the sound of gunshots carry that far? Jack thought as he stared at her gray eyes.

"Excuse me, sir," she said to Jarvis, "but I need to get where you are."

I must've made a better impression than I thought earlier, Jack thought to himself. Everything and everyone around her faded away.

Jarvis glared at her. "What for?" He turned to Justus. "Where's the doctor, Justus?"

"She *is* the doctor, sir," said Justus, glancing at Jack.

Jack's eyes widened.

"Go back and get Dr. Gilbert," said Jarvis.

The woman spoke up. "Dr. Gilbert is delivering a baby, so if you'll excuse me, I can help Mr. Taylor."

Jarvis frowned at her before holding out a hand to Justus. "Help me up."

Justus pulled him to his feet.

"Everybody get back and let the woman check him out." Jarvis turned to meet Link and several lawmen pushing through the crowd. He met them over by the body.

Jack whispered loudly to Justus, "I knew she wasn't a hypochondriac."

"What?" she asked.

"I think he's a little addled, ma'am," said Justus.

Jack watched the *doctor* untie the napkin to look at the wound.

She looked up in alarm. "You've been shot?!" She leaned him forward to look for an exit wound in the back. "It passed through. Can you lift your arm?"

Jack winced as he tried, but he couldn't lift it.

She carefully felt his arm near the wound. "The bullet must've nicked the humerus, but it doesn't feel like the bone separated. I still need to clean it out good, stitch it up and immobilize your arm." She looked around at the crowd of people. "Justus, would you please let somebody know that we need to take Mr. Taylor out of here so I can properly treat the wound?"

"Yes, ma'am."

She gently retied the napkins around his arm, and laid her hand on his bare chest.

Jack almost jumped at the touch, intensely aware of her hand over his heart.

"You're pale as a ghost, and your heart is about to beat out of your chest," she whispered. "What happened here? Who shot you?"

Jack swallowed, trying to think of a logical explanation. "A man tried to shoot Mr. Baldwin, and I tried to stop him."

She turned around and saw a man lying on the floor. She looked back at Jack. "Is he dead?"

"I think so."

"Maybe I'd better go check. Is anyone else injured?"

"I don't know."

She stood up and walked over to Justus, who was waiting patiently to get Mr. Baldwin's attention. The group of men parted for her.

"Mr. Baldwin, is there anyone else that needs my attention?" She looked down at the man at their feet.

"No, he just needs an undertaker. How's Jack?"

"The wound needs a few stitches, and it looks like his arm is fractured, and I'd like to take care of that away from all of this."

"Justus and Link, take Jack up to my room. You can treat him there, Miss..."

"It's *Dr.* Synatzske."

"Where are you from?"

"I should tend to Mr. Taylor," she said, ignoring his question. She turned around and walked back to Jack, pulled his shirt back over his shoulders, and picked up his suit coat. Justus helped him up and started to put Jack's right arm over his shoulder, but Jack shook his head.

"I can walk." He wasn't sure that was a true statement since he felt light-headed, but he didn't want to seem helpless in front of the lady doctor. He glanced at her, still trying to get used to the fact that she was a doctor. She didn't look old enough to be out of school.

One of the lawmen spoke up. "We need to talk to Jack."

"I told you what happened, Frank," said Jarvis. "Jack saved my life, and the man was shot during the scuffle. It's a wonder the boy wasn't killed defending me, and for what? The man was out of his mind."

"We still need to talk to him."

"Well, let him get patched up first, and then you can talk to him. He isn't leaving the premises."

Justus and the doctor flanked Jack as Link followed them out of the restaurant toward the stairs.

Link spoke up behind them. "Take the elevator-- he's in no shape to walk the stairs."

Jack stepped onto the elevator, and steadied himself as the ornate box rose to the second floor. Link led them down the hall to Mr. Baldwin's second floor corner room. Link unlocked the door, and Justus helped Jack into a chair beside a table. The furniture and the room were much too fancy for medical purposes. Jack hoped he wouldn't bleed on something he couldn't afford to replace.

The doctor asked Justus to fetch some hot water.

"These rooms have hot water piped to them," said Link.

"I doubt it's boiled water," said Dr. Synatzske, waving Justus on. After he left the room, she added. "That'll give him something to do besides stand around and fret."

"I'm sure he needs to get back to work—he doesn't have to stay on my account," said Jack.

"He just wants to help," she said.

Link snorted. "I'll be back with the marshal to talk to Jack in a little while." He closed the door behind him, and the latch clicking shut sounded loud in the opulent room.

Jack watched the lady doctor set out a pair of scissors and several other metal tools, including a needle and thread on a towel on the table beside him.

The room was cool, but Jack could feel the sweat beading on his forehead with the thought of her poking around with a needle on his busted arm. He was relieved he hadn't eaten any breakfast yet, which lessened the chance of embarrassing himself by throwing up.

She picked up his right hand and removed the cufflink so she could pull the sleeve off.

He tried to lighten the mood when she started on his left cuff. "If you insist on removing my shirt, ma'am, I should at least know your first name."

She smiled as she guided the shirt around to the left side and carefully pulled it down and off of his injured arm. "It's

Kitty."

"Dr. Kitty. That has a nice, friendly sound." He turned away when she removed the bloody, makeshift bandages.

"I'll try to be as gentle as possible."

"I'll try not to act like an infant."

She rewarded him with another smile.

Justus walked in with a silver teapot and bowl on a tray. He was breathing hard like he had run downstairs. Kitty moved her satchel to the floor so he could set the tray on the table.

"I sure hope that's coffee," said Jack. "I haven't had any yet."

"Sorry, your wound takes precedence," said Kitty.

Justus spoke up. "Is it all right if I get him some coffee?"

Kitty nodded her head as she concentrated on cleaning the still oozing wounds.

Jack watched Justus hurry out of the room. Then he swallowed, trying to keep the bile down.

"Can you tell me exactly what happened now?" Dr. Kitty asked, not taking her eyes off the wound.

"Mr. Baldwin, Link, and I were sitting at the table about to order breakfast, and all of sudden this man came up and began accusing Mr. Baldwin of destroying his family. But he had him confused with someone else because he called him… Ashton, I think it was."

"How odd!"

"He said his father hung himself right before they were evicted from their home, and Mr. Baldwin threatened to get the law in there if he didn't leave. He told me to escort the man out of there, and then everything happened so fast. I started to get up, and the man drew a gun on Mr. Baldwin. I swiped at the pistol as it went off. Then we were rolling around on the floor." He paused, trying to remember. "I tried to take the pistol away from him-- I think it fired several more times, and one of them hit my arm. I finally head-butted him and got the pistol away from him…"

Jack stopped in mid-sentence when she pushed the hair back from his forehead, and touched it light as a feather.

"You have a good-sized hematoma from that."

"Is that serious?"

"It's a fancy name for a bruised bump. I was trying to impress you."

"Oh, really? What's your diagnosis?"

"You're obviously very hard-headed. The bump should go down soon. Go on."

"Where was I?"

"You got the pistol away from him…" She went back to working on his arm.

"Right, and the gun went off again, but the strange thing is… I wasn't touching the trigger. I was holding the cylinder. But maybe I accidentally squeezed the trigger. I don't remember."

"That's understandable."

Jack was silent again for a moment. "I didn't mean to kill him, though. I've never come close to doing anything like that."

He noticed she'd stopped touching his arm and glanced at her. She seemed to be lost in thought.

Justus came through the door carrying another silver coffee service on a second tray. He set it down on a smaller table beside the massive, four-poster bed, then picked up the table to move it to the right side of Jack. He poured a steaming cup and handed it to him.

Jack noticed the older man was still breathing heavily.

"You'd better sit down and rest, Justus, before your heart gives out on you." He blew on the coffee before taking a sip. It settled uneasily on his stomach, so he set the cup down on the table.

Justus continued to stand. "I'm fine, Mr. Jack, but you sure gave us a scare."

"Dr. Kitty will have me patched up in no time at all."

Justus smiled. "Dr. Kitty?"

"My classmates used to tell me with that name, I should've chosen a career in veterinary medicine."

"Nah, it's a beautiful name, ma'am."

"Why, thank you, Mr. Johnson."

"Can I do anythin' else for you before it gets too crowded in here? I think the marshal is headed this way."

"I think we have everything we need; you've been a tremendous help."

"Looks like the boy is in good hands, ma'am. I'll be takin' my leave now."

"See you on the street, Justus," said Jack, "and thank you for fetching Dr. Kitty."

Justus smiled and gave him a wink. "Yes, sir."

He opened the door to a horde of faces, and stepped back to let Jarvis Baldwin, Link, Marshal Frank Davis, and a couple of deputies Jack wasn't familiar with enter the room.

"It's time you left," Link said sternly to Justus. "And shut the door behind you."

"Yes, sir." Justus glanced at Jack before closing the door. Jack frowned at Link.

"We're not quite finished, gentlemen," Kitty addressed them, and then said to Jack, "I'm sorry, but this is going to hurt a bit."

Jack gritted his teeth, letting his irritation with Link draw his attention away from the needle and thread moving up and down at the edge of his peripheral vision.

"He can still answer some questions while you're working on him," said Link.

"We'll give them a few minutes," said Jarvis.

"I'm fine," said Jack. "Ask away."

"We've already heard Jarvis's and Link's statements about the incident," said Marshal Davis, "but we need to hear from you, too."

Jack glanced at Jarvis. "This man walked up to the table and started accusing Mr. Baldwin of ruining his family, and then he pulled a pistol on him, and I tried to stop him. I think the gun went off several times as we wrestled around on the floor, and I was able to get the pistol away from him. Then there was another shot, and... then he was dead. I don't know how that happened."

"He saved my life, Marshal." Jarvis turned to Jack. "You've never shot anyone before, have you, Jack?"

"No, sir."

"You could've been killed."

"I didn't even have time to think about what I was doing."

"Well, you saved my life, and I owe you a huge debt."

Jack shook his head. "I was in a better position to act.

Anybody would've done the same thing."

"I guess you didn't see Link diving under the table."

Jack tried not to grin at that comment.

Link frowned. "Did you notice when Jack lunged at that man, he pushed the pistol straight towards me-- I would've been shot if I hadn't acted so quickly."

"Did the assailant happen to mention his name or his father's name or where he was from?"

"Not that I recall," said Jack, looking at Jarvis.

"He didn't say."

One of the deputies said the only thing they found on his person was some money and a train receipt from Dallas dated a week before.

"Ask around the hotels and boarding houses; see if you can come up with a name so we can try to contact his next of kin," the marshal told his two deputies. "Did somebody go fetch Digger Hearn?"

"Yes, sir."

The marshal turned to Jarvis and Link. "In the meantime, gentlemen, if either of you remember anything else that might help us identify this man, let me know."

"Thank you for responding so quickly, Frank," Jarvis said, shaking each of the lawmen's hands as they prepared to leave.

"I'm sorry he's dead, Marshal," said Jack. "I didn't intend for that to happen."

"Jarvis is right. If you hadn't been there, we'd be contacting *his* next of kin. Right now it looks like a clear case of mistaken identity and self-defense."

"Link, go downstairs and make sure everything's in order before Jack heads home."

"What?" Link asked.

Jarvis glared at him. "Make sure *everything's* in order and out of sight."

Link nodded and walked out with the lawmen.

"What do you mean, *before I head home?*" asked Jack.

"You're not coming into work today."

"I'm fine, sir."

"You're not fine, and don't bother coming in tomorrow, either." He walked over to an armoire and grabbed a folded shirt and laid it on the bed. "Put this on when you're finished." Then he walked over to Jack. "Thank you for what you did for me down there, son. You saved my life." He offered his hand.

Jack grasped it. "I'm glad I was able to help, sir."

"Well, I'm glad *you* were there. I guess it's obvious I keep Link around for his brain, not his brawn." he said, smirking. He finally looked at Kitty. "Take all the time you need here. Is his arm going to be all right?"

"Yes, if he gives it time to heal."

"You're from Galveston, aren't you?"

Kitty looked up sharply. "How'd you know that?"

"There's a medical school down there, right?"

"Yes, that's where I earned my degree."

"And you're the spitting image of someone I used to know there. Do you look like your mother?"

"I look nothing like my mother," she said, picking up her satchel.

Jack noticed she avoided looking at him.

"Coincidence, then." He started for the door. "I'd better get to the office. I'll send Link back up here to help get you home."

"I can get home just fine by myself," said Jack. "And Mr. Baldwin?"

Jarvis looked back. "After what you did today, I think it's time you started calling me by my first name."

"Yes, sir."

"Did you want to tell me something?"

"Yes... uh... I'm not sure where that last shot came from."

"What do you mean?"

"My finger wasn't on the trigger."

"It could've misfired."

"I don't know..." Jack looked away.

"You're probably not thinking straight right now, but that's completely understandable."

"Maybe you're right. It all happened so fast."

"Rest and recuperate this weekend, and I'll see you Monday." Jarvis closed the door behind him.

Kitty exhaled loudly as she finished tying the bandage to his upper arm.

"What's the matter?"

"I don't think Mr. Baldwin cares for me."

"He's probably not used to a woman doctor."

She unfolded the clean shirt and carefully pulled the left sleeve up Jack's injured arm. "That's obvious, but I think there's more to it than that."

"Like what?"

Kitty shook her head and draped the shirt over his shoulder. "I'm probably imagining it. Put your right arm in and let me get this buttoned up for you. It's a little big on you, but that'll help when you're trying to get it off. You're going to have to do a lot of things with just one hand for the next few days."

Jack's heart started pounding again with her so close. "You have the most unusual colored eyes."

"I wish they were brown."

"Why?"

Kitty shrugged her shoulders. "I would prefer a color that doesn't attract so much attention. Your blue eyes are rather startling to look at."

Jack couldn't help but smile at the thought that she'd noticed something about him. "I have my father and grandmother to thank for that."

She walked over to the armoire and retrieved a couple of handkerchiefs. "I hope Mr. Baldwin doesn't mind us borrowing these, but I need to make a sling for your arm." She began tying two corners together. "I'm not sure I should mention this, but something's not right about that last shot."

"What do you mean?"

"You were holding the pistol with your right hand?"

"Yes."

Kitty draped the sling over his shoulder and looked him squarely in his eyes. "Then you didn't shoot that man."

Jack stared at her. "How do you know that?"

"The bullet entered the right temple."

When Jack paused, she continued. "*His* right temple. You were holding the revolver in your right hand. If you had shot him, you would've hit him in the left temple, or if his head was turned, the bullet would've hit his face or forehead."

Jack shut his eyes, recalling the image of the dead man branded in his mind. "You're right!" He looked back at her. "I didn't shoot him, thank God. But who did?"

"Does Mr. Baldwin carry a gun?"

"He does, but I never saw it out. Why wouldn't he admit it if he'd fired the shot? I don't think the man should've been killed. I'd already wrested the pistol from him."

"Maybe Mr. Baldwin has something to hide."

"Why would you say that?"

Kitty finished tying the sling around Jack's neck. "Forget it. Now keep your arm as immobile as possible so the bone will start to fuse back together. I can give you some laudanum if it becomes too painful for you. Can you stand?"

"Of course I can stand-- he didn't shoot me in the leg," Jack said as he quickly stood up.

He grabbed the edged of the table and sat back down when the room started spinning. "Dang, what's wrong with me?"

"Let me see, a perfect stranger almost killed you while you defended your boss... you were shot and lost some blood, so I'd say you're acting quite normal right now. You need help getting home, so sit right there and I'll go find Mr. Link."

"Anybody but him-- please. How 'bout Justus! Go fetch Justus across the street. I'll even pay him for his time."

"All right."

Monday morning…

J ack saw Justus slowly shaking his head as he walked towards the older man. He knew his hair was uncombed; his tie was only half-tied, what he could see of his shirt was solid wrinkles, and his left coat sleeve hung empty on his arm.

"If you don't mind my asking, Mr. Jack, but what in the heck are you doing here?"

"I wanted to thank you for taking me home the other day."

"You're welcome."

"Now help me up." Jack grabbed the armrest with his good hand, and Justus pushed him up on the shoeshine stand. He turned around and sat down hard, like that bit of effort took everything out of him.

"You don't look so good."

"It's hard to dress with one hand. Has she come by yet?"

"No, but ain't you seen her since she patched you up?" Justus started dusting off his boots.

Jack shook his head. "Mr. Baldwin--Jarvis sent Dr. Gilbert to check on me later; I don't think he trusted that Dr. Kitty was capable of taking proper care of me."

"Dr. Gilbert?"

"No, Jarvis, but Dr. Gilbert told me she did a good job-- that he wouldn't have done anything different. Part of me was kind of relieved he came instead of her that first night because I had to ask for some laudanum to help me sleep. I had no idea a little wound could hurt so much."

"You be careful with that stuff." Justus started smearing the blacking on the first boot.

"What do you mean?"

"I seen laudanum drive people plum crazy. It grabs a hold of them and won't let go-- kinda like liquor does with some folk."

"I guess that's why Dr. Gilbert only gave me enough for a couple of days. The pain wouldn't let me rest."

"You still look tired."

"Yeah, but I can't get behind on my work. And my boots actually do need polishing today."

Justus snickered.

"Well, I just need to see her, that's all."

"I sure won't refuse your nickel." Justus wiped off the excess blacking from the boot.

Jack slumped with fatigue. A minute passed silently between them as he watched Justus get into the rhythm of polishing and popping the rag.

Neither one of them noticed Kitty walking towards them until she placed the newspaper on Jack's lap. He looked up and couldn't help but straighten up and grin.

Kitty returned the smile. "How's your arm?"

"I was hoping you could tell me," Jack answered. "I thought for sure you'd come back and check on me over the weekend."

Kitty frowned. "Didn't Dr. Gilbert check on you?"

"Yes, but…"

"Didn't he tell you why I didn't come?"

"No."

"Mr. Baldwin told him in no uncertain terms that he wanted Dr. Gilbert to take care of you, not me."

"That's not his decision," Jack said, suddenly angry. "And Dr. Gilbert had nothing to say but praise for your work."

"Don't get upset about it; I'm used to people preferring a male doctor over me."

"Well, I don't. I mean, Dr. Gilbert's a good doctor, but in this case, I would prefer you taking care of me, I mean, my arm."

"Thanks for your vote of confidence," she said, then lowered her voice. "And I think I figured out why Mr. Baldwin wanted you to take credit for killing the would-be assassin." She pointed at the newspaper. "You're front page news. That ought to boost your popularity."

Jack stared at his own face taking up a substantial area of the top half of the paper. "Where did they get that photograph? That was taken back when I started practicing with Jarvis."

"Looks like your campaign has begun."

Jack looked up. "How did you know I was planning to run for office?"

Kitty's cheeks flushed pink. "I... make it a point to learn something about my patients."

"So you still consider me your patient?"

"Well, temporarily, yes."

"And from this point on, you're still my doctor."

"And that'll be a nickel, Mr. Jack."

"That was fast." He reached into his coat pocket and pulled out a silver dollar coin and handed it to Justus.

"This early in the morning, that's gonna take all my change."

"I don't want any change. It's yours."

Justus stared at it, and then looked up at Jack like he'd lost his mind. "That's worth twenty shines." He started to hand the coin back, but Jack stopped him.

"I took you away from your chair for at least that much in lost revenue last Thursday."

Justus shook his head. "I was glad to help. That's what friends do, right?" He held out the coin again.

"Yes, but I'm a customer, too, and you won't stay in

business if you're away from this chair. I have a selfish motive here, Justus. I want to make sure that you'll continue to be here when I need you." Jack started to climb down, and Justus helped him.

"Yes, sir. I'll be here."

"Then it's settled."

"I need to get to work," said Kitty. "Do you want to come by the office now?"

Jack shook his head. "I have to go to work."

"Then stop by before you go home so I can check your wound. You still look a little peaked. I'm not sure you should be working today."

"I've had three days to lie around doing nothing; I'm perfectly fine. I don't need my left hand to write or turn the pages of a book."

"Hold on a minute." She set her satchel on the side of the stand and reached up to finish tying Jack's tie.

Jack forgot to breathe for a moment.

"Try to stay out of trouble," she said as she gave the tie a gentle pat, "and I'll see you this evening."

Jack watched her walk down the street to Dr. Gilbert's office. She turned at the door and glanced back at him before disappearing inside.

Jack grinned. "She looked back at me, Justus."

"She's probably wondering why you're still standing here like a lump on a stump," he said. "Hey, this may not be the best time to ask, but I was wonderin' what kind of lawyer are you?"

Jack turned and looked at Justus. "Are you in trouble?"

"Nah, I'm just curious. Do you work with trials... like defend people and all?"

"I mostly do research for Link and Jarvis, but they're going to throw a few bones my way to give me some practice as a trial lawyer. I could stand to hone my debating skills for the political arena." He glanced at the front page again. "And the future is coming at me faster than I thought."

"You'll do good."

"Thanks. I guess I can count on your vote, right?"

Justus's smile faded. "I'd be proud to vote for you Mr. Jack, if I can."

"What do you mean, 'if you can'? Negroes have the right to vote."

"I've voted every year since the law started letting us vote, but things are changing. Do you know anything about a poll tax?"

"Yes, it's coming up for a vote soon. The government is trying to tax everything these days. That's nothing unusual."

"But did you know a lot of families rarely have cash on hand? They're living on credit until the crop comes in, if they make a crop that year, and most years they stay in debt. Those people wouldn't get to vote. But for people like me, the poll tax is one to two days' pay. Did you know a lot of folks would have to choose between voting or feeding their families that day? Which would you choose?"

Jack felt like the wind had been knocked out of him. "I didn't realize that."

"And if we can't vote, who's gonna remember us in that big granite building up the road? Things ain't getting' better for us, Mr. Jack, and they won't until somebody speaks on our behalf."

"Let me do some asking around. I really haven't put too much thought into this poll tax, but I promise you, Justus. I will."

Justus nodded his head. "Thank you, Mr. Jack. Thanks for hearing me out."

Jack thought about what the man said as he walked the short distance to the law office of Jarvis Baldwin.

At mid-morning, he asked Link if he thought the poll tax was necessary.

Link didn't hesitate. "A poll tax will weed out the ignorant and the slackers from our elective process."

"But what if people can't afford it?"

"They'll find the money if it's important enough to them. If it's not, we don't need their vote."

Jack shook his head in frustration. "But don't they need representation just like everybody else?"

"They can't help how they are; either that or they don't want to change the way they are. The poll tax is a humane way to raise the quality of the electorate. You wouldn't want your opponent to get elected just because he was able to sway a bunch of ignorant sheep by promising them the moon, do you? Now *that's* dishonest. Not the poll tax." Link waited for a response.

Jack offered nothing.

"Don't you have something more important to be working on?"

Jack turned and walked back to his desk. He disliked Link and detested much of what came out of his mouth, but he wanted to get an accurate picture of both sides of the poll tax-- the reasons for and against it. He didn't like the idea of someone getting elected to office through deception and bribes, but immediately truth stabbed his conscience with the realization that Jarvis seemed to be leading him down the same path by letting everyone think that Jack had shot the assailant.

He exhaled slowly, knowing he had to set Jarvis straight on that. He would not start his campaign on a lie. Today was not the day to confront him, though. He felt like even the simplest thought muddled his brain.

At noon, he straightened his desk and told Emery, one of the clerks, that he was heading home. He ripped his picture off the front page of the newspaper and dropped in the wastebasket on his way out.

J ack awoke to the sound of knocking. He looked around to get his bearings and realized he had fallen asleep in the armchair behind his desk. The feeble light coming through the windows told him it was dusk.

The knock rapped louder.

"Hold on," he said in a gravelly voice. He cleared his throat and said louder, "I'm coming."

He pushed the chair back and rose unsteadily, regretting the late nap, but unable to fight the fatigue. He opened the door to find Dr. Kitty standing there with her black bag. She looked concerned.

"You didn't come by, so I assumed you were feeling fine, but then Justus told me you left work at noon."

"He doesn't miss a thing." Jack pushed his unruly hair back from his forehead.

"Your bruise is quite colorful, but it's fading. Why didn't you come by the office?"

"It meant walking two more blocks than I needed to, and that just seemed too far. I don't know why I'm so tired. How'd you know where I lived?"

"Justus told me. Would you mind if I checked your arm?"

Jack stepped back and let her enter. He walked over to his desk chair and sat down heavily.

"May I turn on the light?"

"Of course, I'm sorry." He started to get up.

"I'll do it." She turned around and pushed the light switch button by the door.

Jack watched her walk to him and set her bag on his desk. She glanced around the room. "I like your house."

"It has somewhat of a reputation."

"Because *you* live here?"

Jack chuckled. "No. Do you remember a big trial going on several years ago--it made the news around the state."

Kitty shook her head. "I'm not familiar with much of anything that happened in Austin before I arrived. Well, or anyplace else for that matter."

"The accused was a man named William Porter, and he skipped the country right before he was supposed to stand trial. His wife was dying of consumption, though, so he came back and turned himself in. My landlord told me William Porter lived in this house."

Kitty's eyes widened. "Really? What was the man on trial for?"

"He embezzled money from First National Bank. They sentenced him to five years in prison, but he was released about six months ago."

"Do you think he'll want his house back?"

"Nah. He just rented it, like me. I heard he followed his daughter and in-laws to Pennsylvania. I imagine they moved out of state to avoid the scandal. Some of my law professors made their students attend the trial as part of their course work."

"But not you?"

"That was the year before I got here, but I think I would've enjoyed watching the proceedings. They say Porter is a writer of sorts."

"His prison record will probably hurt his writing career. It's hard to get away from your past."

Jack waited, thinking Kitty would explain that comment, but she moved closer and began removing the sling.

"Let's take a look at your arm."

"I had no idea something so small could make me so weak. I feel like I'm trudging through a mud bog when I walk."

"It's good you're only three blocks from your office, but you probably should've taken a hack. Too bad the streetcar doesn't pass in front of your house." Kitty gingerly removed his shirt with as little as movement to his arm as possible.

"The trolley is two blocks over, and I'm almost to the office by the time I reach it."

Jack tried to act like a lady removing his shirt was something that happened all the time, but his pounding heart betrayed him.

"It takes a while for your body to recover from this kind of shock." She started to remove the bandage.

"When did Dr. Gilbert check on this last?"

"Saturday morning." He tried not to flinch when she pulled the last bit of gauze from the wound.

"It looks a little fevered. Maybe that's why you're feeling so weak. That and the fact that you were fighting for your life a few days ago." She dug a bottle out of her bag and opened it.

"I had it all under control."

"Except the part where your boss killed that man and claimed you did it. Have you had a chance to talk to him about it?" She poured something on a piece of cloth and started dabbing it gently on both of the wounds.

Jack shook his head. "I didn't feel up to debating him. He's already denied it, and I'm not sure if that was to further my political career by painting me a bigger hero than I actually was… or if he's hiding something. Either way, I don't like it."

Kitty felt around on his upper arm. "The bone isn't separated… that's good. But until it starts to heal good, I want you to continue to keep it immobile."

"Can I use my fingers?"

"Yes, if you can do it with no movement to your upper arm. You can even turn your wrist a bit without moving the humerus." She held his left elbow and hand and demonstrated it. "Let the sling support the weight of your arm, all right?"

"Yes, ma'am."

"Have you had any supper?"

"No, ma'am."

"Do you have anything in the house I could fix for you?"

Jack shook his head. "I usually eat downtown, but don't bother. I can get something in the morning."

"Can I help you into a nightshirt?"

Jack could feel himself blushing. "I... don't sleep in a nightshirt."

"It's too chilly to sleep bareback."

"I have some long johns I sleep in, but I can dress myself."

"Are you sure?"

Jack nodded, feeling a bit uncomfortable talking about his underwear. And he wasn't about to tell her he'd been sleeping in the same shirt Dr. Gilbert helped him change into Saturday morning.

She packed up her bag. "I live in a boarding house only two blocks from here. Mrs. Gerwick usually has some kind of stew or soup on hand, so I'll bring you a bowl."

"That's not necessary--"

"Doctor's orders. You need to keep up your strength."

"I'm feeling better already. Dr. Gilbert's wife packed a basket of food for me, too, but I finished that off yesterday."

"Daisy is a saint. I'm so fortunate to have known her in Galveston. She's the reason I'm practicing with her husband in Austin."

"Galveston-- were you there during that big storm?"

Kitty nodded. "I spent the most terrifying night of my life riding it out with my mother in an office building downtown. I didn't think we were going to survive; thousands of people didn't. And I spent days on end at the hospital afterwards; we were so overwhelmed with the injured and dying. I'm actually relieved I'm not on the island anymore. The storm completely washed away our home, and we lost everything except what we could carry with us downtown during the storm. My mother's still there, but she now lives in a sturdy house near the center of the island."

"Does Jarvis know your mother? I remember him asking

you something about her."

"No, he was mistaken." Kitty looked uncomfortable. "I'd better get home so I can bring you back some supper."

"I'd rather you not walk in the dark."

"The moonlight tower lights up the entire neighborhood."

"Then let me rephrase that. I'd rather you not walk by yourself. Are you familiar with that series of murders that took place a while back?"

"I heard about them—the 'servant girl murders', right? But that was back in the eighties."

"Some people think the person who committed those murders was actually Jack the Ripper-- the same serial killer in London."

"That's what Mrs. Gerwick told me, along with more gruesome details than I actually cared to hear." Kitty shivered. "Are you trying to frighten me? Because if you are, you're doing an admirable job of it."

Jack felt a twinge of remorse. "Sorry, Doc. I didn't intend to scare you." He stood up. "Wait just a minute." Jack walked out of the room and came back with an undershirt.

"What are you doing?"

"I'm escorting you home."

"That's not necessary." She picked up her bag. "You need your rest. Weren't you feeling weak earlier?"

"My legs are fine, and I can carry the soup back myself."

"Are you sure?"

Jack smiled. "I'm sure."

"After that conversation, I wouldn't mind the company. But I know all that happened years ago. The killer is long gone." Kitty set down her bag and removed the sling from his arm so she could help him into the long-sleeved knit shirt. She replaced the sling and draped his coat over his shoulders, then retrieved her bag again.

Jack walked to the door and opened it for her.

She stepped out of the house, saying, "You do realize, Mr. Taylor, that with your wounded limb, *I* would have to be the one to defend us if we were set upon."

Jack closed the door and followed her down the steps. "I can still use my hard head."

Kitty laughed. "I feel so much better now."

Jarvis was out of the office on Tuesday, but the following morning Jack didn't have to wait long to see him. Jarvis called him into his office within minutes after his arrival.

"How's the arm, son?" He cautiously shook Jack's right hand.

"Better, thank you. I don't know what happened on Monday. I felt like I couldn't put one foot in front of the other. I'll make up my time, though."

"Don't worry about it. It's noticeable when you're out, but I was concerned about you. You're an important part of this firm."

"I feel like I don't do much more than Emery does around here."

"That's about to change. This office mostly handles contracts and investments, but Link is already selecting cases for you to work on."

"What kind of cases?"

"The kind we know you can win. We're going to build a successful reputation for you. And it's going to help your case that our firm is expanding, too. We're opening another office in Houston to handle the work pertaining to the oil business over there. We'll add more to our staff here, too. All of our efforts will show you're connected to a successful, profitable firm."

"Sounds impressive."

"Oil is the future, Jack. It's going to help put you in office, too."

Jack paused.

"What is it?" Jarvis asked.

Jack took a deep breath. "I wanted to talk to you about the shooting."

"That's past history. Don't let that unfortunate event weigh on your mind."

"But it *has* bothered me because I think you're giving me credit for something I didn't do."

"You saved my life. I wouldn't be standing here today if you hadn't intervened. Did I remember to thank you?"

"Yes, sir, a number of times... but I know now that I didn't shoot him."

Jarvis didn't speak for a while. "Jack, I'm going to be completely honest with you. I admit I did fire that last shot, but it was only because I was afraid someone would get killed-- namely you. He'd already shot you once, remember? And several more shots went off wildly while y'all were wrestling around on the floor."

"But why didn't you tell the marshal that?"

"I don't know... I guess I was afraid he might feel obligated to look into *my* past, and there are a few things that I need to keep buried there-- things that would damage my reputation here. And I didn't want to hurt your campaign in any way."

"Did you know that man?"

"I don't recall ever seeing him before that day."

"What did you do in your past that you wouldn't want the marshal to find out about?"

"Have a seat." Jarvis gestured to the armchair in front of his desk, and he settled in his leather swivel chair behind it. "I'm telling you this in confidence, and it involves the law, but I assure you I'm an innocent man." He picked up his cup of coffee, took a swig of it and spit it back in the cup. "Emery!" he boomed, "Bring me some hot coffee!" He looked at Jack. "Do you want a cup?"

Jack shook his head. "I'm fine."

Jarvis waited until Emery left before he spoke again. "I used to play cards, and I was pretty good at it. I made my living that way for most of my younger years. But nine years ago I made the mistake of playing at a rough table. When I caught one of them cheating, he pulled a gun on me, and I was forced to shoot him in self-defense. Unfortunately, the man died a few hours later, and the other two claimed I shot him in cold blood, so I left town before the sheriff arrested me. I'm wanted in Kansas for a murder I didn't commit."

Jack was shocked. Jarvis Baldwin, one of Austin's most respected citizens, was a wanted man. "Why didn't you stay and try to clear your name?"

"It was my word-- a stranger-- against two local men. They would've strung me up."

"You're sure about that?"

"I have no doubt. You ever heard of Henry Brown and William Robinson?"

"Brown rings a bell."

"You might recognize Robinson by his alias-- Ben Wheeler."

"I've heard of him. Wasn't he lynched for robbing a bank?"

Jarvis nodded. "In Medicine Lodge… Kansas."

Jack frowned. "Kansas."

"And Brown and Wheeler were outlaws turned lawmen who'd cleaned up Caldwell, Kansas. But after a while they decided living right didn't pay enough, so they told everyone in Caldwell they needed to go track down a murderer, but they actually headed over to the Indian Territory to rob a bank. Two of the bank officers were shot, and the cashier sealed the vault right before he died, so the robbers didn't get a dime before they got away. A posse caught them and brought them back to town where a mob lynched them. No due process, no trial. That could very well have happened to me because it was my word against theirs. If I wanted to live, I had to run."

Jack nodded.

"Well, that incident scared me so badly that I eventually quit gambling, and I started looking for more respectable ways to earn a living. I decided to study law, and it didn't take long for me to obtain a license to practice before I came to Austin. And I think I've done a lot of good since I moved here."

"Did Link come with you?"

Jarvis nodded. "I actually apprenticed under him."

Jack was shocked. "But you're his boss!"

"We're partners, but I'm in charge because we started the practice here with my money. I value his expertise, though."

"Does he know about your past?"

Jarvis nodded. "And I know about his, so we trust each other."

"Do you still have the desire to gamble?"

Jarvis chuckled. "Yes, but I've learned to satisfy it through legitimate speculations, especially in the oil business. And it's paid off more than I ever dreamed it would." He paused for a moment. "I hope my confession to you doesn't change your opinion of me, Jack."

"I have to admit it's a shock to hear that story, but I understand why you ran. I'm glad you told me, and I am grateful you were trying to protect me that day." He looked down at his arm. "A busted arm's a lot better than my family having to plan a funeral."

"Speaking of your family, do they know what happened to you?"

Jack's eyes widened. "Oh, crap...sorry, sir. I hadn't thought about that. If Momma sees that newspaper story from Monday, she's going to catch the first train down here."

"Why don't you send her a wire that you're fine?"

"Good idea." Jack stood. "Would you mind if I took a few minutes to do it now? I'd like for you to meet my parents some day, but not under these circumstances. My mother can be a bit forceful when she's... worried."

"I understand; go on."

Jack wasted no time getting to the Western Union office, but it took a lot longer trying to figure out how to say in as few words as possible the message he needed to send to his parents. He finally ended up with:

Disregard newspaper story STOP Am fine STOP Don't come END Jack

His steps were much lighter on the way back knowing he'd dodged a bullet there. He waved at Justus before looking up at the impressive building that held the key to his future. He paused to read the gold lettering on the large window, including the names of the lawyers listed. It never ceased to amaze him to see his name connected with this law firm. His future looked bright, and he couldn't help but thank the Lord for his job.

He entered the lobby and stopped in his tracks when he saw a beautiful woman talking with Emery. No, that wasn't right. She was talking loudly *at* Emery. Emery looked too scared to speak.

"There he is!" said Emery, pointing and looking relieved.

The woman turned around and her gloved hands shifted to her hips. Jack immediately recognized that pose.

"Mother?"

"And just when were you planning to let us know you'd been shot, Jack?"

"You didn't get my telegram, Momma?" he said, knowing she didn't.

"No, I did not! When did you send it?"

"A little while ago," he mumbled sheepishly. "How did you find out so soon? Did you see the newspaper?"

"No, but news travels faster than the newspaper. Do you not know how to use a telephone?!"

Jack frowned. "Mother, your telephone line just works with the other five telephones in Grace."

"We have eight phones in town now, but I meant you should've called and left word in Waco. Your grandfather's bank has a long distance line."

"I forgot about that. I... just didn't want you to worry."

She walked over to him and embraced him on his right side. "How could I not, sweetheart? I thought the worst."

"I'm fine, Mother. Where's Dad?"

"Your father's in Fort Worth. You'd better be glad he hasn't heard yet."

"I'm actually more scared of you," he said, leaning down to kiss her net-covered cheek. "You didn't come down here by yourself, did you?"

"I'm perfectly capable of traveling by myself." She stepped back. "Let me look at you." She turned him this way and that, careful to not touch his wounded arm.

"I'm all right." Jack felt like a six year old again. Emery and the other clerks seemed highly amused by it.

"What'd the doctor say about your arm?"

"She thinks the bullet just nicked the bone, and it went clean through. It'll heal up fast."

"She?"

"The doctor's a woman."

His mother raised her eyebrows. "And how did all of this happened?"

"Let me go ask Mr. Baldwin if I can take you across the street for coffee. In fact, I'd like you to meet him first." He took her by the arm and led her down the hall to Jarvis's office.

It was empty.

Link followed them into the room.

"Oh, Link, I'd like you to meet my mother, Mrs. Mercy Taylor. Mom, this is Link Segal."

"Hello, Mr. Segal." She offered him her gloved hand.

"The pleasure is mine, Mrs. Taylor."

"You have an unusual first name."

"I don't tell too many people this, but it's short for 'Lincoln.'"

"Lincoln?!" Jack said.

Mercy smiled. "That's an honorable name, and another lawyer at that."

"I think my future career was set when they named me," Link said, smiling back. "You sure did a good job raising this young man. We have big plans for Jack."

Jack did a double take. This didn't sound at all like the Link he knew and normally disliked. The man sounded almost congenial.

"Why, thank you," said Mercy. "And I'd like to meet the man that changed my son's life. Is Mr. Baldwin here?"

"I just spoke with him a little while ago," said Jack.

"He had to meet with a client. I'm sure he's going to regret missing you. Will you be in town long?"

"Only until morning."

"Maybe we can eat dinner with him later," said Jack. "Will you be seeing him, Link?"

"Probably."

"Tell him my mother's here, and we'd like to meet him for dinner at the Driskill if he's available." He looked at his mother. "Say, 5:30?"

She nodded.

"I'll tell him. And why don't you take the rest of the day off to spend with your mother?"

"I've already taken too much time off since…"

"Jarvis won't mind, in fact, I'm sure he'll insist on it. Did you know your son saved Jarvis's life?"

"I don't know anything other than my son was shot."

"You need to tell her what happened, Jack. And Jarvis knows how important family is. I'll pass on your message about dinner." He turned to Mercy. "Mrs. Taylor, I'm so pleased to have made your acquaintance. Jack has told us a lot about you."

"Thank you, Mr. Segal. And tell Mr. Baldwin that I'm looking forward to meeting him. I hope you'll join us for dinner, too."

"I'll try my best. Have a wonderful visit with your son." Link turned around and walked back to his office.

Jack stood there staring after him. "I haven't told him anything about you."

"He was just being polite."

He took his mother's arm and walked her back down the hall.

"He seems like a very nice man."

"That's just it, Mom. He's not. I've never seen that side of Link before."

J ack didn't have the opportunity to introduce Jarvis to his mother at the Driskill that evening. A bowl of beautiful orchids was sent to their table along with a note saying Jarvis and Link were suddenly called to Houston concerning the oil business and would be gone for at least a week.

Jack regretted his mother missing the chance to meet his benefactor, but was relieved Link wasn't going to join them.

After explaining what happened with the shooting, the day had proved very pleasant spending time with her. As an adult now, he enjoyed getting to know her apart from her role as the woman who raised him. He'd taken her for granted most of his growing up years, but now he was discovering things about her he had never noticed before. She had a wicked sense of humor, and sometimes a temper to match. Usually that flared when something frightened her-- like learning her son had been shot. She had a good business head on her, which surprised him when he learned she handled most of the bookkeeping when it came to his parents' horse business.

Mercy Taylor was head-turning beautiful-- blonde, blue eyes, porcelain skin, tall and slender build. He didn't even notice the burn scars on her left forehead and cheek because they'd been there since before he was born. When he was old enough to realize not every mother had scars like that on their faces, he asked her about them one day. She refused to talk about it. He had to learn from his cousins that she almost died in a barn fire trying to save a little girl, and there was something about a bad man involved, but he still hadn't heard the whole story.

His father Jimmy was half Apache and well known and respected in Central Texas, especially when it came to raising and training horses. His mother was quite the horsewoman, too, and together, they built a successful business on their place in Grace, Texas, west of Waco. Jack was also good with horses, but he wanted to do more than that as a career.

Jack inherited his father's piercing blue eyes and olive skin, and his lighter brown hair from his mother. He had two younger sisters; one married her long-time beau four years ago, and the youngest would marry this May. His mother was over the moon getting to prepare what she called the *event of the year* in Grace. But as small as his hometown was, most any event could claim that title. He wouldn't dare tell that to his mother, though.

His father's parents, Matthew and Julia Taylor, founded Grace back in the 1850's. But a few years after they had arrived, an Apache brave named Nantan Lupan kidnapped Julia and her youngest son Justin. It took Matthew six long years to find them, and by then, Jimmy was born-- the result of the forced relationship between Nantan and Julia. The encounter meant the death of Nantan, and Matthew allowed Julia to bring Jimmy and a little orphaned girl named Faith home with them. Matthew learned to love Faith, but Jimmy was a constant reminder of the anguish Nantan had caused for his family all those years. It took a long time for Matthew to stop blaming Jimmy for what happened and to accept him as his adopted son. Jimmy caused a lot of heartache in his growing up years, but it came to a head when he took his brother Justin's girlfriend away from Grace, leading everyone to think she had drowned in the river. Justin eventually figured out the truth and chased them across Texas to bring them home.

Jack still didn't quite understand the whole story, and his older cousins didn't even know themselves what all had happened and why. But all was forgiven, and eventually Jimmy and Mercy fell in love and married. Jack was their firstborn.

His grandfather Taylor passed away last year, and his grandmother Meemaw told the family at Christmas that Faith, the Apache girl Julia brought home, was actually Jimmy's half sister. His father Jimmy seemed extra pleased that everyone could know it now. Jack learned his grandmother spared her husband's feelings all those years because she was afraid he would be bitter towards Faith as another reminder of Nantan's harm to his family. And Meemaw's plan worked. In a very short time after Faith's arrival to Grace, Matthew Taylor learned to love her like his own daughter.

Jack smiled at his mother, chattering on about the wedding plans for his youngest sister Biriney. The middle sibling Mae was twenty-two, and expecting her second child.

"You've hardly touched your food, Momma," said Jack. "It's getting cold."

"I'm not that hungry." She grabbed the yeast roll and handed her plate to him.

Jack scraped the roast beef and potatoes onto his plate and set the empty one aside.

Mercy wrapped the roll in her hanky and slipped it in her purse. "For later," she said. "I've been doing all the talking; tell me more about your plans."

"Jarvis is giving me more experience in the courtroom to start building a resume of successful court cases."

"He's thinking of everything, isn't he? I regret not meeting him today."

"Maybe we can plan something with him well ahead of time when you and Dad come to town. I'm starting to familiarize myself with the legislative process, and a constituent has already asked me to check on something for him." He stuffed a big bite of potatoes in his mouth.

"Really! Someone knows you plan to run for office?"

"You met him today," Jack mumbled.

"Don't talk with your mouth full, dear. It's uncouth for a future legislator to eat like a pig in public. And I met a number of people today."

Jack swallowed. "Justus Johnson - the shoe shine man."

"Really? What would he be interested in when it comes to the law?"

"He's concerned about the poll tax coming up for a vote soon."

"Oh, that. Well, at least he gets to vote."

"That's what he's concerned about-- that the poll tax will knock a lot of people out of a chance to vote because they don't have the money to pay for it. Justus told me that the poll tax is about a day's wage or more for him."

"I don't know why women don't have that right either; we have just as much, if not more horse sense as men. Maybe that's something else you can work on, too."

"I'm not even in office yet, Mother."

"It's a given. How can anyone in their right mind not vote for you?" She reached across the table with her napkin and wiped a bit of potato from his chin before he realized what she was doing.

"Mother!" he whispered sternly as he leaned away from her. "I'm not five years old." He looked around to see if anyone had noticed.

A middle-age woman at the next table smiled at them.

Jack felt the red creep up his cheeks.

"Sorry, sweetheart," she said, smiling back at the other woman. "I'm sure she's a mother, too. Seems like it was only yesterday when I was doctoring your scraped knees and giving you baths."

"I think I'm finished," he said, motioning to the waiter. He signed the receipt and stood to pull out his chair for his mother.

Mercy stood and let him help her into her coat. She leaned over and picked up the bowl of orchids.

"What are you going to do with those?" Jack asked.

"I'm going to take them home with me. Orchids are my favorite flowers. Didn't you know that?"

"No."

"I assumed you told Mr. Baldwin. I wonder where he was able to find them this time of year?"

"He has a way of making things happen when he wants to. I wouldn't be surprised if he demanded that those flowers bloom today just for you."

Mercy laughed as they walked out of the restaurant. "I think somebody has a greenhouse around here. I'd love to have one, too, but then I'd have to learn how grow things. We have too many good gardeners around Grace that I take advantage of. But nobody grows these around town. They take a lot of fuss and care."

"Like my mother?" Jack teased.

"You're a funny bunny," said Mercy.

They walked east to the end of the block and turned right, heading south.

"You're fortunate to live so close to your work. But are you neglecting Lonesome Joe?"

"Yeah," Jack admitted. "I don't ride him but once a week, if that much."

"He's going to get fat and lazy."

"He already *is* fat and lazy."

"He's from champion stock! His father was Redeemer!"

"He must've taken after his mother."

"Then find somebody to ride him regularly." Mercy stopped walking and grabbed Jack's arm. "What is that glow over those buildings? Is something on fire?!"

Jack put his hand over his mother's. "No, Momma. That's just the moonlight tower over on 2nd Street. Austin has them all over town."

"Like street lights?"

"Yes, but much, much taller."

"How progressive of Austin."

They started walking again, but Jack could feel her shaking. He knew she was deathly afraid of fires, and knew it was because of the fire that scarred her face and almost took her life. He wasn't about to tell her the supposed reason the moonlight towers were erected.

"Can I ask you a question, Mother?"

"Of course."

"I know only a little about the barn fire in Brownwood." He felt her tense up. "What were you doing there? You weren't kin to the Samuels, although I think of them as family now since Aunt Faith is so close to them and cousin Grace married Finn Samuel not too long ago."

Mercy said nothing for a number of steps.

"I don't want to bring up bad memories for you, but I'd really like to know the truth."

She nodded her head. "My father... your Grandfather Locke and I had a huge disagreement, and I ran away from home."

Jack was surprised. "You ran away from home?!"

"I was... incorrigible in my younger years."

"That's hard to believe."

"Oh, honey, you don't know the half of it."

"Did you know Dad then?"

"Yes, but I thought he was a scoundrel at the time."

Jack chuckled at that. "Really? What changed your mind?"

"My father hired him to find me and bring me home, and I got to know him on that trip home. He was the one who suggested going to Brownwood and working for the Samuels' after I still hadn't resolved the problem with my father."

"What was that about?"

"It's not important now, but I'm so thankful that I had the opportunity to live with and work for the Samuels. They taught me so much at home and at the general store, and especially how to love and respect others."

"They adopted all those kids, didn't they?"

Mercy nodded. "Eleven, not counting Caitlin, your Uncle Ethan's daughter who stayed with them for a while."

"That was such a sad time for the whole family when she died."

"We didn't think Finn would ever get over that. Do you remember when he came and lived with us that first summer?"

"Not much, other than I worshipped the ground he

walked on and couldn't wait until the next summer when he'd come back. But you saved Caitlin's life years before in that barn fire, right?"

"Yes," said Mercy, unconsciously tugging the netting down over her cheek. "And I'd do it again, if I had to."

"I never learned why that man wanted to hurt you. Was it a random attack?"

Mercy shook her head. "Why do you want to know all of this? It happened so long ago."

"I've always wondered about the event that caused you to hide half of your face from the world. You're beautiful, Mother, even with the scars. I don't know why you're so self-conscious about it."

"That's because you've grown up seeing me no other way than like this."

"Nobody thinks it's as bad as you do. Did you know that man?"

"Not really, but it all stemmed from something that happened on the road outside of Fort Worth when your father was bringing me home. We missed the stagecoach that day because of me, and I insisted that we leave town that same day. I was very spoiled and selfish back then and used to getting my own way. So your father searched all over for a carriage so we could leave. The only thing he could find was a brand new funeral hearse, and I threw a hissy fit when I finally recognized what it was. But later, we realized it probably saved our lives."

They had arrived at Jack's house on 4th Street. Jack opened the gate and let his mother pass.

"A funeral hearse saved your lives?"

"It sounds ludicrous, but it's true."

He held her arm as they walked up the steps.

"Hold that thought, Mother, and let me warm up this room so you can continue."

He held open the door for her and turned on the light. Then he fetched some kindling from the back porch and stoked the pot bellied stove, coaxing the embers back to life. He pulled a second chair over by the stove for his mother, and turned his desk chair around to face it.

He caught his mother watching him.

"You seem to be managing quite well with just one arm." She took off her coat and draped in on the back of the chair.

"The doctor said I'll be able to use it before too long, but until then, I can handle most everything just fine. Would you like something to drink?"

"Do you actually have anything to offer?"

Jack grinned crookedly. "Water, and I'm sure it's cold."

"No, thank you, but you're a dear to ask." She looked around the sparse room. "You definitely need a wife around here."

"It's just a place to sleep, and you're changing the subject. Tell me how the funeral hearse saved your lives."

They sat down at the same time, and his mother continued.

"We met some bad men on the road; they intended to rob us until they saw the hearse. And I believe they would have if their leader hadn't put a stop to it. They thought we were carrying a body, and out of respect for the dead, he let us pass. We learned at the next stage stop that the stage coach we were supposed to have ridden in had been robbed, and a man was shot."

"Y'all were very fortunate then."

"Those men's faces were covered during the stage robbery, but they hadn't bothered to hide them with us, so I was able to give the Texas Rangers a good description of the men and even a couple of their first names after our encounter with them."

"That was very brave of you."

"Not really. I assumed I would never see them again, but several months later when I was in Brownwood, the one named Hank walked into the Samuel's store. I recognized him immediately, but he didn't recognize me. Caitlin's father Ethan had met up with them on the road somewhere, and he had unwittingly brought them to Brownwood after sharing all kinds of information about it, including their new bank. Without Ethan's knowledge, they planned to rob the bank. After Hank left the store, I told Mr. Samuel about him, and he made me go out the back door and head to the house a couple of blocks away to tell his wife to make sure all the kids were accounted for and off the street, since he figured there would be some gunfire if the bank was robbed.

"I didn't see him, but Hank saw me leaving the town square and by then he remembered me. They found out in Fort Worth that our hearse wasn't carrying a body after all, and they must've figured it was our fault that the law was after them. I didn't know it, but he followed me to the Samuel's house and hid in the barn. Caitlin was out there playing with some kittens, but she told me later that she hid when she saw the strange man come in the barn. I ran out there to bring her inside and walked right into his arms."

Mercy shuddered at the memory. "He took great relish in slapping me around before he realized the barn was on fire. Caitlin said later that she watched him smoke a cigarette before I got out there, so we figured that's what caught the hay on fire. I couldn't find Caitlin at first-- she froze where she was hiding, and by the time I found her, fire had surrounded us. We made our way to the inside stalls and I grabbed a horse blanket hanging on the top board and dipped it into the trough and covered Caitlin with it as I carried her through the pen. The hayloft was burning fiercely above us, and I remember something burning fell on me and…the horrendous pain that followed. I don't remember anything after that. Your father told me that we'd made it outside before I collapsed, and Caitlin dragged the wet blanket over me and walked out into the big pen where he saw her. He crawled back into the smoke and somehow found me. It took a long time for me to heal."

Jack reached over and grasped her hands. "I'm so sorry you had to go through all of that."

"It made me a stronger person, and it helped teach me that my looks weren't everything."

"Then you should stop hiding behind your veil."

She smiled. "I still have a bit of vanity, but I mainly wear it because I don't like people staring at me."

"They stare at you because you're beautiful." He knew that pleased her to hear that, but he also knew that she'd learned to be self-effacing.

"And you take after me, you handsome devil."

Maybe not entirely modest, Jack thought, with a grin. "Did you fall in love with Dad after he saved your life?"

His mother rewarded him with a smile. "No. I fell in love with him during that trip from Fort Worth traveling in that funeral hearse, but I didn't realize it until after I'd moved to Brownwood. After the fire I figured he couldn't love me because of my scars."

"And we see how that turned out."

"Do you know that he told me that he thought I was more beautiful after acquiring these scars than when I was flawless and spoiled?"

"That sounds like Dad."

"Your father, more than anyone else, taught me that love means self-sacrifice and trust and patience. He even sold his prized horse to repay a debt I owed, but we got him back eventually."

"Was that Redeemer?"

Mercy nodded her head.

"I know it wasn't easy dredging up all those memories, but thank you for telling me." He squeezed her hand and let go.

His mother smiled. "I need to be reminded how blessed I am that your father didn't give up on me, and now I have three beautiful children. Do you know how proud I am of you and your sisters? I can't believe you're all grown up and ready to take on the world."

"Or at least the state of Texas," said Jack, smiling.

"You're a Taylor, son. Don't forget who you are or what we taught you. I've seen power corrupt and ruin men faster than anything."

"Don't worry, Momma. I won't forget."

In Jarvis's absence, Jack fell easily into an evening routine of going by Dr. Gilbert's office to let Kitty check his arm, which was more of an excuse to see her than anything. But she let him escort her home, and he would stay to eat supper at Mrs. Gerwick's boarding house. He found her cooking similar to Vestal's, his grandmother's cook back home, and Mrs. Gerwick charged him less than the restaurants downtown.

But the best part was spending time with Kitty.

On Saturday, Jack invited her to visit the Capitol grounds, so she packed a picnic basket, and he rented a hack to take them. When Jack turned the horse onto Congress Avenue heading north, the Capitol dome rose up in the middle of the road before them, half a mile away. Seeing the stately building never ceased to amaze him. People said the building was constructed of red granite quarried from around Marble Falls, but Jack thought it actually looked more pink than red.

The trees with their bare branches did little to hide the grandeur of the building where Texas laws were birthed and enacted.

Jack slowed when they entered the park area. A number of people walked the grounds. Some day he would have an office in this magnificent place.

He pulled up beside a young live oak tree, climbed down and tied the reins to a limb. "Do you want to walk around a bit before we have our lunch?"

"Yes, I need to warm up. That wind is a little brisk."

Jack helped Kitty alight from the hack. They walked towards the east side of the Capitol and around it to the north.

"Look!" Kitty touched his arm and pointed up. "Is that a statue of a woman on top of the dome?"

Jack looked up and nodded. "The Goddess of Liberty."

"I've never noticed that before. What's she holding up?"

"A star. You'll see a lot of five-pointed stars around here. We seem to be quite proud of our lone star."

"And other than the color, the building looks very similar to pictures I've seen of the U.S. Capitol, doesn't it."

"I think they patterned it after theirs. But did you know that ours is actually taller than the Capitol in Washington?"

Kitty shook her head. "Is that legal?"

Jack laughed. "In Texas, it is. I don't know if they did it on purpose, but reading about some of the egos that have walked these grounds, I wouldn't be a bit surprised if that was the intent. We were our own independent republic at one time."

"I wish I'd paid more attention to that part of school," Kitty said. "What exactly is a republic?"

"In a republic, the sovereignty is in each individual person; individual freedom is paramount. In a democracy, the sovereignty is in the group; the majority rules; the minority has few or no rights."

"That's hard for me to understand."

"You're not the only one. I think the general public and lawmakers alike tend to stir both concepts together and apply whichever principle proves most favorable for them on any issue. Our country is supposed to be a republic rather than a democracy, but too often the majority can hurt the minority. Justus brought that up this week, and it's really made me stop and think."

They paused to let a couple of young women pass in front of them. Both smiled at Jack as they walked by. He returned the smile and held up a hand in greeting. They giggled and waved back, and kept looking back at him until they walked into the building.

"What was that about?" Jack looked down at his clothes. "They were acting like I forgot to put on my pants or something."

Kitty snickered. "I think they recognized you from your picture in the newspaper."

"You think so?" Jack looked back towards the door.

"I do," said Kitty. "I think with your popularity right now, you could easily be elected if you ran this year."

"This year? Jarvis said I needed some experience behind me. He was thinking about '04." They continued to walk.

"Have you thought about what your platform would be?"

"Not entirely, but I know I want to make things better for folks. Justus mentioned the poll tax recently, and he brought up some troublesome things about it that I hadn't thought of. I've been doing a little research and came across something called the Black Codes."

"What's that?"

"The short version is that they were laws passed right after the Civil War that prevented Negroes from having the same civil rights and liberties that everyone else had."

Kitty frowned. "Lincoln ended slavery, but that sounds like just another form of enslavement."

"Too many people think Negroes are inferior, and if a person is even as little as one-eighth Negro, they're subject to these outrageous laws."

"Do you know any Negroes besides Justus?"

"Not really. Grace had a few Mexicans, but no Negroes. I'd see them in Waco. I just didn't realize how differently the law treats them than us. How can they improve themselves if the laws knock them down every time they try to get up? It's not fair, and I didn't realize it until Justus asked me to think about the poll tax for someone like a sharecropper. They can't ever get ahead to get out of that situation, much less have extra money laying around to use for voting."

"You know taking a stand against that law would be very unpopular among a lot of people around here."

Jack looked at her. "How do you feel about all this?"

"What you're talking about is admirable, but you need to be careful. Your political career could end before it's even started. What else do you support?"

"I think a safe workplace for employees and a healthy environment for creating businesses and jobs are important, and that would increase commerce and the State's revenue, which would allow us to stay within our budget."

Kitty raised her eyebrows. "I'm impressed! And do you know how you're going to accomplish those things?"

Jack gave her a sheepish look. "I haven't the slightest idea."

Kitty threw her head back and laughed, and Jack couldn't help but laugh with her.

"But I'm working on it! I have stacks of reading material at home and at the office, with Jarvis's blessing. I'm learning the process of turning a bill into a law and all the steps that takes."

"Sounds like you're already in office."

"When I commit to something, I jump in with both feet."

"I like that you research the issues and think for yourself."

"I hope I can still say that after a few years. I'm already feeling the pressure to compromise my convictions."

"Really? But you're not even in office." Kitty stopped walking. "Oh, let me guess. Link and Mr. Baldwin."

Jack smiled ruefully. "Yeah."

"They seem to be the manipulative sort."

"Link, more so than Mr. ... than Jarvis. They just want me to be a good lawyer, but I'm not sure I would make a good trial lawyer."

"Is that required for you to be a legislator?"

"No, but I need to be able to debate well, if that's what it takes to campaign and later, convince constituents and lawmakers to agree with good legislation."

They took a wider turn to walk into the park area on the west side of the Capitol.

"I thought my job as a woman doctor was hard, but I think you have a tougher road ahead of you."

"Do you want me to take you inside the Capitol?" Jack asked.

Kitty shook her head. "Not today. I'd rather you take me on a tour when the Legislature is in session. I want to see what you're talking about when it comes to making laws."

Jack's eyes lit up. "I'd love to show you."

"And I'm getting hungry. Tell me more about how Texas became a state while we walk back to get the basket."

"Texas governed itself for ten years without any outside interference, but it wasn't that Texas didn't want to be annexed to the United States. As early as the end of the Revolution in 1836, Texans voted overwhelmingly in favor of annexation, but the current U.S. administration was afraid of war with Mexico, and others said the anti-slavery sentiment in the U.S. was the biggest obstacle, so Texas withdrew the annexation offer."

"What changed the U.S.'s mind?"

"Great Britain was getting a little too friendly with Texas, primarily because they benefitted from commercial trade with us. They didn't have to deal with the American tariff system or the issue of slavery, and they wanted to prevent the U.S. from expanding further west. Great Britain had no plans to take over Texas, but their comfortable relationship was enough to spur the U.S. government into agreeing to add Texas as a state."

"You've done some serious studying."

"I've always enjoyed history, but I had to dig much deeper to prepare for my legislative career. I've learned so much more about Texas on my own than I ever did in school."

"I preferred the science classes. Galveston was a great place to study nature."

"I'd think the fact that you lived on an island would limit your ability to study nature."

"You'd be surprised what you could find on that little plot of land-- the tide pools, the beach and gulf, and the flora, although the storm damaged a lot of it. The city leaders are making plans to build a sea wall and raise the elevation of the island to protect them from future storms."

"How could they raise an island? There's only so much dirt on it to work with."

"They plan to dredge sand from the bay floor to build up the land. I don't have the mental capacity to even come up with an idea like that, much less figure out how to do it. Just like I can't imagine designing a large building as this, and with a dome roof topping it. How does it keep from falling in on itself?"

"You just tapped into a stunted part of my brain. I know very little about construction."

"Me neither. But I can admire the finished work."

They walked up to the hack and Jack grabbed the basket.

"Where would you like to dine, M'lady? The warm steps of the Capitol?"

Kitty reached over and retrieved a folded quilt. "I don't mind sitting on the ground, but let's pick a spot on the sunny side of the building, away from that north wind."

They found a place tucked in a southwest-facing corner of the front of the Capitol where the grass was still green. Kitty spread out the quilt and sat down. Jack set the basket between them and removed the cup towel covering the contents.

"What did Mrs. Gerwick pack for us?"

"Ham and leftover biscuits, and apple pie from last night's supper."

Jack grabbed a biscuit and a piece of ham and took a big bite.

"I wish I could've met your mother when she was here."

"I can't wait for you to meet her, but later."

"Why?"

"She might make some premature assumptions about us."

"Oh."

"And she might start making some premature plans."

"Oh!" Kitty's eyes widened.

"Don't get me wrong. My mother is a wonderful person, but I don't want to put you in an uncomfortable position."

"I understand."

Jack took another bite and glanced around the Capitol grounds. "Everyone's staring at us again. Are we insane to have a picnic lunch in the middle of winter?"

10

Jarvis returned from Houston on Friday, eight days after Jack's mother returned home to Grace. Link stayed behind to work with the newly hired employees of the newly established office, closer to the Spindletop oil field near Beaumont where Jarvis's early investments had finally proven extremely lucrative. Jarvis told him the first gusher brought in 100,000 barrels a day, which wasn't his, but he had invested in land and wells near it, which were already paying off. The huge profits would easily finance Jack's campaign and more.

Jarvis had mentioned on a number of occasions that he saw a possible governorship in Jack's future. But the more Jack learned about the weakness of the governor's position and its lack of formal power, he decided that the House was a good place to start his career, and possibly the best place to stay in public office.

Emery stuck his head in the door. "Mr. Baldwin wants to talk to you."

Jack looked up from the midst of a stack of papers. "I'm not quite finished with…"

"He wants to see you now, and I don't think it's about cattle rustling or petty theft."

"All right." Jack stood up and straightened his tie. He slipped his left arm in the sling and walked down the hall, running his fingers lightly over the smooth bead-board wainscot that lined the walls at a height of five feet. A dark green wall-paper above it complimented the dark wood.

He knocked on the door, and Jarvis spoke from the other side.

"Come on in, Jack."

Jack opened the door, noticing his employer's desk was clear except for a single paper in his hand. He wondered how the man could work without a cluttered desk.

"Good morning!"

"Good morning, sir." Jack walked over and shook his hand. "How was Houston?"

"Very satisfying. We're headed in the right direction with this new office."

"How long will Link be there?"

"Until he knows that everyone can do their jobs. I figure he'll be back sometime next week."

Jack nodded, feeling entirely too relieved about that.

"Have a seat. I need to talk to you about a couple of things."

Jack took one of the seats facing the desk.

"When's your next court date?" asked Jarvis.

"Tuesday."

"Who's deciding the case?"

"Judge Martin."

"Good. He doesn't waste any time. How do you feel about your case?"

"I think it's solid. The evidence is--"

"Remove the phrase 'I think' from your vocabulary," Jarvis interrupted. "Just say, 'We have a solid case.' Otherwise, you don't sound as confident as you should."

"Yes, sir. The stolen cattle were located on my client's property, but since they were there during the time between his working cattle days, he wasn't aware that a rustler was using one of his traps to hold stolen livestock. We're convinced the thief was my client's neighbor that owned the land next to the trap. A deputy found a hide with the stolen brand curing in this neighbor's barn, so we know he butchered at least one of the steers. My client isn't rich, but he has plenty of his own cattle and no reason to steal more, and his reputation is stellar, unlike the neighbor's. He confessed to taking the one steer, but denies that he stole the rest of them. But I thi-- but it's obvious that the neighbor was just using my client's place to cover his own misdeeds. The deputy involved will testify to that fact. And we have plenty of character witnesses for the defendant."

"Good; that should be a quick win for you." He leaned back in his chair. "I've spent a lot of time thinking this past week, and I'm convinced if we play our cards right, we could have you running in this year's election."

"I don't think… I don't believe… I'm not ready yet, sir!" Jack stammered.

"You're three years older than the minimum age for this office; you're the talk of the town after saving my life; and you're smart, Jack. You'll be ready. You've been preparing for several years now. It's time to jump in the water and start swimming."

"But I've never given a speech before."

"You've debated and talked in your classes, right?"

Jack nodded.

"It's not much different in front of less educated people. We'll give you ample opportunities to hone those skills, starting small and ending big."

Jack sat there dumbfounded. "I thought I'd have more time, but I have to admit I'm eager to start working on it. This is what I've been planning for ever since you brought me to Austin."

"I know you'll be ready."

Jack smiled. "Kitty mentioned the possibility of me running this year."

"Kitty?"

"Dr. Synatzske."

"When did you see her?"

"I've seen her every day since my mother left."

Jarvis didn't look pleased.

"Do you know anything about her?"

Jack bristled. "Why do you ask?"

"When you're in public office, you'll be scrutinized about everything. It's important to make sure the people you surround yourself are above reproach."

"She's a doctor! Other than a preacher, I don't know any other profession more noble than that."

"I'm not asking these questions to upset you, Jack, but we have to check anything that your opponents might use against you. Do you know anything about her family?"

"Her mother works as a housekeeper for a well-known lawyer in Galveston. Her father died when she was young."

Jarvis nodded his head. "Sounds like you won't have any problems concerning her."

Jack took a deep breath. "Aren't the issues more important than who I'm seeing?"

"The voting community is a fickle beast and unfortunately, one wrong step can cause you to lose favor. You have to consider everything that you do in light of how the general public will view it. That's just a part of politics."

"I'm beginning to see why you prefer to stay out of the limelight."

Jarvis smiled. "I'm too old and tired to face all of that scrutiny. And even if I did want to run, you know the reason I can't. So my talents and assets are best used elsewhere."

"How did you even find me?"

"Link sent out inquiries around Central Texas. Somebody recommended you; at the moment I don't recall who that was, but I believe he was from Waco."

Jack's brow furrowed in thought. "My mother's parents live there; my grandfather is president of a large bank."

"Maybe it was him. What do you think you'd be doing if you were still in Grace?"

"Breaking and training horses," Jack said without hesitation. "And don't get me wrong, I like horses, and my parents are content to live out their lives in Grace, but I want to do more. I want a leave a mark on this state-- to make life better for folks."

Jarvis pushed back from his desk. "I think you're well on your way to do just that. I'd like to see your opening statement on my desk today, and since the case is fairly open and shut, I want you to work on your closing argument, too. I don't know if Link will be back in time to help you polish them, so I'll take a look at them."

Jack stood. "I appreciate your help." He held out his hand. "And I didn't mean to get a little hot about Kitty. You know much more about this process than I do."

Jarvis grasped his hand firmly. "That's what I'm here for. And I see a big future ahead of you, Jack."

"Thank you, sir."

Jack walked out of the office, convinced he was on the winning team. "Get me some coffee, Emery!" He boomed. "We have work to do, and I need a clear head."

On Sundays, Jack normally rode his horse to First Baptist Church on 10th and Colorado Streets, a good ten blocks or so from his house and nine blocks from the livery. Sunday had become the only consistent time during the week he rode Lonesome Joe. But this Sunday, he stood in front of the stall and confessed to his old friend that he had to take a hack to escort a pretty lady doctor to church; that it wouldn't be too ladylike for her to ride double behind him. He heard Louis, the livery boy, snicker at that statement. He leaned forward to scratch behind the horse's ears and lowered his voice, promising to find time to ride Lonesome soon.

After church, he joined Kitty and some of the other boarders, mostly unmarried school teachers, for Sunday dinner at Mrs. Gerwick's table. He started to feel quite confident with his conversational skills when the young ladies giggled or agreed with every comment he made. But later Kitty shrunk his head back to a normal size by telling him he could've babbled absolute nonsense and all those girls would've thought he was President Theodore Roosevelt.

Jack felt a pang of regret that women weren't allowed to vote.

The rest of his waking hours that week were spent on the trial.

* * *

Link came back Thursday evening, Jack learned on Friday. He saw Link sitting beside his client when he walked into the courtroom. He talked himself out of feeling intimidated by Link, telling himself that Link was only there to help him. He knew he needed to improve his public speaking skills, and learning to keep Link out from under his skin had to be good practice for politics. That thought alone created a genuine smile when he shook Link's hand.

Jack presented his closing argument that morning, and the judge decided for the defendant well before the end of the day. Link made sure the newspaper people talked to Jack and his client on the courthouse steps, and on their walk back to the office he critiqued Jack's closing statement.

"You had good eye contact with the judge, and normally, whether it's the judge or a jury—that is who you focus on to win over. But since you are running for office, that audience at your back is made up of voters, so turn around and convince them, too, of your client's innocence. And if you connect with them now, you'll have their votes later when they see your sincerity and commitment to the truth of a matter."

Jack nodded, and had to admit he was impressed with Link's advice. "Where did you learn all of this?"

"Through lots of practice."

"Where?"

"I started in Illinois and eventually ended up in California."

"Is that where you met Jarvis?"

Link nodded. "He came to me for some legal advice and showed an interest in learning about the law." He glanced around before continuing. "He said he told you about his problem in Kansas."

"Yes. I have to admit that really shocked me."

"Sometimes we get on the wrong side of the law through no deliberate fault of our own. In his case, it was his word against two yokels in their own stomping ground. He did the right thing by running, although it hasn't be easy for him with that hanging over his head. But on the other hand, it was the catalyst that changed the direction of his life."

"How did you end up working together?"

"He talked me out of making the biggest mistake of my life, which is all I'm going to say about that. Instead, I followed him to Texas to open up a law firm with him, and it's been the best decision of my life."

"And you know his real name?"

"Yes, and that's all I'll say about that, too. He'll tell you if he thinks you should know."

Jack nodded. "Do you ever plan to get back into trial lawyering?"

"Nah, it's too much work, and it involves dealing with people."

Jack chuckled. "What do you mean by that?"

"People are emotional and messy. I prefer to keep them at arm's distance, no, make that *across the room* distance."

"How did you end up defending people?"

"I enjoyed the environment and challenge of a debate. I liked the winning part of a trial much more than the part about righting wrongs."

"Pardon me for being blunt, but that all sounds rather aggressive and indifferent."

"I think of it as competitive and objective. Don't ever make the mistake of getting emotionally involved with your clients, Jack. That's a liability that could potentially hurt you."

"Do you miss the challenge?"

Link shook his head. "I take pleasure in winning in different ways now, one of which is going to land you in office come November, and another pays significantly better."

"Now you sound hardnosed and greedy."

Link actually smiled. "Determined and ambitious. Somebody has to do the background strategy and finances of this campaign while you're out there smiling and shaking hands and winning votes."

"True."

"And that's why *you're* running for office, and I'm not."

Jack paused right in front of Dr. Gilbert's office. "I need to step in here for a minute-- I haven't had Ki--the doctor look at my arm all week, and…"

"I'll see you back at the office. Congratulations on your win."

"Thank you." He stood there for a moment watching Link walk away. They had actually conversed as peers, and for the first time Jack felt comfortable enough to rib him a bit. Maybe the man wasn't as unfeeling and insufferable as he originally thought. And he was loyal to Jarvis, in spite of his boss's checkered past.

He stepped into the doctor's office and walked over to speak to Mrs. Leigh, the nurse who did double duty keeping order in the front room and as well as helping care for patients.

"Hello, Mr. Taylor. Haven't seen you in a while! Take a seat, and I'll let Dr. Synatske know you're here."

Jack steered clear of a couple of coughing children and stood by the window watching the bustling street, people hurrying to and fro. The buildings downtown were getting taller and grander. The most recent census said Austin's population was over 20,000 residents. The city was growing; the state was growing. He was learning about the problems associated with growth, and planned to stay one step ahead of them. He felt like this was where he was supposed to be. He took a deep breath and smiled. It felt good to know where he was heading.

"Mr. Taylor?"

Jack turned around.

"Dr. Synatske will see you now," said Mrs. Leigh.

He headed down the gray-walled hall and turned left into the examining room.

He was surprised to see it was empty.

He looked around the room while he waited for her. The walls were also painted gray. The examining table and rest of the furniture in the room were a dark wood, possibly walnut. A tall chest of small drawers and matching shelves beside it contained an array of apothecary jars. He realized he'd been standing most all day, so he pulled out the swivel rolling chair from the desk and sat down.

He turned it to face the desk, and glanced at a stack of

papers, the top one half-covered with notes. He looked at her handwriting, neat with very straight lines. He wrote half-printing and half-cursive, and his writing tended to slant down the page as he wrote across it. Penmanship wasn't an area in which he excelled in school.

Footsteps in the hall made him look up and swivel away from the desk. He stood when Kitty walked through the doorway.

She paused and looked at a chart. "Let's see... your name is... ah! Mr. Taylor. Haven't seen you lately." She looked up and smiled, and then looked down again. "Now what was it that we were treating you for? Dropsy? Flux? Lock jaw?"

Jack chuckled. "I deserve that. I didn't mean to neglect you this week." He walked over to her. "I've missed you terribly."

She held the chart against her chest as she faced him. "I've missed you, too. Is the trial over?"

"Yes! And we won!"

"That's good news! So you won't be so busy this weekend?"

"I promise to not look at the next case until Monday morning."

"Good, now let me look at your arm. Have a seat on the table."

She removed his coat and the sling, and unbuttoned his shirt far enough for her to slide it down his left arm.

He'd finally learned to calm down with her this close. Now he simply enjoyed it. She examine his arm, gently pressing around the stitches. He fought the urge to flex it for her sake, but was afraid he might do it some harm. At the same time he hoped it didn't feel like a mashed potato to her.

He watched her face, watched her eyes taking in everything. Her skin was so clear, and even after a long work day she smelled... clean.

"You smell good."

She blushed a bit. "I wash my hands all day long."

"Dr. Gilbert usually smells like medicine."

"He's always mixing something up for his patients." She

turned around and walked to a counter and started gathering things on a tray.

"Is everything all right?"

"Yes, although I probably should've removed your stitches several days ago. Everything looks like it's healing nicely."

"Good. And do I have to wear this sling anymore? My arm feels like it's wasting away."

"Just a few more days in the sling just to remind you not to over-exert it, then you can take it off." She set the tray beside him and picked up some tweezers and a very pointed pair of scissors.

"You were right about something," Jack said.

She smiled. "I'm always right about something."

"Jarvis and Link want me to run for office this year."

She stopped and looked up at him. "I knew it! But will we ever get to see each other again?"

"No, that's why I stopped by… to tell you I can't see you until after the election in November."

She pulled a little hard on a stitch.

"Ow! You know I'm just kiddin'!"

Kitty smiled mischievously, and then it faded. "I'm afraid that statement's not far from the truth. You'll be so busy campaigning you'll hardly have time for me."

"I'll make time, I promise." Jack lifted up her face with his right hand. "And I keep my promises. Are you busy next Saturday?"

Kitty shook her head. "I don't know enough people in Austin to have a social life yet."

"I have Jarvis's box seats for the opera."

"I thought they turned the Millett Opera House into a skating rink."

"Yeah, but I'm talking about the Hancock on 6th Street. I'd like to invite the Gilberts and my cousins who'll be in town for the weekend."

"Grace… and what was her husband's name?"

Jack nodded. "Finn."

"That's right. I only met him briefly." Kitty's face lit up.

"That'll be such fun! Who's performing?"

"I don't have a clue, but it'll be a pleasant evening for all of us together."

"I haven't seen Grace and Finn since the storm in Galveston! We were so afraid they hadn't survived the night. And then I spent the next week helping at the hospital and missed telling them goodbye."

"They'll be surprised to see you living up here now."

On Saturday Jack rented a carriage to pick up Kitty for their evening at the opera. Grace and Finn were staying with the Gilberts, so they planned to come with them and meet Jack and Kitty at the opera house. He was relieved to learn that John Philip Sousa and his band were performing that evening. He knew he could stay awake during a rousing performance of songs like Sousa's fairly new *Stars and Stripes Forever*. But he was surprised to learn that most of the evening's performance was an operetta called *El Capitan*.

"At least it's in English," Jack whispered to Kitty after it started. He looked around at the four empty seats in the box. "Wonder what's keeping them?"

"Dr. Gilbert was probably delayed by a patient," Kitty whispered back. "I'm sure they'll be along soon."

Ten minutes later, his cousin Grace hugged him from behind, and reached over to do the same with Kitty. Jack stood and turned to shake Finn's and Dr. Gilbert's hands, and nodded to Daisy as she sat down behind Kitty. Jack offered Daisy his seat, but she insisted that he sit next to Grace, and Finn sat in the second row with the Gilberts.

When Grace and Jack continued to talk, a matronly lady in the next box shushed them.

"I'm sorry we didn't get here sooner to talk," said Grace,

"but we'll catch up later."

"Who's keeping the baby?" asked Jack.

Grace pointed back at the Gilberts and put her finger to her lips before smiling at the woman glaring at them.

After the operetta, Sousa played a number of his well-known marches, including *Cotton King* and *Semper Fidelis*, and ended the evening with *The Stars and Stripes Forever*, which brought everyone to their feet clapping in time.

Jack talked to Grace above the din. "We missed y'all at Christmas."

"We hated not seeing everybody, but Johnny was too sick to travel," said Grace. "He's doing much better now. I can't wait to see everyone at MeeMaw's, and we plan to go on up to Brownwood to visit Finn's family and Aunt Faith and her family, so we'll get to see everyone eventually."

"That's good. I know MeeMaw is anxious to see that boy. How old is he now?"

"John Taylor Samuel is five months old, and he'll turn six months before we get back to Dalton. Momma cried when they saw us off. She's convinced he'll be half grown by the time we return." She leaned over to speak to Kitty. "It's so good to see you, Kitty! I had no idea you lived in Austin now."

They turned around to face the others while the theater emptied, and Jack let Grace slip between them so the two women could talk. Jack looked around the group. His cousin Grace, blonde-haired with those Taylor blue eyes, was quite the head-turner. She had fled to Galveston back in 1900 after Finn refused her very bold and public proposal. She didn't realize Finn had lost all of his investments in his brother's business, and he was flat broke. But he ended up following her to Galveston just days before the storm, which killed over 6,000 people. They barely survived the harrowing storm and were married before they left the island. They settled on Grace's parents' ranch in Dalton, which they would inherit someday. Finn's brother Joseph ended up selling their patents and recouped almost all of Finn's money he'd lost.

Finn was seven years older than Grace, but they were a

good match. Grace had chased him for years, but Finn was reluctant to commit because of a tragedy in his teen years. His first love was Jack's cousin Caitlin from Brownwood. Finn saw her fall from a wagon when the horses got away from her, and she died soon after. He blamed himself, and it took him a long time to get over the loss.

Jack looked at the tall doctor and his petite, red-headed wife. Kitty's voice talking to Grace interrupted his thoughts.

"I wouldn't be here if it weren't for Daisy and Dr. Gilbert. And I was so surprised to learn that you were Jack's cousin."

"Texas is getting smaller all the time!" Grace turned to Jack. "Did you know the Gilberts?"

"Only by reputation, and because you told me you'd met them in Galveston."

"Well, Kitty, I don't know how you feel about it," said Grace, "but I'm relieved to be off Galveston Island after that tragic storm. I'm so thankful we survived."

"I have to admit, I'm happy to be much further inland, too."

"And you're a full-fledged doctor now!"

Kitty nodded. "Some of the men around here have a problem getting treated by a woman doctor."

"Not me," Jack piped in. "She patched up my arm just fine."

"We heard about the shooting. What happened?"

"I'll tell you about it later. What about you, Finn? Would you let a female doctor work on you?"

"I don't have any problem with it, as long as I don't have to take off my clothes for something."

"Well, I'm certainly glad to hear that!" said Grace.

Everyone laughed.

Dr. Gilbert spoke up. "I would highly recommend Dr. Synatzske to anyone. I'm proud to have her on my staff."

"Thank you, Dr. Gilbert. I'm so fortunate to be in Austin."

Jack turned and looked at the theater seats below. "It looks like the crowd's thinned out. The Driskill's only a block away, so we can walk to the reception. Afterwards Dr. Gilbert and I can bring the carriages around to get you home."

"Let's go!" said Daisy. She reached over and touched Jack's arm as they exited the theater box. "Thank you so much for including us this evening, Jack. With Joe's busy schedule, we don't get out much these days. And remember to thank Mr. Baldwin for us. This was so generous of him."

Jack nodded his head. "I'll definitely tell him, and I'm so glad we've finally met in person. You made quite an impression on my cousin during that short time in Galveston."

"I wish we could see each other more often, but at least we get to be the stopover for them traveling between Grace and Dalton."

The street was full of well-dressed attendees from the Opera House, and most were heading towards the Driskill Hotel.

"She's all lit up and has her best face on," said Daisy.

"Who?" Dr. Gilbert asked, looking around.

Daisy shook her head. "The Driskill! She's the most beautiful building in Austin."

"She? Why not 'he'?"

"She's too pretty to be a he-- look at all of those beautiful arched windows and columns."

"But what about those men's heads on top of each side?"

"That's just a homage to the Driskill men, like this locket I wear with your picture in it."

"You have a locket with my picture in it?"

"You gave it to me for Christmas, Joe!"

Dr. Gilbert laughed and pulled Daisy into a hug. "I'm just pulling your leg, darlin'."

Finn opened the door for everyone, and Jack he led them through the opulent lobby with its marble floors and towering columns. Grace pointed to the stained glass dome. Daisy said the lobby reminded her of the lavish style of many of the homes on Galveston Island.

They checked their coats and walked into the Grand Salon room where the reception was taking place. Jack had eaten countless meals in this room since he moved to Austin, but tonight it looked more like a ballroom.

Kitty looked up at the frescoed ceiling. "I didn't noticed that the first and only time I was here."

Jack followed her eyes. Texas and American flags graced the ceiling. "Now why have I never noticed that before?"

"You have to look up every once in a while."

An ensemble of stringed instruments played from the corner, and a raised platform was set up nearby. Jack was surprised to see Jarvis and Link talking with a massive man near the podium. They all held stem glasses. Jack noticed the waiters with trays of filled glasses distributing them among the crowd.

"Uh oh."

Kitty looked at Jack. "What's wrong?"

"I think they might be up to something."

A waiter offered his tray to Jack and Kitty.
"What is it?" he asked.
"Champagne."
Kitty declined.

Jack took a glass and sipped it. "What's the occasion?"

"I don't know, sir," the waiter replied.

"What does it taste like?" asked Kitty. "Is it good?"

Jack shrugged his shoulders. "I don't know if it's good or not; I've never tasted champagne before."

"Do you think Mr. Sousa will be attending the reception?" asked Grace, shaking her head at the waiter.

"I've never tasted champagne either," said Finn, helping himself.

Grace's eyebrows lifted.

"Just one glass," said Finn. "I've always wondered what it tasted like."

Dr. Gilbert and Daisy each took a glass. "Was this part of the opera tickets?"

"I don't know."

"This is good champagne," said Dr. Gilbert. "Somebody spent some money tonight."

"I'm not sure what my boss is doing here since he didn't attend the concert," said Jack, "but I'd be willing to bet he knows what's going on. Wait here and I'll go ask him."

Jack made his way through the crowded room towards the platform. When Jarvis saw him, he waved his hand towards the ensemble, and the music stopped.

"May I have your attention, please!" he yelled over the laughter and conversation in the room. "I hope you enjoyed the evening with John Philip Sousa."

A round of clapping, tapping glass and cheers reverberated around the room. Jack stopped and waited for him to finish addressing the crowd.

"He promised to join us for a few minutes later this evening." He paused to let the enthusiastic ovation die down. "I'd also like to take this opportunity to introduce someone else to you." He looked directly at Jack and motioned for him to come up on the platform.

The people in front of him turned around and parted like the Red Sea when they saw him. Several people patted him on the back. Jack gave Jarvis a friendly glare before walking up onto the platform.

"What are you doing?" he whispered to Jarvis before turning around.

"Follow my lead," he whispered back, smiling. Jarvis placed his hand on Jack's shoulder. "Ladies and gentlemen, I'm proud to introduce you to one of the up and coming bright stars in Texas politics. Many of you know that this man saved my life recently, and not only is he courageous and willing to stand for what is right, he's smart and has a heart for helping people. Tonight, Jack Taylor is officially throwing his hat into the ring to become your spokesman in the Texas House of Representatives!"

The crowd roared.

Jack smiled and waved and looked for his friends' faces. He couldn't find them. He started to step away from the podium when someone yelled, "Speech!"

It sounded suspiciously like his cousin Grace.

Jarvis pulled him back and quieted the crowd.

"I'm not prepared," he whispered through smiling teeth.

"Yes, you are."

Jack took a deep breath and looked over the sea of faces, his future constituents. "I really appreciate your enthusiastic show of support. This has been a dream of mine ever since I learned about Texas government. I've always been fascinated by our state's history and how laws are made, and I know most of them were created to make life better for us. But times and industry change, and Texas is growing. We need to be prepared for that growth. I promise I'll do my best to represent everyone fairly." Suddenly, Justus came to mind, and he couldn't think of anything else to say.

"I... would appreciate your support in November. Thank you." He looked at Jarvis, who started clapping, which cued everyone else to follow suit.

Jack started to step down again when Jarvis grabbed his arm and pulled him over to the huge man standing off to the side with Link.

"I want you to meet someone," he said.

Jack was over six feet, but he still had to look up to meet this man's eyes.

"Jack, this is Edward Green, the chairman of the state Republican executive committee. Edward, this is who I've been telling you about."

Jack offered his hand, and the big man grasped it firmly.

"My friends call me Ned. I've heard a lot of good things about you, Jack."

Jack grinned. "I hope they're true. I'm honored to meet you, sir."

Jarvis spoke up. "We heard talk about you taking a run for the governor's office, Ned."

"I've heard the speculation, too, but I assure you, I'm not the one doing the talking. I have to admit I do enjoy Texas politics." He smiled at someone behind Jack. "Ah, there you are, Katherine. I'd like to introduce you to a new friend of mine."

Jack turned around and faced a beautiful brunette.

"This is Jack Taylor, hon. He's planning on running for office in November."

"Hello," she said, offering her gloved hand. "I'm Katherine."

"My pleasure, ma'am." He took her hand, surprised that a woman would offer a firm handshake like a man, and met her eyes, startled by their color.

Ned slapped him on the back. "Poor kid ain't old enough to know what he's getting into with these nasty politics. But I've decided we're going to help him."

Jack turned to Jarvis, who stood there with a smug look on his face. "Have you met Jarvis Baldwin?" he asked Katherine.

Jarvis spoke first. "Yes, Katherine and I are… old friends… from Galveston."

Jack looked back at the woman. Her mouth was smiling, but her eyes weren't.

"Hello… Jarvis. I happen to live in Dallas now."

"Small world!" said Ned. "Kat's so busy with philanthropic work these days, we hardly ever get to see her anymore unless we kidnap her and take her with us, which we try to do regularly." He nodded at someone and waved. "Excuse me, Jarvis. I need to speak to someone."

Jack watched the big man work his way across the room, but Jarvis's odd tone of voice brought him back.

"So, you're calling it *philanthropic work* now, Pearl?"

The smile disappeared from the woman's face. "The storm changed a lot of people's lives, Jarvis. That's all behind me now, and I would appreciate you showing some manners in front of your… protege."

"He's much more than that, I assure you."

She turned to Jack. "I truly hope you know who you're getting in bed with here."

Jarvis laughed. "Interesting choice of words, darling, but then I suppose you speak only of what you know. Does Ned know who you really are?"

"Ned knows enough. Does Jack know who you really are?"

"Yes."

Jack frowned at his boss's rudeness. "I have no idea what

either of you are talking about, but I need to get back to my guests." He nodded to Katherine, "I'm happy to have made your acquaintance, Mrs. Green."

Jarvis laughed out loud. "Good heavens, Jack. They're not married. She's just a beautiful, but common...."

The glove muffled the sound of Jarvis catching her hand before it hit his face. He brought it to his lips. "I'm sorry, Pearl, I didn't mean to ruffle your feathers."

Jack was speechless. The look of anger on Katherine's face told him she still might do something regrettable. He took her by the arm and pulled her off the platform and into the crowd, most of whom seemed oblivious to what had just transpired.

"I am so sorry... Mrs... Katherine," Jack whispered.

"Williams. My last name is Williams."

"I've never seen my boss act that way before. I don't know what to say." He smiled and nodded as they made their way acrosss the ballroom.

"Unfortunately, I've seen that side of Jarvis on numerous occasions," she said with a pasted smile on her face. "If I'd known he was in Austin, I would not have come."

When Jack waited for her to elaborate, she didn't.

"Where are you taking me?"

Jack stopped. "I don't know. I just thought I needed to separate you two."

Katherine chuckled. "You remind me of someone quite chivalrous I used to know."

"Jack!" A voice rose above the din.

He looked around and saw Grace and Finn making their way toward them. Grace about knocked him down with her hug.

"Congratulations, cousin! How exciting! Did you know about this?!"

Jack laughed. "No, I didn't. I was as surprised as you were."

"Grace? Finn?" Katherine said. "What are you doing here?"

Grace turned around and yelled a small scream of delight.

"Katherine?!" She threw her arms around the older woman. Finn stepped up and embraced her, too, like he knew her well.

"Now, I definitely don't believe this," said Jack. "Everybody around here seems to know Katherine except for me. How do y'all know each other?"

"We met in Galveston… just days before the storm, and we actually left the island together," said Grace. She turned back to Katherine. "Have you seen Marguerite lately?" She told Jack that Marguerite was a friend to them both. "I think about her so often, but her letters are getting fewer and farther between."

"She still lives in Houston," said Katherine, "but when she comes to Dallas, she stays with me. I saw her a few months ago."

"What are you doing here?" asked Grace.

"I came with my friends Mabel and Ned Green from Terrell." She turned to Jack. "I'm sorry you didn't get to meet Mabel. She wasn't feeling well this evening." She turned back to Grace. "Ned's involved with the Republican party and is seriously considering supporting Jack's run for office. And I have to say after only a few minutes around this cousin of yours, that seems like a wise decision."

The others walked up, and Jack introduced the Gilberts. He pulled Kitty to stand beside him.

"Miss Williams, this is Dr. Kitty Synatzske, a woman doctor, mind you, and she and the Gilberts used to live in Galveston, too. Do y'all know each other? Would you believe that Grace and Finn know Miss Williams?"

Jack noticed Grace's blue eyes were as wide as saucers. Finn kept looking back and forth between Katherine and Kitty with a concerned look on his face.

Daisy offered her hand. "How do you do, Katherine? I don't believe we've met." Dr. Gilbert nodded in greeting.

Katherine grasped Daisy's hand, and then offered hers to Kitty. "What an honorable profession, Kitty. I'm sure your mother is very proud of you. I know I would be."

Kitty took her hand and stared at the comely woman.

After an awkward silence, Katherine withdrew her hand. Jack noticed the color drained from Kitty's face.

"Are you all right?" he asked.

She nodded her head slightly.

Katherine quickly spoke up. "I don't want to take any more of your time. I'm sure Ned's wondering where I am, and I need to go check on my friend Mabel." She turned and hugged Grace again. "How long will you be in town?"

"We're leaving tomorrow afternoon, but we'd love to see you before we go. Where are you staying?"

"Here at the Driskill."

"We'll be going to church, but how about meeting for lunch? Or we could just meet in the lobby and visit for a while."

"Lunch sounds wonderful. Marguerite told me you have a little one now."

Grace beamed. "Yes, and we'll bring Johnny, too."

"It was an honor to meet you all," Katherine said to the Gilberts and Jack. She looked at Kitty. "Congratulations on becoming a doctor. And I love your name, Kitty." She turned around and walked away.

"What a beautiful woman," said Daisy. "I can't believe I never ran into her in Galveston. I would've remembered *her*."

Jack turned Kitty to face him. "You look pale as a ghost. Do you need to sit down for a bit?"

She shook her head. "I'm not feeling too well at the moment. Would you mind taking me home?"

"Of course. I need to go get the carriage, though."

Grace spoke up. "Kitty, if you ever need to talk…"

She looked sharply at Grace. "About what?" She didn't give Grace time to answer before turning to Jack. "I'll walk with you."

"But you're not feeling well."

"The walk will help me more than anything."

They said their goodbyes to the other two couples, and Jack promised to meet them here at noon the next day.

He walked Kitty to the coat check desk and gave the clerk

her number and waited for him to retrieve her cape.

"You know," Jack said, "the whole time I was talking with Katherine, I was thinking that she looked so familiar. It just now dawned on me that she reminds me of you, but older, of course."

The clerk handed him the cape, and Jack dug in his coat pocket for a coin to tip him. When he turned around to put the cape around Kitty's shoulders, she wasn't there.

He looked around and saw her going out the door.

Jack followed her, cape in hand. When he stepped outside, he noticed that Kitty wasn't heading back to the carriage. She had turned towards home. At the end of the block Jack caught her by the arm and stopped her, but not without a tug of war. She was sobbing.

"What did I do?" he asked as he wrapped the cape around her. "Did I leave you alone too long? I honestly didn't know Jarvis was going to do that."

She let out a wail of frustration and shook her head. "I want... to go... home," she said between uncontrollable hiccups.

Jack had never seen Kitty act this way. He seemed to be facing a little girl rather than a woman. And he had no idea what he'd done to cause this.

"Do you want me to get the carriage?"

She shook her head. "Walk... home."

"All right."

They walked for a while without talking as they continued to head east. Jack felt obligated to fill in the silence, hoping it would stop the tears.

"Did you know the streets running east to west downtown were originally named after trees?"

She shook her head.

"This one was Pecan Street, and a lot of folks still call it that. And the street I live on was called Cedar. And let me see, there was a Pine Street, and Live Oak and Hickory and..."

Jack continued to ramble on until they reached the gate to the yard of Kitty's boarding house. He held his hand on the gate, but didn't open it. Kitty was calm now, but silent. The light from the front window illuminated her face.

"Please tell me what's upset you. I'm so sorry if I offended you somehow. I'm a little dense about reading people, and I have no idea what I did."

Kitty put her hand on his arm. "It wasn't you, Jack." She took a deep breath, still ragged from crying. "Finn and Grace know. I don't know how they found out, but I could tell from their expressions that they know."

"Know what?"

Kitty looked away. "I thought I'd gotten away from all of that when I left Galveston."

"Away from what?"

"That woman."

"What woman?"

"Katherine."

"So you knew her?"

Kitty nodded, refusing to meet his eyes. She didn't elaborate.

Jack waited, and finally broke the silence. "Tell me, Kitty. What is it about her that upsets you so?"

Kitty looked down, and when she spoke, it was barely a whisper. "She gave birth to me."

Jack was shocked. "Katherine is your mother?! I don't understand. I thought your mother lives in Galveston."

"Katherine didn't raise me," she said, looking up. "My real mother Juju raised me. Katherine gave me up when I was little. I'd never met her in person before this evening."

"But you knew who she was."

She turned her face into the light. "Look at me! I'm the spitting image of her. I didn't know that until a number of people on the island started making comments about it."

"Why is that so bad? You're both beautiful."

The tears began spilling over her eyelashes again.

"Did she treat you badly?"

She shook her head. "I didn't know her name was Katherine until tonight; I only knew of her by reputation… and she went by the name of Pearl."

"Jarvis called her Pearl earlier."

"Oh, no." A moan escaped her lips, and Kitty's eyes grew wide. She put her hand over her mouth. "Then Jarvis knows, too."

"Knows what?"

When she spoke, it was only a whisper again. "That the woman who gave birth to me is a prostitute."

Jack's head started spinning. He racked his brain trying to remember anything about Katherine that might have given him a clue about her profession, but he saw nothing that told him she was a woman of loose morals. But then she was with Ned Green... and they weren't married, but she mentioned a Mabel, too. Then he remembered her almost slapping Jarvis when he spoke rudely to her.

"Maybe she's changed," he said.

"How would you know that?"

"She became upset with Jarvis when he called her Pearl. She almost slapped him right there in front of everybody."

"Really?"

"Even if she lived that way, that's not who you are. She didn't raise you."

"I know that. And I don't know how hard things must have been for her to even choose that lifestyle-- maybe it happened *because* she became pregnant with me..."

"You don't know that."

"That's not the worst of it, Jack. Don't you see? If we continue to see each other, any mention of my connection with a prostitute could ruin your chances for office."

"How would people find out?"

"Jarvis knows."

"After all he's invested in me, he wouldn't chance letting that get out."

"But he could tell you not to see me."

"Jarvis doesn't run my life."

Kitty put her hand on his face and smiled ruefully. "Oh, my sweet man, he thinks he does. And I could never live with myself if I destroyed your dream."

He grasped her hand and brought it to his lips. "You're not destroying my dream. This has just been a shock for you to see Katherine this evening. We'll talk more about this later, so don't you fret over it. Promise?"

Kitty nodded... barely.

"Can I pick you up for church tomorrow?"

"I don't want to interfere with your plans with your cousins."

"You're more than welcome to come, too."

"You need some time alone with your family. I'll ride with Mrs. Gerwick in the morning."

"We'll sit together."

Kitty nodded. "Good night, Jack."

He leaned down to kiss her gently on the cheek. "Good night, Doc."

Kitty smiled. "I don't think you've ever called me that before."

"I haven't?"

He watched her open the gate, walk into the yard and up the steps through the boarding house door. He waited for her to turn around and wave at him before closing the door like she usually did, but this time she didn't.

14

Jack saw no sign of Kitty at church. When he found Mrs. Gerwick in her usual pew, she told him that Kitty had left the house early that morning after a young boy brought her a note. Jack figured one of her patients needed her.

After church he met Katherine, Grace and Finn at the Driskill Hotel restaurant. That was the first time he'd seen little Johnny since the Samuels couldn't make the family gathering at Christmas. After the meal, Jack was content holding the baby… until he burped up on him. Then he couldn't hand him off fast enough.

"You'll have to get used to all kinds of repulsive things when you have children, Jack," said Grace, laughing.

"I may not have children then," he replied, grimacing as he wiped the curdled milk off of his pants leg with a napkin.

"Ah, but won't you be kissing hundreds of babies while running for office?" said Katherine, smiling.

"Who started that ridiculous requirement for running for office?" asked Finn. "It seems to be expected of politicians now."

Jack's frown grew. "I don't mind kissing babies; I just don't want to be their burp rag."

"You won't mind your own babies burping up on you," said Grace.

"Or worse," said Finn, grinning.

Jack didn't ask.

"How's Kitty feeling today?" asked Katherine.

Jack was relieved someone finally broached the subject he wanted to talk about. "She was upset last night, but I think she was more concerned about hurting my campaign than anything else."

The silence was deafening until Katherine spoke up.

"Ahhh." She folded her napkin. "So you know about my... past, too?"

Jack nodded. "She told me last night."

"You two must be very close for her to tell you her darkest secret. I judged by her reaction that she realized who I was."

"She said it was the first time you'd met face to face, but that she'd known about you for several years now." He noticed Katherine's eyes were puffy, like she hadn't slept well.

"I've dreamed of that moment for twenty years, but it didn't turn out like I'd hoped." Tears welled in her eyes. "But I was... I still am willing to stay out of her life forever if it meant saving her the embarrassment of being associated with me. That was one reason I left Galveston. The island had become too small, and she looked so much like me." She leaned toward Jack. "That life is behind me now, and I have Grace and Finn to thank for that. They encouraged me to leave and even offered me a way out of there." She looked at each of them. "I'll never forget what you did for me. But I want Kitty to know that life is behind me now. Could you tell her for me?"

"Yes, of course. But wouldn't you rather tell her yourself?"

Katherine shook her head. "I don't want to impose. I've never expected any kind of relationship with her, but I've kept up with her." She smiled. "She has no idea that I financed her medical school. I'm so proud of what she's accomplished. And I bought the house her mother is currently living in. That's the least I could do for the woman who raised my daughter. Juju kept the name I gave my baby girl, too. My mother used to call me 'Kat,' so Kitty was as close as I could get to my own name, which most people in Galveston never knew."

"Jarvis called you Pearl."

Katherine nodded. "That's the name I used in the business, and I hoped to never hear it again, but he brought it up last night."

Grace spoke up. "What about Kitty's father? Would he ever try to come back into her life?"

Katherine shook her head. "I'm not sure who her father is. It could be Jarvis, for all I know. He visited our establishment since well before Kitty was born, but other than last night, I hadn't seen him in years." She looked up at Jack. "Tread carefully with him, Jack. The Jarvis I knew wasn't an honorable man."

"Maybe he's changed… like you have."

"I hope so. Can I ask you to please not tell Kitty any of what I've told you? All I want for her is her happiness, and I regret that I've brought shame to her life."

Grace reached over and covered Katherine's hand with her own. "You deserve happiness in your life, too, my friend. I hope Dallas is treating you kindly."

"I've made some good friends. And with the help of Ned, I've made some good investments, so I can't complain."

Jack spoke up. "I know I'm being bold asking you this, and you don't have to answer, but I'm curious about your relationship with him."

"We're friends and business partners, that's all. I know that's probably hard to believe, but it's true. Ned is one of the kindest and most generous men I've ever met and supports several of the charities I work with. I actually introduced him to my friend Mabel, who used to be in the same *business* I was, and I wouldn't be surprised if he marries her some day. But right now his mother won't allow him to marry at all. She's afraid every woman is only after him for his money."

"Who's his mother?" asked Finn.

"Have you ever heard of Hetty Green?"

"Ned is connected to the *Witch of Wall Street?*"

"Unfortunately, that's her."

Finn continued. "I heard a horrible story about her son breaking his leg, and she took him to a free clinic to get treated.

But they recognized her and made her leave, so she took him home and swore she'd fix it herself because she was too cheap to get him proper medical help, and they ended up having to amputate his leg. Was that Ned?"

Katherine nodded. "He did lose his leg, and he does wear a prosthesis, but he told me he lost his leg after years of unsuccessful treatment. Maybe he's just covering for her. She doesn't sound like she's been the best mother to him, but he loves her in his own way."

"He must have a kind heart to be able to put up with her," said Finn.

"And it looks like he's going to throw some support towards my campaign," Jack said.

"That's good news."

"Have you ever heard of the *Black and Tan* faction of the Republican Party?" Katherine asked Jack.

"No, I haven't."

"One of Ned's best friends is William McDonald. He's very influential in the Republican Party. He lives in Fort Worth, but he's in Austin right now and might be another good connection for you. Ned met with him right after we arrived."

"I'll try to look him up." Jack turned to Finn. "Well, how's ranch life going for you? That's quite a change of pace from teaching, isn't it?"

"It's worlds apart, and I still have a lot to learn about the management side of ranching, but I love it. I much rather prefer an actual saddle than being saddled to a desk."

Everyone laughed.

Jack told Katherine that Finn used to come work for his father during the summers. "So he's not a complete greenhorn."

"Your father was a tough taskmaster, but I needed it. I was a little off-track at that time of my life."

"That's hard to believe," said Katherine. "Jack, do you remember me telling you last night that you reminded me of someone chivalrous I once knew?"

"Yes, of course."

She looked at Finn. "Would you believe I was referring to this gentleman? Finn and Grace gave me the courage to change my life over two years ago. I'll never forget what they did for me."

"We're so glad we met you, Katherine," said Grace.

"And you helped *us* more than you know," said Finn.

"We hope that you and Kitty can get to know each other some day," Grace continued.

Katherine shook her head. "I dare not let myself even hope for something as wonderful as that. I wouldn't want her to have to deal with the disgrace of my past. It gives me joy to know she was well taken care of in her younger years and is so happy now." She glanced at Jack. "And to have become a doctor! I'm amazed at her courage to enter a field that has always been dominated by men. I hope and pray she stays strong. It breaks my heart to think people could hurt her because of this noble profession she chose."

"Kitty's tough," said Jack, "but I'll keep an eye on her."

Katherine took a deep breath and smiled. "You don't know how happy I am to hear that. And Dr. Gilbert-- I'm so glad she is under his wing. I had heard of Daisy by reputation on the island, but we'd never met face to face."

"Speaking of the Gilberts," Finn said as he looked at his pocket watch. "We need to go pick up our luggage and tell them goodbye so we can get to the station before too long."

"Well, this whole weekend has been such a treat with the opera and eating in a fine restaurant and especially running into family and friends," said Grace. "My cup is full!"

They all stood and Jack shook Finn's hand and hugged Grace as she held little Johnny.

Katherine embraced Grace. "Thank you so much for including me today."

Katherine reached into her beaded purse and brought out a small card. "Here's my address in Dallas. Please keep in touch."

Grace took it and handed it to Finn. "We will. I promise."

"Would you mind giving me one, too?" asked Jack.

"You're my only connection to Mr. Green."

"Of course." She placed another card in his hand. "And you'd better not call him 'Mr. Green' to his face," she said, smiling.

"Yes, ma'am," Jack said, ginning back and then looking solemn. "I'm really glad we met, Katherine."

"Me, too." She offered her hand, and he held it for a moment before letting it go. Finn left to settle up with the waiter.

"I had no idea I would ever get to see you two again," Katherine said to Grace, then spoke to Jack. "I'm relieved someone close to Kitty knows the burden she's been carrying about me. I had no idea I would ever run into her outside of Galveston. I thought I was protecting her by leaving. I hope my scandalous past won't become known and affect her job... or your ambitions either."

"Don't you worry about that," said Jack.

"That's true," added Grace. "Jack's a Taylor, and the Taylors have survived plenty of scandals through the years."

Jack looked confused. "We have? What scandals?"

Grace laughed and then stopped. "Are you serious? Jack, dear, every Taylor generation has had its own scandal. Our grandparents, my parents and your father; your own parents..."

"My father? My parents?"

Katherine interrupted. "I'll leave you two cousins to reminise. Keep in touch, Grace."

"I will, Katherine. Goodbye." Grace kissed the baby on the head. "Now where's your father?" She started to walk away from the table.

Jack stopped her. "What scandal about my parents?"

"Oh, Jack, you know our family's history—it's full of scandal."

"It is?"

"We've always known them as family stories, but stop and think about it—Meemaw and my father getting kidnapped by an Apache; then after years of living as an Apache, PaPa Taylor brings Meemaw home with your father who's half Apache."

Jack looked around, remembering the other people in the restaurant. He took her by the elbow and walked her out into the foyer. He'd never thought about his heritage being scandalous until that moment.

"Did you realize how hard it was for Julia Taylor and her Apache children when they came back? It took years for people to accept them."

"I'm one quarter Apache."

"So?"

"I never thought about that affecting my life negatively."

"It hasn't; your parents are well thought of, but it started off rocky."

"How so?"

Grace raised her eyebrows. "If you don't know, Jack, I shouldn't be the one to tell you."

"Mother told me she'd run away from home, and that my father was hired to go find her."

"Whew! I'm glad you know about that. Mother said it was the biggest scandal of the year in Waco when your mother ran off with that gambler. Then the buzzard abandoned her in Fort Worth, but your father tracked her down and brought her home." She lowered her voice to a whisper. "Then when she ran away again, this time to live with the Samuels in Brownwood, that created a whole new scandal as to why. We've grown up with these stories and don't give them a second thought, but believe me, they were all scandalous in their time. Our family has always stood by each other, though, so we never let the gossipmongers get the best of us."

Jack tried to keep his breathing steady to hide the shock of why his mother ran away from home. "You're right. I hadn't really thought about all of that as not being normal."

15

As Jack left the Driskill, his thoughts reeled with what he'd learned about his mother. So *that* was the 'disagreement' she had with her father all those years ago—running off with a man... a man who wasn't his own father. Jack tried to push it to the back of his mind when he stopped by the boarding house to see if Kitty had returned, but Mrs. Gerwick told him no. She reminded him that Kitty sometimes called on patients outside of office hours, which alleviated some of his apprehension. He thanked her and left.

He untied Lonesome Joe's reigns and patted him on the neck. "Looks like it's just you and me today, boy. Where should we go?" He laughed when the horse's ears perked up. "How 'bout down by the river? It's been a while since we've ridden there."

He mounted his horse and turned north on Trinity to pass by Kitty's office on 6th Street just in case she might be there, but it was locked and dark. He glanced at the big Tom Moore cigar sign on the Ziller building and smiled when he thought about his Grandfather Locke letting him take a big puff on his cigar when he was around eight years old. That cured him from ever wanting to try to smoke anything after that.

Jack paused to let a streetcar pass and looked up at all the wires criss-crossing the intersection of Congress Avenue before he turned Lonesome Joe south. Things were changing fast in Austin.

The electric streetcars proved a great improvement over the mule-drawn ones, but electric power wasn't without its vulnerabilities. Less than two years before, a flood on the Colorado River broke the Austin Dam and destroyed the powerhouse that provided electricity for the street lights and trolleys. The streetcars had to return to mule power during the nine months it took to build a steam plant to make electricity. Jack remembered businesses using candles and kerosene lanterns for light, and was glad somebody made the effort to get the power going again.

He heard the electric streetcars were losing money, though, and rumors said the company would sell out soon. He hoped somebody would turn things around; the trolleys considerably lowered the horse and buggy traffic on Austin's streets, and it was bound to get heavier. He knew he took a lot for granted when it came to all the conveniences of city life, but he couldn't have that attitude in office. That's where changes for the better happened, and he needed to educate himself about a lot of things in Austin and the surrounding area if he was going to represent these people.

He crossed Fifth Street and looked toward the large Newman and Co. windows advertising ladies' underwear and fancy goods. Several young women pressed their faces to the glass, looking at a display of some fancy party gowns. He wondered if Kitty might like something from this store, but then he wasn't sure he would feel comfortable visiting an establishment that openly advertised ladies' undergarments.

When he reached the bridge over the Colorado River, he decided to go see for himself where the Austin Dam had crossed the river not so long ago. He turned right and took Lonesome Joe along the bank heading west. He figured he had traveled around three miles or more when he started seeing giant blocks of granite scattered in the middle of the riverbed. A little further, and he saw the remains of the wall of the dam on each side of the river, and the huge hole created by the flood waters that had acted like a battering ram.

The powerhouse on the north side was destroyed. He'd heard eight people had died inside when a wall of water washed over the dam. He dismounted and walked his horse past the debris and tried to imagine what the lake must've looked like on the other side. The granite wall was tall; he guessed fifty or sixty feet high. It was hard to imagine flood waters flowing eleven feet higher than the dam itself. That was a tremendous amount of water. He wondered if replacing the dam and the powerhouse would be an issue for his constituents.

His constituents. He still didn't know too many people outside of his work. Maybe he'd better start talking and listening to voters real soon. The November election was less than nine months away.

He remounted Lonesome Joe and turned a little north and east, away from the river this time. He decided he might stop and meet a few folks on his way home. He rehearsed in his mind how he'd introduce himself and ask them what the government could do for them.

The first few houses he passed were quiet. Some folks took their day of rest seriously. He decided he'd talk to people only if they were outside and looked like they were interested in talking. He saw several people napping on the front porches of their modest homes. He waved to a few. One elderly man just stared at him when Jack spoke to him. He rode on.

After riding through a wooded area, he came upon a community of sorts. Most of the houses were small, box houses with board and batten sides. And all of the people he saw were Negroes. That surprised him. He thought the majority of the Negro population of Austin was located on the east side of town.

"Hello!" Jack hollered and waved at a couple of young boys near the road.

The shorter one tentatively waved back, the taller one ran towards a house nearby.

"Is this where you live?"

The little boy nodded his head.

"Is your dad home?"

The little boy shook his head.

An older man wearing a flannel shirt and overalls stepped onto the porch. Jack could see the other boy peaking around from behind him.

Jack dismounted and led Lonesome over to a post to tie him. "Hello, sir."

The man nodded once. He wasn't smiling.

Jack walked over to him and offered his hand. "How are you, sir? I'm Jack Taylor."

"You wantin' to buy my place?" The man didn't take his hand.

"No, sir." Jack thought that was an odd greeting and started to withdraw his hand, but then the man grasped it.

"I apologize for my rudeness, but the only white men that's visited our neighborhood lately have been trying to talk me into selling my property. I figured you were just another swindler."

"No, sir. I'm running as representative for your district."

"Not much different." The old man chuckled. "And you come all this way out here to talk to me?"

"And anyone else who'll listen."

"What was your name again?" he asked.

"Jack Taylor."

"Well, I'm Hiram Mathis."

"Pleased to meet you, Mr. Mathis. Have you voted before?"

"Yes, sir. A couple of times."

"That's good. I was wondering if you have any concerns that I might take with me if I'm elected."

Hiram looked shocked. "You're asking *me*?"

"Yes," said Jack. "I want to find out what my constituents are thinking; what their needs are. For example, you're fairly close to the river; would you want to see the Austin Dam rebuilt?"

"We sure enjoyed fishing on McDonald Lake, but that's the least of our problems right now."

"What do you mean?"

"They're trying to run us off our land."

"Who is?"

"I don't know-- speculators, I guess. Austin's growing out this way and suddenly our land has become very valuable to some people. And they're telling us *we're* on the wrong side of town. But we were here first. Governor Pease allowed us to buy our lots years ago. This house and the little bit of land it's on is mine, and I don't intend to move."

"I don't blame you."

He swung his hand around. "I built this house myself."

"That's very commendable of you."

"How much time do you have?" Hiram reached into his pocket and pulled out a timepiece. "We're actually meeting at the church about this very thing in less than an hour. Some of my neighbors were threatened and attacked last night. And two weeks ago a barn burned; they're convinced somebody set it."

"What did the marshal do?"

"We didn't tell the marshal. We'd heard the people coming around might even be lawmen."

Jack shook his head. "I know Marshal Davis personally, and he's an honorable man. You need to report this."

"Can you stay for the meeting? We're gonna talk about how we can protect ourselves and our property."

Jack thought for a moment. "Sure."

"Praise the Lord!" Hiram's smile looked like a picket fence with a few pickets missing. He pointed to a ladder back chair. "Come have a seat, Mr. Taylor, and let me bring you a cup of coffee."

The coffee was strong and bitter, and Jack and the old man sat on the porch and visited until it was time to head to the church.

He told Jack that somewhere in this area housed the quarters for Governor Elisha Pease's slaves who worked his Woodlawn plantation just north of here. After the emancipation, Pease gave land to some of his favorite former slaves and sold land to others. They called their neighborhood

Clarksville after Charles Clark, also a former slave, who had moved to the area and established a community for freed slaves.

Hiram told Jack that he was twenty-six years old when he became a freedman back in 1865.

"Did I tell you I built this house with my own hands?"

"Yes, sir," said Jack, smiling.

Jack gazed at the proud man and tried to imagine what it was like to have been the property of someone else with no control over his life. The concept refused to come together in his mind.

"My son and his family live with me. They tell me I need taking care of, but I think I'm the one taking care of them," he laughed. He suddenly turned around and spoke toward the young boy sitting in front of the door. "Where's your brother, Crew?"

"I dunno."

"Go find him and tell him to wash up. We're fixin' to leave for the church. You make sure he gets his shoes on, too."

"Yes, sir," the boy said.

"It can be freezin' outside and Albert Lee runs around barefooted. You'd think he'd catch his death a cold, but he's the healthiest one of the bunch. Beats all I ever seen."

Jack smiled.

"My son and daughter-in-law are already at the church getting everything ready for the meetin'." He stood and stretched. "Lemme go get my baby girl; she's still sleeping."

Jack watched him enter the house and close the door. He glanced around the porch while he waited. An old, threadbare cotton sheet partially covered a variety of plants in different sized coffee cans nestled up against the wall. The board and batten walls had never seen paint, faded to a dull gray. A rocking chair held court amidst a variety of cane and ladderback chairs. A faded checkerboard with a half finished game sat on a crudely built table. He smiled when he saw that most of the checkers were actually crown cork bottle caps.

The porch stood two steps off the ground, packed hard

and bare from lots of traffic. A pile of sticks leaning up against the porch made him recall his younger years when he fought many a battle with sticks he and his cousins gathered up that miraculously turned into swords or pistols or rifles.

Hiram stepped outside with a bundled up, sleepy-eyed little girl. She stared at Jack.

"How old is she?"

"Rachie's three." He kissed her on the cheek. "I wasn't supposed to let you sleep this late, but we won't tell Momma, will we."

The little girl shook her head and smiled shyly.

"Ah, she's startin' to wake up now. Baby girl loves her sleep, almost as much as her grandpappy does." He hollered for the boys and stepped off the porch and started across the yard. "It's not too far to the church. You can ride if you like."

"Nah, I'll walk my horse beside you." He untied Lonesome. "Would the kids want to ride?"

Crew's eyes widened as he looked to his grandfather for permission.

"You want to?"

The boys enthusiastically nodded their heads. Jack lifted each of them up on the horse and then reached for Rachie. She buried her head in her grandfather's neck and hid.

"Baby girl, you're getting too big for PawPaw to carry you very far."

By the second house they passed, though, Rachie decided she wanted to sit with her brothers. Jack lifted her and sat her in front of Crew. He placed her tiny hand on the saddle horn. Her dark skin felt smooth and thicker than his own. He realized he'd never touched a black person's skin other than a quick, calloused handshake.

About five minutes later, Jack tied Lonesome Joe to a hitching rail at the side of a clapboard-covered church. Hiram took Rachie into his arms, and the boys helped themselves down from the horse. Jack tried not to notice the glares from a group of men gathered around the entrance as he walked towards the door.

"What's this, Hiram?" A man with arms like sledge-hammers stepped forward.

"Everything's fine, gentlemen. He's not what you think."

"What's he doin' here?"

Jack spoke up. "I'm Jack Taylor, and I'm running for the legislature, and I just want to get to know my future constituents."

The men stared at him, and their silence was deafening. Then someone snorted, and several guffawed.

"You're here to listen to us?" Big Arms looked at Hiram. "Is he for real?"

Hiram nodded. "Either that or he's crazy," he said, grinning at Jack, "but we've been talking on the porch for a while, and he wants to know what's going on here in Clarksville."

The group parted and let them through. Jack nodded at several of the men. Most still weren't smiling, and it looked like they trusted him about as far as they could throw him. But one man's eyes were different; he thought he caught a glimpse of hope in there.

16

The sanctuary was about half-filled with people of all ages talking, but as soon as they saw Jack, the talking ceased and everyone stared. He hoped he didn't look as uncomfortable as he felt.

One man stood up and stepped out into the aisle.

"Mr. Jack? What you doin' here?"

A familiar face came into focus in the sea of black. Justus Johnson stood in front of him.

Jack never wanted to hug someone so badly in his life, but he settled for a handshake. "Justus! I'm so glad to see you. I didn't know you lived in this neighborhood."

"For thirty years. Hello, Hiram. Where did you find this young man?"

"He just showed up on my porch this afternoon."

"I rode out toward the old dam site and was heading back to Austin. I had no idea this community was even out here."

"I thought he was trying to buy me out."

Someone hit the pulpit several times with a gavel to get everyone's attention.

Justus gestured behind him. "Come sit with me. I need to talk to you."

Hiram said he'd join his family across the aisle. He shook Jack's hand. "It's been a pleasure, Mr. Taylor."

"Please call me Jack, and thank you for taking the time to talk with me today."

They took their seats.

A middle-aged man addressed the congregation. "I call this town meeting to order. And since it's a called meeting, the only thing we're going to discuss is the incident last night and how we're going to protect ourselves from these speculators trying to force us out of here. If you haven't heard by now, a confrontation at the Alexander's place got out of hand last night, and Ira held his own against two men, but a third one knocked him out cold with the butt of his rifle. He was unconscious for several hours, so we weren't even sure if he was going to make it or if he'll be right in his head from now on. How's he doing, Justus?"

Justus stood up. "He knows us, Reverend, and that's a good sign, the doctor tells us. He's just powerful sick and so dizzy he can't stand."

Jack jumped in his seat when the room exploded in "Praise you, Jesus!" and "Glory to God!" and "Hallelujah!" responses. This was unlike any church meetings he'd attended, which were reserved to the point that a quarter of the congregation--young and old, slept through them. He kept having to remind himself that this wasn't a church service.

Justus's voice rose above the others. "He only remembers bits and pieces of what happened last night. The doctor's been with him all day, so we're hopeful he's going to be all right."

"Praise God!" said the Reverend. "We've all been praying for him, and we'll continue to pray for him."

A loud chorus of 'amens' and various expressions of affirmatives filled the room.

When Justus sat down, Jack leaned over and asked, "Who's Ira?"

"My son-in-law, Liberty's husband. That's why they're not here." The room quieted down, so Justus lowered his voice. "I need you to take the doctor home."

"I just have my horse. Does he live far?"

"It's Dr. Kitty."

Jack's eyes widened."Kitty's here?"

Justus nodded. "I sent my grandkids to fetch her this mornin'. We wouldna bothered her, but Liberty thought Ira was dyin' he was throwin' up so much. But now it's gettin' late, and I don't want my grandkids in Austin after dark, and my son shore can't escort her home without getting' lynched. In fact, why don't we slip out now."

"If you think it's best."

Justus stood and stepped out into the aisle. Jack followed.

Hiram stood up. "Excuse me for interrupting, Reverend, but I'd like to introduce the guest I brought today. He's Mr. Jack Taylor, and he's looking for our vote so he can represent us."

People started mumbling among themselves; some even laughed outright.

Jack wasn't sure what to say. "I hope you'll let me come back to one of your regular town meetings so we can talk."

"Thank you, Mr. Taylor," the preacher said. "We would appreciate that. But until then, we could use somebody's help with these land speculators. They're not going to run us out of our homes just because they think we're on the wrong side of town. We were here first."

That comment drew cheers and hollers.

Jack nodded. "I didn't know this was going on, but I promise I'll look into it." He turned and followed Justus out of the church.

One of the men he saw earlier with Big Arms stepped out to block their way.

"This is my youngest son, Jonathan," said Justus.

Jack held out his hand, and the young man took it. Jack figured he was around his age or a little older.

"I hope you can help us," he said. "We're going to defend our homes, no matter what it costs us."

"Get in there and find out what we can do about this, Jon, and I'll talk to Mr. Taylor... Jack... about it."

"My father told us about you-- that you're a lawyer. I hope you can help us."

"I'll do my best."

"Thank you, sir."

Jack nodded again and walked over and untied Lonesome Joe. He led his horse as he walked beside Justus.

"How far are we from downtown Austin?" asked Jack as they walked along.

"Just a couple of miles, and that's the problem. The city's growin, and some people think Clarksville's in the way. Did you know they built a home for Confederate Civil War veterans right next to our community? Can you believe that?! Most of them men are just plain crazy, and there's some that are downright violent. Our womenfolk live with the fear of someone escapin and causin' harm around here."

"Has that happened before?"

"Patients have escaped a number of times. We'd heard about a lot of attacks that happened on the grounds, but nobody's mentioned any harm takin' place outside of there, thank heavens. The preacher keeps tellin' everyone—especially the children, to stay away from there. If a Negro gets within sight of it, the veterans holler every nasty thing they can think of. We've always steered clear of that sad place, but its presence hangs over us like a dark cloud."

"You think they built it there to intimidate y'all?"

"I don't know, but it's been here for twenty years, and we still ain't left. But now they're resortin' to more drastic measures. They're even threatenin' to close the school."

"I'm going to check into all of this. You have every right to be here."

"Thank you, Mr. …Jack." Justus pointed to a house. "That's my home, and next to it is Liberty and Ira's. We're right on the southeast edge of the community, so they've been botherin' us the most."

"Whose barn burned down?"

"The Jacksons' barn just north of here. We're all gonna help them re-build as soon as we can cut enough lumber for it. We got a lot done yesterday, and Ira came home to find some men harrassin' my daughter. He's mighty protective of Liberty, and when one of the men pushed her, that's all it took for him to start swingin'. It's a wonder they didn't kill him."

"They shouldn't have been here in the first place."

"Come on inside. You need to take the doctor home. She was kind enough to come, but I'm sure she's exhausted."

Both Justus's and Liberty's houses looked similar to Hiram's-- simple wood frame with board and batten walls, but Liberty's was covered in a whitewash. And unlike most of the unpainted houses he saw in the area, this one's piers underneath the porch all along the front of the house were covered by a short wall of stacked rocks.

The sun lay low in the sky, and the air felt quite chilly. Jack looked around the neighborhood, much of it hidden by dense trees. If he hadn't stumbled across Hiram's house, he never would've guessed a good-sized community thrived in these woods west of Austin.

Justus opened the door and let Jack enter the house. The warmth from a pot-belly stove on the far wall felt good on his cold cheeks. Three children looked up from eating supper at a table and stared at Jack. The youngest began to cry.

Justus quickly stepped around Jack with his arms outstretched, reaching for her. "It's all right, Dinah. PawPaw's here." He picked up the little girl and held her tight as he rocked her back and forth. "There, there, sweetness. Don't cry. I've brought a good friend of ours."

Jack was shocked to realize that the mere sight of him had frightened the children.

"This is Mr. Taylor, and he's gonna help PawPaw and your daddy keep those bad men away."

The little girl kept her arms wrapped around Justus's neck and her face against his cheek.

"She's still shook up about what happened last night," Justus whispered.

"She saw it?"

"They all did, unfortunately." He turned toward the other children at the table. "This is Hadassah-- did you know that was Queen Esther's Jewish name?"

Jack smiled. "No, I didn't. Hello, Hadassah. That's a beautiful name."

The girl just looked at him.

"Where's your manners, girl?" Justus said.

"Thank you," she said quietly.

"And this is Ethan, Liberty's youngest son. Where's Marcus?"

"He hasn't left Daddy's side," said Hadassah, "except when we went to get Dr. Kitty. Is she gonna to stay the night?"

"No, Mr. Taylor's come to take her home."

"Will Daddy be all right?"

Justus nodded his head. "Daddy's gonna be fine. He just needs to rest for a while."

Jack saw movement in the corner of his eye. He turned to see Kitty standing in a doorway. She looked shocked, but then her face melted into relief. She walked over to him and embraced him.

"What are you doing here? I didn't tell anybody where I was going. I didn't even know where I was going except that Justus's family needed me."

"And you're an angel for comin' Dr. Kitty," said Justus.

"I ended up at a town meeting, and Justus was there. He told me you were here, and asked if I'd come take you home."

Another woman walked into the room. Jack could see no resemblance to Justus; she must've taken after her mother. She looked like she hadn't slept all night.

"Berty, come over here and meet my lawyer friend I was tellin' you about."

The comely woman straightened her shoulders and walked over to Justus. "Mr. Taylor, I'm so glad to meet you. I hope you'll be able to help us."

"Now I haven't talked to him about that. I didn't think it would come to this," said Justus.

Liberty told the kids to go their room. She waited until they closed the door before speaking again. "Somebody's gonna get killed with these charlatans pesterin' everybody to sell out. But we're not leaving. This is our home."

Justus turned to Jack. "The speculators started off by comin' by and making offers-- most of them laughable, but now they're sendin' bullies to harrass us, and they hurt Ira bad last night. If I'd a just been here, maybe I could've stopped it from goin' as far as it did."

"You don't know that, Daddy, and it could've been you that got attacked. I don't think you could of survived what they did to Ira."

Jack spoke up. "Let me do some checking to try to find out who's behind all of this. I'll talk to Marshal Davis to see if there's something legal we can do to prevent this from happening again."

A boy that looked to be about twelve or thirteen entered the room. "Daddy's asking for you, Momma. I think he's hungry."

"That's a good sign, daughter," said Justus.

Liberty smiled. "Thank the good Lord. Tell him I'll be right there, Marcus." She grasped Kitty's hand. "I can't thank you enough for coming, Doctor. I told Daddy I didn't believe any doctor would come out to Clarksville, but he said you were different. You tell us what we owe you--"

"Don't worry about that now. I want to check on Ira again before I leave." She turned to Jack." I'll be right back."

The two women left the room.

"You really think we can do somethin' legal to keep those buzzards away from here?"

"I'll try my best to find something."

Jack thought the old man was going to cry, but instead he grasped his hand and squeezed it hard.

"Thank you, my friend."

17

Kitty said as she and Jack rode along, "These winter days are short. It gets dark so early."

All Jack could think about was Kitty's hands gingerly touching the sides of his waist. He had offered to let her sit in the saddle and him behind it, but she refused.

He noticed Lonesome Joe's ears flattening, and the horse started to get skitish. "Whoa, boy." He looked down and behind him. "Are you touching his flanks?"

"I don't know."

"Hold your feet away from him. He's goosey about that area."

"That's how I'm holding on."

"Hold onto me, and prop your feet against my legs if you need to. He'll pitch us both off if you keep touching him there."

"Sorry." She pulled her doctor's bag from between them and placed it in front of him, scooting closer. One of her hands grasped the handle of the bag, the other reached around his middle. "Is this all right?"

"I'll hold the bag, you just hold onto me," he said.

She did as he asked. "I'm glad it'll be dark by the time we get to town; this is quite scandalous, you know, for a lady to be riding this way."

Jack hadn't thought about that. "Do you want me to drop you off behind the Gerwick house?"

Kitty giggled. "No, I don't think anybody will see us…but will it hurt your campaign if someone does?"

Jack hadn't thought about that either. "I really don't plan for this election to change the way I live."

"You may not have a choice."

He growled under his breath. "I don't like that part of politics."

Someone hollered loud to their right. Jack and Kitty both jumped. He pulled back on the reins.

"What was that?" Kitty asked.

Jack noticed the lights of a large house on a rise. "I think it came from over there."

Several voices began yelling at the same time.

"That must be that old soldiers' home Liberty told me about," said Kitty.

"I think you're right. I'm glad you were able to help Justus' family, but the next time you decide to head over this way, send word to me, and I'll come take you." He touched his heels to Lonesome's side to get him walking again.

"Justus's grandkids were with me.They know their way around here, and they didn't walk us by this place."

"That's good. Justus said this area's not too safe sometimes. I'm going to try to find out who's causing so much trouble at Clarksville. They're lucky Ira wasn't killed."

Kitty was quiet for a moment. "That's the first time I've been in a Negro's home."

"Me, too, now that I think about it."

"It wasn't so different from the house I grew up in back in Galveston."

"What'd you think it'd be like?"

"I honestly hadn't ever thought about it before. I saw Negroes in Galveston, but I never really knew any. They lived their lives and we lived ours. I enjoyed talking to Liberty, though."

"What's she like?"

"Smart, like Justus, but she doesn't hide it."

He chuckled. "You noticed that about him, too?"

He felt her chin on his back nodding in agreement.

"He's had a lot to overcome," said Jack. "I didn't realize they had so much stacked against them."

"I need to go back and check on Ira soon. Head injuries are very unpredictable. I asked Liberty what doctor they used, and she told me they didn't have a doctor. They have a mid-wife in Clarksville who helps deliver babies, but for everything else they take care of themselves. She said their community has had more than their share of deaths because of the lack medical care. Galveston is opening a Negro hospital this year. I just assumed the other larger cities in Texas had places for Negroes to get medical attention, too. I guess I assumed a lot of things."

"I wonder if any of the white doctors will treat them."

"I don't know, but I'm going to talk to Dr. Gilbert about it. Maybe we can do something for them."

"You know that would probably kill his business."

"Maybe we could treat them in the back."

"You'd still lose a lot of white clients when word got out."

Kitty sighed. "How did things get this way?"

"They've been this way for a long time."

"I guess I thought if I treated everyone respectfully, that made me a good person and all was right in the world. But there are a lot of things that aren't right in the world, and I didn't bother to notice."

"I guess we see what we choose to see and are blind to everything else. I'm learning that it takes some effort to see beyond the end of my nose, and I'm seeing some ugly sides to life I hadn't faced before. At the church, I told them I'd check into what's been happening out there, but I'm not quite sure where to start. I have to admit I was a bit uncomfortable being the only white person in their church meeting."

"Were they rude to you?"

"No, nothing like that. It was just different. They put up their guard towards me, but at the same time they felt free to express themselves there… and loudly. I hadn't seen that side of them before. They've always been in the background—living their lives, I assumed, like we lived our lives... just not together. Their faith in the Lord seems strong, but they didn't have a lot of faith that I could do anything to help them."

"Think you can?"

"I hope so. I didn't realize I had to prove myself to them, too. But when I think about it, I don't have a history of abuse and mistreatment. Nobody owned me like a piece of property to do whatever they wanted to do with me. I don't know what that's like to overshadow every dealing with a white person."

"Momma always treated everybody equally, well, except for her boss. She thinks he's some kind of prince, especially after he gave her his house after the storm."

"But he—" Jack caught himself before he finished, remembering Katherine's request. "That was generous. Where did he live after that?"

"He bought a mansion on Broadway for next to nothing-- the owners fled the island, vowing to never return."

"I read about the storm in the papers, but I can't imagine how bad it must've been."

"Worst night of my life. I thought the building we were in would collapse at any minute, and the wind-- I've never heard anything so terrifying, almost as if it was alive and trying to devour us. The weeks afterward were hard. There were so many dead and missing, and the hospital was damaged and overwhelmed with the injured-- we had to step over people laid up in the halls. And most of them had no homes to return to. I think we all worked on just a couple of hours of sleep each night for the first week. Momma and Lucius eventually came and forced me to go home and rest. But I was back the next day, and the next. I lost count of the days."

"I'm glad you live up here now."

"Me, too, but the least little thunder cloud that comes up still gives me the shakes. I'm terrified of storms."

"You said your mother treated everyone equally. Who taught her that?"

"Well, you know our faith teaches that, but not everybody

lives it. Momma knew what it felt like to be an outsider. She and her husband immigrated from Germany—they couldn't speak a word of English when they stepped off that ship in Galveston."

"You don't think of him as your father?"

"I used to, but I really don't remember him. He died in a wharf accident when I was two or three years old. Ever since I found out about…Katherine, it was hard to think of him as my father. I have no idea where my ancestors are from."

"You could ask Katherine-- in a letter, I mean."

Kitty was silent for a moment. "Maybe. I still can't come to grips with what she did all those years. It embarrasses me to think about it, and I'd be humiliated for people to know that the woman who brought me into this world was a… prostitute. I wonder if she even knew who my father was?"

"I sort of gathered that she didn't."

"Y'all talked about me?"

Jack bit his tongue, regretting bringing that up. "She asked how you were doing is all. They were concerned about you since you said you weren't feeling well."

"How did that turn into the topic of who my father was?"

"I think Grace asked if he might ever try to come back into your life if he knew about you. That's when Katherine said she wasn't sure who the father was."

"I keep asking God why this happened to me. What have I done to deserve this?"

"You know God doesn't work that way."

"I wonder if Dr. Gilbert would let me go if my true parentage ever got out."

"I don't think he works that way either."

She sighed. "You're right. But I was terrified people might connect us somehow at that social after the opera. It was such a shock to see her face to face."

"She wanted me to tell you that her previous life is behind her now-- ever since she left Galveston. Finn and Grace helped her get out."

"But the past still follows her… and now me. And it scares

me to know that Mr. Baldwin knew who she was. What if he makes the connection?"

"Don't worry about Jarvis."

"He's a powerful man, Jack."

"Kitty?"

"What?"

"Don't worry about Jarvis."

Jack felt the side of her face lean against his back.

Before Ned Green left town that week, Jack asked if he would introduce him to his friend William McDonald. He offered to meet them at the Driskill where Ned was staying, but Ned suggested another place for coffee: the Capitol.

Jack thought that the gesture was symbolic; surely Ned was giving him a vote of confidence by asking to meet there. Jack rehearsed a few humble-sounding lines about him not working in his future office yet.

Walking up to that awe-inspiring granite building never failed to get his blood pumping. He stopped at the door and turned around to look down Congress Avenue toward the Colorado River, trying to imagine what it looked like when Mirabeau Lamar first saw this place over sixty years before. It was Indian territory then, and this little settlement called Waterloo perched precariously on the edge of the wild frontier. He tried to remember how many capitals the Republic of Texas had-- three or four? before finally settling on Austin... twice... after a tug of war between Sam Houston and Lamar. But Austin has been the only capital the *state* of Texas has ever had.

Jack turned and touched the granite stone before entering the foyer, walking to the Rotunda area. He stopped and looked up at the magnificent dome, like he did every time he came to the Capitol.

"Jack!"

Ned waved at him from an elaborate, wood-framed doorway halfway down the hall, so he headed that way. The smell of coffee reminded Jack that he hadn't had a cup yet. Ned greeted him with a handshake and pulled him into the room.

"Good morning, Jack!"

"How you doing, sir?"

"Great, great. Bill's not here yet." He nodded toward a service cart. "Help yourself to some coffee and breakfast. I started without y'all."

He sat his big frame down at a table and continued to speak in-between bites.

"Sorry we couldn't meet at the Driskill, but we have to put up with that kind of crap until we can change these damn laws. Then hopefully, people will eventually follow suit because their conscience tells them to."

Jack set down his coffee and a plate of biscuits, jam and butter next to Ned. He hadn't the slightest idea what Ned was talking about. And the man kept talking.

Jack nodded as he chewed, as if he understood everything Ned was saying.

"… now they're trying to bring back that damn poll tax."

Jack's ears perked up. He understood that one.

Ned continued. "They tried to instigate the poll tax back in the 70s, but it was voted down because they figured it'd hurt the poor white vote as much as the black vote, but dang if it's back again." He looked at the door. "There he is." He put his palms on the table, and started to rise. "Good morning, Bill!"

The man motioned with his hand. "Stay seated, my friend."

And Jack understood everything then as he stood up to greet Bill McDonald, a black man.

"This is who I've been telling you about, Bill-- Jack Taylor. Jack, this is my friend and partner in crime, William McDonald. But call him Bill."

"How do you do, sir?" Jack asked, shaking his hand.

"I'm fine, thank you. Ned is quite impressed with you."

"Hope I don't disappoint him."

"Get you some breakfast, Bill. Hope you don't mind that we started without you."

Bill chuckled. "Guess you noticed, Jack, that patience isn't one of Edward's qualities, especially when it comes to eating."

Ned laughed. "I see something I want, I go after it. And these biscuits and ham are worth going after. Why don't you bring me a couple more of them-- no, just roll that cart over here closer so I don't have to get up again."

Jack started to go help.

"Sit down, Jack. Bill can take care of it."

Bill rolled the cart to the corner of the table and poured himself a cup of coffee. "I guess you see where our name comes from."

"Pardon me?" Jack said.

"The 'Black and Tan' faction."

"Oh, yes, sir."

"Ned wouldn't let us call it the 'Black and White' faction."

Ned snorted. "I've yet to see anybody with purely white skin, or even purely black skin, for that matter. We're all shades of tan and brown. Can't understand why people put so much store into skin color. But would you believe there's a group daring to calling themselves the 'Lily Whites?' Inside, they're black as sin."

Jack watched Bill unfold a napkin and place it in his lap.

"You don't know that, Ned. These things take time." Bill said calmly.

Ned's napkin was stuffed into his collar. Jack hadn't even bothered to unfold his. He took a bite of biscuit with one hand and subtly pulled his napkin into his lap with the other.

"We took a beating from them two years ago, but we're going to get control back." Ned looked at Jack. "Bill was in charge of the Republican Party for several years after Cuney died."

Jack looked at Bill, surprised that a black man had held such a powerful position.

"Are you familiar with Norris Cuney?" Ned asked.

"No, sir."

"For over a decade, Cuney was in charge of the Republican Party…"

"Go back further, Ned. That doesn't mean much until Jack knows where Norris came from."

"You knew him better than me."

"All right." Bill took a swig of coffee and wiped his mouth with his napkin. "Norris Cuney's father was a wealthy plantation owner over by Hempstead. Colonel Cuney had lots of land and cattle, and over a hundred slaves. He was also involved in politics, so on the surface, it seemed natural that his son would go into politics, right?"

Jack nodded.

"But the problem, you see, was that Norris Cuney's mother was a mixed-race slave, so even if Norris was only 1/4 black or less, he was still a slave by the principle of *partus sequitur ventrem*, meaning 'that which is brought forth follows the womb.' His mother was a slave, so he was a slave. But his father granted him his freedom when he was thirteen and sent him to a boarding school in Pennsylvania for his education. One of his sisters was sent to Europe, and passed as a white in society, from what we heard. The Civil War interrupted Norris's plans for college, so he came back to Texas and continued to learn on his own. He accomplished a lot living in Galveston…"

"Galveston?" Jack interrupted. "I've met more people with connections to Galveston this past week."

"A lot of people have come and gone from Galveston; it's a port city and the world passes through there," said Bill.

"It's a more progressive society down there," added Ned.

"I may have to visit it and see for myself," said Jack. "How did Mr. Cuney get into politics?"

"He became friends with people like Pinckney Pinchback over in Louisianna—first black governor of any U.S. state. Unfortunately, he only served 35 days, but we'll take any step going forward," he said, smiling. "Then Norris was elected as alderman in Galveston and started getting appointments to positions in the Republican Party and worked his way up. He served as a delegate to every national convention for something like twenty years… a very capable man.

"After the Civil War, the Reconstruction Act attempted to integrate the Negroes into the political process, and I really have to commend the Republican Party for making the effort to include us. Men like Governor Edmund Davis genuinely supported the rights of Negroes, and Norris respected that and was loyal to him."

Ned added, "A lot of white Republicans resented Cuney as their party chairman, in Texas and outside of it, too. But his efforts helped register over 100,000 Negro voters before he was ousted."

"And all of his hard work is about to be destroyed."

"Why's that?" asked Jack.

"The Democrat Party is allowing outrageous voting laws to keep Negroes from voting; things like 'white primaries,' literacy tests, and the illiterate whites are getting around it because they're grandfathered in."

"And it looks like the poll tax has a good chance of passing this year," said Ned.

"All those efforts are essentially going to wipe out the Negro voters, and we'll almost be back where we started."

"What happened to the Republican Party?" asked Jack. "You said they supported the Negroes."

"When one of Sam Houston's sons was president of the state League of Republican Clubs a while back, he started promoting these segregated, 'lily-white clubs' within the local clubs, and it spread like a disease," said Ned.

"Election fraud has been rampant in the counties where the black vote was strong," said Bill. "Black men have been kept from voting by gunpoint, or the ballot counting was done in secret and the white candidates declared the winners. Or defeated white candidates challenged the voting results on a technicality, seized the court house and declared themselves the winners. Black leaders have been assaulted and run out of town."

"And some have been murdered with no consequences for the guilty," said Ned. "It's like we're going backwards instead of forwards."

Jack shook his head. "Why don't we hear about these things?"

"The news would be all over the country if these atrocities were committed against white people, but it's not very newsworthy for them to happen to Negroes," said Ned. "Or if the story is printed, it's biased or downright false. And too many of us allow ourselves to turn a blind eye to injustice. If we don't know about it, then we don't have to do anything about it."

"I learned something a few days ago that bothers me, but I'm not sure what to do about it," said Jack. "I told my boss that some people are trying to force a Negro community to sell their property and move because Austin is expanding in that direction. My boss told me to let it go—that it'll kill my political career before it even starts if I poke my nose in places I shouldn't. I want to help them, but I also think I can do a lot of good for everyone if I get elected."

Bill smiled sympathetically. "That's a tough choice."

They sat there in silence until Ned slammed his fist on the table, rattling the china and Jack.

"That chaps my hide," said Ned loudly, then lowered it. "But maybe you don't have to choose between the two. We need to get you elected, but in the meantime, tell me where this place is and who to talk to there. I know some people who can do some checking around to find out who's behind those harrassments. That way your name won't be connected with it."

Jack didn't realize he'd been holding his breath until he exhaled loudly. "That sounds like a good idea. Clarksville is the name of the community—it's a couple of miles west of here. I just happened to stumble upon it last Sunday, and come to find out, a man I know from downtown lives out there with his family. Three men beat up his son-in-law Saturday night—Ira was out of his mind until the following day. Before that a barn burned down in the neighborhood, and they think it was deliberately set. Speculators used to just pester them about selling out, but they're getting more violent, and they're afraid somebody's going to get killed."

"What's your friend's name?"

"Justus Johnson."

Bill spoke up. "I like that name."

"He's a good man, too. He shines shoes across from the Driskill. Do you want me to introduce you to him down there?"

Ned shook his head. "I could use a good shine, and that's a good excuse to meet him, but I think it's best that we're not seen with him at the same time. I'll just let him know that someone's going to come to talk to him and his son-in-law about what happened."

"I met his daughter and kids out there. It shocked me when Justus's little granddaughter start crying when I came into the house—just because I was white."

"There's fear on both sides. I hope for all of our children's sakes we can change that in our lifetime," said Bill.

"Did anybody see you?" Ned asked Jack.

"Only the whole community—I went to one of their town meetings and introduced myself."

"Well, that was noble and unwise of you," said Ned.

"Why? I was asking for their vote."

Bill spoke up. "If that poll tax passes, you probably won't get too many of their votes. Nobody will."

"That's what Justus told me."

"I think I need to get my shoes shined, too, before we leave town," said Bill. "I'd like to meet this friend of yours."

"When you talked to Jarvis, did you tell him Justus was involved?" asked Ned.

Jack shook his head. "No, but he knows Justus. I believe he'd want to help him."

Ned glanced at Bill. "I think you need to be careful about using Justus's name; we don't want to bring any more trouble his way. And be careful about what you say around Jarvis—"

"You don't think he had anything to do with sending those

men out there, do you?"

"No, not at all. Jarvis and I go back a ways, and I'm pretty sure not much goes on around Austin that he doesn't know about."

Jack sat back in his chair. "He's done so much for me... I can't imagine—"

"All I'm saying, Jack, is be careful with this Clarksville matter. I don't want you to walk out of here thinking less of your boss. Every dealing I've had with Jarvis has been above board and honest."

"Ned, I think you're right about telling whoever you ask to investigate what's going on in Clarksville to keep Justus's name and especially yours out of it." Bill pulled a pocketwatch from his coat. "Now, if you men will excuse me, I have another meeting to attend." He stood and offered his hand to Jack.

Jack stood and grasped it.

"It's been a pleasure making your acquaintance, Jack. I hope to see your name on the roster in this magnificent building next year. Don't get up, Ned. Finish your breakfast. I'll see you at the station later."

"All right, my friend." Ned nodded, and watched him walk out the door.

"Bill is always looking out for my bum leg, but it's actually my size that hinders me more," he said, chuckling. "What'd you think of him?"

Jack smiled. "I'm impressed."

"Bill's one of the sharpest men I've ever met. He's going to do some great things in his life in spite of the disparity. He's been talking about opening a bank, and he'll figure out a way to do it before too long."

"He seems much more qualified for public office than me. Why hasn't he run?"

"He and Cuney have been able to do more from their positions in the Republican Party than they ever could do in office, and they don't have quite as big a target on their backs as the elected officials do. But with all the good they've done, we're losing ground fast. If you get in, you'll learn pretty quick that politics is a mean bull pen."

"I'm not looking forward to that part."

"A few years ago, a Dallas newspaper reporter called him 'Gooseneck Bill,' in a column, and everybody picked it up. Makes my blood boil when I hear it. Can you imagine calling the governor, 'Duckmouth Chuck'?"

Jack shook his head. Just the thought seemed preposterous.

"But for Bill, it's acceptable because he's a Negro. One more bit of advice, Jack. Don't go spouting my name around. My reputation will not help your campaign, but my money will."

"Your reputation?"

"I have a couple of big strikes on my record. My involvement with Bill and the Black and Tan Faction is one. And the other has to do with the woman I live with. I consider us married, but we don't have a piece of paper that says we're legal. We have our reasons, and I don't need to get into why, but it's a family issue and I plan to remedy that some day."

"Can I ask you a question?"

"Shoot."

"I can see you're not afraid of taking risks. But what was it that made you decide to work with Bill?"

Ned looked straight at Jack. "I got to know the man behind the skin. And I learned we weren't that different after all."

19

itty glanced at Louis, the livery boy, holding the reins driving the one-horse buggy as they headed to Clarksville. She was counting on Jack taking her, but his schedule suddenly filled. His campaign was already taking over his life... their lives.

"How old are you, Louis?"

"Thirteen."

"Why aren't you in school?"

"I know how to read and write."

"That's just the beginning of your education."

He shrugged the comment off his skinny shoulders. "Momma needed my help, so she let me quit. This is really pretty country out this way. I haven't been out here before."

"It is pretty. I love the trees. Do you read?"

"I ardy said I could read."

"That's not what I meant. Do you like to read books?"

"I don't have time to read."

"Do you have any books?"

"Do we have to keep talking about this, Miss?"

"No, we don't."

"What are we going out here for?"

"I'm checking on a patient, and I appreciate you taking me."

"Mr. Taylor's paying me."

"I'm thinking about coming out here twice a month, or maybe even once a week, if needed. Do you think you can take me those times, too?"

He looked at me. "Will I get paid for all those times?"

Kitty nodded. "Yes."

"Then, sure!" He actually grinned at her. "Can I start calling you Doc?"

"Why?"

"I can't say your last name."

"What about Miss Doc?"

"Yeah, that'll work."

"In the future—hopefully every other Thursday, you could pick me up behind Dr. Gilbert's office after lunch to head over here, and we'll be here 'til supper, but I'm hoping for us to get home before dark. I haven't worked it all out, yet, but I'll have some kind of idea by the time we leave today. Do you think your mother will let you?"

"Momma won't mind as long as I'm bringing home some money."

"Wonderful! You'll have some wait time over here, but I'll bring some books to keep you company."

His face fell and shoulders slumped, punctuated by an unintelligible sound.

"You'll get paid to read, Louis. I don't know any other job as enjoyable as that."

"But I don't like to read."

"You just haven't found the right book is all."

They rode the rest of the way in silence, broken only by Kitty giving the boy directions until they came within sight of Liberty's house. They could see several children playing on the porch.

"Hey," said Louis. "You didn't say we were coming to niggertown."

"Stop the buggy, Louis."

Louis pulled up on the reins.

Kitty turned in her seat. "That's rude. This community is called Clarksville. I don't ever want to hear you say that other word again!"

"Everybody calls it that, but I didn't know there was one on this side of town, too." He looked at her suspiciously. "I don't know if Momma'll like me coming here."

"I can always hire someone else." Kitty said sharply.

"No, no. I can do it. But I don't have to talk to them, do I?"

"I'm not sure I've hired the right person for this job. Jack told me I could depend on you."

"You can, Miss Doc." He looked conflicted for a moment. "But they're colored people."

"Does that make them of any less worth than you?"

"Well, they were slaves."

"Not because they deserved to be. Can you imagine someone coming into your home and stealing you and taking you to a foreign country, selling you like you were a horse and forcing you to work hard for nothing?"

Louis shook his head. "But why didn't they fight 'em? Why didn't they run away?"

"I'm sure many did, but those folks usually didn't live very long."

"But why was slavery ever started if it was so wrong?"

"Evil has been in this world since the Garden, but it's up to us to recognize it when we see it and do something about it."

"I don't think a lot a people see it as evil."

"When people grow up with something wrong, they assume it's right and don't give it much thought. Do you go to church, Louis?"

"Yes, ma'am."

"Do you listen any while you're there?"

"The part about hell fire got my attention."

"There's a lot more to God's teaching than hell fire, and that has to do with loving and helping people right now. Did you know that many of the people in Clarksville are Christians? So if you and I are Christians, that makes us brothers and sisters in Christ with many of these people. What do you think about that?"

Louis sat there with a skeptical look on his face.

"Part of this job calls for you to be respectful. The Alexanders and Mr. Johnson are some of the nicest people you'll ever meet, and they're no different than you or I... No, I take that back. They are different from you and me because they and their ancestors have had some horrendous wrongs committed against them for many years. They just want to live their lives and raise their children in safety, but life's not treating them as fairly as it's treated you and me. These folks have no doctor to help them, and people have died because of it. We're going to do something good here, Louis, if you want to be a part of it."

"I need the money."

"I don't want your mother to be upset about this, so you tell her where you're bringing me, and that you're not in any danger, and ask if it's all right for you to keep bringing me."

"Yes, ma'am."

"And if she doesn't want you to come, I understand. But other than your mother, you don't have to tell anyone else about what we're doing because some narrowminded people are bound to get upset with us."

"You don't have to worry about me tellin' anybody, Miss Doc. I'd be crazy to—"

"Louis!?"

"Sorry."

"All right. Let's go."

Kitty directed Louis to drop her off in front of the Alexanders' home, and to tie the horse to the tree between the two houses.

"What do I do then?"

"Take a nap, stretch your legs. I shouldn't be too long this time."

She climbed down from the buggy and grabbed her bag. "Would you rather come in with me?"

"No," he said rather quickly.

"All right. I'll be out in a little while. If you need something, come knock on the door."

"Yes, ma'am."

She turned and walked up to the porch and spoke to Hadassah and Dinah as she paused on the steps. "Hello, ladies. I've come to check on your father. Is your mother here?" Little Dinah came over and took Kitty by the hand and led her inside. She walked her right through the house and out the back door. Liberty stood by a tall, roughhewn table, elbow-deep in chicken feathers. A few were caught in her hair.

"Oh! Dr. Kitty! I didn't know you were coming today!"

Kitty couldn't help grinning. "I wanted to check on Mr. Alexander."

"Don't you laugh at me. Haven't you ever plucked chickens before?"

"I'm happy to say I only tried it once, and I did such an awful job and cried, no, wailed so loudly for that poor chicken that my mother never asked me to do it again."

Liberty laughed. "Yeah, crying didn't do me no good. My momma didn't let me off the hook. Ira wasn't in the front room?"

"No."

"Dinah, go find your daddy and tell him Dr. Kitty's here to look at his head."

"I'm sorry I didn't give you fair warning. I wasn't sure I would be able to take off from work to come."

"That's no problem—I'm almost finished here. You go on inside and let me clean up and get this chicken in the pot. I'll be there shortly."

Kitty retraced her steps back into the house and set her bag on the table.

Dinah brought her father by the hand from the bedroom. He walked with a home-made cane. The little girl hadn't said a word since Kitty had arrived.

"Hello, Doctor."

"How are you feeling, Mr. Alexander?" She had to look up at him. He was well over six feet.

"Thank you, sweet pea," Ira said to his daughter. "Why don't you go play with sister now."

Dinah dropped his hand and headed out the front door.

Ira pulled out a chair and sat down. "I feel sick to my stomach, and I'm dizzy much of the time; I don't trust myself walking without this cane."

Kitty examined his head. "That's to be expected with your injury. It takes time to heal."

"I'm afraid I'm gonna lose my job. Liberty's brother is filling in for me, but he can't do it for much longer, and they won't hold that position for me."

Liberty kicked open the door and walked in with a headless, plucked chicken in each hand, then turned around and kicked the door shut.

Kitty watched her rinse the chickens in a tub of water, and was relieved to see her chop the feet off before she dropped the whole chickens in a deep kettle and poured water over them. Then Liberty picked up the chicken feet and scrubbed them a bit before dropping them in the pot, too.

Kitty looked away, hoping her face didn't betray her revulsion.

Ira snickered. "Liberty don't let nothin' go to waste 'round here."

"Are y'all talking 'bout me?" Liberty carried the kettle over to the fireplace and hung it on the trammel and swung the crane over the blazing fire. She wiped her hands and turned around to face them. "How 'bout chicken and and dumplings for supper?" she asked her husband.

"Sounds good to me."

"It's going to take a while for those tough old birds to get tender, but you're welcome to stay for supper, Dr. Kitty," Liberty said as she walked over to stand beside Ira.

"Oh, no, we'll be heading back soon," said Kitty.

"We?"

"A livery boy brought me out here."

"It's chilly outside—doesn't he want to come in?"

"No, I told him I wouldn't be long."

"Well, tell me how my husband's doing. He gets real dizzy and almost falls."

"That's common with a concussion, but it should get better with time. Do you have any saltines? They help with the nausea."

Liberty shook her head. "But Daddy might—he brings them home sometimes."

Kitty continued. "And the best thing you can do for yourself, Ira, is rest and give yourself time to heal."

Liberty squeezed his shoulder. "I've been telling him that."

"I feel like I've rested enough. And as soon I can stand without grabbing the walls, I'll be back at work, Berty."

"I know, hon. Hope you don't get tired of chicken."

"I need to do some work on our chicken house; something's gettin' after our chickens at night," he explained to Kitty.

"Marcus can do it if you'd just tell him what to do," said Liberty.

"Yeah, sometimes it takes longer to tell him than it would for me to do it myself."

"But that's how he learns."

"Dr. Kitty don't wanta hear about all this."

Kitty actually enjoyed hearing them talk. But she remembered the other reason she came. "I have an idea I wanted to talk to you about."

But screams from the porch interrupted her.

20

Ira yelled Hadassah's name as he jumped up, took three big steps toward the front door, tilting further with each step until he fell over the rocker.

Liberty and Kitty darted past him and out the front door. Hadassah and Dinah stood on the edge of the porch screaming and crying. Liberty grabbed Hadassah.

"What's wrong?! Stop yelling and tell me what's wrong!" Dinah buried her face in her mother's skirt.

Kitty looked around and saw nothing alarming. She turned toward Justus's house. The horse and buggy tied to the tree looked normal, but two boys rolling around in the dirt on the other side of it didn't.

The shock of blonde hair amidst the tangled limbs told her Louis was involved.

Kitty ran across the packed ground and around the buggy. Marcus was the other culprit. It horrified her to see them trying to beat the daylights out of each other. She screamed Louis' name, trying to get him to stop, but they were oblivious to her shouts. That made her mad, so she tried to grab each of them by the hair and somehow got pulled down into the scuffle. She felt a stinging pain when one of them popped her in the mouth.

Liberty was right behind Kitty, dragging Marcus away from the pile.

"What do you think you're doing, Marcus Joshua Alexander?!"

Kitty picked herself up off the ground, spitting blood, and dusting herself off. She was so angry, rational words refused to come. She glared at Louis, who was already on his feet staring wide-eyed back at her.

She walked over to a hat on the ground, picked it up, and threw it in the buggy. The horse would've bolted if he wasn't tied to the tree.

"That's not my hat, Miss Doc," Louis said.

She glared at him again, walked over to the buggy, retrieved the hat, and handed it to Louis. "Then you give it to Marcus… with an apology." She spit again and wiped her mouth.

"But—"

"NOW!" she growled in a low voice.

Liberty was still yelling at Marcus, so Louis had to wait until she was finished.

When they finally realized he was standing there, Louis handed Marcus the hat and mumbled, "Sorry."

"And what do you say, Marcus?" said Liberty.

Marcus wouldn't even look up. "Sorry."

Kitty turned Louis around to face her. "You're done with this job."

Louis looked shocked. "But I—"

She stopped him. "I thought I could count on you, Louis, to be a decent human being. Now what, may I ask, was this about?"

Louis looked at Marcus for an explanation, but he said nothing.

"Marcus?" Liberty glanced at Kitty. "Oh, Dr. Kitty! You're bleeding!"

Marcus looked up at her, then jerked his arm away from his mother and bolted around the buggy.

"Marcus!!" Liberty started to follow, but stopped.

Ira came around the buggy holding Marcus' collar. The boy was crying. "I'm sorry, Daddy! I'm sorry!"

"Calm down, son." His eyes widened, too, when he saw Kitty. "What happened out here?"

"Don't worry about me—I'm fine," said Kitty. "Now, what did Louis say to you?"

"But Miss Doc—"

"Hush, Louis, and let Marcus speak."

Marcus wouldn't raise his head. "It wasn't his fault, Miss. I started it."

"Oh, my Lord, Marcus. What's gotten into you?" said Liberty.

"Let him speak, Momma," said Ira.

Marcus wiped his nose with his coat sleeve. "I come home from school, and I saw this horse and buggy here, and I thought those men had come back, and I wasn't gonna hide this time. I know Daddy still ain't well, and I needed to be the man of the house. I told him…" he looked at Louis, "I told him he'd better git off our property or else, and he told me he wasn't leavin' and I told him I was gonna make him leave and he said I could try, so… I tried." He looked at Kitty. "I didn't know he brought you, Miss. I didn't mean to hurt you."

"You didn't hurt me, Marcus," said Kitty. "I'm tougher than I look."

"Are you gonna call the marshal?" he asked Kitty.

Liberty turned away, overcome with emotion.

"Over this? Of course not."

Kitty turned to Louis. "I'm sorry I assumed the worst about you. "

"I'm sorry I might've hit you, Miss Doc."

Kitty tried to keep from grinning, and then grimaced. She touched her busted lip.

"I never seen a grownup lady get in a fight like that before."

She laughed out loud at that one. "And don't you tell anybody I did!" She noticed no one else was laughing. "How 'bout we start over." She took a deep breath. "Louis, I'd like you to meet one of the bravest young men I know, Marcus Alexander. Marcus, I'd like you to meet one of the hardest-working young men I know, Louis Miller."

They just stood there awkwardly.

"It's all right to shake hands."

Louis offered his hand, and Marcus took it.

"You go to school?" Louis asked.

Marcus nodded.

"You read?"

Marcus nodded again.

"You like to read?"

"Yeah," said Marcus.

Louis glanced at Kitty.

"It's getting late, and I know you need to get back to supper, Liberty," said Kitty, "but I wanted to discuss that idea with you. We can do it another time." She started walking to the house. "I need to get my bag."

Liberty told Marcus to walk his father back to the house and bring Dr. Kitty's satchel back.

"And check on my chickens!" she hollered across the yard. She turned back to Kitty. "Now tell me about this idea of yours."

Louis went around to untie the horse.

"I'd like to come out maybe twice a month, or more, if needed, and I'd like to meet your midwife."

"You want to come out as a doctor?" Liberty asked.

Kitty smiled. "What else?"

Liberty's eyes filled again. "You'd do that for us?"

"If we can work it out. I'll need a place to see people—does your church have a smaller room we might use?"

She nodded enthusiastically. "I'm sure the Reverend wouldn't mind."

Marcus trotted up with Kitty's bag. A couple of girls walking by on the road spoke and waved at Marcus. They wore a mishmash layer of clothes instead of coats. He didn't even acknowledge them, but he nodded his head toward Louis before he turned back to the house.

Louis nodded back.

Kitty smiled and looked at Liberty to see if she noticed, but she was watching the girls on the road.

"Now that's a family that really needs our help. They're

squatting on a place a few blocks over. Their momma died from the cholera a couple of years ago, and since then their daddy lets 'em run wild. I told Marcus to stay away from them or they'd get him in trouble for sure. Their grandparents originally came from Oklahoma—they'd been slaves of the Chickasaw Indians—"

"The Indians had slaves?"

Liberty nodded. "Thousands. After the Emancipation, the Indians set 'em free, but those poor folks didn't know where they belonged. The girls' momma told me the Chickasaws were supposed to grant her parents full citizenship in their nation, but they didn't. Daddy calls them lost souls—wandering around without a place to call home." Liberty looked around her. "That's why it's so important for us to keep this little plot of ground. It's the only thing my father ever owned, and it's the only home my family's ever known."

Kitty reached over and squeezed her hand. "I'm sure Jack will put a stop to it. And I'm going to come every other week to begin—Thursdays if that's all right, and if you'll make arrangements with your church."

"Yes, of course. Thank you so much, Dr. Kitty." She followed her around the buggy to speak to Louis. "I'm so sorry, Louis, for Marcus fighting you. You understand he thought he was defending his family, right?"

Louis looked baffled. "I just figured I wasn't welcome here."

"No, it's not that—"

"I'll explain it to him on the way home," said Kitty.

"Miz Alexander?" Louis asked. "Why did Marcus think we were gonna call the marshal?"

"Child, if he struck a white woman, our men and boys have been hanged for much less."

21

Jack opened the big door to let Louis bring the buggy inside the livery. His smile melted into a concerned frown when he saw Kitty's face.

Kitty patted Louis's arm. "Thank you for doing a fine job today."

Jack looked at Louis. The boy looked like he was facing a firing squad.

"And ask your mother if you can do this two more times this month starting next Thursday."

"Yes, Miss Doc." He climbed down to unhitch and tend to the horse, casting glances toward Jack every so often.

Jack helped Kitty down from the buggy.

"What happened out there?" he asked.

"Ira's still on the mend; he's having dizzy spells, but I hope they'll go away soon. He's worried about his job. And Liberty and I decided every other Thursday would be a good time for me and Louis to go out there."

She reached back for her bag and opened it up to retrieve some coins for Louis.

"I'll get that," said Jack. He pulled out four bits and walked over and handed it to the boy.

"Thank you, Mr. Taylor."

"Would you like to tell me what happened to *Miss Doc*?"

The color drained from the boy's face.

Kitty walked over. "I tripped and my face hit the bag handle. Go on and finish your work, Louis, so you can get home."

"Yes, ma'am."

"Why didn't you say that in the first place?"

"Was that what you were asking? I'm sorry. Could you walk me home?"

"Of course, I can walk you home." He took her bag for her; her clean, shiny unscuffed bag, he noticed.

"Good night, Louis!" Kitty said, walking out of the livery.

"Good night, Miss Doc."

They walked the first block in silence before Jack spoke up. "You gonna tell me the truth now?" He mentally lined up his points of contention. He would get the real story out of her, no matter how long it took.

"I had to break up a fight," she said.

Jack stopped walking. "What?!"

"I was inside talking to Liberty and Ira, and Louis was waiting in the buggy. Marcus came home from school and thought those men had come back. He was trying to be brave defending his family by running Louis off."

"Louis is just a scrawny kid. How could Marcus have thought Louis might have been one of those men?"

"I think his fear kept him from thinking straight, and he knew his daddy couldn't do anything. He was trying to be the man of the house."

Jack lifted her chin to get a better look at her busted lip. "You're no bigger than those boys. How'd you stop them?"

"I promise you, I'd never done anything like that before," she said, smiling sheepishly, "but I got mad when those boys seemed to ignore me when I was trying to break them up, so I went for their hair and ended up right in the middle of them."

"You got in the fight?"

Kitty nodded. "And they stopped; well, at least when Liberty pulled Marcus away, but not before I got popped."

Jack looked back at the livery.

Kitty reassured him. "Louis….both boys felt so bad about

it. It was just a big misunderstanding."

He started chuckling. "I wish I could've seen it."

Kitty slapped his arm, but couldn't help but grin herself. "I can be pretty mean if I need to be."

"I'll remember that." He took her arm and started walking again. "I'm really sorry I couldn't take you myself today. Other than brawling, how did Louis do?"

"Fine, except we had to have a little talk about watching his language and what I expected of him. I don't know if his mother will approve of his going out to Clarksville, but if she says he can, we're definitely going to keep it under our hats so as not to attract any additional trouble."

"Good idea."

"Did you find out anything about who's behind the attacks?"

"No, but someone's working on it for me. Jarvis wasn't happy about me going out there earlier."

"You told him?"

"I thought he could help, but that isn't going to happen. He forbid me to get involved—said it could kill my career before it even started."

"What are you going to do?"

"I'm going to find out who's paying those thugs, and then we're going to put a stop to it. But I was advised to keep Justus and me out of it."

"That's wise. Who'd you talk to?"

"Katherine's friend, Ned Green," Jack spoke before thinking.

"Oh."

"Ned's supporting my campaign, but he isn't going to advertise it. Seems he has a tarnished reputation, too."

"Why does that not surprise me?"

"I shouldn't have mentioned her name; I'm sorry."

"No, don't be. I don't want you to ever think you have to keep things from me; and I always want to be honest with you."

"Like falling and hitting your face on your bag?" Jack said.

"That was for poor Louis's sake. He was scared to death you'd whip him for what happened. I never had any intentions of keeping the truth from you."

"I'm glad to hear that. I really wanted to be with you today, but my schedule's getting busy. We have a lot to do before the election in November."

They stopped at the gate in front of the boarding house.

"Are you hungry?" he asked.

She nodded. "Starving."

"Take this immaculate bag inside... and then I can take you to the Driskill."

She took the satchel. "I'll need to change out of these wrestling clothes, too," Kitty said, smiling crookedly.

He reached up and touched her face. "I'm sorry—"

"Oh, hush! I'm fine." She turned and stepped through the gate, holding it for him. "Come sit on the porch. I won't be long."

"Get a heavier coat—the wind's picking up. Looks like the weather's changing."

22

Jack pulled his hat down lower on his head and turned his collar up to keep the north wind from licking his neck as he turned down Trinity Street. He smiled, thinking about the kiss he just shared with Kitty on the porch of the boarding house after a very pleasant evening at the Driskill, his second such evening that week. That erased the mild irritation he felt towards Jarvis for inviting himself to join them for a while. He had finished his supper, but decided to have his coffee at their table while they waited for their dinner. Jarvis was polite towards Kitty, but Jack knew something was eating at him. He asked if Jack had learned anything about the men who were harrassing the residents of Clarksville, and Jack could honestly say he didn't even know who to ask about it, other than Jarvis. He felt no need to mention that Ned Green had offered to help out. The nagging question Jack had about Jarvis' possible involvement in the Clarksville incidents was put to rest, though, when Jarvis said he would do some asking around himself.

Jack turned west on 4th Street and walked quickly to his house at the end of the street. He took the steps two at a time and reached for the door when a shadow moved in the corner of his eye. He whipped around to face it, fists clenched.

"Didn't mean to startle you, Mr. Taylor," the voice said quietly.

"Who are you?"

The man tilted his head down, as if to hide his face further, but that wasn't necessary. Jack could see nothing recognizable.

"I'd rather not say, if you don't mind. But we do have a common acquaintance…Ned Green."

Jack exhaled with relief. "Of course. Would you like to come in out of the cold?"

"No, sir. I just need to tell you what I learned, and then you can forget we even talked."

"So you found out who's behind the harassment at Clarksville?"

"I found out who's after the land—it's a company that moved into Austin last year. *Sloane Developments* is the name, and it sounds like they've convinced a number of people to invest in them with the promise of big returns. They're buying up land north and west of Austin as cheaply as possible, dividing it up and turning around and selling it at huge profits."

"Sounds legal."

"Except for the part about forcing people to sell. And I'm not absolutely positive Sloane hired the thugs. Wheatsville is getting the same pressure as Clarksville."

"Wheatsville?"

"It's another freedman town northeast of Clarksville; about 300 people live out there. And it's not just land developers trying to run them out. Austin's putting the pressure on them, too—passing restrictions prohibiting them from raising livestock within the city limits and upping their building quality. I heard some city garbage wagons dumped trash on the streets of Wheatsville on the way to the dumpsite, which got the town written up."

"Someone from Clarksville told me they were talking about closing the schools and providing no city services to force them over to east Austin."

"Yes, sir. The pressure's coming from several sources, not just that one land development company."

"This is a lot more complicated than I realized."

"I need to get going. If I hear anything else, I'll contact you. I posted a letter to Mr. Green saying what I just told you."

"That's good," said Jack. "What if I need to get a hold of you?"

"You won't have any reason to. I could lose my job over this, so please don't ask me to identify myself. I don't like what's going on any more than you do, and I'll do whatever I can so long as my livelihood isn't threatened. My family depends on me."

"I understand," said Jack. "I appreciate your help." He reached his hand out, and was surprised when the man grasped it awkwardly with his left hand.

"You're welcome, Mr. Taylor," the man said before stepping off the porch and disappearing into the night.

Jack opened the front door and stepped inside without turning on the light. He walked through the dark room to the potbelly stove and opened the fire door to add some kindling, then stoked the glowing coals until a flame appeared. He left the iron door open, pulled his desk chair up close and sat down, watching the fire. He held out his hands, feeling the comfort of the warmth as he thought about what the stranger had said.

How could he help the people of Clarksville and Wheatsville without getting involved and making it a public issue? Ned Green advised him to stay in the background, but who would speak up for them? He figured he could wait until after the November election to do something, but what if someone was killed in the meantime? He couldn't live with that kind of guilt.

He shook his head, like that would settle his thoughts into some kind of order. He wished Ned was still in town, but he and Bill McDonald had left days before. Jack decided he'd better write and ask Ned's advice before he took any action, whatever that might be.

His career and future was neatly planned out; how could it get so complicated before it even started?

* * *

Jack left the house a little early the next morning so he

could talk to Justus. The older gentlemen already had a customer.

"How you doin', Mr. Jack?"

"I'm fine, Justus. And yourself?"

"I can't complain," he said, chuckling. "Life is good."

Jack knew better than that. He squeezed the older man's shoulder, and then grabbed an old newspaper and leaned against the wall.

"I'll be right with you soon as I take care of Mr. Watson here."

"No hurry."

"Any good news to report?" asked Justus.

Jack looked sharply at him.

"In the paper?"

"Oh." Jack glanced back at the page. "Looks like China's empress made it illegal to bind women's feet."

"What?!" That came from Mr. Watson.

"They bind little girls' feet so they stay small. They even have a drawing of it." He held the paper for both men to see.

"All they've done is folded up the foot," said Mr. Watson, visibly shuddering. "Looks like that's gotta hurt."

Jack read some more. "The ideal size of their feet is three inches!"

"Why would they do something like to their womenfolk?" said Justus, shaking his head.

Jack kept reading. "Only the upper class did it; it says it's a symbol of beauty and sign of status—showing the women didn't need to work. But then they're crippled the rest of their lives."

"Barbaric," said Mr. Watson. He pulled out a coin from his pocket and handed it to Justus. "Aren't you glad we live in a country that doesn't allow stuff like that, Justus?"

"Thank you, sir. Yes, sir."

Jack glared at him as he walked away. Then he climbed up on the chair. "What does he know?" he grumbled to himself.

Justus smiled. "'Bout the same as you did not too long ago."

Jack watched the top of the graying man's head as he dusted off his boots.

"People don't have to do nuthin' about nuthin' if they don't know nuthin'," said Justua as he started wiping the blacking on the left boot. "That's the safest place to be—busy and blind."

"I'm sorry, Justus."

"Didn't mean to make you feel bad. Hope I didn't offend you."

"No offense taken. But I learned something last night."

Justus looked up, then glanced from side to side.

"I found out who's trying to buy your land."

"Who?"

"I think the less you know the better. Let me handle it."

"Don't you git yourself in trouble for us, Jack."

"I won't. I'm going to see what kind of legal recourse we can take."

"You think the law would help us?"

"I think it depends on how good your lawyer is," said Jack, grinning. "But I did find a case that might interest you. Have you ever heard of Elizabeth Freeman?"

Justus shook his head.

"It happened up in Massachusetts eighty-something years before the Emancipation. It was a county court case, and Elizabeth Freeman was one of the plaintiffs in *Brom and Bett v. Ashley*— she was the 'Bett' in that case. She and Brom were slaves suing their owner for their freedom."

Justus stopped buffing. "Slaves sued their master?"

Jack nodded his head.

"Did they git beat for it?"

"No, they—"

"Killed 'em."

"No, Justus! They won their case. The jury decided in their favor and awarded them $30 in damages."

"They won?"

"Ashley appealed to the Supreme Judicial Court, but abandoned it some months later."

"How did they win?"

"Massachusetts had recently adopted its consitution, which said that 'men were equal, free, and independent of each other.' Bett had overheard someone reading that and figured it applied to her, too. The case really damaged the slavery system in Massachusetts."

"How would that work for us?"

"I'm not sure yet, but it gave me hope that we might have a chance in court, if we have to go there. I want you to tell your grandkids about 'Mumbett'; that's what her family and friends called her. It wasn't until after she won the case that she gave herself the name Elizabeth Freeman. She ended up going to work for her lawyer's family after that... for pay."

"I like this Mumbett." Justus grinned as he popped his buffing rag. "Looks like this is gonna be a good day after all. Maybe even a good week."

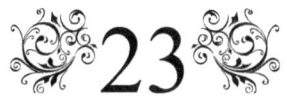

23

Two weeks later, Deputy Ben Stephens walked into Sloane Developments downtown and handed Axel Sloane an injunction letter on behalf of the citizens of Clarksville and Wheatsville.

The deputy reported back to Jack at the marshal's office, saying that it looked like Mr. Sloane was going to "bust a gut" before Ben left the office.

"He said he was going to sue you for slander and he didn't know what this was about along with a number of choice words I'd rather not repeat. I imagine you're going to hear from him."

"I figured as much," said Jack. "I'm hoping he doesn't realize there's not much legal teeth in that letter, but if he does come after us, we have a pretty solid case that they're behind at least Clarksville's harrassment."

"They probably have a passel of lawyers."

"They have two, and they like to bend the law to get what they want."

"So you know what you're up against."

Jack nodded.

"What about the city workers dumping trash?"

"I don't know if the drivers decided that on their own, or if their superiors ordered them to do it, so I'm going to go directly to the men first and ask them."

"You want me to come along?"

"No, let's keep it quiet until I find out who's behind it. If they were ordered to do it, I'll bring another injunction for you to deliver to their boss. I want them to know that somebody's watching what's happening in those communities; and they're not going to get away with their harrassment."

"What does Mr. Baldwin think about all of this?"

"I'm about to find out. I'm sure he'll have a few choice words for me, too," said Jack, with a wry grin. Then it disappeared. "But I can't turn a blind eye to what's happening out there." Jack offered his hand. "I appreciate your help, Ben."

He grasped his hand firmly. "That's my job."

"Could you tell Marshal Davis when he returns? I want him to know what's going on."

"I will."

* * *

Jack stared at Jarvis's face. He didn't realize skin could turn that color of reddish-purple.

Jarvis finally found his voice. "You.. did… what?!"

"You really don't want me to repeat all of that, do you?"

"Why? Why did you go and do something so stupid?"

"I'm trying to keep somebody from getting killed. And I didn't deliver the letter myself. Ben delivered it to Sloane."

"Who in the hell is Ben?"

His head is going to explode. Jack started to step back, but caught himself and stood his ground. "He's new to Austin's police department, but he's got a good head on his shoulders. I thought it'd be more effective for a law officer to deliver it."

Jarvis stopped and asked, "Was your name on the letter?"

Jack nodded. "I didn't see any way around that."

Jarvis turned around and faced the bookshelf, saying nothing for a good minute. It seemed more like an hour to Jack.

Jarvis finally turned around. "Do you realize what you've done? You've put yourself directly in Sloane's sights now, and you'll probably get a visit from his goons. I don't know if your campaign will survive this if it gets out that you're taking up for the niggers now. And you can be sure they're going to let everyone know. "

Jack felt like someone had punched him in the gut. "I thought being a public servant meant helping people when they needed help—especially those who can't help themselves."

"Why didn't you come talk to me first? Better yet, why couldn't you leave things alone? They'll take care of themselves."

"How can they help themselves when everything's against them? They can't defend themselves going up against whites—they'll be the ones accused and hung for it, Jarvis. And it's not just Sloane. The City's doing its dead-level best to drive them over to the east side, too."

"Why couldn't you wait until after the election?"

"It may be too late by then. I had to at least try."

Jarvis placed his hands on his desk and leaned into them, exhaling loudly.

"I'm sorry if I've disappointed you and your plans for me, but I'm not sorry for what I've done."

Jarvis looked up at him. "You don't even know what you've done, Jack. Let me think about this for a while; Link and I will come up with something to save your career."

"But—"

"And we'll try to help Justus and—what was that community called?"

"Clarksville."

"—and Clarksville, too."

That surprised Jack. "Thank you, sir."

"Now get out of here before I change my mind."

Jack obliged; wasting no time getting back to his office.

* * *

Jack walked out of the building a little after four and glanced at the words scrawled on a piece of paper Emery had given him. The young clerk had proven himself useful in discretely gathering information, and in this case, the name of one of the men on the garbage wagons. He frowned when he noticed where the man lived— right in the middle of Guy Town, Austin's vice district close to the river. He decided he'd better not stroll through that part of town. He turned around and headed for the livery. Lonesome Joe needed to be ridden anyway.

"Louis!" he hollered, walking through the open door. No answer. Thursday. Thursday meant Louis was with Kitty. He walked through the barn. "Patrick!?"

An old man peered out from the loft above him. "Hey, Jack! You need a hack or a horse?" He threw an armful of hay down into a stall.

"I've come for Lonesome Joe."

"I'll saddle him for you."

"No, stay where you are…I'll do it. I just wanted somebody to know I was taking him out for a little while."

"You know it's his supper time, right? He's not gonna be too happy with you."

Jack laughed. "I think you're spoiling that fat boy." He grabbed the bit and walked over to Lonesome's stall. The horse stood in front of the trough and looked at Jack like he'd understood every word they'd said. But he didn't look put out as much as he looked sad… and pitiful. "All right," Jack relented. "Throw him a little hay, Patrick, while I saddle him!"

Patrick laughed and dropped some hay into the trough.

A little later than he intended, Jack rode a contented Lonesome Joe out of the livery and headed toward Guy Town. He knew more from hearsay about this side of town than anything else. He'd received plenty of invites from his college buddies in previous years, but he never joined them. He'd heard university students probably kept most of the establishments open; that, and Congress when it was in session.

He recalled Jarvis advising him to stay away from Guy Town, and in the next breath telling him that anytime he needed a woman, to let him know. He said he knew the right women to contact, and they would come to him.

It wasn't that Jack hadn't thought about it, he'd thought about it plenty of times. But the idea of being so intimate with a strange woman who opened herself up to a different man every night made him cringe.

When he tried to explain that to Jarvis, the older man said that sex was nothing more than a man relieving himself, and that it wasn't any more important than a man eating or urinating. He said it was unhealthy when a man didn't partake regularly.

Jack made the mistake of saying that he believed that kind of relations was meant for the marriage bed.

Jarvis almost shouted that it was expected that men come to the marriage bed experienced—that no woman would want an ignorant man in her bed.

"How would a virgin know any different?" Jack said aloud, then looked around to see if anyone was within hearing distance. It bothered him that the man he looked up to had such little regard for women or the sanctity of marriage. He wanted the kind of marriage his parents had, and his grandparents. He knew they were faithful to each other. He couldn't even imagine them not being loyal to each other.

Jarvis told him that when he was fourteen years old, his father took him to the town whore to make him a man—that it was a rite of passage for young men. A few nights later Jarvis sent Jack up to his room in the Driskill to 'fetch' something, and a scantily-dressed woman met him at the door and started crawling all over him.

When Jack finally disconnected himself from her arms, he marched downstairs and up to the table where he'd left Link and Jarvis minutes before.

"Well, that was much faster than I thought it'd be," said Link, trying to keep from laughing.

Jack couldn't speak for a moment, he was so angry.

Jarvis seemed surprised at Jack's response. "Was she not to your liking, son?"

"Son?" Jack finally found his voice. "My father would never do that to me."

"I don't think your parents are as blameless as you think."

"How would you know?"

"Forget it. I was just trying to help. My father did it for me, and I'm glad he did."

"Where's your father today?"

The seconds of silence spoke volumes.

"I left home when I was seventeen, and I never saw him again," he said.

"And you're passing a tradition on to me from a man you don't respect enough to keep in touch with? I'll pass." Jack turned around and walked away.

"Hey, handsome!" a sultry voice broke into his thoughts.

Jack looked around; he was at least a block into Guy Town and hadn't even realized it. He found the body that the voice was attached to on the porch of a two-story house. He turned Lonesome towards her.

The woman seemed too old to be doing this kind of work.

"Looking for some fun, Cowboy?" she smiled at him enthusiastically, but her eyes looked tired.

"'Evenin', ma'am," said Jack, touching the rim of his hat.

"A gentlemen, even. What you lookin' for, honey?"

"Just information."

Her face fell.

"Could you tell me where 245 West 3rd Street is? I see there aren't any numbers on the buildings."

"We don't go by numbers 'round here—everybody knows where everybody is. Who you lookin' for?"

"A man by the name of Tug Spencer."

She eyed him warily. "Is he in trouble?"

Jack shook his head. "Some friends of mine could use his help."

She pointed down the road. "Turn right at the drugstore; he's a few houses down, across from the blackmith shop."

"You said a drugstore?" he said, a little incredulous.

"Yeah, and a grocery store and a tailor's and—"

"Got it."

"Real people live here, too," she said.

"Yes, ma'am, sorry," he tipped his hat again.

"The name's Sofie... if you ever need anything... or if you prefer someone younger, Sage and Ginger come in after dark."

"I appreciate your help, Miss Sofie." He turned Lonesome down the road.

He turned right at the drugstore and watched for the blacksmith shop. A piano started playing a lively tune; laughter came from another house. Guy Town was waking up for the night, and he needed to do his business and get back into Austin.

He came up on the blacksmith shop and looked left. A white picket fence stretched across the front, and that's as far as it went, dividing a line between the road and yard. The fence extended no further towards the house. Jack dismounted and tied Lonesome to the gate post, struggled with the latch before he opened it and walked up to the house. Something smelled good coming from that direction, reminding him that it was close to supper time.

Jack rapped on the door and waited. A woman yelled at someone to answer the door. In a litte bit a young boy came to the door and just stood there.

"Hello," said Jack. "Is your father home?"

The boy shook his head.

"Who is it, Chigger?" the woman yelled from inside.

"I dunno," he yelled back. "He wants Papa."

A short woman came up to the door, wiping her hands on a dishtowel. "Can I help you?" she asked.

"Is this where Tug Spencer lives?"

"Yes... is he in trouble?"

That was the second time in the past five minutes someone asked him that. Jack's curiosity was piqued.

"No, ma'am; I'm hoping he can help some friends of mine." That was the second time in the past five minutes he'd used that excuse, too, but he thought the explanation was accurate enough.

"Tug's not home yet, but I expect him any minute. You're welcome to wait out here."

"Thank you, ma'am." He struggled opening the gate again and gave up and walked around the end of the picket fence.

He wondered if Tug might run if he saw him, so he grabbed Lonesome's reins and walked across the street to the blacksmith shop, closed up for the evening. He tied the horse to a post and sat down on a bench to wait. The sun had disappeared in the southwest, but he could still see in the graying light. He spoke to several passersby.

Ten minutes later, he watched a man come walking down the south side of the road.

Jack stood up when he saw the man stop and reach for the gate, which he had no trouble opening. He'd used his left arm to open the gate, but his right arm remained bent and close to his chest... unmoving.

With a start, he knew his answer without even asking the man. Tug Spencer was the stranger that visited him in the shadows on his porch. The knot in the pit of the stomach just tightened.

The orders to dump trash in Wheatsville had come from higher up.

24

J ack walked into Jarvis's office the next morning. His boss gestured for him to sit down.

"Link and I had a long talk over supper last night. He's going to take care of the Sloane situation, so I don't want you to mention that name, or talk to anyone associated with that company. I don't even want you to walk by that building before you're elected."

"I appreciate what you and Link are doing, but will Sloane's thugs keep harrassing the people of Clarksville?"

"No, Link will handle that."

"I found out something last night."

Jarvis' eyebrows met in the middle. "Didn't I tell you to steer clear of—"

"I didn't involve myself in anything; I just learned that the garbage wagon drivers were instructed to dump trash in Wheatsville from somebody higher up. Looks like the city was responsible for that."

Jarvis rubbed his forehead and took a deep breath. "Let me try to explain this to you in a way I hope you can understand. At this time in your life, Jack, you are not in the position to do anything about that situation other than hurt yourself and your reputation. You have absolutely nothing to influence or leverage any change for the better. And they will destroy you and your chance to make things better, which is getting elected as a lawmaker. What good will you be able to do for Clarksville and Wheatsville if you're not elected?" He leaned back in his chair to let Jack ruminate on his words.

"But the truth—" Jack began.

"Sometimes the truth must be deferred until you have a better chance to win," Jarvis interrupted. "Otherwise, you may be opening Pandora's box. What if your raising awareness of what's going on out there causes more harm to them than good—unintentionally, of course."

"How could it? They're being wronged. But you said Link is going to put a stop to it, right?"

"Jack, don't you realize that Sloane won't be the only one going after them? They're just the first to notice where Austin's heading, and Clarksville and Wheatsville don't fit nicely into Austin's plans. Running off one speculator right now is just a temporary solution. If you make public what's happening out there, you're waving a flag to let other opportunists know something valuable is out there, and they'll try their hand at getting their property. Those people have years of struggle ahead of them."

Jack felt a sick feeling in his gut. It hadn't even occurred to him that his efforts were just a temporary solution, or that his actions could cause more problems for those communities.

After a moment, he stood up to leave.

"I know your intentions are good, Jack, and I admire you for that. But sometimes good intentions aren't enough to change the way things are. Do you understand what I'm saying, son?" Jarvis asked, almost in a gentle tone.

Jack nodded, and walked out of the room. He turned right, though, instead of left that led to his office. He pushed open the back door that opened up to the alley, slamming the door behind him.

"Such a big problem-solver you are, Taylor," he mumbled to himself. He kicked a can, scaring a stray cat to flight.

Then he did something that he hadn't done since he was a little boy.

He wept.

* * *

Jack avoided seeing Justus the rest of the week, but he honestly hadn't had time to see Kitty either. He buried himself in his work and election plans since he realized how much he still needed to learn in order to win this seat. He envied the presidential candidates who allowed their party leaders to campaign for them. Presidential candidates were supposed to appear nonpartisan so it would be like they would represent all of the people. For years, it was considered beneath the presidency for candidates to publicly promote themselves, but he noticed that was changing. In the last two presidential elections, William Jennings Bryan spent his entire campaigns on speaking tours when the other candidates stayed home.

He pushed aside the stack of newspapers on his desk to look at his calendar, which used to be so pristine and... empty. Now it was covered in ink. Link told him he needed to choose a couple of important issues to focus on, but to stay away from very divisive and controversial topics, and to be knowledgeable about any subject or current event that people might bring up. Link said Jack could basically use the same speech, but he needed to add something that applied to the particular group of people or organization he was speaking to.

His list of notes was getting longer – prohibition, railroad regulation, population growth, economic production, segregation, land development, farmers and the price of cotton and corn, ranchers and the price of beef and sheep, credit, debt, manufacturing, flour milling, lumber industry, meat packing, labor unions, churches, social clubs, women's suffrage, the Interstate Commerce Commission...universities... education.

Jack ran his fingers through his hair and groaned. He felt like he was back in school.

Someone quietly knocked on the door.

"It's open," said Jack. He smiled and sat up straighter when Kitty stepped through the door.

"Are you too busy for lunch?" He noticed she was carrying a covered basket.

"Is it lunch time already?" He stood and walked around the desk to greet her.

"Do you normally work on Saturdays?" she asked.

"Is it Saturday? I was wondering where everyone was." He laughed when he saw the concerned look on her face. "I'm pulling your leg. Here, let me move some of this stuff." He cleared off half of his desk and pulled up a chair for her. "Mrs. Gerwick?" He lifted up the cloth.

"Mrs. Gerwick."

"I love her fried chicken." He grabbed a chicken leg and paused in mid-bite. "I'm sorry I haven't been by to see you this week. Things are getting—"

"I understand, Jack." She set two plates and forks on the desk, along with several small Mason jars of green beans and buttered potatoes. She unwrapped a linen napkin containing several biscuits.

"This is great," he said, with a mouth full of food.

"When was the last time you ate?"

"I had coffee for breakfast," he said, not bothering to slow down.

"Coffee isn't breakfast; it's a catapult for your brain."

"What?"

"Nevermind; I brought some hot… by now it's probably warm tea," she unwrapped another mason jar and poured a cup. "Mrs. Gerwick added a little sugar back at the house since she didn't have anything sweet to send you. I hope you don't mind." She poured herself a cup, too.

"Mind? If I shut my eyes, it's like I'm back at home eating in Vestal's kitchen."

"Have you checked in with your family lately?"

Jack shook his head. "Have you?"

Kitty smiled. "I write my mother every week, and she does the same for me. I hear about her rheumatism acting up and the latest debutante her handsome boss is seeing—they get younger every year. And she usually includes a good recipe she's found, like I have time to cook."

"Wait, go back to the handsome boss. How old is he?"

"I'm guessing around thirty, maybe?"

"That's not so old. Was he ever interested in you?" Jack asked.

"Oh, no. *I* was terribly infatuated with Lucius for years..."

An odd feeling washed over him... was this what jealousy felt like?

"...but he never saw me as anything but JuJu's little girl, always under foot, always trying to get his attention." Her eyebrows raised. "You'd never believe who he was besotted with for a short time."

"Who?"

"Grace."

"My cousin, Grace?"

Kitty nodded. "I honestly think he wanted to marry her."

"Really? But what about Finn?"

"If Finn hadn't shown up when he did, he might've lost her. On the day of the big storm, Momma and I had come to Lucius's house because it was higher on the island than ours. Grace was staying there—"

"With Lucius?"

"She was good friends with his sister; that's how she knew him, but he offered his home to her and stayed at his office downtown until she got her own apartment. In fact, Daisy helped her lease an apartment in her building, which was close to the beach. Grace was supposed to move in that day, but the storm prevented it, thank heavens, because that huge apartment building washed away. Lucius sent a hack to bring us downtown where he thought it would be safer for us, but Grace refused to come. She knew Finn was on the island looking for her, but they kept missing each other, so she told Mom and me that she was going to stay there to wait for him. Then when we got downtown, there was Finn waiting for her at Lucius's office. And in the middle of that dangerous storm, he went after her. By then the streets were already flooded and buildings were crumbling and the wind-blown objects were already killing people. I honestly thought we would never see Finn again, or even Grace for that matter. And Lucius just stood there and watched him go. I think that showed between the two of them who truly loved Grace."

"I'd heard that Finn had gone after her and that they had survived the storm, but I hadn't heard that part of the story."

"Lucius has always been good to Mom and me, and I will forever be grateful to him, but my obsession with him crumbled that night. I realized he always paid someone else to do his chivalry for him."

Jack felt relieved about that part. He set down the half-eaten biscuit. "Speaking of chivalry, this knight in shining armour fell off his horse."

Kitty smiled like she thought he was about to tell her something funny. The smile disappeared when he didn't return it. "What is it, Jack?"

"I found out that Sloane Developments is behind the harrassments at Clarksville."

"But that's good news, right? Now you can stop them."

"Yes and no. Jarvis told me that Link is going to take care of it to keep my name out of it, although I sent them a letter with my name signed to it. I don't know how Link is going to keep Sloane from causing problems for me—whether he'll pay them off or dig up something scandalous they wouldn't want known to use as leverage. But Jarvis made me realize something I hadn't even thought of. He said that Sloane won't be the only speculators going after Clarksville, and that if I made it public, it'd be like waving a red flag to others to try to get ahold of their property."

"Do you think that'll actually happen, or was that Jarvis trying to get you to drop it?"

"Have you ever heard of Wheatsville?"

Kitty shook her head. "No."

"It's another freedman community a few miles northeast of Clarksville, and somebody ordered the garbage wagons from Austin to dump trash in their streets so they'd get written up by Austin officials. They're threatening to close the schools and stop services to try to get the Negroes to move to the east side of town."

"That's not right! We have to make it known."

"Jarvis said that before I should try to change anything, that I needed to be in a position of authority—that I have nothing to leverage any kind of change. Right now, all it would do is sink my chances of getting elected. But once I'm elected, I would be in a better position to fight these injustices."

"But it's not right."

Jack nodded his head. "I'm learning that this world is a lot more complicated than I ever realized. I see three choices ahead of me. I can go on in life with my blinders on and do nothing about it; I can try to do something about it right now and sacrifice my career as a lawmaker; or I work my way into a place where I can do something about it."

"I hate to admit that Jarvis may be right," said Kitty. "But you know you're having to give up something with every one of those choices."

"Yeah."

"It has to be number three, then."

"That's what I'd decided."

"And you're going to have to distance yourself from me, too, until after you're elected."

"No!"

"I'm not going to stop going out to Clarksville, and that could hurt you."

"I can't even think about not seeing you, Kitty."

"You survived a week without me," she teased.

"Because I knew I'd see you eventually," he said, rising. He walked around the desk and pulled her up into his arms and spoke into her hair. "I don't think I can do this without you. Just knowing you're close and that you're mine..." he grabbed her arms and pushed her back so he could see her face. "You are mine, aren't you?"

"Yes, Jack," she said, putting her hands on each side his face, pulling him toward her lips. "I'm yours."

For the next several months Jack and Kitty saw each other discreetly; they even kept it from Jarvis, at Kitty's insistence. Jack didn't want to, but she was convinced Jarvis had made the connection between her and Katherine.

Jack made the rounds to talk to most every organization, church, and business in the city and surrounding communities, and some of them twice. By August, he felt like he had the election in the bag.

The sun was barely up when Jack pulled out his key to open the door to the firm *Baldwin, Segal & Taylor*. He smiled at the recently re-painted sign. Jarvis told him he wasn't an official partner yet, but that the name recognition would help him in November. In the past few weeks, Jack started opening the office in the morning, much to Emery's annoyance. But Jack let him continue to make the first pot of coffee, which he regularly complimented the younger clerk on.

Jack glanced down the street. Justus was setting up his chair a little earlier than usual.

Jack pocketed the key and walked across the intersection. It had been a while since he'd checked on the older man.

"Good morning, Justus! You're up early."

Justus turned around with a grin. "You know what they say about the early bird?"

"Something about getting the first worm?"

"Nah, the early bird gets the first nickel."

Jack laughed and climbed up on the chair. "How are things going for you, my friend?"

"I can't complain," said Justus, wiping off Jack's boots. "You sure been busy. I think we're gonna see your name on the roll in that big pink building up the street, from what I hear."

"I hope so. I'm sorry I never made it back to one of y'all's town meetings, Justus, but that'll change after I'm sworn in."

"I know. We want to see you elected, too." He started smearing the blacking on Jack's boots. "I appreciate what you already done for us."

"Link took care of that."

"But he wouldna if you hadn't started the ball rollin'," said Justus. "That man couldn't care less about us."

"He's not as bad as I once thought."

"Well, Miss Doc has helped us out so much, too. She's not gettin' any grief over her goin' out there, is she?"

"No; few people know about it."

"God bless and keep her." Justus began wiping off the excess blacking.

"Anybody else been pestering y'all about selling out?"

"Nah, but we've heard they may not open the school next month—that the kids'll have to go all the way over to east Austin if they want an education, but that's miles away. They think they're gonna draw us away from our property by holding that over our heads."

"I'll check on it."

"You be careful." Justus began pulling the rag back and forth over Jack's boot, drawing out the shine.

"I will."

* * *

Kitty grasped a scrawny arm and pulled the young girl up to a sitting position on the table. She glanced at Liberty as she helped her put the dirty, tattered shirt back on. It looked like a man's shirt.

A breeze came through the open window. Kitty turned her face toward it and shut her eyes for a moment, letting it cool the sweat on her brow.

"What's wrong with me?" the girl asked.

Kitty turned back to face her. "Nothing's wrong with you, Winnie." Kitty rolled up the girl's too-long sleeves and then clasped the thin hands in her own. "How old are you?"

"Thirteen."

"You're going to have a baby, sweetheart."

Liberty made an involuntary groan. "Child, you're just a baby yourself."

Kitty continued. "Do you know how babies are made?"

The girl shook her head.

"Has a man touched you down here?" Kitty gestured briefly over the girl's lap.

The girl looked uncomfortable and shook her head again.

"You can't make a baby all by yourself. A man has to share part of himself with you for that to happen."

Winnie began to cry. "Do we have to tell Daddy?"

Liberty put her arm around her. "That baggy shirt won't be enough to keep it from him much longer, girl." She looked at Kitty. "How far along is she?"

"I'd say five months, give or take a few weeks, but you need to eat better, honey. You're skin and bones; it's all going to the baby."

"Daddy's gonna be mad."

"Do you want us to talk to him for you?"

She shook her head.

"What about the father, Winnie? Would he be willing to take care of you and the baby?" asked Liberty.

She slid off the table. "I gotta go." She ran out the door.

"Wait, Winnie!" Kitty started down the hall after her. "I need to tell you…" but she stopped when she saw the dozen faces still waiting in the sanctuary to see her. She pasted a smile on her face. "Who's next?"

Later, when they were turning the makeshift examining room back into a Sunday School room, Kitty asked Liberty,

"What do you think we should do about Winnie?"

"I'm not sure, but I'm thinkin' she isn't gonna tell her father, and I don't know if we'd be making things worse for her if we approached him" said Liberty.

"He's going to find out before too long."

"I would not be comfortable around Hokee when that happens; he's an angry man, mad at the world ever since his wife died. I'm afraid he'll beat Winnie when he finds out she's with child."

"What about the Reverend? Do you think he would talk to Mr. Hokee?"

"It wouldn't hurt to ask. It's getting late and you and Louis need to get on home. I'll talk to the Reverend when I see him."

"Thank you, Liberty," Kitty said, wiping the sweat off her brow. She walked to the door that opened up to the outside and hollered. "Louis! Come take a load to the buggy!"

No answer.

She stepped outside and looked around. "Louis!!" she yelled louder.

He and Marcus came running around the church. Each of them had several good-sized fish.

"Look what we caught, Miss Doc!" said Louis. "Marcus took me to his secret fishin' hole."

"He swore he woodunt tell anybody," said Marcus solemnly.

"I swore," said Louis apologetically, like he thought Kitty would actually ask him.

Kitty grinned at the thought. "I swear I won't ask, then." She looked down at the boys' rolled up pants and bare feet. It looked like they had done some wading, too. "Where are your shoes, Louis?"

"They're in the carriage."

"You walked barefoot all the way to the river?"

"We walked on the tracks most of the way."

Kitty smiled. "You look like Huckleberry Finn and Tom Sawyer."

Marcus said, "You mean Huckleberry Finn and Jim."

Kitty was impressed. "So you've read it?"

"Yes, Ma'am."

"What are y'all talkin' about?" asked Louis.

"She's talkin' about a book," said Marcus, "a book you ought to read."

Kitty continued. "I wasn't referring to a slave, Marcus. I see two boys—two friends out fishing. I stand by my words. And I have to say those are nice-looking fish."

Marcus beamed. "Is Momma still here?"

"Yes, she is."

He walked over to the door and hollered, "Momma, I caught us some supper!"

Liberty came to the door and fussed and fawned over the catch. "Daddy's gonna be so pleased to have some good catfish tonight. Why don't you head on home and get them skinned and cleaned up for me? I'm almost finished here."

"You can go on, too, Liberty. Louis will help me close up."

"Thank you, Dr. Kitty. Everything's in order."

"Louis, could you load the buggy? But first go wrap those fish in some of that newspaper I hope you already read."

"Yes, ma'am."

She turned back to Liberty. "I can't tell you how much I appreciate your help; you're a natural at this. Have you ever thought about doing some serious training?"

Liberty smiled ruefully. "For about one minute, then I folded up that dream and put it away."

"But—"

"Where would I go? I can't leave my family and we can't pull up and move to where you got your training. They probably don't admit Negroes there. And then how would I pay for it? Did you pay for your doctor degree?"

Kitty realized at that moment how much she had taken for granted—her mother's and especially Lucius's generosity. She shook her head.

"You seem to forget that I don't live in your world."

Kitty felt like a barrier suddenly appeared between them. "I'm so sorry."

"I didn't mean to make you feel bad. That's just the way things are."

"I don't like it, Liberty," said Kitty. "I don't like it one bit." Then she did something she'd never done before. She reached across the barrier and wrapped her arms around Liberty. "I'll teach you what I know."

Liberty chuckled as she returned the hug. "You just now figurin' that out, professor? I've already been attending the school of Miss Doc for months now."

26

Emery walked into Jack's office and handed him a sealed letter with *Mr. Jack Taylor* scrawled on it.

"Where'd you get this?"

"Justus brought it over this morning while you were out. How'd it go over at Beth Israel?"

"Very well, although I only spoke to the Ladies Auxilliary, but they have some influence on their husbands' votes, and they fed me good while I was there." He looked at the envelope. "Did Justus seem upset to you?"

Emery shook his head. "Nah, he was his usual good-natured self."

"All right, thanks," Jack said dismissively, breaking the seal. He smiled when he recognized Kitty's neat cursive handwriting on the inside. He looked at the outer writing again and realized she had disguised it.

He leaned back to read the note, then sat up straight in his chair to look at the clock. He stuffed the letter in his suit pocket and hurried out of the office.

"I'll be back after while," he yelled to Emery as he headed out the door.

He ran the three blocks down Brazos Street and turned west to get to the red brick Houston and Texas Central Railroad station sitting on the corner of Congress and 3rd. He had recently visited the grand opening of the new station at Link's suggestion, and it proved to be profitable to meet the officers of this successful railroad company, now owned by Southern Pacific. He entered the building, hoping the trains were running late that day, and made his way to the first open ticket window.

"Excuse me," said Jack, trying to catch his breath. "Has the train... left for Houston yet?"

The man glanced at a wall clock. "Twenty-eight minutes ago. Didn't you hear the whistle?"

"No, I don't... even notice them... anymore."

"Were you supposed to be on it?"

"No, sir, I just... wanted to see someone off...," he took a big breath. "Thank you."

Jack turned around and headed to the door. Outside, he pulled his handkerchief from his pocket and wiped his brow, noticing the strong odor of oil in the air. He'd learned from his previous visit that the locomotives had begun using oil to power them rather than steam. One of the railroad officials proudly mentioned it in his speech. Jarvis was pleased to hear about another use for oil.

Jack noticed another moonlight tower on the corner, which he hadn't seen before. He smiled, remembering one of the first conversations when he and Kitty had talked about those monstrosities. He returned his handkerchief to his pocket, and felt the letter. He pulled it out and read it again, staying in the shade of the deep overhang.

Dearest Jack,

A wire was delivered to my office early this morning with a message from Lucius that my mother has had some kind of apoplexy, which is a bleeding in her brain. Dr. Gilbert was kind enough to let me take some time to go tend to her since I'm her only family. Lucius offered to hire someone, but I need to be there. Justus will tell Liberty for me. Could you tell Louis that we won't be going to Clarksville again until I return?

The storm was frightening, but this terrifies me in a different way. Please remember Mama in your prayers. I'm praying she has the clarity of mind to know me and hear everything I need to tell her, things I should've told her years ago. I just assumed she would always be there.

I know you are busy, but if you get this in time, my train leaves at 11:10 a.m. if you can see me off. If I don't see you, I'll write as soon as I know more.

Forever yours,

K

Jack folded up the letter and slipped it back in his pocket. He wiped his face again and walked over to the empty tracks, feeling the weight of regret with every step. He couldn't remember ever feeling lonesome in Austin before… until now. His heart wanted to catch the next train and follow her, but his head knew he had commitments to keep. The election was less than two months away now. But if she needed him… he would go.

He decided he would wait for her letter before acting.

* * *

Kitty stepped out of the train station holding her hastily packed suit case. She stood there for a moment and breathed in the smell of Galveston Island, a mixture of fish odor and brine. The powerful sense of familiarity and nostalgia washed over her.

She'd learned through her mother's letters that the city began building a seventeen foot seawall this year, and that they planned to raise much of the island's elevation behind it. That meant building it up with sand up to a level of 17 feet behind the seawall, sloping down one foot for every 1,500 feet to the bay on the other side of the island.

What seemed even more inconceivable to Kitty was raising every structure with jackscrews, and their location determined if they would be raised a foot or up to eleven feet. All of the sewer, water and gas lines, along with utility poles for electricity and telephone service, would also have to be raised. She could not imagine how they would begin this massive undertaking, but she had to admire their tenacity. She'd chosen to abandon the island to live away from the path of those terrifying storms. Even if another one never came again during her lifetime, one was enough, and it scarred her forever.

She glanced at the sky as she walked down the street to Lucius's office, where she planned to rent a hack to take her to the hospital. The sun had set as the train traveled across the bay bridge, but the sky was cloudless and nonthreatening in the fading light. She felt the salty breeze linger on her face and licked her lips out of habit. Most of the businesses had closed several hours earlier, but a number of people were still on the street.

Kitty paused when she reached Lucius's office. The brick building looked immovable now, showing little evidence that the wind almost collapsed it two years before while she and her mother prayed fervently inside. Lucius wasn't a religious man, but he was on his knees with them that night.

She tried the door, but it was locked, so she rapped on it loudly.

"Is that you, Kitty?" a voice spoke from above.

"Yes, Lucius, it's me!" She stepped out in the street so she could see him above the canopy.

"I'll be right down!"

The handsome head disappeared before she could utter a response.

Kitty smiled. Patience had never been one of the man's virtues.

A key grated in the lock, and Lucius was out the door enveloping her in his arms. "It's been too long, little girl. How are you?"

Kitty was more shocked than anyone when she burst into tears. She had not shed one tear on the long trip, convincing herself that her mother's illness probably wasn't as serious as it sounded.

"There, there. Your mother's a tough woman; she'll pull through."

Kitty nodded as she wiped her nose, feeling like the 'little girl' he called her. She took the handkerchief he offered.

"Come inside. I'll call Tom to take us to the hospital."

Kitty finally spoke her first words. "How bad is it?"

He set her suitcase by the door and walked her to a sitting room.

"Let me call Tom first; I told him to be on call, but it'll still take a few minutes for him to get over here. Have a seat, and I'll be right back tell you what the doctor told me. Fix you some coffee or tea."

The coffee was lukewarm, but the water for tea felt hotter, so she dropped some ground tea directly in the teapot to steep and sat down on the sofa closest to it. She felt like a limp dishrag.

Lucius came back in and sat down beside her. "The doctor told me he's seen a lot worse cases of stroke than your mother's, but it's still serious."

"When did it happen?"

"Late yesterday afternoon sometime. I came home from work and found her lying in my kitchen, unable to get up. I called Tom, and he helped me get her to the hospital."

"Thank you so much, Lucius."

Lucius shook his head. "She's my family here, Kitty. You both are. When I found her, she tried to talk, but I couldn't understand her—"

"She wasn't unconscious?" Kitty sounded hopeful.

"No, and she can move one of her hands, and she knew me."

Kitty felt such a relief. "I can't wait to see her."

"Did you get something to drink?"

"No, the coffee's cold and the tea is steeping."

Lucius stood and poured the lukewarm tea in a cup for her. "Sugar?"

Kitty nodded.

Lucius stirred in some sugar and handed her the cup on a saucer. "I'm sorry it's not hotter."

Kitty took a swig. "It's fine." She didn't realize how thirsty she was. She drank the rest of the amber liquid and set the cup and saucer down.

"More?"

"No, thank you. I guess I didn't drink that like a lady, but it was very good."

Lucius chuckled. "You can drink it however you like. I can't believe you're working now."

"I've been working for years."

"I meant as a doctor. Little Kitty is now a doctor."

"Little Kitty is all grown up now, Lucius. And I realized recently how much I've taken for granted in my life. You and Momma spoiled me," she said, smiling. "Did I ever thank you for providing for my education?"

"I'd like to take credit for that, Kitty, but I can't."

That took her by surprise. "I always thought it was you."

"What did your mother tell you?"

"She said a benefactor provided a scholarship. I don't know anybody else who had the means or the desire to help me, other than you. Who was it?"

Lucius smiled and took her hand. "Your *benefactor* wanted to remain anonymous, and I've respected her wishes all these years."

"Her?"

"She also bought my old house for you and your mother."

"I thought you—"

"I have to say that I did let her have it at a rock bottom price. And don't forget, I always remembered your birthday and Christmas," he said, in an attempt to redeem himself.

"You've always been good to me, Lucius, but if you didn't pay for those things, who did?" Kitty sat there mentally going through the names of women in Galveston she knew were well off enough to pay for a modest house and a university degree, but she didn't have a close relationship with any of them.

Relationship.

The answer came like a bolt of lightning. Her eyes widened at the thought. "Katherine?" she whispered.

This time Lucius was surprised. "You know her?"

"I've known about her for a couple of years, but I met her in person in Austin last February."

"She's an exceptional woman."

"She was a prostitute!" Kitty fired back.

"You don't know why she ended up in that life. Maybe she was forced into it."

"But she stayed in it all these years. She doesn't even know who my father was."

"That's probably a blessing."

"I feel such shame about that. I was conceived in a moment of lust, not love. Not commitment. What an awful heritage I have to pass down to my children."

"That's something you wouldn't need to tell your children. But I've known Katherine for years—"

"—as a paying customer?" Kitty said spitefully.

Lucius paused, like he was weighing his answer.

"Oh, Lucius, no."

"Only in the beginning. Then we became friends, and she let me handle her finances. I have the utmost respect for your mother."

"She's not my mother!"

Lucius backtracked. "You're right. Juju raised you. But you need to know that Katherine has kept up with you all of your life, making sure you and Juju were well taken care of. She was the one who insisted that I hire your mother after I moved to Galveston. Everything I learned about you from Juju, I shared with her. But she chose to stay out of your life—not that she wanted to, but she didn't want to bring shame to you or your mother. That was one of the reasons she left Galveston; you two look so much alike, and she was afraid people would make the connection."

"Finn and Grace helped her leave." The tears flowed freely down Kitty's cheeks again.

Lucius nodded. "And she's turned her life around since then." He retrieved his kerchief from the cart and wiped away the tears. "I didn't tell you this to make you sad, ma cherie, but I wanted you to know how much she's done for you because she loves you. She's always loved you."

The sound of the door opening and shutting interrupted them.

"Mr. Roderick?" a voice called out.

Lucius stood and walked to the door. "We'll be right there, Tom. Can you load the bag by the door?" He came back to Kitty. "Juju thinks I'm your benefactor; that was also at Katherine's request. She didn't want to diminish your mother's role in any way."

"Then why did you tell *me* the truth? Why didn't you just let me keep on believing this benefactor was you?"

"Because I thought you needed to know what she's done for you, and I'm sure she'll be upset that I told you."

"It doesn't make me feel any better to know this, Lucius."

"It should."

"Now all I can think about is that the house my mother lives in and my medical degree was paid for by men having... physical relations with that woman."

"Kitty..."

"It's the truth."

"I hope you can learn to forgive her. She's trying to learn to forgive herself." He offered her his hand and helped her stand.

"Why didn't she quit years ago if she felt bad about what she was doing?"

"Maybe she felt trapped."

"Now I feel like the one trapped since you told me the truth. I don't want to owe that woman anything, Lucius."

"Katherine never intended for you to know what she's done for you, so why would you think she would ever want you to feel like you owed her?"

Kitty refused to let that thought sink in. "I'm ready to go see Momma."

The street lights glowed by the time Tom pulled the carriage to a stop in front of the John Sealy Hospital. Only a few windows were lit. Kitty stared at the building where she had spent so much of her time training and working towards her medical degree. Latched onto that memory was the nightmare week following the storm. She suppressed a shiver.

"We won't be long, Tom," said Lucius, helping Kitty down.

"I'll be staying the night," she said, reaching for her bag.

"It's past visiting hours. We'll do good to even get in to see Juju tonight."

"I know the rules, but I have a history here, too, Lucius. Momma needs someone with her 'round the clock. They don't have the staff for that."

"I'm glad somebody around here has some clout. They kept running me off." He took the bag from her hand and offered his arm as they walked up the steps and through the doors. The hall was quiet and dimly lit as they made their way to the nurses' desk in the center of the first floor.

"Psst!" someone made a noise behind them. "The next visiting hours are at ten in the morning."

Kitty and Lucius turned around to see a young woman walking toward them, obviously a nursing student.

"The last visiting period ended at 6:30," she said rather sternly. Her face softened when she looked at Lucius. "Oh, it's you."

"How are you, Miss..."

"Gabby... I mean, Miss Jones," she said, her face blushing. "I'm so sorry, but I'm not allowed to let visitors in at this hour."

"Hello, Miss Jones," said Kitty, pulling her attention away from Lucius. "I'm Dr. Kitty Synatzske, and I need to examine Jewel Synatzske."

Gabby's face showed recognition at the name. "I'm so glad to meet you, Dr. Synatzske! Actually Nurse Crain told me that you'd be coming. She wasn't sure exactly when, but she knew you'd get here as soon as you could."

"How is Nurse Crank doing?" asked Kitty.

Gabby's eyes widened, and she stifled a giggle. "How'd you know about that?"

"This is where I got my degree; I learned a lot from her, but she didn't make it easy for me or anybody else."

"You are exactly right," said Gabby. "Follow me. I know you're anxious to see your mother."

Gabby led them to the long hall on the left, but stopped at the first room. She whispered, "Nurse Crain put her as close to our desk as possible. She stayed on after her shift and only left your mother's side a little while ago."

Kitty was touched to hear that. "She and Momma are friends."

"I gathered that," said Gabby, opening the door. She turned on the light and walked into the room. "I'm sorry to disturb you, Mrs. Synatzske, but your daughter's here."

Kitty paused. She had rushed across Texas to see her mother, but her feet suddenly felt like lead. She felt like a little girl again.

Lucius touched the back of her arm. "Are you all right?"

Kitty took a deep breath and nodded, and stepped into the room.

Gabby was on the left side of the bed, so Kitty walked around to the right.

The right side of Juju's mouth turned up in an effort to smile.

"Oh, Momma," Kitty said, leaning down to kiss her forehead. "I came as quickly as I could." She grasped her mother's calloused hand, and sat on the side of the bed, noticing the left side of her face drooped like it had stopped working. "Lucius brought me over."

Juju nodded and gave him a half-smile. She tried to say something, but it was garbled.

"You're welcome," said Lucius.

Kitty looked around at him in surprise, wondering how in the world he figured that out.

"She's always thanking me," he said. "Wasn't that what you said, Juju?"

Juju nodded her head slightly.

Gabby walked over to the door and stood there, staring at Lucius.

"Well, I've worn out my welcome here last night and several times today already," he said as he set Kitty's bag in a chair, "so Miss Jones can see me out." He walked over and gently picked up Juju's paralyzed hand and kissed it. "Sleep well, m'lady. Don't you worry about a thing here or at the house. I'm not as helpless as you think."

Juju smiled crookedly again.

"I'll check in on you tomorrow."

Kitty reached over and squeezed his hand. "Thank you for taking good care of Momma, Lucius. You do know that you're our knight in shining armor."

"Always." He patted Kitty's hand and gave them a heart-stopping smile before turning his attention to Gabby.

After their footsteps died away, Kitty said, "I wonder if that man is ever going to settle down?"

Juju made a noise, and it took a moment before Kitty realized she was chuckling.

Kitty smiled back. "You know I was infatuated with him for years."

Juju nodded and touched her chest twice with her good hand.

Kitty's mouth dropped open. "No, ma'am! Not you, too!" Kitty started giggling.

Juju made several loud grunt noises, which Kitty assumed was laughter, but then her mother's face skewed up, and she began to cry.

"Oh, Momma, don't cry. It's all right."

Juju looked confused.

"Sometimes this ailment gets laughing and crying backwards; that's normal, so don't let it upset you. Things will get clearer for you in time." Kitty reached for her hand again. "Why don't you shut your eyes and rest, and I'll be right here. I'm not going anywhere, Momma... well, maybe to the toilet every once in a while," Kitty said, smiling.

Juju shut her eyes and sighed.

Kitty sat there looking at her mother's hand, so different from her own. Kitty's olive skin was flawless, except for a small white scar on top of her left thumb. Her mother's pale skin didn't hide the blue veins or liver spots. Kitty's fingers were slender and tapered at the end; Juju's short fingers were just as wide at the tips as they were at the base. The pads of Kitty's fingers and palm were soft and smooth; her mother's were marked and calloused from years of manual work.

Kitty leaned down and kissed it, turning the palm to hold it against her cheek for a moment, shutting her eyes and taking in the feel of it, remembering the countless times her mother held her face in those hands, wondering how something so rough could be so gentle. The tears began to fall again from her eyes.

When she looked at her mother's face, Juju was watching her. Her mother's tears came quietly this time, but Kitty knew from her eyes that they weren't sad tears or even confused tears.

"I love you, too, Momma."

28

Jack received a letter from Kitty on the fifth day after she left, written the morning after she arrived in Galveston. She said her mother knew her, but was sometimes confused. Juju was confined to bed because half of her body was paralyzed. She couldn't speak, but she seemed to understand when spoken to. Kitty said she had seen worse cases of stroke than her mother had experienced, but that recovery would still be slow. She planned to take her mother home as soon as possible to keep the costs down. She could do everything herself, she said, and told Jack not to worry or think about coming down there. She hoped to be back before the election.

Jack wanted to ask Jarvis for some time off, but then he'd have to explain why. So for now he begrudgingly decided to sit tight and try to be content with communicating through letters. He sniffed Kitty's letter again and smiled, knowing she had added the perfume sparingly to her letter because she only wore it on Sundays. He wondered if she knew how tortuous it was for him to smell her perfume with her not attached to it. He folded up the paper and slipped it back into the envelope and placed it in the back of the middle desk drawer with the first note Kitty had sent through Justus.

Ned Green was in town, and Jack was supposed to meet him for lunch at the Driskill. He was relieved to tell him that the Sloane speculators had not approached anyone in

Clarksville for months now, thanks to Link and Ned's help. But he knew it was a matter of time before someone else would start pressuring them to move. The City had backed off, too, when they learned that someone was watching them. The threat of a lawsuit was enough to stop them... for now.

Jack grabbed his coat and hat and headed down the hall.

"Emery, I'm meeting someone for an early lunch," he said, "I'll be back by one."

The young clerk raised his head from his work at the desk and nodded.

Jack donned his hat and had his suit coat on by the time he opened the office door to the street. He glanced both ways as he secured a couple of buttons and timed his crossing between a freight wagon and a carriage. He entered the Driskill and walked quickly down the hall, through the restaurant, and past the elevator to the stairs and took them two at a time to the second floor. He was only a little out of breath by the time he rapped on the door at the opposite end of where Jarvis's room was.

A hotel employee let him into the room. He had just finished setting up a table for dining and seemed to be waiting to leave. Jack noticed this was a suite of rooms, rather than a single room like Jarvis's. Ned came out of the bedroom, booming.

"Jack! So good to see you! Come on in here." Ned walked over and handed the man a folded up bill. "Everything looks great. Thank you, Tony."

Tony left the room with a huge grin on his face.

Jack figured Ned just doubled his wages that day.

Ned turned his attention to Jack, offering his hand.

Jack tried not to grimace when the big man crunched his fingers in a very firm handshake.

"Get comfortable; there's a hatrack behind you."

Jack obliged, glad to shed himself of the coat he'd just put on. Late September in Texas still felt like the middle of summer.

"Sit down and help yourself." Ned pulled the silver cloches

off the plates and set them on the floor.

"This is a nice change of pace," said Jack, digging into a plate of roast beef slathered in gravy, with potates and green beans on the side.

"The food or the atmostphere?

"Both. And before I forget, when you see Katherine, tell her that Kitty's mother had a stroke. She's gone down to Galveston to take care of her."

"I'm sorry to hear about that, but who's Kitty?"

"Someone Katherine knew in Galveston."

"I'll tell her."

"I appreciate that, and I appreciate you backing me in this election."

"I know my money can help you get elected, but it's getting to the point that my name may do you more harm than good. It's getting vicious out there."

"I'd be proud to be seen with you anywhere, Ned."

"You must've not heard the latest stories."

"Let me see, was it the story that you took 'two streaks of rust running from 'Not Much to Nowhere' and turned Texas Midland Railroad into a profitable business? Or was it when you brought the first automobile to Dallas a few years ago?"

Ned laughed. "I have to admit that caused quite a commotion. Nah, it's just that I'm in the crosshairs of a lot of people in Dallas right now, especially because of my relationships with Mabel and Bill McDonald. If a former mayor gets elected again, he's vowed that the first thing on his agenda is to run me out of town. But Bill's convinced that with my help he can get the Blacks to vote for that former mayor's opponent."

"There you go."

"Money can buy a lot of things, Jack, but it can't buy real respectability. Oh, people fake it when they're around me if they think they'll profit from being nice to my face, but I know what they're saying behind my back. And I really don't care what they think about me—I live my life as I choose. But I don't want to pull you down, too, especially if you don't have the resources to rise above it."

"I feel very confident about the outcome of this election," said Jack, with a full mouth. He realized most every time he'd seen Ned Green, food was involved. "I heard people are still trying to talk you into running for governor."

"It's tempting, but I don't think even *I* have enough money to pull that off. I can accomplish more out of the limelight." Ned set his fork on his empty plate. "Don't let your guard down, Jack. People's opinion can turn on a dime, even if it's just hearsay. Too many don't even bother to learn the truth; they prefer to live in a constant state of flux. I guess it makes them feel more alive getting all tore up over other people's business than actually getting out and living life themselves."

"I've been careful."

"Elections are very volatile events, especially if race is involved."

"Everyone's been so kind."

"About thirty years ago in Colfax, Louisiana, a hundred and fifty Negroes were killed because of a contested election. White Democrats overpowered Republican freedmen and a group of black state militia. And most of the freedmen were murdered after they surrendered. The handful of perpetrators that were prosecuted and convicted were soon set free, thanks to the U.S. Supreme Court that declared that the protections of the 14th Amendment only applied to what state governments did, not the actions of individuals. For years, it was open season on Negro Republicans and even some white Republicans.

"After Lincoln was assassinated, Andrew Johnson became president, and he did everything he could to block efforts to force Southern states to create equality for Negroes. His efforts allowed all these 'Black Codes' to be set up. He did more damage while Congress was in session, but the Republicans came back and passed things like the Freedmen's Bureau Bill and the Civil Rights Act that clarified that all persons born in the U.S. were citizens. In fact, everything but the 14th Amendment was passed even though President Johnson vetoed them. He missed getting impeached by one vote."

Jack didn't even realize he'd stopped eating.

"But what I took the long way around to tell you, this same president prevented the Louisiana governor from sending the state militia and U.S. forces to get things under control. Secret societies like *The Knights of the White Camelia* and the *Ku Klux Klan* were getting away with murder. 1868 was the worst year in Louisiana—over a thousand people were murdered in an eight-month period."

"I haven't heard of those groups before."

"They were started by Confederate veterans. The KKK was made up of low-class whites and the Camelias were upper crust. There's another group called themselves the *White League*. They were more aggressive and military-like."

"Are they still around?"

"They've for the most part gone underground since Congress passed several laws against groups like that, but I wouldn't be surprised if they reared their evil heads again. The political climate's changing and we're losing ground."

"How so?"

"Well, for one, it looks like that damn poll tax is going to go through soon, but I think we can hold it off going into effect until after the election."

"That's good. I'm going to need those votes."

"For every law to right the wrongs during Reconstruction, five more have cropped up to knock them down."

"Those Black Codes."

"Right. Reconstruction supposedly did away with those, but they're back with a vengeance under these Jim Crowe laws across the south. Ten years ago a man named Homer Plessy decided to test Louisiana's 'Separate Car Act' for railroad cars, and he was arrested for sitting in the 'white car'. Mind you, Plessy was only 1/8 Negro and passed as a white man, so he wasn't arrested until after he identified himself as black. The case went all the way to the Supreme Court, where only one Justice sided with Plessy."

"We studied that case, but I didn't realize Plessy was almost white."

"Nobody is 'almost white', Jack, much less all white. You skin everybody, and we're the same. And Plessy's skin color didn't give him away; it was his claim to be 1/8 black that got him arrested. Color should never have been an issue, but with the Supreme Court's decision, they put a legal stamp of approval on segregation and stigmatizing Negroes as inferior, in spite of the 13th and 14th Amendments. I know I have some moral failings in my life, but I can still see the wrong in that plain as day. When are people going to wake up?"

Jack just shook his head, afraid he might say the wrong thing again.

"Now eat your pie before I eat it," said Ned.

Jack took a big bite of apple pie as the corners of his mouth turned up. The apple pie tasted much better than the foot in his mouth.

29

Kitty allowed the tears to fall as she poked through the sun-baked plants in her mother's garden. Nineteen days had passed since Kitty had arrived back on the island, and she hadn't even noticed her mother's fall garden, much less tended to it. And now everything was dead. She dumped the bucket of water on some plants anyway, hoping the garden would forgive her and come back to life.

Her feet felt like lead walking to the back steps. She was starting to question her decision to bring her mother home over two weeks ago, determined to take care of Juju herself and stop depending on other people's charity. She sat down on the third step and wept some more. She never cried in front of her mother; she didn't want Juju to see the toll it was taking on her. On top of all the effort Kitty was making, she hadn't seen much improvement in her mother's condition. As a doctor, she knew this was a long term process, but as a daughter, she had hoped her mother would be much more improved by now.

Kitty wasn't sure if she should resign from Dr. Gilbert's employment and move back home and hire someone to care for her mother during the day while Kitty earned an income, or hire several people to take shifts caring for her mother so she could return to work in Austin. She could try to come down as often as possible, but knew that would be difficult and even more exhausting, not even considering the additional cost.

Either way seemed impossible.

Friends from church brought food by the first week after Kitty brought her mother home. Some came to sit with Juju while Kitty ran errands. But the visits were getting fewer and farther between them. Maybe Kitty gave them the impression that everything was fine, that she could handle it herself.

But it wasn't fine.

"Lord, I don't know what to do," she whispered. "We're almost out of money, and I have to start working again. I hoped and prayed you would heal Momma, and that we could go back to the way things were, but I don't see any change in her. Is she going to be like this for the rest of her life?"

She crawled out of the sun and sat in one of the chairs on the porch and propped her feet on a second chair. She noticed the stains on her skirt and knew she needed to do laundry that day, too. She'd put that off for far too long.

"I'm so tired. I don't know where to go from here, but I trust that You do. If You could speak this world into being, surely You can show me what my next step is."

She looked up, waiting for the answer to come like manna from the sky.

It didn't.

After a few more minutes, she glanced at the wringer washer in the corner of the porch.

"All right, all right. I see you."

She stood up and unbuttoned her skirt, letting it drop to the floor. She picked it up and dropped it in the tub. Then she unbuttoned her blouse and set it aside. She smiled, thinking about how her mother would scold her for standing on the back porch with only her bloomers and camisole on. She doubted anybody would be around, much less peering into the backyard of an elderly woman.

Kitty stepped into the kitchen to put the water on to boil and walked through the house to gather up the rest of the laundry. She peeked in the library off the foyer where she had set up a bed for her mother. Her eyes were closed, so she tip-toed around the bed, picking up stray linens and towels.

"Dee?"

Kitty stopped in mid-reach and looked up to smile at her mother. 'Dee' was easier for her to say than 'Kitty'.

"I've been a little lax on the laundry, Momma, but today everything's getting washed, including you! And as soon as one of your friends comes over, I'm going to figure out a better way to wash your hair, too. A soapy washrag isn't working anymore." She dropped the load on the foot of the bed and got down on her hands and knees and looked under the bed, pulling out another towel and a couple of stockings. She ignored the track the towel left on the dusty floor.

"I was wondering where I'd left these," she said as she stood up.

"Meshy... guh." Juju smiled crookedly.

"I can't help it if I'm messy. You spoiled me."

Juju frowned.

"What is it, Momma? Are you thirsty?"

Juju reached over and touched Kitty's bloomers.

"I needed to wash what I had on. That skirt was so dirty, it almost stood by itself."

Juju reached higher.

"I refuse to wear a corset down here, Mother. In fact, most days I don't even wear one to work. I don't know who decided women were supposed to wear those tortuous contraptions, but it's restricting and unnatural. If we have to wear them, why aren't men required to wear them, too?"

Juju snorted.

"And as to why I'm running around in my knickers, I'm completely out of clean clothes. I'm going to go upstairs and borrow something of yours while I do the laundry, all right?"

Juju nodded.

"Or I just might stay in my bloomers all day long," she said, gathering up the pile on the bed and sashaying across the room. Kitty looked over her shoulder, hoping the sound Juju made was laughter.

It was.

She almost dropped the pile of dirty laundry in the foyer

when someone knocked on the door. She could see the silhouette of a woman behind the sheer panel.

"Just a minute!" she said loudly, looking around for a place to stash the laundry. She opened the hall closet and chunked the pile in it and grabbed Juju's coat, which smelled like mothballs. Juju always put mothballs in the pockets before storing it after the last cold spell each year, which meant it stayed in the closet most of the year.

She quickly buttoned the coat as she walked over to the door, hoping it was one of Juju's friends. Then glancing down at her short mother's even shorter coat, hoping it wasn't someone who'd care what she was wearing. But whoever it was, she needed their help.

Kitty opened the door, and at first, she didn't recognize the woman beneath the fashionable hat.

Then she recognized the eyes.

Katherine Williams.

"What are *you* doing here?" Kitty whispered. She started to step outside to talk, but noticed the open window to the library. Instead, she grabbed Katherine's arm and pulled her into the house, through the parlor and dining room, and into the kitchen.

"Why are you here? Momma could've seen you!"

Katherine shook her head. "I heard your mother had a stroke…"

"How'd you learn about that?"

"Jack told a friend of mine, and I contacted the hospital… and they said it was very serious… How is she?"

"She's fine. Why did you come?"

"I… thought you might need some help."

Kitty smirked. "And just how do you think *you* can help?"

"I can cook a little," she said, then glanced at Kitty's clothing, "and I do know how to wash clothes."

"Do you think you can just come down here and take Momma's place?"

"No! Of course not! I… didn't want you to be alone in this."

"We're not alone. Momma has plenty of friends helping."
Katherine nodded. "That's good. I'm so glad to hear that."
She looked around and noticed the back door. "I'll just slip out the back so your mother won't know I was even here."

She turned at the door and smiled, but her eyes said otherwise. "I'm so sorry if I upset you, Kitty. That wasn't my intention. I just knew what you were going through, and I didn't want you to be alone." She opened the screen door and shut it as softly as possible.

Kitty stood there, frozen for a moment. *What just happened here?* How would Katherine have the slightest idea what Kitty was going through?

She pushed open the screen door, not bothering to catch it before it shut with a loud bang as she ran down the steps. "Wait!"

Katherine had just opened the back gate.

"How could you possibly know what I'm going through?"

Katherine glanced at the house. "Can your mother hear us?" she asked quietly.

Kitty lowered her voice. "Why did you say that?"

She shut the gate and turned to face Kitty. "I was a little over half your age when my mother died, and I was trying to take care of her. That was an unbearable burden to place on a twelve year old's shoulders." Katherine's voice broke as she said, "I blamed myself that she died because I didn't know how to help her."

"Why didn't you ask for help?"

"My mother wouldn't let me. Her family disowned her when she became pregnant out of wedlock. *I* was the reason she had no connections to her former life. She chose *me* over respectability, and she was too proud to admit she'd made a mistake."

Kitty stared at her. "Is that why you didn't choose me?"

Katherine's face fell. "No, child. Of course not. I had lost any semblance of respectibility a few years after my mother died. I didn't want to raise you in that world. My life was already ruined…I didn't want to ruin the most precious thing in the world to me. I'm so sorry to interrupt your taking care of your mother. I just know how hard it was for me... but good heavens! You're a doctor, not a young, scared, ignorant girl who didn't know what she was doing." She smiled like she was embarrassed. "I let my emotions take over, and I really don't do that very often." She turned to open the gate, like she couldn't get away fast enough.

"Lucius told me what you did for me... and for Momma."

Katherine froze, but didn't turn around. "He wasn't supposed to."

"He told me that, too."

She turned and faced Kitty. "I didn't want you or your mother to feel obligated in any way. I just—"

"I don't."

Katherine nodded her head. "I just wanted you to have a chance in life." She turned again.

Kitty grabbed her arm. "I'm not very young, and I'm not ignorant..." Tears filled her eyes. "But I'm scared," she whispered. "I'm scared I might lose her, no matter how hard I try."

"Oh, honey..." Katherine said, reaching for her.

But Kitty put her hand up. "No."

But Katherine grabbed her anyway, and pulled her to her chest. "I'm so sorry," she whispered.

Kitty tried to wriggle away, but Katherine held on.

Kitty began sobbing and letting herself be held, refusing to let the ugly thoughts come, for once. She didn't know how long they stood there, but she knew one thing by the time she pulled away.

She wasn't alone anymore.

"What can I do to help?" Katherine asked.

"I don't want Momma to see you."

Katherine nodded. "I understand."

Kitty stood there, trying to organize her thoughts.

"Do you always smell like mothballs?" Katherine asked, with a faint smile.

Kitty looked down and snorted. "I guess that's the first

thing I need to start on—washing clothes. But I need to go to the grocer's… and I need to bathe Momma…"

"How 'bout I start the laundry while you make a grocery list, then I can go pick up those things while you bathe your mother. Then you can strip her bed and I'll wash the bedclothes…"

Kitty kept nodding at Katherine's words as they walked back to the house. Her steps even felt lighter since half the weight of the world had been lifted off her shoulders.

She noticed the chair where she'd been sitting not too long before, crying out to God for help. She felt a tingle on the back of her neck when she realized God had answered that prayer… and in a way she never would've chosen.

But she was grateful for the help, in whatever form it came. And Juju would never know otherwise.

30

Kitty opened her eyes in the still gray light and stared at the knot of gauze at the top of the canopy. She looked at the translucent curtain surrounding her bed, remembering where she was. She sat up in bed. What was she doing up here when her mother was downstairs by herself?

Then she remembered.

Katherine was here.

All of the memories of the previous day flooded in. She sniffed her nightgown sleeve; it smelled like lavendar. It felt good to be in clean clothes again. How did Katherine manage to turn the tedious chore of laundering into something special?

And the woman talked Kitty into sleeping in her own bed last night instead of the pallet on the floor of the library. Katherine said that she would keep an eye on Juju, disguised, of course, with her hair covered in a bonnet and tinted glasses covered her eyes. Kitty introduced her as "Kay" when she decided she needed help to wash her mother's hair.

She was surprised at how helpful Katherine had been, especially since she thought her skills were limited to one thing. Kitty lay back on the bed, knowing she needed to get up and go check on Juju. But since her mother wasn't alone, Kitty thought it would be okay to close her eyes for just a little longer...

The sun was shining bright when she opened her eyes again. The mornings were finally feeling cooler like fall was knocking on the door. She tried to remember what day it was, and couldn't. She knew it was well into October, though, and thought about Jack. His election was less than a month away. She tried to make her letters as lighthearted as possible so he wouldn't feel like he needed to come down here. She missed him so much, and the thought of moving down here permanently away from him made her chest ache to think about it.

Kitty still had no idea what she should do about that. But right now Katherine provided a temporary fix. She sniffed the air. Was that bacon?

Her stomach rumbled as she threw the bed clothes and fought her way through the gauze. She wasted no time dressing, other than to take in the scent of lavender in her day clothes. She would have to ask Katherine how she did that. Juju used plain old lye soap and starch to launder, and Kitty assumed that was what everyone did. Sometimes she splurged and bought Borax. Kitty paid Mrs. Gerwick at the boarding house to do the little laundry she had. Doing these tedious chores made her appreciate her mother all the more.

She quickly rebraided her hair into a single braid to the right side of her face. Who did she need to impress? This past week Kitty felt like a housebound hermit with only a handful of opportunities to get out of the house to run to the market when a friend stopped by to sit with Juju.

She headed downstairs and into the library to check on her mother. Juju's eyes were closed, and her breathing was steady. She looked around at the mostly empty shelves, realizing the room was no longer a library. When Lucius lived here, the shelves were full, mostly gained when he bought the house from a widow. Kitty was fairly certain that Lucius had read very few of the books. Appearances were very important to him, so he took the books to help fill the even bigger library at his mansion on Broadway, and he continued to acquire many more that she was sure he didn't touch again once they were placed in the shelves.

But she still loved him, in spite of his faults. And he loved her mother and would do anything for her. His calls and visits came fewer and farther between, though, but Kitty understood why. She knew it made him sad to see Juju that way.

Kitty stayed busy, too, reading up on the sparse material on treating patients with apoplexy, usually sitting next to her mother's bed. Nurse Crain loaned her several nursing journals that discussed the care of stroke patients. She knew from her schooling that the bleeding occurred on the opposite side of where the stroke manifested itself through paralysis. She snorted out loud when she read that one nurse wrote that 'alcohol intoxication should be considered' as a cause of cerebral apoplexy.

Juju's eyes fluttered open.

"Sorry, Momma," she said. "I just read that drinking spirits could cause your condition. I thought I hid all those bottles well enough before I left for Austin."

Juju shook with what Kitty hoped was laughter. She figured the sun would quit shining before her mother would take a drop of liquor.

Kitty dropped the journal beside the chair and stood up. "We need to move your limbs or they'll stop working." She picked up her mother's left arm and began gently bending it back and forth at the elbow. "Kay will help me get you into your chair in a little while. Maybe we'll have some visitors today. And Nurse Crain is on the lookout for a rolling chair we can borrow so we can sit on the porch or eat in the dining room all together."

Juju's head jerked in several directions, and Kitty couldn't tell if she was agreeing or disagreeing with her. She laid her mother's arm down and walked to the other side of the bed to pick up her right hand. But Juju pulled it away.

"Nuh!" she said, quite clearly.

"I know it's probably uncomfortable for you, but we have to move your muscles or they'll atrophy." She grasped her mother's arm, and Juju pulled it away.

Kitty stared at her. "What's the matter, Momma? Are you in pain?"

Juju moved her head awkwardly back and forth.

"I'm glad you're able to move your right arm so well." Kitty thought of something. "Do you think you can write?"

Juju made a noise that didn't sound like her 'no'. Kitty walked over to the shelves and found a pencil and a large receipt. She grabbed a book and brought it back to the bed, turned the receipt over and placed it on the book in her mother's lap. She sat on the bed and arranged her mother's fingers to hold the pencil, then realized she needed to prop her mother up a bit so she could see what she was writing. Kitty pulled her mother's good leg up and held the book against it, and Juju began to write…

…scribbles.

She filled up half the page with illegible markings before a recognizable word appeared.

gO

"Go! That's great, Momma!"

Then after more scribbles, another

/\ome

"Aome?" Kitty looked at Juju. "Home? Don't be silly."

Juju dropped the pencil and grasped Kitty's arm. She tried to speak, but Kitty couldn't understand what she was trying to say. Juju felt around for the pencil and struggled to write again.

/me OLd /\ome

"Me old home?" Kitty read aloud.

"She wants you to put her in an old folks home and go back to Austin," said a voice behind her.

Kitty turned around to see Katherine holding a tea tray.

Kitty turned back to her mother. "You want me to put you in a home for the elderly? You're not that old!"

Juju made a sound like she was frustrated. She pointed to the paper.

"I'm not going home, Mother. My place is here with you."

Juju looked angry.

"You can get as mad as you want to, but I'm not going home until you're on your feet."

"I thought we could have a spot of tea," Katherine said with a bad British accent. She walked around the bed and set the tray on a side table. "I think you are stuck with us, Mrs. Synatzske, whether you like it or not. Now, you like two cubes of sugar in your lukewarm tea, right?"

Juju's expression changed when she looked at Katherine. Was it amusement? Katherine looked like a badly dressed character out of an even worse play. Juju looked back at Kitty and rolled her one good eye. Kitty threw her head back and laughed for the first time since she'd returned to Galveston.

Then she caught another look on her mother's face... relief, maybe?

And then love.

Kitty knew that look without a shadow of a doubt. It hit her so hard, she quickly leaned down and kissed her mother's forehead before stepping around the pocket door and covering her mouth to quietly let the tears fall.

31

The three women sat on the front porch facing the gulf. Kitty and Katherine flanked Juju sitting in a rolling chair.

The beach was a good seven blocks away, and the view used to be blocked by hundreds of homes and businesses. But the great storm that hit two years before had swept most everything clean all the way to the beach, and much of the structures had yet to be rebuilt. They could see more of the ocean on the horizon than houses.

"Who knew we'd ever have an ocean view, Momma?" said Kitty, grinning.

Juju nodded her head.

"The breeze sure feels good," said Katherine. "Have you heard from Jack?"

"Yes, things are getting even busier for him since the elections are just weeks away."

"Do you plan to go back for the elections?"

Kitty glanced at Juju. "I really hadn't thought that far ahead. He sounds confident that he's going to win, but I know he'd still want me to be there."

"Then you need to go back."

"But I can't…"

"At least for the elections. Juju and I will be just fine."

"I don't know…"

Juju nodded her head and made a noise.

"See! Juju agrees with me, and you need to be there for him on one of the most important days of his life. Jack is going to be a great representative..."

Kitty raised her eyebrows at Katherine.

"...from... what I hear."

Kitty quickly changed the subject. "I'm curious about where you're from, Kay, and your family."

Katherine gave her a sharp look and then looked at Juju.

Juju stared straight ahead.

"Well, my family's from Louisiana—New Orleans, but I grew up in Houston, and eventually we came to Galveston. I don't think I ever met any of my kinfolks. No, that's not right. When I was very young—maybe six or seven, one of Mother's brothers visited us in Houston, but I don't remember much about him."

"Our family came from Germany. Mom and Dad came to Galveston by ship. Do you know where your ancestors originally came from?"

Katherine leaned her head against the tall rocker and began rocking. "I think they were French. But that could be entirely my imagination. My mother didn't talk much about them, and it was so long ago."

"Momma," Kitty touched her mother's arm, "Kay's mother passed away when she was only twelve years old."

Juju turned her head toward the right and reached out her good arm for Katherine's hand.

Katherine grasped her hand, and looked Juju in the face.

"Momma's sorry for your loss," said Kitty, noticing tears filling Katherine's eyes.

"Thank you," said Katherine, obviously touched by the simple gesture. "Now, can I get either of you something to drink?"

"I'm fine," said Kitty.

"Fine," said Juju.

Kitty and Katherine stared at Juju and then each other.

"Mother! We understood that word!"

Juju looked at them in surprise. "Fine."

"Yes! Fine!" Kitty stood up.

"Fine, fine, fine."

"Yes, Momma! You're going to be fine, fine fine!"

* * *

Kitty sat at the table watching Katherine stir the gravy with a spatula in the cast iron skillet.

"Where did you learn to make gravy?"

"I asked Mrs. Cotulla at the market."

"You mean you've never made gravy before you came to this house?"

Katherine shook her head. "I have to admit that those dumplings I made last week was my first attempt at gravy."

Kitty laughed.

"But I went back and told Mrs. Cotulla that I had followed her instructions to the letter, and still had lumps, and she told me her secret was to use a spatula to keep the lumps from forming."

"Could you teach me? Momma always did the cooking, and I always seemed to be busy except when it was time to eat."

"Of course, but this batch is done; I'll show you from the beginning on the next batch." Katherine picked up a dishtowel and used it to move the heavy skillet from the hot surface. "You thinking about the future and cooking for someone special?"

Kitty felt the heat rise to her face.

"Don't be embarrassed."

"I'm not embarrassed… well, except for the fact that I'd make a horrible wife since I was more interested in science and medicine than household science."

Katherine continued talking as she readied a tray for Juju. "I'm forty-two years old, Kitty, and I'm a shining example that you really can teach an old dog new tricks. I've learned more about cooking these past couple of weeks than the rest of my life combined."

Kitty remembered with a start what Katherine did for a living for many years. She realized she hadn't thought about that for days. She wondered how she came to be sitting in her mother's kitchen talking to a former prostitute that just happened to have given birth to her.

Katherine turned around and faced her. "I'm sorry."

"For what?"

"For reminding you of my past."

"What are you talking about?"

"I can see it in your face, Kitty, and I'm sorry for putting—"

"Stop saying you're sorry. I know you're sorry." Kitty stood up to leave the room.

"Wait, I need to talk to you about something."

Kitty slumped back in the chair.

"I want you to go to Austin this weekend so you'll be there for the elections."

Kitty sighed. "I want to... I need to... but I don't know if—"

"Please go and let me do this for you and Juju. I assure you we won't starve. We may eat the same dishes over and over again, but we'll be fine."

Kitty couldn't help smile at that thought. "But who'll sit with Momma so you can go to the market or any other errands that need to be done?"

"I'll stock the pantry before you leave, and Lucius would be happy to come if I have any other reason to leave the house."

"He hasn't been here all week."

"Then he's due for a visit, and I won't be gone long. And my friend Marguerite is coming to visit her family. I'm sure she won't mind helping out."

Kitty sat there weighing her options.

"Do you have money for a ticket?" Katherine asked.

Kitty nodded her head, and didn't want to admit that was about all she had. "I need to go back to work soon, too. Dr.

Gilbert's been far too kind to hold my job for me. I'm thinking about moving Momma up to Austin with me and hiring someone to take care of her during the day."

Katherine nodded. "I'm available."

"What about your life in Dallas?"

"I'd rather be where I'm needed."

Kitty felt hopeful at the thought that Katherine could make it possible for her to go home, but then her heart fell.

"What?"

"Jarvis knows who you are. And if we're together, he's going to make the connection, if he hasn't already."

Katherine frowned. "I don't trust the man, but he doesn't even have to know I'm in town. How often do you see him?"

"Never. I avoid him like the plague. I don't want to do anything that might jeopardize Jack's election."

"Then we'll make the move after the election. But what would Jarvis do? He would never sabotage Jack's chances; he's invested too much in him."

Kitty hadn't thought about that. "You're right."

"Why don't you leave tomorrow instead of Friday, and you can start looking for a house to rent. I'll even split the cost with you."

"No, you've done too much already," said Kitty. "I feel like I'm taking advantage of you."

Katherine shook her head. "No, you're not. I feel like for the first time in my life, I'm doing something that matters, Kitty. Please don't take that away from me."

"But what if Momma takes a turn for the worse while I'm gone?"

"Then I'll send you a wire, but you know she's been improving daily, and you've shown me everything that needs to be done."

"Are you strong enough to move her by yourself?"

"I'm as strong as you, and Juju's able to help some, too, now."

Kitty sat there, letting the thought of seeing Jack seep into her mind, and it felt good. She hadn't let herself even entertain the thought because she thought it was impossible. She needed to be there for him; she wanted to be there for him. And now she might be able to move back to Austin.

Kitty looked up at Katherine. The impossible looked possible. "Are you sure?" she asked, giving her a chance to back out.

Katherine beamed. "I'm sure."

"I need to reimburse you for the groceries you bought, and I should be paying you for what you're doing."

Katherine shook her head. "That's not necessary."

"How are you supporting yourself?"

"I received some very good financial advice from Ned Green and invested my savings well. What it earns isn't a lot, but it's adequate for my needs. I won't be a burden to anyone."

Kitty realized at that moment how alone Katherine was. She was forced to take care of herself from a very young age and had survived a business that would have destroyed most women.

"Why are you doing this for us? I don't like the feeling that I owe you."

"Kitty, you're looking at it the wrong way. The debt has always been mine, and I'm so grateful that you're giving me the chance to repay it. So don't you give a second thought to thinking that you owe me." She turned back to the stove. "Your mother's food is getting cold."

Kitty watched Katherine spoon gravy onto a plate of shredded roast, mashed potatoes and carrots and set it on a tray that already held a cup of water and a napkin with a fork and spoon. She pulled the hair cap out of her apron pocket and covered her hair and put on the tinted glasses before she picked up the tray.

Kitty stood and reached for the tray.

Katherine shook her head. "I'll feed Juju; you go to the train station and get your ticket." She walked out of the kitchen.

Kitty's mind started racing. Was this really happening? Was she free to go to Jack? Was the dream of returning to Austin to work possible now? She needed to get a ticket and then send a wire to Jack that she was coming home for the election. And wash the few clothes she'd brought. Then pack.

That part wouldn't take long.

Jack stood on one of the large, second story balconies at the Driskill, waving at the cheering crowd filling the street. He noticed Justus and Liberty standing in front of his shoe shine chair, and her children atop it. He waved at them, and then scanned the throng for one face. He spotted Dr. Gilbert first, standing head and shoulders above much of the enthusiastic horde, and there she was, laughing with Daisy. Kitty turned and gave him such a look, it took everything he had to keep from jumping off that balconey and taking her in his arms and yelling to the world that she was his.

The time spent apart from her in Galveston made him realize that he never wanted to go through that kind of separation again. He was relieved to hear about her plans to bring Juju back to Austin, along with Katherine to help, he was surprised to learn. Kitty seemed nonchalant about the fact that her birth mother would be taking care of her adoptive mother, like that was something normal that happened all the time. He wondered what had happened in Galveston for Kitty to accept Katherine's help.

Jack planned to make Kitty his wife, and now that the election was decided, he was determined to ask her soon, before she returned to Galveston. He wanted to make the proposal special, but he hadn't even had time to think about it. He also planned to tell Kitty that she didn't have to look for a house to rent—that she and her mother and Katherine could move into his house, and he would take her boarding house room until they were married.

Things were falling into place perfectly.

Jarvis placed his hand on Jack's shoulder, bringing him back to reality. He realized he would need to tell Jarvis about his plans with Kitty soon.

"We did it, son!"

"Yes, sir. Thanks to you and Link."

Link stood at his right.

"We're a good team."

Link offered him a cigar, and Jack declined. "They smell good, but my grandfather cured me of ever wanting to smoke. I got sick as a dog after he let me puff on his a couple of times."

Someone yelled, "Speech!" and the crowd began to chant it.

"I hope you prepared something," said Jarvis.

"Yes sir; you taught me well, and I've had plenty of practice these past months." Jack held up his hands to quiet the crowd.

"Thank you, Austin! Thank you, everyone who supported me in my run for office."

The crowd rewarded him again with enthusiastic yells and applause.

"I'm very humbled and grateful for your vote, and I want you to know that when you voted for me, you voted for yourselves because I plan to represent each and every one of you in that magnificent granite building up the street."

He had to pause until the people quieted again. He pulled a paper out of his inner jacket pocket and unfolded it.

"I want to read something to you written by a man named Francis Bellamy about ten years ago in celebration of Columbus Day and our nation's flag. It says, '*I pledge allegiance to my Flag and to the Republic for which it stands, one nation, indivisible, with liberty and justice for all*'. Now Texas doesn't have a pledge to its lone star flag, and I hope we do some day. But the part that appealed to me most in this pledge is the last phrase, 'with

liberty and justice for all'. That's what I want to represent in the
Capitol up the street: freedom and equal justice for everyone,
not just a select few or for a certain class of people. And we
have a ways to go in this area."

"You're treading on thin ice," Jarvis whispered under his
breath.

"I hope you'll stand with me on this," Jack said even
louder.

The crowd applauded.

"I want you to look around and take pride in what's been
accomplished in Austin and central Texas these past seventy
years. The people who founded this town had a vision, and we
are reaping the benefits of so many hard-working people that
have gone before us. I hope we never forget that. But I want us
to have a vision, too. I want us to think of the future and the
legacy we'll be leaving our children and grandchildren. That's
on our shoulders; that's our responsibility to make this city and
Texas the best it can be."

The crowd cheered.

"No single one of us can do it alone. We have to work
together. I admit I'm young and still have a lot to learn, and I'm
willing to do that. Are you willing to work with me?"

The crowd cheered even louder.

"Thank you again for electing me to represent you! God
bless Austin, and God bless Texas!" Jack yelled at the top of his
voice. The volume of noise from the mass of people yelling was
deafening. Jack could see Liberty and her husband waving their
arms. He looked across the crowded street. He couldn't even
see Kitty or the Gilberts anymore.

He waved back, dismissing the crowd.

An intoxicating fire surged through Jack's body at that
moment. He liked that his words could incite such passion and
enthusiasm. He was excited about the days to come, personally
and professionally.

"Jack!" A familiar female voice spoke from behind him.

"Mother?" Jack turned around to see his parents beaming.
"You came!"

"Of course we came!" Mercy Taylor grasped him tightly. "We are so proud of you!"

She finally released him so his father could greet him.

Jack grinned at his father. His blue eyes seemed even paler against his dark skin. His father was tall, taking after his mother's side rather than his Apache father.

Jack grabbed him in a bear hug.

"It's been too long, son," said Jimmy.

"Your father thought it would take days to count the ballots or we would've been here sooner. Did you even sleep last night?"

"A little, but I want to introduce you to the man who made all of this possible," Jack said as he turned around to face Jarvis.

The man was no where to be seen.

"What about me?" said Link.

Jack shook his head. "I'm sorry; of course you helped make this possible. Mother, you remember Link?"

Mercy extended her hand. "I most certainly do. How are you, Mr. Segal?"

"Couldn't be better at the moment."

"And this is my father, Jimmy Taylor. Link Segal, the brains behind this campaign."

Jimmy offered his hand. "Thank you for teaching my hard-headed son a thing or two."

Everyone laughed.

Link shook his hand. "Stubborness and perseverence are traits he's definitely going to use in this job, so you see, he was in training."

"Now that's a positive way to look at it," said Jimmy.

"You've done a great job, Mr. Taylor. Jack is an exceptional young man, and we're very excited about his future in the state legislature."

Jack looked through the open door. "Where's Jarvis? I want him to meet my parents."

"You know him—probably taking care of some detail related to your campaign."

Mercy spoke up. "We are so grateful for Mr. Baldwin's influence and support in Jack's career. I am not leaving town before I shake his hand."

"Are you hungry?" Jack asked his parents. "Let's go downstairs and eat a late breakfast then. I haven't had much to eat since the polls closed."

"I could eat," said Jimmy.

"Your father can always eat," said Mercy, "but he doesn't get fat like other men his age. He's as fit and handsome as he ever was. But I, on the other hand—"

"Mother..." Jack smiled apologetically at Link.

"You're embarrassing your son, wife," said Jimmy, who looked like it didn't bother him one bit.

"He's not embarrassed, are you, Jack," said Mercy, linking her arm through Jack's and turning him toward the door, not waiting for his response. "Come on, darling." She looked over her shoulder. "Would you care to join us, Mr. Segal?"

"I would love to, but I also have matters to attend. Enjoy your breakfast. I'll see you later, Jack."

Mercy led Jack down the hall.

"I need to tell you that someone's waiting for me in the restaurant that I'd like for you to meet," said Jack.

"This person wouldn't happen to be a certain young lady doctor, would it?"

Jack stopped. "Now how could you possibly know that?"

"Keep walking. Your father's hungry. Grace mentioned something about it when they visited back in February. I waited for you to tell me about her at Biriney's wedding, but since you didn't mention it, I assumed that nothing came of it."

"We've had to keep a low profile around Jarvis. He didn't want any hint of a scandal to hurt my election chances."

This time Mercy stopped. "Scandal? What kind of scandal?"

Jack cringed inside. *Why did he even mention that?*

"Keep walking. Dad's hungry. Did I say scandal? This lack of sleep has fogged up my brain. I meant that Jarvis wanted me to appear completely dedicated to this campaign—like I had no other interests occupying my time."

He glanced at his mother and smiled, but her expression told him that she wasn't swallowing that explanation.

"I'll explain later."

Jack led his parents into the dining room, but had to shake hands and acknowledge people all the way across the room to an occupied table in the corner.

Kitty stood to greet them.

"Mother, Dad, this is Kitty…I mean Dr. Kitty Synatzske. Kitty, this is my parents, Mercy and Jimmy Taylor."

Kitty smiled and shook their hands. "I'm so happy to finally get to meet you both in person. Jack hasn't told me nearly enough about you."

Everyone laughed. Jack seated Kitty, and Jimmy seated Mercy.

"What do we call you… Dr. Synatzske?" asked Mercy.

"No, please call me Kitty. That title's only used when I'm working." She unfolded her napkin and placed it in her lap.

"So you're the one who doctored Jack's arm after he was shot," said Mercy.

The interrogation had begun. Jack reached over and squeezed Kitty's hand.

"Yes, ma'am," she said.

"Was that how you two met?"

Kitty glanced at Jack and smiled. "No, we actually met at a shoe shine stand across the street."

"I saw her one morning, and then I kept getting my shoes shined every day just to see her pass by." He turned to Kitty. "Did you notice I was stalking you?"

Kitty laughed. "By the second day, I noticed. Did you notice that I made it a point to take Justus a newspaper every morning?"

Jack nodded.

"That was because I wanted to make sure you noticed me."

"I thought you did that out of the goodness of your heart."

"I still do it, even when I don't see you." She turned to Mercy and Jimmy. "I thought he was going to wear the leather off his shoes from Justus shining them so much."

Mercy laughed. "Oh, Jack. You're going to have to work hard to stay ahead of this smart lady here. I think we already have a lot in common, Kitty."

"Uh oh," said Jimmy. "That's a dangerous thing."

33

Two days after the election, Jack walked into Jarvis's office and sat down in front of the desk.

"We did it!" Jack beamed. "I still can't believe it's happened."

"Of course we did it," said Jarvis, smiling. "You worked hard for this, son, but you'll have some time to rest up before you're sworn in. Have your parents left?"

Jack nodded. "I saw them off this morning. I'm so sorry you didn't get to meet them. I kept looking for you."

Jarvis shook his head. "That was my fault; I got pulled away with work. I'm sorry I missed them."

Jack leaned forward in his chair. "I need to confess something, too."

Jarvis waited.

"We've kept it low-key because of the election, but now that it's over and we've won, I'm going to ask Kitty for her hand in marriage."

For a moment, Jarvis said nothing, and Jack couldn't tell if he was angry or sick.

He felt obligated to defend her. "Kitty may have come from humble stock, but she's educated and beautiful and most importantly, I love her. "

Jarvis looked away before he finally turned to Jack spoke. "I'm not sure where to begin… no, I know exactly where to start. Did you know her mother's a whore?"

"Yes, sir, and she wasn't the one that raised her."

"That'll make little difference in the public eye."

"Katherine's put all of that behind her, and I think she deserves a chance at a respectable life. She's been down in Galveston helping Kitty take care of her mother, who's recovering from a stroke."

"That's commendable, but there's more to Kitty's past than you realize. What do you think it will do to your career when people find out your future wife is a Negro?"

Surely he didn't hear that right. "What are you talking about?" Jack stood up. "I'm not going to sit here and listen to you insult her."

Jarvis stood up, too. "So being associated with Negroes is insulting now?"

"I didn't mean it that way..."

Jarvis walked around the desk. "I didn't want to have to tell you this... I didn't think I'd have to when I thought you stopped showing an interest in her. Sit down, Jack, and I'll tell you what Link found out in New Orleans."

Jack shook his head.

He pulled a chair up close to Jack's. "Please sit down. You want to know the truth about your future bride, right? You don't want to go into a marriage blind. I know I can't tell you what to do with your life; I can just tell you what I know."

Jack sat down numbly.

Months ago when Link and I went to Houston to open up our office over there, I asked him to go on to New Orleans. Pearl... I mean, Katherine once told me that her family was from New Orleans, so Link did some checking."

"That wasn't your business."

"You're young, Jack, and you don't know all the pitfalls out there waiting to swallow you up. It's been Link's and my job to watch your back—we stopped the trouble in Clarksville for you, didn't we?"

Jack sat there.

"Didn't we?" Jarvis asked again.

Jack reluctantly nodded.

"And it kept your reputation intact. You know that could've destroyed your chances to get elected."

"You don't know that for sure."

"Yes, I do. I've seen good people turn vicious when it comes to race. They wouldn't forgive you, Jack, for taking the Negroes' side."

Jack's heart felt like it dropped to his stomach. He didn't want to hear this, but he had to know. "What did Link find out in New Orleans?"

"Well, he didn't learn anything from the whites, but he learned plenty from the coloreds. Katherine's mother—her name was Jane—came from a well-known, upstanding family there. Years before the Emancipation Proclamation, New Orleans had its own culture of free black people—many of them mulattos. You know what a mulatto is, don't you?"

"I assume they're mixed."

"Right. Well, Jane fell in love with a mulatto. They said he was trying to change things for the coloreds. He was respected in his community and well-to-do, but that didn't matter. You just don't mix the two. Jane got pregnant, and relations between a black and white is against the law in most places. They didn't know for sure if this mulatto was strung up by Jane's family because of their relationship, or if it was because of his political dealings…"

"They hanged Katherine's father?" Jack felt sick.

Jarvis nodded.

"And they got away with it?"

"Most did and still do. After that, her mother fled New Orleans. Her family told Jane she could come home if she got rid of the baby, but she chose the baby over them."

"Kitty told me Katherine was only twelve years old when her mother died."

"That's tragic, but I tell you all of this so you know that makes Katherine a quadroon, and Kitty's an octoroon."

Jack looked at Jarvis. "That doesn't amount to much."

"Have you heard of Plessy vs. Ferguson? One-eighth

Negro blood was enough to throw Plessy in jail for sitting in the white section of the train."

"But he had to tell them he was one-eighth Black. We don't have to tell anybody about Kitty's heritage. Katherine doesn't even know her own history."

"If Link found out, someone else is bound to. This world is getting smaller all the time. And in this job, you're going to have enemies, Jack. They'll turn over every stone to find something to destroy you, and Kitty's past will do just that."

The walls felt like they were closing in. Jack didn't want to hear anymore. "I need to go."

Jarvis grabbed his arm. "With your position, you can have any woman you want. This is your future, Jack. Don't throw it away."

"I don't plan to." He pulled away from Jarvis's grasp and couldn't get out of there fast enough. He didn't want to face anybody in the front office so he turned toward the right… to the door leading to the alley.

He didn't slam the door this time. He looked up and down the alley, not wanting to draw any attention to himself. The stray cat didn't run off this time, and rewarded Jack by rubbing up against his leg.

"What's your story?" he said aloud.

He grimaced as he heard Jarvis's words echoing in his mind. It felt like something started gnawing on his insides. How could life be so perfect one moment, and then so confusing the next?

He started walking down the alley. He could hear the world going on as usual only a building width away on Brazos Street with all the dressed up facades. He looked around at the peeling paint and boarded up windows. The alley was the part no one wanted to show—where the garbage was dumped and flaws were tolerated. No one bothered with pretenses here.

His own world had changed just as drastically.

Even the air felt different. Something had shifted in his life, and he had no idea what he should do with the information Jarvis had dropped in his lap.

Jack was standing in front of the livery before he realized it. He hadn't seen Lonesome Joe in weeks. He stepped inside and called out, "Louis!?"

Patrick shuffled out from the shadows. "Well, hello Mr. Taylor! I'm sorry, but Louis is in school."

"Louis goes to school?"

"Miss Doc insisted on it, and I think Louis doesn't mind so much anymore."

Jack smiled. "That's good to hear." He knew Kitty was determined to make something of that boy. "I'd like to take Lonesome out."

"Let me get your saddle."

"No, Patrick, I'll do it."

"Yes, sir, and congratulations on your election. I voted for you."

"Thank you. I appreciate it."

Jack retrieved his saddle and rigging and walked over to Lonesome Joe's stall. He dropped it in the empty trough and turned to his horse.

"Hello, old boy," he said, rubbing the horse's nose. "Looks like you've been rolling around in the mud." He put a halter on Lonesome and tied the lead rope to the fence rail. He picked up a worn brush and began brushing the mud off the horse. "I know that feels good," he said when he noticed Lonesome leaning into the brush, "but don't get used to it."

Jack lost track of time brushing the horse. He didn't have to think about saddling the horse either, something he had done from as far back as he could remember. He switched out the halter for a bridle, threw the blanket on, followed by the saddle, which he cinched up. Then he led Lonesome out of the stall.

"We'll be back later, Patrick!" Jack called out.

"Have a good ride!" the old man's voice responded from somewhere.

Jack stepped up in the saddle and walked Lonesome out of the barn. He avoided Congress Avenue as he headed down to the river. He pushed Jarvis's words out of his mind and focused on the trees still hanging onto their leaves since the first freeze had yet to arrive. Some of the trees' leaves had turned yellow and red and every shade between. A small dog ran out towards them and started barking, but Lonesome didn't seem too concerned.

Jack came to the river and turned right, taking the same path he took all those months ago. But he didn't want to see any of his constituents today. When he came within site of the destroyed dam, he climbed down and let Lonesome graze. He picked up a few pebbles and tossed them into the shallow water.

"Lord, it seems like I talk to You only when I can't figure out how to handle something on my own, and I apologize for that. But I'm not sure what I'm supposed to do with what Jarvis told me."

He grabbed bigger rocks and cast them as far as he could, and he kept throwing them, gradually choosing progressively larger stones, eventually to the point that he could only lift them waist high to hurl them only a yard or two.

Jack stood there heaving from exertion, staring at the remaining base of the destroyed dam, trying to imagine the water running eleven feet over the top. He couldn't. Everything around him looked so peaceful and tranquil. How could it all change so drastically after one storm?

If nothing else, all that rock chunking cleared his mind. One thing he knew for certain.

He couldn't imagine his life without Kitty.

itty breathed in deeply as the buggy bumped along. Almost two months had passed since her last visit to Clarksville, and she was looking forward to seeing everyone. She glanced over at Louis holding the reins. The boy had grown at least half a foot since she first met him. He even had a little facial hair showing.

"Have you learned anything new in school?" she asked him.

"Nah."

"Oh, come on. You can learn something new every day if you just pay attention."

Louis glanced at her. "Are you still learning something new every day?"

"Of course. I'll keep learning for the rest of my life."

"Tell me something you learned today."

"I learned that you are beginning to look and act like a man, and I'm so proud of you continuing your education."

Louis looked away, but not before Kitty saw the corner of his mouth turn up.

He stared straight ahead when he asked, "You think I look like a man?"

"I think you'll be shaving before too long."

"Miss Doc!" Louis's face flushed. Even his ears turned red.

Kitty stifled a giggle. "I'm sorry. I didn't mean to embarrass you."

"Momma won't let me shave yet. She thinks I'll cut my throat with that straight razor."

"She's probably having a hard time adjusting to the fact that her little boy is growing up."

Louis snickered. "Yeah, then why have I been working since I was nine?"

"Are you reading any good books at school?"

"The teacher's making us take turns reading *The Wonderful Wizard of Oz*, but it's a little silly."

"What's it about?"

"You're not going to believe this, but this girl doesn't make it to the storm cellar in time, so she's in her house when a tornado carries it off to a place called Oz where there's talking scarecrows and witches and these little people called Munchkins. The witch is pretty scary... well, there's a good witch, too."

"Sounds interesting."

"I liked *The Red Badge of Courage* better."

"That one I'm familiar with."

They rode along in silence for a while until Louis spoke up.

"I've missed coming out here."

"Me, too."

"Out of all my friends, I like hanging out with Marcus best."

Kitty turned to Louis. "Why's that?"

Louis shrugged his shoulders. "I dunno."

"Are you two a lot alike?"

Louis thought for a moment. "No, but I don't feel like I have to be something I'm not around him. Does that make sense?"

"Yes."

"I mean, if I make a mistake at school, I don't hear the end of it. Same thing if I answer Miss Lesley's question right."

"You call your teacher by her first name?"

"No, that's her last name. Yvette's her first name, but nobody would dare call her that."

"That's good."

"Anyway, I learned it's best to keep my mouth shut at school."

"That's a shame."

"Why?"

"Because mistakes are a part of learning, and you need to be able to express yourself or explain yourself or even defend yourself well with words."

Louis held up his fists, still grasping the reins. "I defend myself with these." He boxed the air with a flurry of his fists, The flustered horse didn't know whether he was supposed to stop or keep going.

Kitty laid her hand on his arm. "Whoa, Jack Johnson. You should be able to do both equally well."

"Who's Jack Johnson?"

"He's a professional boxer from Galveston. In fact, just a few weeks ago he won the World Colored Heavyweight Championship. Boxing's illegal, but they do it anyway."

"You know about boxing?"

Kitty laughed. "No, I can't stand the thought of two men trying to beat each other senseless, but my mother likes it." She paused when she realized both of her mothers liked boxing, another thing they had in common. She smiled, remembering how excited Katherine was when she came back from the grocery store telling Juju that all the town was abuzz about Johnson. "They're saying he's good enough to be the world champion, but he's not allowed to fight the white world champion."

"Doesn't sound like the white boxer's the true *world* champion if he won't fight Jack Johnson."

Kitty nodded. "Some people think if Johnson wins, that black people might start thinking they're equal to whites."

Louis looked at her. "What do you think, Miss Doc?"

"In God's eyes, they are, so that settles it. White people just haven't come to terms with that yet."

"But why are they so poor and ignorant?"

"Maybe they haven't had the same opportunities you and I

have had. Do you think Marcus is ignorant?"

Louis snorted and shook his head. "He's better at school than me. And he knows more about fishin' and skinnin' cats and raising chickens and growing stuff than I do. Did you know he wants to be a scientist?"

Kitty raised her eyebrows. "Really?"

"Yeah, can you imagine that?"

"Yes, I can."

They were within site of the church.

"Louis, I want you to help me unload first, and then I want you to go Mrs. Alexander's and tell her I'm here today. You and Marcus may have to go around and pass the word. We may not have many come, but I want them to know I'm back and will continue to come on Thursdays like before."

"You're not going back to Galveston?"

"Only to bring my mother back up here until she's well."

Louis let out a whoop.

Kitty laughed. "Did you miss me that much?"

"Nah, I need the money," Louis said, then the red started creeping up his face. "And.. and I missed coming out here with you, too."

"Well, I know where I stand now."

"I didn't mean to hurt your feelings, Miss Doc," he said, looking sheepish.

"No offense taken. Your honesty is refreshing, Louis. Now let's get this buggy unloaded so you can get on your way."

Within an hour, the church was half full of people. Some just wanted to come say hello, and Kitty was glad they felt comfortable enough to do that. Liberty and Kitty worked almost to sunset, which came much earlier this time of year.

They visited while they packed up everything and set the room to order. Liberty shared that while Kitty was away, she had taken care of a few things: setting a broken finger, stitching up a gash on a man's leg, mixing up concoctions for upset stomachs and headaches, assisting the midwife with two births, and staying with a family during the last hours of an elderly grandfather's life.

"I cried more than they did," said Liberty. "They ended up having to comfort *me*! I couldn't stop thinking that it could've been my daddy lying there struggling to breathe, and it broke my heart. I don't know what I'd do without my father."

"What happened to your mother?" Kitty asked, but on second thought added, "Or if it's too painful, you don't have to tell me."

"Oh, I'm fine now. Time will do that. I was only ten when we lost her, but back then I thought I wasn't gonna live through that. For years Momma thought she was barren, but then she finally had my older brother, five years later she had me, and then ten years after that she had my younger brother Jonathan."

"She died in childbirth?"

Liberty nodded. "We didn't have a midwife back then, and we were on our own. Momma told Daddy what to do when I was born, and she did the same with Jonathan, but something was wrong. Jonathan was fine, but Momma died two days later, and we didn't know why. Daddy wouldn't let me sit around and mope, though; he and my brother had to work, and I had to take care of the baby."

"That was a lot of responsibility for a ten-year-old."

Liberty smiled. "It's a miracle Jonathan survived at all. I didn't know what in the tarnation I was doing."

Louis peeked his head in the door, waiting for Kitty to notice him.

"Good, Louis. You can start loading up." Kitty said her goodbyes to Liberty, arranged the chairs like she'd found them, and carried her bag out to the buggy.

"It'll be dark by the time we get home," said Louis.

"Yes, and I'm sorry. I did too much catching up with folks today; next time will be better.

Louis turned the horse toward the road.

Someone shouted from behind. Kitty grabbed the buggy frame and peered around the side. A young girl was running after them.

"Stop the buggy, Louis."

Kitty climbed down and met the girl, who burst into tears. "Calm down, hon. What's your name?"

"Di...nah."

"What's the matter?"

"My... sister..." she said, in-between sobs, "Winnie."

"Winnie?"

The girl nodded her head, sobbing. "Baby's coming... Winnie's... hurtin' bad."

"Is your father home?"

She shook her head. "Just me... an I dunno know... what to do."

"Come on," Kitty said. "Climb up and tell us how to get to your house."

Louis scooted over as far as he could. "I gotta get home, Miss Doc."

"I know, Louis. You're going to drop off Dinah and me at her house, and then I want you to go to Liberty's house and tell her to meet me at Winnie's, then you go back to Austin and find Jack... Mr. Taylor, and tell him that I need him to come get me, and you tell him how to find me."

Louis turned the horse and buggy around, and Kitty made him repeat what she told him.

"Two things... don't forget."

"Yes ma'am."

Dinah directed them to her home about five blocks away from the church. It looked like nature was doing its best to reclaim the old box-shaped house; trees and overgrown brush almost buried it. Grass had grown up unrestrained in most areas, except for a well-worn path to the door.

Kitty grabbed her bag and stepped down. Dinah climbed off the buggy and ran up the path. Kitty sent Louis on his way and followed Dinah.

The porch steps were in need of repair.

"Watch out for that second step," said Dinah. "It'll put you on your face."

Kitty pulled up her skirt and stepped over it. Dinah slipped through the darkened, open door.

Kitty followed, but paused by the door to let her eyes get accustomed to the dark room. In the quickly fading light, she could see it was one long room that ran the width of the house. The front part contained a bevy of mismatched furniture and an overturned crate, including a table and three chairs towards the back. Newspaper covered most of the walls and part of the floor.

This room had four doors – two on each side. The closest ones were closed; the farther two were open. A dim light glowed from the one to the right, so she headed towards that one. She could hear Dinah trying to calm Winnie.

The room was lit with a single candle.

"Winnie, Miss Doc's here."

The young girl was curled up under a quilt, facing the wall, whimpering.

"Hello, Winnie."

Kitty walked over to the bed, a stained and torn ticking-covered mattress lay on wood slats across two rough-hewn posts on the floor.

"Dinah, do you have any more candles?"

"In the kitchen."

"Could you bring a couple more in here? And I need you to get a pan of water and heat it. Do you have a stove?"

"No, but we have a fireplace."

"Then get a fire going and we'll heat up the water that way."

Dinah left the room.

Kitty gingerly sat down on the mattress, hoping the bedframe would hold her. She reached over and put her hand on the quilt covering the girl.

"Everything's going to be all right, sweetheart."

Winnie stiffened and started crying out. She turned over and looked at Kitty, her eyes wide with fright.

"I know it hurts, but this pain is normal. Here, grip my hand until it passes."

Winnie squeezed hard. Kitty held up her watch locket and faced it toward the candle to read the time.

"Your body is getting ready to have this baby, so it's going through some powerful changes."

"It hurts... so bad."

"I know, but it'll be over soon." Kitty let her watch fall against her chest and reached over to feel Winnie's head.

After a moment, the girl scooted closer to Kitty.

"Has it passed?"

Winnie nodded.

Dinah came in and lit two more candles sitting in glass jars, placing one on another overturned crate, and the other on the sill of the window. An old shirt was tacked over the bottom half. Dinah tied it up away from the flame.

"Do you know when your labor pains started?" Kitty asked.

"My back started hurting..." she looked at Dinah, who finished the sentence for her.

"Around noon. I still gotta put the water on." She left the room.

"Winnie, do you have any clean cloth around here?"

She shrugged her shoulders.

Kitty looked at the newspaper-covered walls. She got up and walked to the door. "Dinah, try to find some newspapers that haven't been unfolded. Or bring the cleanest you can find."

Kitty looked around the room. A few clothes hung on hooks on the wall.

After a moment, Winnie spoke. "Papa brings papers home so we can shut out the cold."

"And you can read them at the same time," Kitty said, smiling.

"I can't read."

"Don't you go to school?"

Winnie shook her head and stiffened again. She started groaning and looking afraid.

"Squeeze my hand," said Kitty, looking at her watch again. "That was less than a minute since the last one. This baby's going to be here before too long."

Kitty stood up. "I need to check you before the next pain comes." She rolled Winnie on her back and lifted up her ragged dress. The girl was all belly, like the baby had taken what little nourishment Winnie had. The rest of her body was emaciated.

Dinah brought in a stack of newspaper.

"I want you to unfold them—are your hands clean?"

Dinah shook her head and set the stack of papers on the edge of the bed.

Kitty stood up. "I need to wash my hands, too." She opened her bag and grabbed a bar of soap.

The fire from the kitchen lit their way, and they stepped down into the room, which was directly on the ground. The floor was covered with some kind of flagstone.

"Did your father build this house?"

"No."

Kitty waited for her to elaborate, but then remembered Liberty telling her they were squatters.

Kitty stopped and looked for the sink, but Dinah kept going, heading out the back door. Kitty followed her outside to a well beside the house. She watched Dinah lower a bucket down on a rope into a dark hole. Kitty shuddered when she realized how deep it was before it finally hit the water, and then Dinah pulled it back up. She poured the water into an old cooking pot, and they stood there scrubbing their hands.

The sun had set. Kitty's watch said that last labor pain occurred at 6:21 p.m. A chill hung in the air. The days were still comfortable until a norther hit. She glanced at the well and the clutter around it, and was glad it wasn't light enough to see everything more clearly.

Winnie started yelling again.

When Dinah started to wipe her hands on her dress, Kitty stopped her. "Just wave your hands in the air; don't touch anything."

They hurried back to the bedroom. "Spread the papers

thickly over the mattress and under your sister," Kitty instructed her.

Kitty checked Winnie. "It'll be just a little while longer, but you'll get through this."

"What the hell are you doin' in my house?!" a deep voice spoke from the door.

Kitty stiffened, but pulled Winnie's dress down before turning. The man filled the doorway, and in the candlelight, he looked ominous.

Kitty took a deep breath. "I'm Dr. Synatzske, Mr. Hokee, isn't it? Your daughter is about to have her baby."

"You need to get out a here."

"Do you know how to deliver a baby?!" Kitty asked him.

"People done it all through time. People are still here in spite of your kind. We can handle it ourselves."

"My kind?! You don't even know me."

"You can walk outta here on your own two feet, or I can drag you outta here."

Winnie grabbed Kitty's hand. "Don't go," she whispered.

"I'm not going anywhere." Kitty sat down on the edge of the mattress, rattling the papers. She hoped that came across as confidence rather than the fact that her legs were shaking so badly she wasn't sure they wouldn't hold her up. "Why can't I help your daughter, Mr. Hokee?"

"We don't take charity."

"This isn't charity; it's a medical issue." She squeezed Winnie's hand, hoping she wasn't frightening the girl even more. "Can I speak to you in the kitchen?" Kitty was convinced she could reason with the man using the frightening statistics of women dying in childbirth. Winnie's case was even more dangerous because of her age… and the baby was coming early. Kitty stood up a little more confidently.

Hokee didn't say a word, like he was thinking it through.

"Don't leave me," Winnie said, reaching for her, then crying out when another pain started.

"I'm not going anywhere, Winnie. I'll be right back."

Kitty walked towards Hokee. Winnie cried even louder.

Hokee stepped aside to let Kitty pass.

Kitty walked out of the bedroom and was halfway to the kitchen when he grabbed her by the arms and began forcing her towards the front of the house.

Kitty tried to wrench herself away, to no avail, then stiffened her legs and dug in her heels, plowing up newspapers across the floor, but that didn't slow the man down one iota. He lifted her off the ground like a thrashing rag doll, walked out on the porch, set her down hard and shoved her roughly towards the steps. Kitty struggled to keep her balance, and recovered quite nicely until she hit the second step. Next thing she knew she was kissing the ground in front of the house.

35

K itty felt a sharp pain in her left wrist as the door slammed behind her.

That made her mad.

She could still hear Winnie screaming. Kitty got up and dusted herself off with her good hand. She licked her lip, the salty metallic taste of blood told her she'd busted her lip… again.

"Lord, help me," she said under her breath, feeling like she was taking on the devil for that poor girl.

Dinah had tuned up, too, crying and yelling at her father.

Kitty marched around the house, praying she wouldn't step on a rattler in the tall grass. She paused at the back door, listening. It sounded like Dinah and Hokee were still at the front part of the house, so she slipped in the back door. The fire Dinah had built in the fireplace to heat the water made her feel exposed. She walked to the door of the kitchen, dropping to her knees to peek out. She could hear them better than see them.

"We don't need her," Hokee yelled at Dinah. "Now git in there and help your sister."

Winnie was screaming hysterically. Kitty crawled out of the firelight of the kitchen toward the back wall. She gathered up her skirt to keep the newspapers from rattling, but she doubted

Hokee and Dinah could hear a train whistle in that house, as loud as they were yelling at each other.

"No, Papa! I don't know what to do. Listen to her!"

Hokee grabbed her arm and started pulling her toward the bedroom. Dinah put up a pretty good fight for being such a scrawny girl, but Kitty cringed when Hokee started slapping her.

Kitty was on her hands and knees behind a small table, but she stood up when Hokee started hitting Dinah. She had no idea what she would do, but she couldn't stand there and watch the man beat his daughter. At that moment, Dinah jerked her arm away from him.

"You can slap me all you want to, Papa, but I ain't gonna watch Winnie die."

They stood there at an impasse, chests heaving. Finally Hokee let out a string of expletives and looked toward Winnie's room. The screams were nonstop.

Kitty froze, waiting for him to see her.

"Go get her," he finally said.

Dinah bolted for the door.

"I'm here…" Kitty's voice broke, so she said it again. "I'm already here." She stepped into what little light made its way from the kitchen.

The look on Hokee's face sent a wave of fear through her gut, but she stood her ground for Winnie's sake.

Dinah ran over towards her. "Thank you, God!" she said, wiping her bloodied nose and then looking at her hand. "Now I gotta go wash my hands again."

Kitty didn't wait for Hokee to say anything. She ran to the bedroom and tried to calm Winnie down. When she checked her, she could see the top of the baby's head.

"Winnie, we're amost there. When the next pain comes, I want you to push as hard as you can." Kitty leaned over and matched her voice to the hysterical girl. "Winnie, stop yellin' and listen to me!"

Winnie screamed in agony. Kitty's left wrist throbbed with pain. She wasn't sure she could do this with one hand.

Kitty went back to end of the bed and got on her knees. "Push, girl! Come on, you can do this!"

Liberty's face appeared at the head of the bed.

"Oh, thank God!" said Kitty, under her breath.

Liberty began rubbing Winnie's forehead and telling her how good she was doing.

Kitty had no idea where Hokee was at the moment or what he was doing.

Dinah spoke from the door. "I washed my hands, Miss Doc!"

Kitty glanced at her, standing there waving her hands in the air like a revival preacher. She realized her own hands had been crawling around in the dirt recently.

"Dinah, you take Mrs. Alexander's place and calm your sister down. Everything's going to be fine." She looked at Liberty. "I need you to come down here with me."

The noise coming out of Winnie was a loud whimpering.

When Liberty was on her knees against the low bed, Kitty whispered in her ear, "I need you to deliver this baby."

Liberty's eyes widened. "Why?"

"I hurt my wrist and won't be able to hold the baby. I'll tell you exactly what to do."

Liberty nodded her head, then Kitty saw her glaring at the door where Hokee appeared.

"Everything's fine, Mr. Hokee," Kitty assured him, and then firmly to Liberty, "Everything's fine."

Hokee turned around, disappearing from sight.

Winnie started up again. Kitty climbed on the bed with her.

"All right, Winnie, I need you to push now. This baby's almost here. Come on, push! Dinah, get up there behind her and help hold her head and shoulders up. Push, sweetie!"

"It's coming!" yelled Liberty, looking up at Kitty.

The baby's head appeared, but Winnie collapsed back against her sister.

"Rest a bit, then on the next one, we're going to find out if you have a baby boy or baby girl."

Dinah looked excited. "Did you hear that, Sissy?"

Winnie opened her eyes, then shut them tightly again, grimacing with the pain.

"She's pushing!" yelled Dinah.

"One more big push, Winnie… that's it." Kitty guided Liberty to help get the baby's shoulders through, and then it was done.

"It's a boy, Winnie!! You have a baby boy!" Liberty cried. Liberty turned him over and and patted his tiny back, trying to get a response out of him. The baby let out a squeak, and then let the world know he had arrived.

"He definitely has your lungs, girl!"

Winnie's exhausted face lit up. "Can I see him?"

"Let me get him cleaned up. Dinah, hand me some of those towels I brought," said Liberty.

"Bring the water in here, too, Dinah," said Kitty.

Kitty sat back on the floor and watched Liberty. The woman knew what she was doing. She laid the baby on one of the towels, and tied the umbilical cord close to the baby before cutting it. She dampened a towel and gently wiped off the baby, talking sweetly to him. Then she wrapped him in a clean towel and placed him in Winnie's outstretched arms.

Kitty loved watching a new mother's face.

"Look here, Dinah. Looky what we got."

A movement caught in the corner of her eye, and Kitty saw Hokee standing at the door.

"You have a grandson, Mr. Hokee."

"One more damn mouth to feed," he said before he turned and walked away."

Liberty looked at Kitty. "What is wrong with that man?"

Kitty whispered to the girls, "Has your father always been this angry?"

Winnie shook her head. "He misses Momma," she whispered.

"What happened to your face, girl?" Liberty asked Dinah.

"Nuthin'."

"Papa was trying to make Dinah come in here and deliver

my baby after he threw Miss Doc out the house. But Dinah wouldn't do it."

Liberty looked at Kitty. "Is that what happened to your arm? And look at your lip!"

"I fell going down the porch steps." She looked at Dinah. "I forgot about the second step."

"I told you…"

"I know, and I forgot."

"Well, the second step wasn't even there when I come in," said Liberty. "So he threw you out of the house."

"Dinah talked him into letting me stay."

Dinah snickered. "Yeah, she'd already come 'round the house and snuck in the back door."

"You came back after Papa kicked you out, Miss Doc?" asked Winnie.

Kitty interrupted her. "Winnie, we need to talk about taking care of this baby. Do you have anything for him to wear?"

Winnie shook her head.

Liberty stood up. "I brought a couple of old sheets we can tear up and use as diapers. I can see what the ladies of the church can round up tomorrow, but before I go, I want to show you how to feed…have you thought about a name?"

Winnie smiled and nodded, but Dinah spoke for her. "If it was girl, we was gonna name her after our momma, Elizabeth, but we'd call her Lizzie. And if it was a boy, we was gonna call him Seth, after my Papa."

"Your father's name is Seth?" asked Kitty

Liberty hissed, "Your father doesn't deserve you naming your baby after him."

"Liberty…" Kitty touched her arm.

"That reminds me," said Liberty, turning around. "Let me take a look at your arm."

Kitty's eyebrows raised, and she couldn't help but smile. "Who's the doctor here?" But she held out her left arm.

They both noticed the wrist was swollen, and Kitty winced when Liberty gingerly touched it.

"What do you think?" Kitty asked, testing her.

"It's either sprained or cracked, but it doesn't feel like any bones are out of place."

"What needs to be done?"

"We need to make it immobile to give it time to heal... do you have a splint in your bag?"

Kitty nodded.

Liberty rummaged around in Kitty's medical bag and found a splint and pulled out a roll of gauze, too. She placed the splint underneath Kitty's hand and wound it firmly to hold it in place.

"Not so tight that it cuts off the blood circulation, but not too loose," said Kitty, admiring the woman's work. "Good job."

Liberty beamed, then turned to the girls. "Let's get you cleaned up, Winnie, then I'm going to show you how to feed Seth, and I'll be back tomorrow to show you how to take care of this baby."

Kitty stood. "We'll be right back." She walked Liberty out of the room, through the kitchen, and out the back door. "We can wash up out here."

Kitty whispered, "The baby's early, but he seems to be breathing all right on his own."

"I figured she'd have that baby next month."

"Have you seen her since I first examined her?"

"Twice, both times when her father was at work. The Reverend and me came here soon after we found out she was expecting to try to talk Hokee about Winnie, but he cussed us off his property. I was gonna get the ladies from the church to help me round up some things for the baby, but I thought I had more time. It'll be a miracle if that baby survives a month in this house."

"Oh, Liberty..."

"Those poor girls are on their own. That man is absolutely worthless. He couldn't care less about them... or the baby for that matter."

"But they still love him."

"They don't know any better. I know this ain't the Christian thing to say, but I think they'd be better off without him.

36

The horse seemed to know its way well enough, even in the dark, so Jack let it trot all the way to Clarksville. He stopped at Justus's house to find out where this 'crazy man', as Louis had described in his note left at the livery, lived.

Justus and Ira insisted on coming with him when they finally learned from Marcus that Liberty had gone to Hokee's house. Until then, they had simply accepted Marcus's explanation for Liberty's absence was that she was helping deliver a baby.

They all decided Louis and Marcus both needed a lesson in better communication skills.

Justus sat beside Jack holding a lantern; Ira was somewhere ahead on foot. He didn't have to stay on the road like the buggy had to.

"Who is this Hokee?" Jack asked Justus.

"Someone who lost his way somehow."

"What do you mean?"

"His wife died a while back, but he still has has two daughters, and he ain't doing right by them."

"You mean he's not taking care of them or he mistreats them?

"I 'spect a little of both."

"And one of them is having a baby?"

236

Justus nodded. "Yeah. Liberty's tried to help, but he don't want any help."

"Do you think he's capable of hurting Kitty or Liberty?"

"I dunno, but if he's smart, he wouldn't tangle with Bertie. She'd make him regret it." Justus chuckled.

Jack frowned. That didn't seem funny at all.

By the time they arrived at Hokee's house, they heard raised voices.

Jack dropped the reins and hit the ground running, not waiting for Justus. The porch was in shadow, but he could tell people stood on it.

"Kitty!" he yelled out.

One of the shadows pulled away and jumped off the porch to meet him.

"I'm so glad you're here," said Kitty, reaching for him.

Jack pulled her close. "Are you all right?"

"Yes, everything's fine. I just didn't want you to trip on those steps; they're falling apart."

"What's going on?"

"Liberty's giving Hokee... some instructions."

Justus walked up with his lantern. Jack could see everyone's faces. Ira stood between his wife and Hokee.

"I'm coming back tomorrow with some things for the baby, and we're gonna make some changes around here. You know this is no way for your girls to live."

Jack didn't like the look on Hokee's face.

"Ain't none of your business." He looked around. "Ain't none of any of your business."

"Well, until you start taking better care of your family, we're gonna make it our business." She lowered her voice. "And I know how Miss Doc hurt her arm."

"What happened to her arm?" Jack asked, noticing Kitty's wrapped wrist.

"I tripped on that broken step," Kitty said, a little too loudly, Jack thought. "And I didn't do a very good job catching myself. Liberty wrapped my wrist for me." She stepped forward. "And I want y'all to know she did an excellent job delivering the baby. I think Clarksville has its second midwife now."

Liberty couldn't help but grin, and Ira patted her on the back, congratulating her.

Liberty's stern voice softened as she turned back to Hokee. "I don't know your past, Hokee, or the sorrows in your life— I'm sorry about your wife, but you can't quit on your girls. They need you now more than ever. Did you know Winnie named the baby after you?"

Hokee didn't respond.

Liberty sighed in resignation. "Well, Ira and I need to get back to our own children. I'm gonna go tell the girls I'm leaving, but I'll be back to check on them tomorrow with some supplies for the baby."

"I need to get my bag," said Kitty, stepping over the broken step to follow Liberty into the house.

Justus held the light over the steps. The second step was in two splintered pieces. "Me and Ira can come back and help you fix this, Hokee." He held the lamp higher to see the man's face. "Is that all right wi' you?"

Hokee barely nodded. Jack noticed the man wouldn't even look his way.

"We'll come after work when you'll be here." Justus glanced at Jack. "And this here is Jack Taylor. He's our new representative and Miss Doc's beau."

Jack walked over to the side of the porch and extended his hand. Hokee looked like a cornered coyote ready to bolt and run. He finally took Jack's hand, but still wouldn't meet his eyes.

"You have an unusual name, Hokee. Does it mean anything?"

Hokee shook his head and released his hand.

Jack saw the man's demeanor change from a proud, angry stance to a scared, submissive hull right in front of him. He was shocked when he realized that it was his own presence that triggered it.

Kitty and Liberty returned, and Jack took the bag and

helped her down the steps.

"We're gonna fix that tomorrow," said Justus.

Jack noticed Hokee had disappeared.

Everyone said their goodbyes, and Jack walked Kitty to the buggy and helped her up, placing the bag on the floor. She scooted over and Jack stepped up and sat beside her. He could feel her trembling.

"What's the matter?" he asked, putting his arm around her.

"It's just been a long day, and very emotional for everyone." She leaned her head into the crook of his neck. "Have you ever had to be strong for everyone during a crisis, but when it was over, you felt like a limp rag?"

"Not often… does defending my sisters' honor count?"

Kitty chuckled. "I always wanted an older brother to look out after me."

Jack kissed her forehead. "How 'bout I look out after you from now on?"

"I'd love that." She turned her face upwards, kissing his neck and stubbled chin.

Jack couldn't help but turn his head and find her lips. He felt an electric charge to the bottom of his gut.

After a bit, he reluctantly pulled away and said, "I'd better get you home." He flipped the reins to get the horse walking and turned the buggy around to head back to Austin.

"Now tell me what happened back there. You said you had to be strong for everyone."

"Winnie's only thirteen or fourteen and too young to be having a baby, and the baby came early. She was hysterical most of the time I was there. And when Hokee got home, he asked me to leave—he actually expected Dinah to deliver that baby. She's only eleven years old! He didn't want my help and asked me to leave, but I wouldn't."

"You *are* a stubborn woman."

Kitty snickered. "Well, I was afraid they might lose both Winnie and the baby if I left. I'm so thankful the baby came out head-first. It could easily have been a breech birth."

"You lost me there."

"Feet or butt first, which can be dangerous for both the baby and the mother. Liberty got there just in time to deliver him. She's making an excellent nurse. Where did Louis find you?"

"He didn't. Patrick told him I'd taken Lonesome out, so he knew I'd be back eventually. Louis tacked a note on the livery door saying you were delivering a baby at that crazy man's house in Clarksville, and that I needed to go get you."

"How would he know anything about Hokee?" Kitty thought for a moment. "I guess he must've overheard Liberty and me talking about him. I forget he's around half the time, he's so quiet. Or maybe Marcus said something to him."

"Louis left the horse hitched up to the buggy for me, but he forgot to say where this Hokee lived, so I had to go see Justus so he could tell me. Marcus told Ira and Justus that his mother was delivering a baby, but he failed to mention it was Hokee's daughter. Ira's going to have a set-to with Marcus about that; I think I need to have a word with Louis, too."

"What am I going to do with that boy?" Kitty said. "Did you know he was back in school?"

"Yes, thanks to your needlin' him."

"I wouldn't be a doctor without Juju and Lucius needlin' me about school. Well, and Katherine's help, too. I hope Louis understands that education is his way out of a life of struggling financially."

"It's more than that, though," said Jack. "I know educated people that are poor, especially ministers and teachers."

"And doctors that get paid with rabbits and chickens," said Kitty. "If it weren't for Dr. Gilbert paying me a salary, I'd be in trouble."

"Do you accept those kinds of gifts?"

"At first I didn't, but Liberty told me I needed to let people pay in whatever way possible... for their sakes, not necessarily mine. She said it keeps their pride intact, and that charity's all right every once in a while, but too much of it can do more harm than good. People get used to it and then start to expect it, and then they get to the point they forget how to be responsible for themselves."

"What about those who have absolutely nothing?"

"If they're physically able, Liberty gives them tasks like sweeping out the church or gathering firewood, or even helping some of the older folks in the community."

"Did Hokee try to pay you?"

"It never came up, no, that's not right. He did tell me he didn't accept charity, and I wanted him to understand that he didn't have a choice—that it was a life or death situation for his daughter, but I didn't want Winnie to hear me use those words. I guess Liberty will take care of that."

"Sounds like you and Liberty talk a lot."

"Yeah, she told me one of the hardest things for former slaves after the Emancipation was learning to be responsible for themselves. They'd lived several generations with someone else making every decision for them and telling them exactly what to do."

"Kind of like prison."

"Many had no education—it was against the law in most places to teach Negroes how to read and write. And then a law came along and declared them free and equal, when nothing about their lives was equal. Liberty said getting people used to living on charity was putting the chains back on them."

"I hadn't thought of it that way."

"Me neither."

"Justus seems to have adjusted well."

"Do you think if he had a choice of any job, he'd choose to shine shoes for a living?"

"I'll have to ask him."

"I think it's obvious."

"I think you're being presumptuous."

"You sound like a lawyer."

"I am a lawyer, and I think it's important to not make assumptions about people without getting the facts."

"Are we arguing?" asked Kitty.

"I'd say it's more of a debate."

"Of course you would."

"I do rather enjoy debates," Jack said, hoping she wasn't angry. "It's a big part of my job."

He couldn't help but smile when he felt her arm link through his.

"I'm glad you're coming to Galveston with me to bring Momma back. Are you sure about us moving into your house?"

"I wouldn't have asked you if I wasn't."

"That is so generous of you. I'm hoping we'll get Momma back on her feet as soon as possible so you won't be out of your house for too long."

Jack exhaled, letting another debate take place inside his head. He wanted so badly to ask for her hand, but he wanted to make a special occasion of it, maybe at the Driskill. They had a history at that place, from the day he was shot... to announcing his campaign and meeting the woman who gave birth to Kitty... to introducing her to his parents and celebrating his victory... and all the times in-between.

Impatience won out.

"I was kind of hoping we could live together in that house." He felt her stiffen beside him. "No, I meant as husband and wife... you know, married and all." The words weren't coming out of his mouth nearly as smoothly as he'd planned.

She didn't say anything.

"What do you think?" he asked, pulling the carriage to a stop.

"About what?" she asked.

"About what I asked you." This was getting uncomfortable.

"You didn't ask me anything."

"Are you wanting me to get down on one knee?"

"That's not necessary."

He couldn't see her face to judge what she might be feeling, but he was starting to sweat in spite of the cool evening. "Or did you want me to get permission from your mother—maybe I should've waited until after I met your mother this weekend. But I didn't think that would be necessary since you didn't have a father for me to ask."

"What exactly are you asking me?" Kitty said.

Was the woman daft? Jack wondered. "I wanted to ask you at the Driskill or some other romantic place. Do you want me to wait and do it right? I... don't even have a ring."

Kitty sighed; it sounded impatient to Jack. This wasn't going at all like he planned.

"Are you asking me to marry you?" she said.

"Isn't it obvious?"

"I kept waiting for you to ask the question so I could answer you."

"I didn't ask the question?"

"No."

"Oh! Well, then would you marr– "

"Yes, my love!" she interrupted him. "Of course I'll marry you!"

Jack let out a whoop that startled the horse. "Whoa, Tomaté!" he said, pulling back on the reins. "I'm excited, too, but you have to let me kiss my fiancée."

But his fiancée beat him to it.

37

Jack smiled patting the small bump in his inner coat pocket as he walked along the boardwalk on the Strand in Galveston. He didn't have time to shop for a ring in Austin, but Kitty told him that there were plenty of jewelry shops on the island.

He thought about his meeting with Kitty's mother. Juju looked frail sitting in her rolling chair, but her eyes told a different story. She fiercely loved her daughter.

Jack didn't stumble over his words this time, and he made sure Juju was aware of his kinship with his cousins Grace and Finn since Kitty told him her mother thought very highly of both of them. Jack figured it might help his cause.

Juju gave them her blessing. Her words were slurred, but he had no problem understanding her. Katherine seemed pleased, too, and Jack was glad about that.

He stopped at the corner where he had disembarked the streetcar and waited.

Jack thought about the odd arrangement, Kitty's birth mother taking care of her adoptive mother. And it was more than a caretaker patient relationship. They truly seemed to be friends. He wondered if Juju would feel the same if he knew Katherine's actual identity.

But the biggest shock was Katherine's announcement that they wouldn't be coming back to Austin with Jack and Kitty.

Lucius had hired a lady to come in and work with Juju on her speech and teaching her how to use her limbs again. Katherine said that Juju was adamant that a young married couple shouldn't have a millstone tied around their necks to start their marriage. And that Juju wouldn't get well nearly as fast in Austin because Austin wasn't 'home'. Jack figured the women threw that caveat in to help Kitty agree to their plan.

Jack had to admit that Kitty put up a good fight trying to change their minds, but the only thing they agreed on was to have the wedding in Galveston to make it easier for Juju. Jack said his mother would be happy to help; she loved planning social events, although Grace didn't provide that many opportunities for her.

Kitty informed him their wedding wasn't going to be a social event, but rather a small gathering of close friends and family. She told him later that she didn't want to put any undue pressure on her mother.

Jack loved her all the more for not wanting to have a big affair. He knew his mother would be disappointed about that, but she would understand when she learned it was because of Juju's health. He decided his mother could have a 'big affair' back home over Christmas in honor of their upcoming wedding.

He knew Jarvis wasn't going to be happy about his decision, but he was convinced that the man wouldn't do anything to jeopardize all he'd invested to get Jack elected by leaking Kitty's heritage. And very few people knew about her relationship with Katherine, and Katherine's connection to New Orleans.

Jarvis would have to learn to deal with the fact that Kitty would be Jack's wife, no matter what had happened in her family's past. She had no control over that, and neither did Katherine. And he had decided neither of them needed to know about their heritage. They had enough difficulties in their lives.

Katherine mentioned that newlyweds needed time alone, but he had an inkling she was distancing herself from Kitty because of Jarvis… and to protect Jack's own career.

He looked up and down the street, bustling with business. Kitty told him that many residents had left the island after the storm over two years before, and he could still see the scars it left, but it was still a more thriving city than Austin. The talk of building a seawall to protect the island and raise the island's elevation was on everyone's lips. Jack couldn't even imagine an engineering feat on that massive scale.

Jack walked around the corner and looked toward the docks, wondering if he could learn something down here that he could take back to central Texas to boost business. He knew Galveston shipped a lot of cotton out of here. They even had something called cotton presses, which compacted cotton into smaller, denser bales that meant more cotton could be shipped at one time. The same could be done for cotton traveling by rail. He wondered if the cotton gins around central Texas could do the same.

Jack heard that Houston was trying to establish its own port and passage to the sea without having to deal with the Galveston Wharf Company that controlled Galveston Harbor. A deep channel was in the process of being dredged. He wondered what another deep channel port in the area would do to Galveston. And how would that help Central Texas?

He realized anew how much he needed to learn in order to do his job well.

The streetcar started clanging down the street, so he returned to his place on the corner.

* * *

The next day Kitty and Jack attended her former church, and Jack met more people than he could ever remember their names. Most seemed to be so proud that Kitty was a doctor, but Jack could tell by the skeptical expressions on some faces that they weren't too keen on a female doctor. His fiance's courage to work in a field dominated by men continued to astound him.

On the way home, Kitty pointed out some of the well-known mansions on Broadway, and even more empty lots where grand homes used to exist before the storm. He was impressed with Lucius's home. It was a showpiece. Kitty said Lucius offered to let them have the wedding there, but Kitty wanted to keep it small and simple.

They walked to the beach later that afternoon. He was astounded when Kitty told him that the homes and businesses had solidly covered the land up to the beach before the storm. Jack saw where a number of new houses had been built, but by far were the vast, bare stretches of sand that used to be covered with houses and businesses.

The waves rolling up to the beach seemed steady and nonthreatening. The breeze felt thicker down here, somehow, but he knew it must've felt good in the heat of the summer. He looked back toward town, trying to imagine fifteen feet of water rolling over the island, along with an inconceivable wind. How did anyone survive that?

He felt Kitty shudder standing beside him. He grasped her hand, squeezing it reassuringly.

"I was never afraid of the ocean until that day," she said, looking out to sea. "And the wind... it was a constant scream that went on for hours... so loud it covered people's real screams. I'll never forget that sound."

She turned abrubtly, pulling Jack with her.

"So now you've seen the ocean," she said. "We need to get back to pack."

Later at the house, Katherine insisted that Kitty and Jack sit with Juju while she prepared supper for them. Juju's speech had improved greatly, although she still slurred her words.

"See ocean?" Juju asked Jack.

"Yes, ma'am. It's big."

Juju smiled crookedly. "Jekyll and Hyde."

"Pardon me?" Jack asked.

"She's talking about that book with Dr. Jekyll and Mr. Hyde," said Kitty.

"Oh!"

"Have you read that book?" Kitty asked him.

"Several years ago, and it gave me nightmares to think a person could have good and evil inside of them." Jack looked at Juju. "You're comparing the ocean to Dr. Jekyll and Mr. Hyde."

She nodded. "Moshly Jekyll."

"Thank heavens, for your sake, Momma." Kitty reached over and tucked the quilt around her mother's legs. "I don't plan on ever seeing the Mr. Hyde side again."

Juju reached for her daughter's hand. "Tank Katsrun."

"What?" Kitty brought her mother's hand to her own cheek.

"Tank...Kats...run 'fore you go."

"I'm sorry, Momma, I don't understand."

"I think she's saying Katherine," said Jack.

Kitty's eyes widened. "Are you talking about Kay?"

Juju nodded. "I know."

Kitty sat up straight. "You know what?"

"Kay... Katsrun."

Kitty looked at Jack and then back at her mother. "Did you say, 'Kay... Katherine?'"

Juju nodded.

"Are you saying you know who Kay is?"

"Not ...dumb."

"Of course you aren't." Kitty seemed to be at a loss for words. "Are you angry with me?"

Juju snorted and shook her head.

"She showed up several weeks after... it happened, and I was exhausted, and she offered to help... and I let her."

Juju patted Kitty's hand.

"Does she know you know?"

Juju nodded.

"And you're all right with her being here?"

Juju nodded, and tears came to her eyes. "Gave me you."

Kitty's face skewed up as she reached over and embraced her mother as she wept. Juju shed tears, too, but not like Kitty, who looked like she was crying for a whole lot more than this moment.

Jack didn't know whether he should remain seated or give them time alone. He waited a bit before he stood. The women seemed oblivious to his presence. He started walking quietly out of the room when he heard Juju speak again.

"Tank her," she said softly.

"Of course, I'll thank her, Momma," Kitty said. "I never thought I'd say this, but Katherine was an answer to prayer."

38

Jack stood in front of Jarvis's office door and took a deep breath. Back in Galveston, he felt so confident about telling his boss of his engagement to Kitty, but the closer the train got to Austin, the more his self-confidence waned. He and Kitty came back on Monday, but Jarvis was out of the office until Thursday. The wait had been unbearable.

He knocked on the door.

"Enter!" The voice boomed from the other side.

Jack's stomach lurched as he turned the knob. He reminded himself again that Kitty was worth defending. He could imagine a future without Jarvis, but not without Kitty.

"Good morning, sir," Jack said, trying to sound chipper.

Jarvis was scowling.

Not a good sign.

"You lied to me," he said.

Jack was immediately on the defensive. "No sir, I did not lie."

"You told me you had family matters to attend to. You don't have family in Galveston."

"I will. I needed to meet my future mother-in-law and ask for her blessing to marry her daughter."

"You defied me and went behind my back after I told you about that woman's past—a past that could sink your career."

"You and Link are the only ones that know about Kitty's

past; you're the only ones that could sink my career, but I don't think you really want to do that."

Jarvis clenched his jaw and looked away. He didn't look convinced.

"And remember, I know about your past, too." Jack didn't want to use that against Jarvis, but he needed to remind him that he had his own leverage.

Jarvis looked sharply at him.

"I'm sorry, Jarvis, but you can't tell me how to run my personal life."

"Yes, I can." Jarvis paused like he was struggling for the right words to say. Jarvis never had a problem with that before. "I didn't want to have to tell you this way... but there's a chance, although it's a small chance... that Kitty could be my daughter."

"What?!"

"I've known Pearl—Katherine-- for over 20 years, and not in a way that I'm proud of..."

"If you think there's even the slightest chance that Kitty might be your daughter, then why wouldn't you want a relationship with her? She's an amazing, accomplished woman—"

"Let me finish. Have you ever wondered why I chose *you* to give you an education and groom you for public service?"

"In the beginning, yes, but then I began to think you chose me because you thought I could make a difference in people's lives."

"How much do you know about your mother before she married your father?"

"Some."

"I knew your mother back when she went by the name of Florine Locke."

"Why didn't you tell me you knew her?" Jack realized something. "You were avoiding her those times she was here, weren't you."

He was surprised to see Jarvis slowly nod his head.

"Why?"

Jarvis looked haggard all of a sudden, like he was full of regret. "I'm sure your mother hates me. I wish there was a better way to tell you this, but I almost married your mother years ago. I convinced her to run away with me—to get away from her overbearing father. We spent time in Houston and Galveston, and eventually made our way to Fort Worth... where I'm ashamed to say that I abandoned her... after she told me she was with child."

Jack felt like someone punched him in the stomach.

"I don't believe you," was all he could manage to say.

"I was young and selfish at the time, Jack, but I actually had a change of heart and went back for her. I was told that a Mr. Taylor had taken her home to Waco. I figured Mr. Locke would shoot me on sight if I showed my face in town, so I left the state."

"Why are you telling me this?"

"You... are your mother's firstborn, Jack..." Jarvis said, waiting for him to put it all together.

Jack couldn't breathe all of a sudden. He frantically tried to recall what his cousin Grace had told him months before... that his mother had run away with a gambler, and after he abandoned her in Fort Worth, his father found her and brought her home. Then she ran away from Waco again to live with a family in Brownwood. When he asked his mother about the fire in Brownwood, she said she'd run away to Brownwood because she had a disagreement with her father.

Jack grabbed the back of the chair when the room shifted.

No, this couldn't be right. His father was Jimmy Taylor. He was a Taylor. He stared at Jarvis... looking for any signs of resemblance... he saw nothing familiar.

"I've been keeping up with you for some time, son. Your parents have done a good job raising you, but I wanted to be a part of your life somehow. I've built an empire here, and I wanted you to be a part of it, too. It's going to be yours someday."

Jack just stared at him.

"And I didn't want to tell you like this... but since I've had relations with both your mother and Kitty's mother around the times you both were conceived, there's a small chance that you and Kitty are—"

Jack lunged around the desk and pinned Jarvis against the bookshelf.

Jack didn't even recognize his own voice when he spoke. "You destroy my life in one breath, and then hand me your empire on a silver platter in the next? How in your twisted mind could you ever think I would want to have anything to do with you now? I don't know who in the hell you think you are, Jarvis, or whatever your name is, but you aren't my father... and you never will be."

Jack shoved the man away from him and stormed out of the office, heading to the alley.

He slammed the door behind him, which brought the stray cat from down the alley running towards him, rather than away. Jack never lost stride as he scooped up the cat and headed south toward the livery.

He focused on putting one foot in front of the other as he walked along the streets.

"You can't live there anymore, Cat. That place is evil."

Jack wasn't sure if the feline was purring or growling at him.

He ignored the friendly stares of people he met on the street, and just nodded his head at the ones that spoke to him, obviously recognizing him.

He walked into the livery and found Patrick.

"You have mice around here, don't you?" Jack asked.

"Yes, sir."

Jack handed the furry bag of bones to the old man.

"He needs a new home." Jack reached into his pocket and pulled out a handful of bills and coins, stuffing it in Patrick's pocket. "Get him some food, and he'll be your friend for life."

Jack walked over and began to saddle Lonesome Joe. By the time he finished, Cat was enjoying a pan of warm milk Patrick had retrieved from the livery's lone milk cow.

"What's his name?" asked Patrick.

"Whatever you see fit to give him." Jack mounted his horse.

"Where you headed so early this morning?"

"Home," Jack said, with no hesitation. He turned Lonesome toward the big doors.

"Are you all right, sir?" asked Patrick.

Jack didn't even begin to know how to answer that, so he just shook his head and walked the horse out of the barn.

He noticed the wind had shifted from the north, so he pulled his hat down and kept his head low as he traveled into the wind along the backstreets of Austin. He could still see the Capitol through the trees, but the granite looked gray—the color of the cloudy sky.

When he reached the edge of town, he spurred Lonesome into a trot.

"Let's go home, boy."

39

Kitty held the tiny baby in her arms, marveling at his perfectly formed features and softly curling hair.

"Hello, baby boy," she said softly. "What happened, Liberty?"

"They left him on my porch Sunday morning, along with all the things I had collected from my friends from church. I changed his diaper and fed him a little milk, and then I marched over to Hokee's house, but they were gone. I think that was my fault, too."

Kitty waited for her to explain.

"I tried to put the fear of God into that man—telling him he'd better start taking better care of his family, and to not lay another hand on those girls, or else…"

"Or else what?"

The woman looked near to tears. "Or else I'd tell the law that he put a hand on you."

"You did what?!"

The baby's eyes fluttered open. Kitty began rocking him gently.

"I know he pushed you outta his house, Miss Doc," Liberty whispered. "I know that's why you hurt your arm. He knows touchin' a white woman's a hanging offense, but I honestly didn't intend to turn him in. I just wanted him to do right by them girls and his grandbaby. But I ended up runnin' 'em off, and look what they left me with. I don't need another baby to raise."

"Is there some other family that might take Seth?" asked Kitty. "I wonder who the father might be?"

"When I took those baby things over there the next day, Winnie told me that my Marcus was the father…"

"Marcus?!"

"I was fit to be tied by the time I got home, but Marcus swears he hasn't touched her. He said he came across Winnie and a few boys one day out in the woods. They'd paid her a few pennies to show them her privates, and Marcus run 'em off. He promised me that's the only time he's had anything to do with her, and I believe him."

"Maybe Winnie thinks of him as her hero."

"That's what I figured."

Kitty looked down at the baby. "You're one week old today, Seth. We're going to find you a good home."

"The Reverend is asking around, too." Liberty reached for the baby. "I know you need to start seeing patients, but I hoped it would be all right if I brought him today so I could still help. He's a good baby—sleeps most of the time."

"Of course."

"I'm amazed that God designed a woman's body to build something as perfect as this… even in the midst of the worst possible environment."

Kitty smoothed the baby's shock of black hair. "It's miraculous, Libery. And this baby still deserves a chance at life."

* * *

It was well after dark by the time Jack rode into Eddy, and he was still a good ways from Grace. Lonesome Joe was wore out. Jack had taken it easy with the horse since he hadn't been ridden this much since… since he'd ridden him down to Austin four years before.

He was anxious to get home, but he could hardly feel his own face or hands from the cold. He snorted, thinking that these fancy duds he wore made him feel like he was riding butt naked. He groaned, realizing now how reckless he'd been to leave town without thinking things through. He passed a hotel, but figured he didn't have enough money since he emptied his pocket for that stupid cat. At least the cat was warm and fed tonight.

He began to envy that cat.

His cup of coffee and a quick biscuit early that morning ran out half a day ago.

On the edge of town he passed a barn. A few minutes later he turned around and headed back to it. If he could just get out of the wind...

He saw the glow of a lamp through a lighted window in a nearby house so he rode up to it and stiffly dismounted, giving his legs a moment to remember how they were supposed to work. He tied Lonesome's reigns to the porch rail and walked up to the door and rapped on it, standing there rubbing his hands to try to get some feeling in them.

He heard a chair scoot against the floor, and in a moment, the door opened a crack. A man's face appeared, and Jack took off his hat, hoping he didn't look as miserable as he felt. Or maybe looking miserable would get him and Lonesome a night out of the wind.

The man looked like he was straining to recognize him. "Need something?"

"Yes, sir. I'm Jack Taylor from Austin, and I'm on my way home to Grace."

"You're from Grace?"

"Yes, sir. I ended up leaving town a little too hastily and didn't realize the weather was going to turn, and my horse and I don't think we have the strength to go any further before daylight. I was wondering if you'd mind if we took shelter in your barn for the night?"

"Who'd you say you were?" the man asked.

"Jack Taylor. My grandparents founded Grace."

"You're one of those Taylors?"

"Yes, sir."

"Good grief. Come on in here out of the cold." The man opened the door wider and held out his hand. "Name's Yanek."

Jack shook his hand and looked behind him. "My horse…"

"We'll take care of your horse later. Come over here by the fire and thaw out. Your hand feels like ice."

Jack stepped into the room, feeling the warmth hit his face. He nodded to a woman sitting beside the fireplace knitting.

"Ma, this here's Jack Taylor from Grace."

"Evenin', ma'am."

The woman gathered her yarn and stood up. "You're shaking like a leaf. Come over here and take my chair."

Jack wasn't too good at judging people's ages, but he thought the couple looked old enough to be his parents.

"No, ma'am," Jack refused. "I don't want to put you out any."

"Nonsense," she said. "I was fixin' to turn in anyway. Have you had anything to eat?"

Jack paused. His stomach was gnawing on itself, but his manners didn't want to be any trouble to these good Samaritans. But he didn't want to out and out lie.

"You probably haven't eaten all day, right?"

"How'd you know?"

"I raised six boys, and I know that look."

"I don't want you to go to any trouble."

The man spoke up. "It's no trouble. Our last two boys left in August, and Ma still ain't figured out how to cook for two yet. I'd be obliged if you'd finish off that stew I've been eating on for three days."

In ten minutes, Jack was warm and eating leftover cornbread and stew. In twenty minutes, Lonesome was a happy boy out of the wind feasting on a pile of hay. The couple insisted Jack stay in the house, and he didn't put up too much of a fight.

By daylight, he and Lonesome were up and ready to get on the road with full stomachs, and two new friends he planned to repay their hospitality in some way.

The air was cold, but still. Mr. Yanek tried to give him a coat, but Jack wouldn't take it. He couldn't refuse Mrs. Yanek's warm scarf she'd knitted, though, after she'd wrapped that luxurious piece of warmth around his neck. He just couldn't hurt her feelings by refusing it.

Jack broke away from the main road and railroad tracks that led to Waco and headed northwest toward Grace. That would save him a good 20 miles cutting cross country rather than follow the main road into Waco and then turning due west.

He reached up and pulled the scarf across the lower part of his face and sighed with the comfort of it. He realized one of these scarves would make a good Christmas present for Kitty.

Then like a knife stabbing his heart, he remembered.

And he wept.

40

By noon, he'd made it to Grace. He'd made a quick trip home for his sister Biriney's wedding six months before, but he didn't stay long because of the campaign.

He had always traveled by train to Waco since he had moved to Austin, and his father always picked him up at the station in the buggy. He enjoyed that time catching up on the way home.

The Taylors were adamant about the family gathering for Christmas, and unless there was a really good reason for not coming, everyone made the effort to get together. Some came from South Texas where his cousin Grace and her brothers and parents were from. His aunt Faith and her family came from a ranch outside of Brownwood. His sisters and several of his cousins came over from Waco. Some of his aunts and uncles and their children still lived in Grace. His grandmother's home was filled and overflowing during the holiday season.

Hours into the journey, Jack realized he had acted too hastily leaving Austin. He should've waited for the next train. He should've sent a message to Kitty so she wouldn't be worried. He needed to send her a wire today. But beyond that, he saw no future until he learned the truth about his past. And his mother was the one to confront about his father.

He recalled what Katherine had said that day in the Driskill—that Jarvis could be Kitty's father for all she knew, and he felt sick to his stomach at the thought.

He refused to dwell on that slim chance until his mother told him the truth. He prayed there was a good explanation for all of this. But what Jarvis said dovetailed with what he'd learned about his mother's past. Did she go to Brownwood to have a baby? To have him? Did his father marry her to give her some respectability?

He paused at the elaborate brick entrance to his parents' place. That was his mother's doing; his father's tastes were much less pretentious.

His father.

There was a good possibility that Jimmy Taylor wasn't his own flesh and blood, and the pain almost doubled him over.

He wept again.

Jack thought about what his constituents would think about seeing him crying like a baby, and at that moment, he couldn't care less. That all paled compared to what he was facing right now.

He wiped his face with the scarf and decided standing there stalling wasn't going to change anything. He started Lonesome Joe forward. When he looked down the road, he saw his mother running towards him.

What was it with her? She always seemed to know when something was wrong.

He dismounted and let her come to him.

"Jack?! What in the world are you doing here?" She threw her arms around him. Then backed up to look at his face.

"What's wrong, honey?"

He couldn't answer for bawling again, feeling like a little boy rather than the man he was.

She put her arms around him again and held him tightly for a moment, then said quietly into his ear. "Is Kitty all right?"

He nodded, trying to compose himself. "How'd you know I was here?"

"I just happened to look out the window, and I saw

Lonesome Joe standing there at the gate and knew something was wrong."

Jack couldn't help but laugh. "You recognized the horse before you recognized *me*?"

"My eyes aren't as good as they used to be." She linked her arm in his and started walking him to the house. "I knew it had to be you when I saw your horse. But you've never surprised us before, and your father always brought you home from Waco. I could tell you were upset though—just stopping there instead of coming on in."

They walked for a bit in silence.

"Are you hungry?"

"I need to talk to you first," Jack said. "Where's Dad?"

"At the barn, of course. He spends more time with those horses than he does me."

"Good. I need to talk to you alone."

"Then tie up Lonesome at the front of the house, and you can take care of him later."

Jack tied the reins to a hitching post. They walked up the steps to the porch of the two-story red brick house. The house was a smaller version of his grandparents' home—minus one story. Mercy led him to the parlor to the left while she went to get him some coffee. Jack pulled off the scarf and laid it on a table as he looked around the opulent surroundings. He never much cared for this room, so he turned around and followed his mother into the kitchen.

"Let's talk in here," he said, pulling out a chair. "Something smells good."

"Let me fix you a bowl," Mercy said, setting a cup of steaming coffee in front of him.

Jack shook his head. "Let's talk first."

Mercy sat in the chair to his right at the corner of the table. "Now tell me what's wrong," she said, folding her hands together in front of her.

Jack wasn't sure where to start, so he blurted out the first thing that came to mind. "My boss told me he knew you before you were married."

"I've never met your boss… are you talking about Mr. Baldwin or someone else?"

"Jarvis Baldwin is the only boss I have, but that's not his real name. He said you ran away from home and ended up… pregnant in Fort Worth."

Mercy sat up straight like something had poked her in the chest. Her expression started off with shock, then she looked… ashamed.

"Who told you this?"

"Is that why you went to Brownwood… to have the baby away from Waco?"

Tears came to his mother's eyes. She seemed to be at a loss for words.

"Oh, dear Lord, then it's true, isn't it," Jack said, feeling sick again.

Mercy nodded slowly. "I never wanted you to know about that. I didn't want my children to learn about my disgraceful past. I'm sorry that you found out about it."

"And Dad married you anyway?"

"I don't know how it happened, but he fell in love with me and never held any of that against me. Your father is the most honorable and unselfish man I know."

"And you never intended to tell me any of this?" Jack said, raising his voice.

"Of course not. Why would I ever want you to know about that part of my past?"

Jack was flabbergasted. "Because of my father—my real father!"

His mother looked confused.

"Jarvis Baldwin told me *he* was my real father—that he was the gambler who abandoned you in Fort Worth."

Mercy stood up so fast, the ladderback chair fell over.

"Eustace!?"

"That's Jarvis's real name?"

The color drained from his mother's face. Jack reached for her when she started to sit down again.

"Wait!" He picked up the chair and got her seated again.

Mercy dropped her face in her hands.

"I deserve to know who my real father was, Momma."

She looked up suddenly. "Oh, sweetheart, Eustace isn't your father."

"But I'm your firstborn."

She shook her head slowly as she reached over and put her hand against his cheek. "I lost my first baby in Brownwood, Jack. The Samuels gave him their last name and buried him in their family plot. Only a handful of people knew he was mine." The tears fell freely down her cheeks. "He was a beautiful little boy, and I didn't think I was going to survive that loss."

Jack took her hand in his and let her cry. He could see that the pain was still deep and raw, even after so many years. "I'm so sorry, Momma." At the same time, he felt such an overwhelming sense of relief, he couldn't help but cry with her. His mother had given him his life back.

"But then you came along, and—"

"And Daddy knew about the first baby?"

Mercy nodded her head. "If he'd been smart, he would've turned tail and run. But he didn't. He even used his first stud horse to repay my debt to my father."

"You owed your father?"

"Eustace didn't tell you about the money?"

Jack shook his head.

"Then you don't need to know any more about it," she said, looking relieved.

"Grandpa Locke took Dad's horse?"

"He gave Redeemer back," said his father, Jimmy, standing in the doorway. "But even if he hadn't, your mother was worth it."

Mercy smiled. "See why I married him?"

Jack stood to shake his father's hand. Then he grabbed him in a bear hug.

"What's this?" said Jimmy. "Didn't we just see you last week? Aren't we going to see you next month? How'd you get here?"

"I rode Lonesome."

"All that way? It's a wonder the old boy didn't keel over."

"I didn't push him."

Jimmy looked at Mercy and back at Jack. "What's wrong?"

Mercy stood again. "Jack's boss is Eustace Ashton; he told Jack *he* was his father."

Jack watched his father's expression go from pleasant to angry, almost dangerous.

"You told him about Brownwood?" he asked Mercy.

Mercy nodded. "He knows everything... well, almost everything."

"That's why you came home?"

Jack nodded. "I had to know the truth."

He put his hands on Jack's shoulders. "You're *my* son, Jack."

"Momma told me."

Jimmy frowned. "I'm sorry that buzzard put you through that." He turned to Mercy. "Can't the man add? He was at least a year off, if not more."

"I'm sure all of those years are a blur to him. He lived in so many different places, and I realized too late he wasn't the type to settle down with just one woman," said Mercy.

"He told me he came back for you in Fort Worth, but Dad had already taken you away."

"I'm so glad your father got to me first. Back then I was stupid and desperate enough to have taken him back."

"What are you going to do now, son?" asked Jimmy.

Jack grinned with relief. "I'm going to marry Kitty."

His mother screamed and grabbed him in a hug again.

"Have you set a date?"

Jack shook his head. "But it'll be soon."

"But that doesn't give me much time to plan."

"It's going to be very small, Mother, just our immediate families down in Galveston so her motther won't have to travel."

His mother looked crestfallen. "How's her mother doing?"

"Much better, but she still has a long recovery ahead of her. How about you planning something here around

Christmas time for the whole family to meet Kitty."

"That's a wonderful idea!"

Jack couldn't help but laugh watching his mother's expression change so quickly. He could see her mind already working.

"Where's Lonesome?" asked his father.

"Out front."

"Let's go take care of him."

"Don't tarry—lunch is ready," said Mercy.

41

J ack led his father out the front door and down the steps to Lonesome, who had eaten all of the grass he could reach around the hitching post.

"He's fat and out of shape," said Jimmy, walking around, looking over the horse. "Do you keep him at the livery?"

"Yeah, I haven't had much time to ride him," said Jimmy, loosening the reins.

They started walking to the barn.

"Hire a kid to ride him several times a week for you if you don't have the time. Or find some acreage where he has room to run around, or both. You took a chance riding him all this way in the shape he's in."

"I realized after a few hours what a stupid thing I did. I just wasn't thinking straight after Jarvis... I can't think of him as Eustace... after he talked to me. Had you ever met him?"

Jimmy shook his head. "I didn't particularly care for your mother back then, but she didn't deserve what that man did to her. And he took the remainder of her father's money with him. He left her just enough to cover the hotel for a couple of nights. That told me a lot about his character, or the lack of it. I'm not sure what I'd do if I were ever to meet him. I'm so sorry we didn't check him out better before you got involved with him."

"He paid for my education and gave me a job. And he financed my campaign. He's not completely evil. He even helped protect a Negro community when speculators were trying to run them off."

"Most people tend to grow up in more ways than one as they get older," he said, then chuckled. "Like me. I was a terror when I was at home. You wouldn't believe some of the things I did that almost got me thrown in jail. I was a drunk and mad at the world."

"You drank?!"

"Back when I was young and stupid. I'm glad you were smarter than that. But your Uncle Justin and Aunt Allie helped get me on the right track." His father opened the barn door wide.

"I heard a few stories from the cousins, but I thought they were exaggerating," Jack said over his shoulder. He led Lonesome to the middle of the barn and started to unsaddle him.

"Well, you're not going to hear any more about it from me. I've put all that behind me." He walked over to a neat stack of hay bales and cut the twine, loosing the bale.

"Those are good-looking bales," said Jack.

"Momma let me get a new baler from Kansas this year, and it packs 'em really tight." He grabbed an armful and carried it into an empty stall."

"I don't miss that job." He walked Lonesome into the stall, and the horse wasted no time burying his head in the hay.

"We could've used you. Most of the young folk leave town as soon as they can; it's mostly us old geezers."

Jack laughed. "What are you, forty?"

"Forty-five, and I'm feeling it," said Jimmy. "How long are you staying?"

"I need to get back fairly soon, but would it be all right if I left Lonesome here until Christmas? I don't know if he can handle that much riding again so soon."

"That's fine; I'll get him back into shape for you. But that means we'll have to be in Waco by mid-morning tomorrow;

otherwise, you'll have to wait until Monday."

"I'll go tomorrow, then. Can I borrow some money for the ticket?"

"You did leave Austin half-cocked, didn't you."

Jack grinned sheepishly.

They walked out of the stall, and Jack latched the gate.

"Well, to be honest, I thought my world had come to an end."

"I'm sorry you had to go through that. What are you going to do when you get back?"

"Resign from the firm, and I'm considering resigning from office, too."

Jimmy looked alarmed. "Why would you go and do that? You just got elected. What Eustace did shouldn't affect your job as Congressman."

Jack took a deep breath. "If I tell you something, will you promise not to tell anyone… even Mother?"

"I'm not sure; does it have something to do with her?"

"No, not at all, but it may affect what she thinks about Kitty."

"You're probably underestimating your mother."

"I don't want to take the chance of losing either of the two most important women in my life."

"All right."

"Jarvis told me that Kitty is a octoroon. Do you know what that is?"

Jimmy nodded. "Does Kitty know this?"

"No, and I don't plan on telling her. Link, Jarvis's partner, dug it up in New Orleans. Kitty knows nothing about her past."

"I thought Kitty was adopted. How would this Link even know where to start searching?"

"The woman that gave birth to Kitty was a prostitute in Galveston. Jarvis knew her well enough for her to mention that she believed her family was from New Orleans. Katherine is the name of the woman who gave birth to Kitty, but she gave her up to let Juju raise her. Juju is Kitty's mother's nickname.

Her real name's Jewel. "

Jimmy nodded.

"Jarvis thinks Kitty's heritage would eventually come out and hurt my career, but I'm more worried about what it would do to Kitty. She's already going against the flow working as a female physician."

"And you aren't going to tell her?"

Jack shook his head. "She could lose everything."

"But that information may never come out."

"Jarvis told me that I would have enemies in this job, and that they'll leave no stone unturned looking for ways to destroy me. If it was just me involved, I could handle that. But I can't take the chance of letting them destroy her, too." He paused for a moment. "And there's something else."

His father waited for him to finish.

"And you can tell Mother this is why I'm resigning, although I don't plan to use it against Jarvis."

"Sounds like you've thought all of this through."

"That's all I did on the back of that horse. I'm just thankful that you're still my father, and I can still marry Kitty."

"Is what I'm going to tell your mother the truth or made up?"

"It's true, unfortunately. I guess you could say I started my campaign on a lie. It seems so clear now, but at the time, it was so confusing, and I thought I was protecting Jarvis…"

His father looked angry again. "What happened?"

"The day I got shot… at first I thought I had fired the shot that killed the man. We were wrestling on the floor—and I finally forced the gun out of his hand, and it went off, or so I thought. And I wasn't sure how that happened because my finger wasn't even on the trigger. For a while, I thought I was the one who'd killed him. But Kitty made me realize that the pistol I was holding couldn't have shot the man, based on where the wound was.

"She told me I needed to to confront Jarvis about it, and when I did, he admitted he had fired the shot to protect me and anyone else in the restaurant. But he also told me that even

270

though it was self-defense, he couldn't take the blame for it because of his past. He confessed to me that Jarvis Baldwin wasn't his real name."

"His real name is Eustace Ashton."

"Ashton? The man he shot called him 'Ashton', but we all thought he mistook Jarvis for someone else." Jack felt sick. "He told me he'd never seen that man before, but he must have known his father. The reason Jarvis changed his name, though, was because of a different situation. He's wanted for murder in Kansas. He said that he was gambling with three men, and one of them pulled a gun on him during the game. He shot the man in self defense, but the other two claimed it was murder. He said he's lived as Jarvis Baldwin ever since."

"It sounds like he left a string of problems behind him as Eustace Ashton. Do you think he's really changed?"

"I did at the time, and he's done so much for me. But now I realize that Jarvis was protecting his true identity by shooting that man in the restaurant as much as he was protecting me."

"Did they ever identify the man that shot you?"

Jack shook his head. "The man stood there and accused Jarvis of destroying his family, and said that his father had hung himself over losing his business. So it's obvious now that Jarvis knew who this man was without ever having seen him because he was a kid when all that happened. How can someone do such awful things and turn around and do good things, too?"

"I think you just described most of mankind. None of us are completely good or completely bad."

"How does God keep up with all that?"

"None of us can get to heaven *or* hell based on our own merits or demerits, thank God, or I wouldn't have a chance. It's not determined by our good outweighing our bad, but rather us saying 'yes' or 'no' to God by accepting what Christ did for us. That's called grace, Jack. Understanding God's grace took a long time for it to sink in to my hard head. For years I thought I had to be really good to make up for all the bad I did."

"But won't people take advantage of God's grace knowing they can still sin as much as they want to and still go to heaven?"

"God changes the heart, son. I still slip and make mistakes; the difference is that I know it ends up hurting me or someone else. And I don't like living with a guilty conscience. Peace of mind has become very important to me, and I think you're telling me the same thing with what you plan to do when you get back to Austin."

"Jarvis used that unfortunate incident to paint me as a hero, and it was enough to help me win the election."

They walked out of the barn, and Jack shut the big door.

"I think you ought to reconsider resigning, Jack. What if you and Kitty move away from Austin? Your legislative job is only a few months out of the year, and you could have a life more outside of the public eye... in a small town, maybe?"

"Like Grace?"

"There are a lot of towns not too far from Austin you could consider. I'm sure most would be happy to have a new doctor in town. And remember, what you know about Ashton may be the only thing keeping him from hurting Kitty."

Jack nodded. He had thought about that.

"I think you could do a lot of good. We need good people to run our government."

"Have you ever considered public office?"

Jimmy shook his head. "I just know horses, but you, on the other hand—"

They both jumped when a loud bell rang from the house. Jack looked at his father.

"I think I'm going to have to break that bell," said Jimmy.

Jack laughed. "That's the one Momma used to call us kids in for dinner."

"Yeah," said Jimmy, as they started towards the house. "Now she uses it whenever she needs me for something... for anything... even just to tell me something that's on her mind."

"I'll break it for you," said Jack, "since I'm not the one living with her."

"I'll dance at your wedding."

"You dance, too?"

"I think I fell in love with your mother at a dance in Brownwood... she had changed so much while she was over there, and I couldn't take my eyes off of her. I wasn't a very good dancer, but she didn't seem to mind. Then some yokels mistook me for a member of John Wesley Hardin's gang and jumped me."

"You were in a fistfight?" Jack stopped at the porch steps.

"I'll tell you about it on the way to Waco in the morning." He looked up and nodded at the well-worn bell mounted to a column. "On second thought, why don't you just make that thing disappear so Momma won't get it fixed."

"Sure thing," said Jack, grinning.

"You know I love your mother."

"Of course, Pa! But hell's bells—"

"Exactly."

42

Jack spotted her immediately in the small crowd as the train pulled to a stop. While others in the passenger car stood and gathered their belongings, including rounding up boisterous small children, he sat there at the window and watched her for a moment. He smiled when he realized she was wearing the same suit and hat as the first time he saw her from Justus's shoe shine stand almost a year ago. So much had happened since then... the shooting, their relationship, Clarksville, his campaign and election... thinking that he had lost her and his father.

He thanked God that he had lost neither of them.

Kitty pulled off her hat and smoothed her hair as she watched the people disembark. She never seemed concerned about the latest fashion. She once told him her clothes had to be comfortable and functional.

Jack realized *he* was more aware of clothing styles than she was, thanks to his mother. He wasn't sure if that was a blessing or a curse. But it didn't seem to hurt Kitty one bit.

She had no idea how beautiful she was.

He stood and followed the people out of the train, and had barely set both feet on the ground when Kitty almost knocked him down greeting him. Her hat fell to the ground, but she didn't seem to care.

"Are your parents all right? Your telegram said so little."

"They're fine," he said, kissing the side of her head.

"Thank the Lord," she said, hugging him again. "When Patrick told me you'd taken Lonesome and gone home, I thought I'd lost you somehow."

"I'm so sorry I worried you. Come on—I'll explain everything."

"Don't you need to get your bag?"

"I took off with only the clothes on my back. My father loaned me this coat."

He picked up her hat and took her by the hand, walking her away from the train and into an alcove, out of sight of the other people milling about the platform.

Kitty started to speak, but he cut her off by kissing her mouth.

When he finally came up for air, he said, "I don't mean to be so forward with you out here in public, but that's all I could think about on the way home."

"When you say 'home', do you mean here or Grace?"

Jack smiled. "I mean anywhere you are."

This time Kitty pulled his head down to kiss him.

"Your hands are so cold," Jack said, taking her hands in his. "How long have you been out here?"

"Maybe an hour?"

"Let's go somewhere warm so we can talk. I have a lot to tell you." They walked to the corner and turned north.

"The Driskill?" suggested Kitty.

Jack shook his head. "No, I don't want to chance running into Jarvis." Before she could ask him why, Jack told her his mother was going to plan a party for them around Christmas, when the whole family was there. He asked her how everything was going in Clarksville, and Kitty told him about the baby Hokee had abandoned on Liberty's porch.

About two blocks from the railroad station, they stepped into a small café and sat at a table away from the drafty door. Jack ordered coffee for them and decided to order some biscuits and meat gravy.

"Do you want anything to eat?" he asked Kitty.

She declined. "I can wait until supper."

"I know it's early, but I haven't had anything since breakfast."

He began telling her what Jarvis told him on Thursday that prompted him to leave town so abruptly.

"He told you we could be brother and sister?"

Jack waited until the woman delivering his food walked away. Kitty grabbed a biscuit and started chewing… angrily, Jack thought.

"What he told me fit what Grace had told me about my mother going to Brownwood under suspicious circumstances. Then Katherine said Jarvis could be your father for all she knew." Jack noticed Kitty shudder at the thought. "I just knew I had to talk to my mother to find out if it all was true. And it wasn't. I'm a Taylor through and through." Jack didn't feel the need to share his mother's secret tragedy. "But what I did wasn't very smart—me jumping on Lonesome and heading back to Grace without even thinking about what I was doing. It was a hard trip for both of us."

"Where *is* Lonesome? Is he all right?"

"He's fine, just really wore out. I left him with my father. He'll get him in shape, then I'll bring him home after Christmas."

"What do you plan to do about Jarvis?"

"I'm going to turn in my resignation and look for a job elsewhere. I'd just as soon never see his face again."

"He could hurt you."

Jack nodded. "But I know some things about him that he wouldn't want known, so I'm hoping that'll be enough to keep him quiet and out of our lives."

"In your business, you can't help but run into him."

Jack nodded. "That's why I'm thinking about moving away from Austin. I wanted to talk to you about that."

"How can you work as a legislator living away from Austin?"

"It's not a fulltime job; we wouldn't have to move far away."

Kitty was silent.

"I was considering resigning since I took responsibility for that shooting when it was actually Jarvis that did it. He used that to get me elected—painting me as some kind of hero, and I felt obligated to protect him. But I feel bad about that."

"You can't resign," said Kitty. "But what about my job… what about Clarksville?"

"I know I'm asking a lot, but it would make our lives so much easier not being so… visible here."

"Are you saying this because of Katherine?"

That hadn't even entered Jack's head, but it did provide a good reason without him having to explain that he was trying to protect her.

"Don't you want a relationship with her?" Kitty asked.

"I already have a relationship with her."

"Wouldn't you want her to visit?"

He could see that Kitty was torn. "Of course I would." Nix that plan. He decided to put the reason for moving back on Jarvis. "I want to avoid Jarvis as much as possible. But I'll only look at the towns that have train service to Austin, so you can continue to go to Clarksville twice a month if you want. As for your job, I'm sure any community would welcome a doctor."

"Do you know how much it would cost to set up my own practice?"

"No." He waited for her to tell him.

"Me neither… but I imagine it would be a substantial amount of money. Dr. Gilbert is already established here. He runs everything—there's so much more to it that I don't even know about—where he gets his medical supplies, and what about the cost of equipment, furniture… an office… an assistant? It's almost overwhelming to think about."

"Maybe you can work under another doctor."

"I think most feel threatened to hire a woman physician. Dr. Gilbert is the exception, not the rule when it comes to male doctors accepting female doctors."

Jack reached for her hand… it still felt cold.

"I know I've given you a lot to think about, and I don't want to do anything that you're not in agreement with. I'm sorry this is going to complicate your life, but I honestly think this would be the best path for us to take."

She glanced at his plate. "Your food is getting cold." She didn't look happy.

Jack took another bite… then another. He finished the plate in silence.

"We don't have to decide anything now. Just think about what I said, all right?"

Kitty nodded, but she looked… worried.

Kitty let Louis help her into the carriage, proud of the fact that the boy had learned some manners.

"Thank you, Louis," she said. She stifled a yawn as she watched him walk around the front of the horse and climb up beside her on the upholstered seat. He flicked the reins to start the horse forward, heading back to Austin after a long afternoon in Clarksville.

"I think you've grown a foot this past year," she commented, noticing she had to look up to him now sitting beside him.

Louis beamed. "Yes, ma'am, well, not a foot, but Momma fusses that she can't keep me in pants anymore."

She smiled, noticing the deeper voice.

Louis was growing up.

"Y'all looked busy today."

"Lots of runny noses and coughs. It's that time of year."

"Marcus told me something about that mean man."

"Hokee?"

"Yeah, I never can remember that name—I never heard a name like that before."

"I think it's an Indian name."

"A Negro has an Indian name?"

"His parents were slaves to some Indians in Oklahoma. I'm sure they spoke the language."

"Indians had slaves?"

"I guess every culture has its shameful practices. Anyway, what did Marcus have to say about Hokee?"

"He knows were he is."

Kitty turned sharply. "He knows where Hokee is… right now?"

Louis nodded. "They're over in east Austin. His daddy saw him working at the freight yards. He tried to talk to him about the baby, but Hokee wouldn't give him the time of day."

"Did he find out where he lived?"

"I dunno. Marcus didn't tell me that."

"Do you think you could find out where he lives?"

Louis snorted. "I ain't going over there by myself."

"Would Marcus go with you? I'd pay y'all to find out where he lives. You'd have to be discreet, though. We wouldn't want to scare him off."

"I'll ask Marcus next time I see him."

* * *

Kitty walked to the back room of Dr. Gilbert's offices to retrieve her coat. Otherwise, she never would've heard the light rapping on the back door. It had been a long day, but it was Friday, and she looked forward to catching up on her rest the following day… unless she had a house call. Seems like she'd had a number of after hours house calls lately.

Kitty unlocked the door and opened it. No one was there. She stepped out into the alley, and caught a movement in the corner of her eye to the left. A girl was walking away.

"Winnie?!"

The girl turned around and just stood there.

Kitty started walking towards her. Winnie began to cry, covering her eyes with her hands.

Kitty rushed over to her. "Aw, honey." She wrapped her arms around the girl's scrawny frame and let her cry it out.

"I miss him, Miss Doc," she finally was able to say.

"I know." Kitty could feel the girls shoulder blades through the threadbare clothes.

"Is he still with Mrs. Alexander?"

"Yes."

"That's good," she said with a shudder. "I know he'll be all right if he's with her."

"Why don't you come inside where it's warmer?"

Winnie shook her head. "I gotta go home."

"Where do you live?"

"I can't tell you."

"Do you want me to come talk to your father?"

Winnie shook her head again.

"Well, I want to send something home with you." Kitty walked her back to the office. "This won't take long." She pulled Winnie into the back room.

Kitty rummaged through several boxes, half-filling a tow sack with potatoes and onions. She handed it to Winnie.

"Daddy says we don't accept charity."

"You'd be doing us a favor. People have been paying us with food, and we have more potatoes and onions than we could possibly eat."

Winnie looked longingly at the sack, but then shook her head. "Daddy'll be mad at me."

"What if you worked for it? I really need some help here."

Winnie's eyes brightened. "I could do that."

She handed Winnie a broom and asked her to sweep the front hall and waiting room. "I'll work here at my desk while you sweep; it won't take but a few minutes, and you can tell your father you earned it."

While the girl swept, Kitty followed her around, telling her how to make potato soup and fried potatoes and onions.

After Winnie finished, Kitty handed her the sack. "You can tell him you helped clean *Mr.* Gilbert's office downtown."

Winnie beamed. "Yes, ma'am."

"Come back on Tuesday, and you can dust for me, all right?"

"Yes, ma'am."

Kitty walked her to the back door and watched her run down the alley. Winnie turned to wave before disappearing around the corner of the building. Kitty hoped their regular custodian, Mr. Parker, wouldn't notice the little bit of cleaning Winnie had done when he came in the next morning.

The following Tuesday, Winnie showed up at closing time again, and Kitty let her dust around several of the rooms. This time, Winnie took home a loaf of bread with the potatoes and onions. She also asked Kitty if she could go with her to Clarksville on Thursday so she could see her baby.

Kitty wasn't sure that was the best idea, but when Winnie told her she knew she couldn't keep the baby, she allowed her to come.

Kitty walked in the room the church let them use for the clinic. Liberty sat there holding Seth, but her eyes widened when she saw Winnie. She looked sharply at Kitty.

"She just wants to see him."

Winnie walked up to her, never taking her eyes off the baby. "Miss Doc said I could watch him while y'all worked."

Liberty acted like she wasn't willing to hand him over at first, then relented.

Kitty realized baby Seth wasn't going to be raised in another home.

Liberty leaned down and kissed the baby's forehead. "He's a good boy, Winnie. Won't be any trouble to you." She gently handed him over to her.

The young girl began to sway. "How's my little man?" she said in a soft voice. "He looks so... happy, Miz Alexander." Winnie looked up at Liberty. "He looks real happy."

Liberty's face softened. "We're taking real good care of him Winnie. Don't you worry none about him."

"I ain't worried... not when he's with you... and Marcus."

Kitty opened her mouth to say something, and Liberty shook her head.

"Let's go get you two settled in the next room so Miss Doc and I can get to work." Liberty took her to the room across the hall. When she came back, Kitty apologized for springing that surprise on her.

"I thought you'd gone off your rocker bringing that girl back here," Liberty whispered. "Then I thought she'd come to take him back, and that didn't set too well with me."

"I noticed that. Why didn't you straighten her out about Marcus?"

Liberty seemed at a loss for words.

"You want to keep him, don't you."

"Well... if it makes her feel better in her own mind that Seth is with family, then she might not take him back," said Liberty, quietly. "He wouldn't stand a chance in that house."

"Winnie just wanted to see him... to make sure he was all right. She knows he's better off here."

"Does Hokee know she's here?"

Kitty shook her head.

"You're opening up a big can of worms there. Where'd you find her?"

"She found me at the office. They're living on the east side of Austin somewhere. I'm letting her do a little cleaning so she can take food home. Winnie looked like she hadn't had a decent meal lately."

"Does Hokee know she's working for you?"

Kitty sidestepped that question. "Why don't you go bring our first patient in."

She could hear Liberty mumbling all the way down the hall.

44

Jack watched the gray landscape pass by as the train headed east. Field after field lay fallow, ready for the next crop of what he learned earlier was cotton. He felt the train slowing down. The whistle blew, heralding its arrival to the third town he would visit today before heading back to Austin in the morning. He had already taken a look at Round Rock and Hutto.

He couldn't help but smile when he saw the name of the town: Taylor. He wondered if it was a sign. His grandfather first named the small town he founded west of Waco, 'Taylor', but changed it to Grace after he brought his wife and son home after several years of captivity with the Apaches. Jack learned when he was older that his blood grandfather was the Apache who had kidnapped his grandmother and his uncle Justin, who was only a young boy at the time. Jack's father Jimmy was the son of Nantan Lupan, who was killed during the rescue.

Jack's grandfather Taylor raised Jimmy as his own, but Jack learned that those were very difficult years for the whole family because of Jimmy's heritage. His thoughts drifted to Kitty, and how difficult it would be for her if her heritage was known.

At each train station he stopped that day, he learned a little bit about the community. Round Rock was named for a large round rock in the middle of Brushy Creek where wagons crossed. The town seemed to be most proud of the fact the notorious train robber Sam Bass was killed downtown in a shoot-out with two Texas Rangers several decades before. Jack declined an invitation to go see the outlaw's headstone.

As for Hutto, it was a fairly young town like Taylor; both built up when the railroad came through.

Jack stood and stretched, and made his way to the front of the train car to disembark. He would catch the next train back to Austin in the morning. This would give him some time to explore the community and gauge if it would be a good place to set up his own law practice.

He walked into the impressive International & Great Northern train station, and walked around for a moment before stepping up to a short line at the ticket window. In just a few minutes, he started to greet the clerk, but was interupted by a loud whistle.

"Was that the train you wanted?" the man yelled over the whistle. "If it is, you're too late."

Jack shook his head and waved his hand. "I just got off that train."

The man smiled. "Then what can I do for you?"

"I need a ticket back to Austin in the morning, and some information."

"Early or late morning?"

"I'll take the later one. That'll give me enough time to look around. Could you recommend a good hotel?" Jack said as he paid for his ticket.

The man pointed north with his thumb. "Right across the street's the LaGrande."

"One more thing. What do you think of your community?"

The man raised his eyebrows. "Are you a reporter?"

Jack laughed. "No, I'm just looking for a new hometown."

"Oh! Well, welcome! You won't find a more up and coming town than Taylor. Cotton and cattle have brought in a lot of money, and our businesses are thriving. Mansions are going up as we speak. Big things are happening in Taylor. You won't regret moving here, sir."

Someone walked up behind Jack, so he thanked the clerk and stepped away from the window. He exited the station on the north side and walked across the street to the LaGrande Hotel to get a room.

The hotel proprietor reiterated that cotton and cattle were the big money makers around here, and Taylor was one of the biggest shipping points for both in Central Texas. A fire back in 1879 had destroyed most of the businesses in the downtown area, but even more substantial buildings were erected in their place. Two railroad lines connected Taylor, and both were serviced by local machine shops and a roundhouse.

He decided to take a walking tour of the downtown area before supper, and he liked what he saw. He noticed the prominent structures were brick or stone, and most were two and three stories high. Two national banks sat caddy-cornered from each other across a wide intersection. One's first floor was made of rough red stone, and the second and third stories were made of smooth red bricks. The other bank was gray stone with large leaded glass windows.

Plans were underway to build an impressive city hall on the town square. Taylor boasted of two newspapers, several grocery stores, a furniture store and more.

He met Dr. Mack Joseph, who had recently taken over his late father's practice. Jack told him his fiance was a doctor, too, and would be looking for work if they moved to Taylor. Jack was pleased when Dr. Joseph expressed an interest in meeting Kitty. Jack felt sure he could establish a successful law practice here, too.

Dr. Joseph even knew about a house for sale a few blocks away. He enlisted his neighbor Mr. Kyle to take Jack over to show it to him. As they walked along, Jack noticed a number of stately homes lining the streets and asked him what made Taylor such a prosperous town.

"The two railroads coming through gave it a big boost, and it's a hub for shipping cotton and cattle. You probably saw many of the successful businesses and banks downtown." Mr. Kyle looked for a response, so Jack nodded.

"They built these houses," he continued. "What do you do?"

Jack told him he was a lawyer by trade, and that he was just elected as a state representative.

The man raised his eyebrows. "A lawyer *and* a politician?"

Jack waited for the barb, but the man just grinned.

"I guess we need those, too."

They stopped in front of a waist-high wrought iron fence surrounding a gabled, two-story home. An ornate porch wrapped around two sides of the house. Painted shutters adorned the sides of each window along the front.

"This is it," said Mr. Kyle. "Do you think it's too big for you?"

Jack liked what he saw. "It's not too big at all, because I'll have a wife by the time I move to Taylor."

"Well, congratulations!" The man grasped his hand and pumped it.

Jack started to open the gate. "Can I see the inside?"

"Oh, right. Let me go get the key—it's right across the street here at our former mayor's house."

Jack watched him walk quickly to a similar two-story house across the street and looked at the house again.

A baseball bounced off the fence next to him.

Jack leaned over and picked it up. He turned around to see a young boy racing toward him. Behind him on a bare lot, several other young boys waited to resume their game.

"Sorry!" the red-haired boy said. He looked like he was expecting trouble.

"Hello," said Jack.

The boy grinned and said hello back.

"You live around here?"

The boy nodded and turned, pointing to the house where Mr. Kyle stood on the porch.

"So you just might be my neighbor. I'm Jack Taylor." He offered his hand, and the boy stepped forward and shook it firmly. Then he retreated a few steps, like he still didn't quite trust him.

"You have the same name as our town," the boy said. His blue eyes stood out under the shock of red hair.

"Yes, but it wasn't named after my family." Jack glanced at the boy's house. By this time Mr. Kyle was talking and pointing his way. "So your father used to be mayor of Taylor?"

"Yes, sir."

"I'd like to meet him."

"He'll be home later."

"What does your father do?"

"We have a dairy behind the house, and he sells insurance, so if you need any milk or insurance…"

Jack laughed. "You're a pretty good salesman yourself." He noticed the boy eyeing his ball. He guessed he'd interrogated him long enough, so he pitched it back to him.

"Thanks!" he said, turning to rejoin his buddies.

"How old are you?"

"Nine."

"And do you have a name?"

The boy snickered and answered, "Yes, sir. Daniel Moody, but everybody calls me Dan."

"Well, Dan, we might be good friends in the near future."

The boy grinned, and then jogged away.

Mr. Kyle came hurrying back with the key and escorted Jack inside. He walked him through every room, but Jack knew after only a few steps inside the house, that this was the home for him and Kitty. It felt… right.

When Jack asked Mr. Kyle who he needed to talk to about buying the house, the man said, "That'd be Dr. Joseph. It's his grandmother's house."

Jack chuckled. "I think I was waylaid back there."

"Oh, no, sir. This house has been empty for some time, and Dr. Joseph has had plenty of offers on it, but he turned 'em down. I figure he's been waiting for the right people for it."

Jack couldn't help but smile.

That night at the hotel when his head touched the pillow, he had a good feeling about this town. He decided he could take the early train back to Austin because he was already convinced this was the place for Kitty and him to make their first home.

Hopefully, she would agree.

45

Kitty glanced at the clock on the wall. Winnie should have arrived by now. She grabbed a wrap to step out the back of the office into the alley. A norther had blown in several hours before, and Kitty hadn't allowed for it. She pulled the cloth over her head and held it tight to keep it from blowing off as she started walking east, the direction Winnie would be coming from. Kitty hoped the girl was dressed warmly enough to be out in this weather.

A muffled scream rose over the wind.

Winnie? Kitty picked up her skirt and hurried down the alley. A door slammed to her right, so she ran over and tried the knob. She was surprised that it was unlocked. Most of the businesses had closed by this time. The wind caught the door and slammed it back against the wall. She left it open as she stepped into the dimly lit room. She could see rows of shelves filled with stacks of... clothing, perhaps? This must be the back of Jackson's store. She could hear crying from somewhere beyond, so she started going row to row looking down the aisles.

"Winnie!?" she called out. What would the girl be doing in the back of this store? Surely she remembered where Dr. Gilbert's office was. "Winnie, what are you doing in here?"

Dead silence answered.

"I know you're in here, honey. You're in the wrong place."

She walked to the last aisle of the room and looked to the left. A single dim bulb hung from the ceiling. Her heart jumped to her throat when she saw a man standing there holding Winnie with his hand across her mouth. Her eyes were wide and red from crying.

"Winnie?" The word sounded more like a gasp.

"Get out of here," the man said. "This ain't none of your business."

"This is absolutely my business," she said. "Who do you think you are? Get your filthy hands off of her."

"Or what?"

"Or you're going to regret it." Kitty said, having no idea how she was going to make him regret it.

"Why don't *you* leave before you regret it," he said, backing into the shadows and pulling Winnie with him.

Kitty started walking towards him. "I know the marshal, and he doesn't take kindly to men putting their hands on young girls."

The man reached the end of the aisle, then shoved Winnie towards Kitty. The last thing she saw was him pulling the heavy shelves over. All she had time to do was push Winnie down beneath her.

Winnie screamed as Kitty felt the blow of the heavy shelves hit her back and head, but some crates stacked against the wall kept the wood shelves from completely crushing them.

Kitty felt like she was drowning in clothes, and couldn't seem to move. Winnie was pinned beneath her, whimpering. Kitty could hear shouts and more banging around before she laid her head against a pile of stiff men's pants and shut her eyes.

* * *

Kitty felt the cold wind hit her face, startling her.

"Cover her up," a stern voice whispered.

She turned her head, and the world was upside down before something covered her face. She could hear Winnie crying.

"Winnie?" She wasn't sure if she just thought that or if she said it out loud.

She could feel herself trembling. It felt so cold.

Then it was warm.

The floor was hard, but she felt something soft slipped beneath her head. She turned toward the warmth and shut her eyes again.

Someone helped her up off the floor. Once she was upright, she leaned over and vomited, which she correctly identified as stomach bile. That's what you throw up when you haven't had supper, she correctly deduced. *Who said a woman couldn't be a doctor?* she thought proudly before crumbling to a heap.

That wasn't right. She was the doctor here. Doctors don't sit on the floor.

Then she was sitting in the chair. How did that happen?

Dr. Gilbert's face appeared before her.

"Dr. Gilbert?"

He looked very concerned. "What happened, Dr. Synatzske?"

Kitty reached up to touch his face to make sure he was actually there. Why did that take such an effort?

"A girl came to my house and told me you were hurt. Did you fall?" He began to feel around her head. "What are you doing here so late?"

Kitty tried to remember. "Ow!" she said, pulling away from his touch.

"You have a pretty good goose egg back here," his voice spoke from behind her. "How did you do that?"

"The pants fell on me," she said.

Dr. Gilbert walked around to face her. Then he looked around the room.

"Did you lose something?" she asked.

He smiled and shook his head. "No, but I think I need to keep an eye on you for a little while. Do you know who that girl was?"

"What girl?"

"The Negro girl who told me you were hurt."

"Winnie!" Kitty tried to stand, but the room started spinning. She felt afraid for Winnie, for some reason. "Where's Winnie?"

"I don't know; she didn't come back with me. How did she know you were hurt?"

"I let her clean a little bit around here so her daddy wouldn't get mad at her for bringing food home."

"Why would he get mad about that?"

"He's a proud, angry man, and doesn't want any charity, he told me."

"Did he hurt you?"

"No, and I'm not afraid of him." She looked at her still wrapped wrist. "He didn't mean to hurt me. He just didn't want me in his house and pushed me off his porch. Did I tell you he's a proud man and doesn't want any charity?"

"Yes, you did. What's his name?"

"Hokee."

"Hokee?"

"That's Winnie's father."

"Where does he live?"

"Somewhere in… East Austin. Louis might know. He said Hokee worked at the…" the words failed her, "some place." Kitty thought about her last year in school when for an entire year she couldn't remember the word… and she couldn't remember it again.

"I'll be right back." Dr. Gilbert left the room.

Kitty walked her mind back, trying to remember that word… it was a new fangled contraption her mother was so proud of…she used it with a broom…

Kitty could hear Dr. Gilbert talking. Who else was here? She wanted to go to sleep. There were two patient beds in the middle room. She stood slowly and held onto the wall until she made it to the room down the hall. She didn't bother turning on the light; that seemed too much of an effort. She crawled in the first bed and pulled a folded cover over her shoulders. She began trembling like she was afraid, but she couldn't remember why.

"Dustpan," she said aloud, before she went to sleep again. "The word was dustpan."

46

Kitty opened her eyes when she heard voices again. She recognized Dr. Gilbert's voice and... that's all.

"We got him," said a vaguely familiar voice. "He put up a good fight, and Ben got the worst of it, but the man's in jail."

"That's a pretty good shiner, Ben," said Dr. Gilbert. "Why don't you let me take a look at it."

"I'm fine," Ben insisted. "But I don't think he's gonna be for very long with what he did to Dr. Synatzske."

Kitty breathed a sigh of relief when she realized Dr. Gilbert was talking to Marshal Davis and his deputy Ben. She had never felt unsafe on the streets of Austin before last night. Surely that man wasn't from Austin. She remembered the strong smell of alcohol in that back room. Poor Winnie must've been scared out of her mind.

Winnie! She needed to check on Winnie.

She sat up too quickly and grabbed her head.

"I will not throw up, I will not throw up," she said under her breath until the nausea subsided. She reached for the iron footboard to help her up. A stabbing pain shot through her shoulder, and she couldn't help but cry out as she sat back down.

Dr. Gilbert appeared in the doorway and turned on the light.

"You're awake!"

Kitty nodded. "What time is it?"

"Getting close to noon."

Kitty was shocked. "I've been asleep all this time?"

"We've had several conversations during the night."

"We did? I've been here all night?!"

Dr. Gilbert nodded. "With good reason. How are you feeling?"

"Like I've been kicked by a mule. What about the patients?"

"I put the closed sign up and sent Mrs. Leigh home. We'll open later, but this takes precedence."

Kitty felt badly that the doctor had closed his practice, but she was relieved that somebody was pursuing that man. Her head still felt sore, and she gingerly touched the back of her head. She noticed her bun was gone; her mussed hair draped down her back. She felt self-conscious about it when Marshal Davis and his deputy stepped into the room. They removed their hats.

Dr. Gilbert continued. "He must've broken your hair clasp when he hit you."

"He didn't hit me. He pulled the shelves over on us."

"What shelves?"

"At Jackson's Emporium down the alley."

Dr. Gilbert looked at the marshal.

"Harold reported a break-in this morning, but he couldn't tell that anything was taken. One of the shelves in the back was pushed over." The marshal turned to Kitty. "You're saying you were attacked there?"

"Winnie was."

"Who's Winnie?"

"A young girl I've been trying to help. I asked her to come do a little work around the office… after hours," she assured Dr. Gilbert, "so she could take some food home. A lot of people pay us with food, so we usually have plenty on hand. Winnie's father is very proud and doesn't want to take charity, but they desperately need help—especially his daughters…"

"How did you end up in the back of Jackson's store?" asked Dr. Gilbert.

"Well, this man accosted Winnie in the alley and dragged her in there…"

"He found out what you and Winnie were doing behind his back?"

Kitty was confused. "No, I assume he spotted Winnie and decided he would take advantage of her." She looked at the marshal. "I heard you say you had him in jail."

The marshal nodded, "Yes, ma'am, but…"

"Thank God. I'd never seen him before, so I assume he's not from here?"

"But you told me Hokee hurt you," said Dr. Gilbert.

Kitty's eyes widened. "I did? Why would I say that?"

"And you told me the pants fell on you, but it didn't make any sense until Frank just now mentioned what happened in Jackson's store, so I'm assuming that shelf there fell on you."

"Yes, after I confronted that man about his shameful intentions towards Winnie, he pushed her towards me and pulled the shelves over on us."

"You're saying Hokee did that?"

"No, some man I'd never seen before. I think he was drunk."

"You told me Hokee was an angry man and that you didn't want him to find out you were helping Winnie."

Kitty tried to remember what she said. *Dustpan* immediately came to mind. She shook the word out of her head in frustration.

"I didn't even see Hokee last night. Did you put *him* in jail?" she asked the marshal.

Dr. Gilbert answered for him. "The marshal only did what he thought was right based on what I told him, and that's all I could gather from what you told me. I thought Hokee found you and Winnie here at the office and that he attacked you here. If it happened at Jackson's, then how did you get here? And how did Winnie even know where to find me?"

"I don't know." Kitty was close to tears. "Are you telling

me you put Hokee in jail because of what I said? I don't even remember what I said, but Hokee didn't pull those shelves over on us." She put her hand on her mouth. "What have I done?"

"We'll get this straightened out," said Marshal Davis.

Someone hollered from the front of the office.

Ben stepped into the hall. "Back here!" he yelled.

The marshal and Dr. Gilbert stepped into the hall.

Kitty recognized Justus's voice, telling them they needed to come quick, that a crowd had gathered at the jail.

"They're angry, Marshal. I seen this kinda crowd before, and I'm afraid somethin' bad's fixin' to happen."

"No!" Kitty cried, standing. She heard the men heading down the hall.

"Wait!" she yelled at the top of her voice as she staggered to the door and out into the hall. "Wait!"

Dr. Gilbert turned and told her to stay there. When she started to argue, he told her that her presence could make the situation worse instead of better.

Kitty couldn't help but wail at the thought an innocent man might come to harm because of something she couldn't even remember saying.

"Justus, stay with her. It may not be safe for you on the streets either."

"Yes, sir."

The doctor ran to catch up with the marshal.

The weight of what Kitty had done settle on her shoulders. She slid down the wall onto the floor and buried her face in her hands.

"He don't deserve to live for hurting you, Miss Doc."

She looked up at the older man, "But he didn't hurt me, Justus. A stranger attacked Winnie in the alley, not Hokee," she cried. "We have to stop them."

Justus stiffly lowered himself to the floor beside her. He pointed at her wrist. "I know he did that. Berty told me."

"He just wanted me out of his house, and I tripped on that stupid broken step." She looked at him. "You said you've seen crowds like that before.... Were you talking about a lynching?"

Justus looked torn, but he finally nodded his head.

"Oh, dear Lord." She cried again. "I won't be able to live with myself if something happens to him, Justus."

"The marshal'll set 'em straight."

"What if he's too late?" The tears continued to stream down her face.

"Well, why don't we put it in God's hands?"

Kitty nodded and shut her eyes. "Lord, please let the truth come out and the right man be brought to justice. And please protect Hokee. You know he's innocent and doesn't deserve this. I ask this in Jesus's name." Kitty opened her eyes and whispered, "Please don't let it be too late for Hokee."

"Amen," said Justus. He reached over to pat her hand, but withdrew it before touching her. "You're probably the only one who cares, child. People have tried for years to help that man, and he just spits in their faces. I think somethin' inside a him is broke."

"But he's not beyond the grace of God, Justus. Why haven't I been praying for *him* all along, instead of just worrying about his daughters?" Kitty sat up and wiped her eyes. "I think it was Hokee that brought me here last night. He must've followed Winnie and found us. And he had to have been the one to find out where Dr. Gilbert lived and sent Winnie to fetch him. She wouldn't have the presence of mind to figure that on her own with what she just went through. If Hokee didn't care, he wouldn't have come looking for his daughter, and he'd have just left me there in the back of Franklin's store."

"Franklin's store?"

"Some man grabbed Winnie in the alley and pulled her into the back of the store. I'd gone looking for her and heard her crying."

"Well, that's an entirely different story than what's on the streets. People are saying you'd been..." he didn't finish, looking uncomfortable. "You don't know who he was?"

Kitty shook her head. "I'd never seen him before, and I never thought about it being dangerous for Winnie to come here by herself. He must've followed her into the alley."

"Some people think they can take liberties with us without any fear of the law stoppin' 'em. What happened to Winnie ain't nothin' new."

"It shouldn't be that way." She put her hand on the wall and stood up, and helped the old man stand. "You haven't seen Jack around this morning, have you?"

"No, ma'am."

"He's looking for us a place to live after we're married."

"You're getting married?" The old man's face lit up. "That's fine news!"

"I need to find him."

"Dr. Gilbert said for you to stay here. Seeing you might be all it would take for a mob to get out of control."

Kitty took a resigned breath. "Then do you think you could find him for me?"

"Yes, ma'am. I'll go to his house and see if he's home." Justus turned and started toward the front of the building.

"Justus? If there was a hanging, where would it happen?"

"I dunno, but the trusses on the Congress Street bridge are plenty high enough."

"Find Jack, Justus; he'll make this right."

Justus nodded at her before hurrying out the door.

47

J ack stepped off the train, anxious to see Kitty and tell her about the town where they would settle down. Of course, he reminded himself that their new hometown would have to meet her approval, but he figured she would agree, especially since he had a potential job lined up for her.

He headed toward his house to clean up and put on a clean shirt before he saw Kitty. But after walking a short distance, he realized something was happening in town— clusters of people gathered, and others were walking north. By the looks on people's faces, whatever was going on, it wasn't good.

He stepped into the little café he and Kitty had recently visited following his last train trip and asked the proprietor what had happened since he left town the day before.

He learned that a white woman had been raped by a black man, and that there was talk of a hanging.

"Without a trial?"

"That's what I heard, and I think it's happening soon."

"Where?"

"The only trees tall enough for a hanging are along the river or around the Capitol."

"It looked like some people were heading north."

"Then it'll probably take place on the Capitol grounds."

"Oh, dear Lord," Jack said under his breath. "We're more civilized than that, aren't we? Do you know any specifics about the attack?"

"They said the woman was a lady docter."

Jack's heart stopped. "What?"

"That's all I heard."

But Jack had already hit the door running. After two blocks, he turned right and headed for the livery. He'd forgotten Lonesome Joe wasn't there, but Patrick said he could use his horse, Calibre Zane. He felt he had to explain that his granddaughter had named the horse.

"What's going on?" Patrick asked, letting the horse nuzzle his hand while Jack put the bridle on her.

"A lynch mob is gathering."

"Why?"

"I'm not sure, but I'll find out." His stomach lurched at the thought of what may have happened to Kitty. Jack grabbed hold of the horse's mane and mounted her bareback.

"Don't you want me to saddle her?"

"No time," he said. "Wait, do you have a pistol I could use?"

Patrick nodded his head and hurried to retrieve it.

"It's old, but it works, and the chambers are loaded," he said, handing it to him.

"Thanks," said Jack, slipping it into his coat pocket.

"Be careful, Jack."

Jack nodded, walking the horse out of the barn, hoping she'd been ridden lately. Lonesome used to try to pitch him off if he hadn't been ridden in a while. But Calibre Zane seemed gentle enough.

His emotions ran the gamut from anger to sorrow and guilt for not being here. His mind told him to calm down, that it may not be true.

He nudged the horse to a trot, and by the time he reached Brazos Street, he was loping her, and thankful she had a smooth gait or he'd be in the dirt. He hadn't ridden bareback in years. He turned west on 6th Street.

"Jack!" a voice called out.

He turned to see Justus running towards him.

"Where is she?" he yelled back. His voice sounded strangely desperate to his own ears.

"She's fine! She's fine, Jack! The rumors aren't true."

"What is going on around here? I leave town for only a day, and all hell breaks loose! Where is she?"

"At the office, but—"

Jack slid off the horse and ran towards the office. Before he reached the door, Kitty pushed it open and flew into his arms.

Jack held her at arm's length, looking her over. "What happened? Are you all right?"

"I'm fine, but they're going to hang Hokee if the marshal doesn't get there in time."

"Hokee?"

"It'll take too long to explain," Kitty said, looking beyond Jack. "Can you please go stop them?"

"How can I stop anything if I don't know what happened?"

Justus walked up leading the horse.

"I'll explain what happened on the way to the bridge," said Kitty.

"The bridge?"

"Justus thinks that's where they'll try to hang him."

"Someone told me they thought it would happen at the Capitol."

Jack mounted Calibre and pulled Kitty up behind him and turned the horse east and then turned the mare south on Congress Avenue. She told Jack what had happened to her and Winnie at Franklin's Store, and that Hokee had been blamed. By mid-morning, the rumors were that she had been attacked by a Negro, and people were taking matters into their own hands.

"When did the Marshal leave the office?" Jack asked over his shoulder.

"About ten minutes ago."

Jack saw a large crowd gathered at the bridge.

"Hold on," he told her as he kicked Calibre into a lope.

He could see Hokee standing in the back of a wagon with a noose around his neck. The marshal shouted above the din as Ben climbed on the wagon to get Hokee down.

Jack slowed the horse to a walk at the back of the crowd. "Ben's getting him down. The marshal stopped them."

He could feel Kitty press her forehead to his back. "Thank You, Lord."

A gunshot suddenly split the air, and Jack was horrified to see the horse jerk the wagon forward. The deputy fell off the back of the wagon, and with no one in the wagon seat the horse shot forward across the bridge, leaving Hokee swinging. The screams of the crowd framed the nightmare taking place before them.

Jack heard a scream of despair from Kitty as he roughly maneuvered Calibre through the crowd, yelling at people to get out of his way.

48

Kitty buried her face in the back of Jack's coat, trying to erase the image in her mind of Hokee hanging from the bridge. When Jack started the horse foward, she slipped off the back and started to run away... to get anywhere but this place of horror.

Her sobs caught in her throat when she saw Winnie and Dinah clinging to each other and wailing. Kitty ran over to them and gathered them to herself, turning and shielding them from the sight of their father swinging from the bridge rafter.

They all cried loudly, until they were the only sounds in the area. When Kitty looked up, the body was already taken down. A number of people in the back of the mob turned and stared at them. Everything was eerily quiet, and people started to leave until a familiar voice shouted for them to stop.

Jack.

She couldn't see him, but she knew his voice, and he sounded angry.

"We need to get out of here," she said to the girls, still sobbing. "I don't know what's going to happen next."

"What... about... Daddy?" Winnie asked between uncontrollable gasps.

"Mr. Taylor and Dr. Gilbert will take care of your father," said Kitty. The knife in her heart twisted with the knowledge that her words made these girls orphans. "And I'll take care of you. But we need to get off the street right now."

She quickly led the girls to 1st Street and turned right, walking away from Congress Avenue. At the next intersection she turned north on Brazos Street, unsure about where she should take them. She considered her boarding house, but wasn't sure Mrs. Gerwick would appreciate her bringing a scandal into her home.

She kept walking, each girl clung to her side.

After several blocks, the girls turned quiet. Kitty glanced at one, then the other. Their eyes were downcast, their eyes and noses still ran freely.

"Why?" asked Dinah, barely above a whisper. "Why did they do that to my daddy?"

"They thought he was the one that did something bad last night."

"But he didn't!" said Winnie. "He saved me from that man. And you, too. He carried you back to Dr. Gilbert's office."

Kitty stifled a moan. She would have to tell them her part in what happened that day, but not today. "I know, sweetie. But rumors got started, and a mob took matters into their own hands. I'm so sorry Mr. Taylor and I didn't get there in time."

"Daddy whupped up on that man real good last night and told him he'd better leave town or he was gonna kill him. Do you think that's why they hung him?"

Kitty just shook her head. She kept hoping she would wake up from this horrible nightmare, but every sense in her body screamed that this was real—feeling the girls' arms linked in hers as they walked along, hearing their heartrending expressions of grief, seeing the familiar buildings she walked past each day, smelling bread baking nearby...

Put one foot in front of the other, she told herself. *What do I do, Lord? How can I begin to repay the damage I've caused?*

The weight of guilt was almost more than she could bear. A loud groan preceded her own tears of remorse.

They reached the corner of Brazos and 6th Street, and Kitty

saw Justus sitting in his tall chair with his head in his hands.

"Justus!" she called out.

The man climbed down from the chair and met them.

"What are you doing, Miss Doc?"

"I don't know… did you hear…?" She didn't want to say anything more for the girls' sake.

Justus nodded his head.

Kitty walked Justus away from the girls and whispered, "Tell me what to do, Justus. I'm responsible for what happened."

"You didn't know what you was doin', Miss. Don't be so hard on yourself." He looked past her at the girls. "What you gonna do with them?"

"I'm not sure… but I can't take them home with me."

"Do they have a home?"

Kitty nodded.

"Why don't you take 'em home until I can talk to Liberty and see what we can do for 'em."

Kitty exhaled with relief. "I'll pay you something each month—"

"Don't you worry about that right now." He walked over to the girls. "Where do you live?"

Winnie spoke up. "By the cemetery."

"Which cemetery?"

"The one that has all them Confederate soldiers in it," said Winnie, "and famous people."

"She's talkin' about the State Cemetery," said Justus.

"How'd you know who was in it?" Kitty asked Winnie.

"I like to go read the headstones sometimes."

"Not me," said Dinah. "There's ghosts in that place."

"Nu uh! Them's real people restin' there."

"I thought you said you couldn't read," said Kitty.

Winnie nodded. "I can… a little. And I know what a confederate flag looks like."

"Which side is your house on?" asked Justus.

"South side, well, kinda on this corner…" Winnie knelt down and drew the shape of a rectangle with her finger and pointed to the southwest corner, "not too far from the freight yard where Daddy works…" her face skewed up, "worked."

Kitty pulled her up. "We'll wait for you there, Justus."

49

D r. Gilbert and Marshal Davis were trying to hold Hokee up as Ben and another man frantically tried to untie the other end of the rope from the bridge railing. Hokee's hands were free, and he was clawing at the noose choking him.

Jack stopped the horse next to Hokee to let the horse carry his weight. He wrapped his arms around the big man's chest, and the marshal let go to hold the horse in place.

"Just cut it!" the marshal yelled to Ben. "Cut the damn rope!"

Ben pulled out his knife and sawed the rope in two, and Hokee slid off the side of the horse into Dr. Gilbert's arms.

Jack dismounted and let the marshal lead Calibre off to the side. He knelt down beside the doctor, who had removed the noose from the man's neck and was gingerly examining it. Hokee was wheezing, trying to breathe. His eyes were bloodshot and swollen, and his face looked like he'd taken some blows.

Jack asked the doctor. "Is it broke?"

"I don't think so," said Dr. Gilbert, "but his larynx may be damaged."

Hokee's eyes widened when he saw Jack. He tried to say something, but started coughing up blood. The doctor got in his face and told him not to talk, that he was safe.

Hokee grabbed Jack's arm and shook his head.

Jack leaned over and said quietly, "Calm down, Hokee. I know what happened. You were protecting your daughter and Dr. Synatzske. You just focus on getting your breath back. Dr. Gilbert will take good care of you."

Hokee shut his eyes.

The crowd was eerily silent, and Jack looked up, noticing that people were starting to leave. The doctor told Ben to fetch a wagon, that he needed to take Hokee back to his office.

Jack stood up and yelled, "Stop! Everybody stop where you are!" He was a bit surprised when the people did as he demanded.

"There's a reason we have laws in this state, and what happened today is why we *have* to follow the rule of law. A misunderstanding almost cost an innocent man his life today. I know you were reacting out of concern for something you thought had happened. This man helped save his daughter and Dr. Synatzke last night." He turned around to look for Kitty, but she was nowhere to be found. "But you whipped up unfounded rumors into what you thought was the gospel truth, but it wasn't. Every one of you here would have blood on your hands for killing an innocent man today if Marshal Davis hadn't stopped you, and a man who attacked a young girl is still walking the streets free. Go home and and let the law do its job."

The crowd dispersed quietly, and the wagon was retrieved from the other side of the bridge. Only minutes before, the same wagon used for hanging would carry Hokee back to Dr. Gilbert's office.

Jack helped load him into the wagon and then walked around looking for Kitty. Several people apologized to him, and he told them they needed to tell that to Mr. Hokee, not him.

He finally went back to the bridge for Calibre Xane and headed to Kitty's boarding house, hoping she had returned home.

She had not.

Now he was worried. He didn't know when she had slipped off the back of the horse. Maybe she thought they were too late—that Hokee had died.

He slowed at each intersection to look left and right as he headed back to Dr. Gilbert's office, hoping Kitty had somehow returned there. The empty wagon sat in front of the building; a lawman stood beside the door.

Jack dismounted and tied the horse to a hitching post and nodded to the deputy before entering the building. He saw Marshal Davis standing outside an open door.

"I can't find Kitty," he said. "Did she come back here?"

"I haven't seen her," said the marshal.

"She disappeared in all the commotion after the gunshot. Did y'all find out who fired that gun?"

"Not yet."

"How's Hokee?"

He heard a raspy voice from inside the room, so Jack stepped in the room. The doctor was trying to calm him down. Hokee motioned him over with his hand.

"Don't talk, Hokee," said Dr. Gilbert. "You'll make it worse."

Hokee ignored him, trying to speak to Jack.

"Housh... muh housh."

"Your house?" asked Jack.

Hokee nodded, struggling to swallow.

"Muh... guls... saw... me."

Jack repeated what he said. "Your girls saw you?"

"Hang," said Dr. Gilbert. "His girls saw him hang."

"Kitty must've seen them," said Jack. "Where would she have taken them?"

"To Mrs. Gerwick's?"

Jack shook his head. "I already checked. She must've taken them home. Where do you live, Hokee?"

Hokee opened his mouth to speak, but nothing but a rasping sound came out.

"The southwest side of the State Cemetery," the marshal

spoke up from the door. "That's where we picked him up early this morning."

Jack headed out of the room, and the marshal walked him down the hall.

"It's a dogrun house— the roof's about to fall in on half of it. Look for a dead oak tree that's split down the middle out front."

"Thanks," said Jack, nodding his head. He mounted his horse and headed east on Sixth Street towards a side of Austin he'd never visited.

50

Kitty stopped to catch her breath at an intersection.

"How much farther?" she asked the girls. It seemed like they'd walked for miles since the bridge. She felt a little light-headed, and wasn't sure if that was from the bump on her head or the fact that she hadn't eaten anything since noon the day before. Glancing at the girls, they probably hadn't either.

"We're almost there," said Dinah.

"Do y'all have anything to eat at the house?"

"We still have a few potatoes… and maybe one onion," said Winnie. She suddenly stopped walking.

Kitty turned to see why, and the girl's face had turned ashen.

"What is it, Winnie?"

"That's him!" she whispered. She was looking straight ahead.

Kitty looked straight ahead.

Several women gathered in a yard in front of them turned and stared. Children played in the street.

"Where?" Kitty asked. She looked south towards a group of black men standing in front of a place called the Red Rooster.

"Don't look! Maybe he won't see us." She pulled Dinah beside her and started walking stiffly across the street.

Kitty turned around slowly. She saw plenty of Negroes, but not one white man in sight.

Several of the men from the Red Rooster started walking towards her.

One of them spoke. "Ain't you the woman that lied and got the nigger hung?"

She looked around. All eyes were on her, and they weren't friendly. She turned to join the sisters, but they were nowhere in sight.

"Whatchu talkin' about, Muley?" one woman asked.

"This here's the doctor lady who claimed a nigger had his way with her, and they hung him for it."

"I never said that! It was all a misunderstanding," Kitty said, trying to defend herself. She looked around again. A crowd had gathered around the intersection.

She saw a gap and started walking towards it.

"You come to the wrong side a town, lady," a tall, big-boned woman said, pushing her back.

"I just want to help Hokee's daughters," said Kitty, looking around for Winnie and Dinah. "They shouldn't be alone right now."

"We take care of our own," the tall woman said.

The man called Muley spoke up again. "Their daddy was hung without a trial. What should we do about the woman who caused it?"

"An eye for an eye!" someone yelled.

"Maybe she should just disappear," Muley suggested, spurring the others on. "No one would know any different over here."

Kitty darted towards what she thought was the weak link in the crowd—the women, and began pushing her way through. They slapped at her and someone spit on her, but she finally broke through and started running like her life depended on it. She heard footsteps and rocks hissing by, and she almost went down when one hit her in the back.

She kept running until she reached the cemetery, then turned south. She wasn't sure which house was Hokee's; the girls were supposed to take her there. She looked behind her—no one was following her. If she had to knock on every door, she would. She had to get off the street and wait for Justus. Why didn't she tell him to leave a message for Jack? She didn't think this day, which was only half over, could get any worse after the hanging, but it was finding new ways to torment her.

It had never occurred to Kitty that her presence here would provoke people to violence.

She walked towards a small, square house on piers, and a dog came barking out from under the house, forcing her to run again.

"Miss Doc!" Dinah called from the next house. "Over here!"

Kitty hurried toward the open dog-run between the two sections of the house. Dinah hollered at the dog, which seemed scared of her and slunk off. She took Kitty into the right side of dilapidated structure. The left side looked unlivable.

She found Winnie sitting in the corner of the room, knees to her chest, terrified.

"Oh, Winnie," Kitty said, going to sit beside her. "I think you were mistaken."

"He was there," she said firmly.

"I'm sorry we didn't wait for you," said Dinah, "but Winnie was scared."

"I understand." Kitty looked around. Hokee had not improved their living conditions, but something looked familiar. They'd already covered most of the walls in this room with newspaper.

"Are you hungry? I'm famished. Where are those potatoes? I can fix us something while we wait for Justus." She got up and brushed the dust off of her skirt.

Dinah pulled the last of the potatoes from the burlap bag Kitty had given Winnie, along with a small onion. She set a dented pot on the table, and handed Kitty a knife. It was so dull she could barely peal the potato. Dinah lit an oil lamp on the table, providing a little more light for Kitty to work by.

"Where do you cook?"

Dinah pointed to the fireplace. "I liked the other house better."

"Why don't you get a fire going, and we'll have these potatoes cooking in no time." Kitty cut the potatoes and onion in chunks and put them in the pot. She looked in the water bucket and decided to get some fresh water.

"We get it from the well next door," said Dinah, fanning a small flame.

"With the mean dog?"

Dinah snickered. "No, the other side. They don't mind."

"I'll be right back," said Kitty. She stepped through the door and walked to the right in the dog-run towards the back of the house. She didn't want to chance anyone else seeing her and causing another melee.

She didn't have to worry about a broken step at this house; The back had no steps at all, only a two foot drop. She pulled up her skirt to keep from tripping over it when someone grabbed her ankles and jerked them forward, flipping her on her back. She landed hard, knocking the breath out of her. The bucket went flying. She lay there gasping to catch her breath when rough hands jerked her to her feet. One clamped roughly over her mouth, like she was capable of making a sound other than struggling to catch her breath.

The man pulled her against his chest.

"I told you this was none of your business," a voice spoke directly in her ear as he dragged her down the middle of the dog-run.

Kitty thought she would pass out when she recognized that phrase from the night before.

"But then I thought you'd fixed it for me when they hung that man, but here you are." He kicked open the door and drug her through it.

Dinah screamed.

"Shut up or I'll break her neck," the man said.

Dinah slapped both of her hands over her mouth.

Winnie started moaning and rocking.

The room began to go dark. Kitty started yanking at the

hand over her mouth and nose so she could get a breath. She finally bit it as hard as she could, and the man yelled in pain, flinging her to the floor. Kitty pushed herself onto her hands and knees, sucking in air loudly, desperately trying to get air into her lungs.

"You shoulda stayed where you belonged, Miss," he said, rubbing his hand. "You're in our world now."

Kitty turned her head and was shocked when she recognized Winnie's attacker. "You're a... Negro!" she said between breaths, sitting up. She felt the table leg against her back.

The man stared at her for a moment, and then guffawed. "What did you think I was?"

"I thought you were a white man." She tried to remember where the knife was on the table.

The man walked over to a cracked mirror on the wall, took off his hat and looked at himself. "They say I do look like my daddy." He turned towards Kitty. "Why is it that three-quarters of me is white, but I'm still a nigger?" He looked back at the mirror. "Now that isn't fair at all."

"What are you doing here? What do you want with us?" Kitty asked.

"Well, I'm not rightly sure."

"Why don't you leave before you get into more trouble?"

He turned sharply. "Trouble? I couldn't get in more trouble than I already am. I harmed a white woman."

"You put your hands on a young girl."

He glanced at Winnie. "She don't matter."

Kitty grabbed the edge of the table and pulled herself up. "Of course she matters!"

The man looked her up and down. "But the odd thing is, I thought you was one of us last night in that dark room. I thought you must've belonged to that man the way he was whuppin' up on me."

"Hokee was defending his daughter."

"I saw him carry you outta there. He woulda left you if he didn't care. But the ironic thing is... the man helped you and you got him hung."

Kitty's heart sunk when she looked towards Dinah, but the girl was glaring at Muley.

"That ain't true! I know he's lying, Miss Doc." She turned to Kitty.

Kitty wasn't sure what to say. "Now's not the time to talk about it."

"Miss Doc?"

The man turned back to the mirror to put his hat on. "It don't matter what I do now cuz I'm a dead man if y'all walk out of here," he said as easily as he might have made a statement about the weather.

Kitty felt a sinister shift in the room, and she knew she had to do something. She looked toward Winnie, willing her to look up. But the girl kept crying quietly with her head down. But Dinah… Dinah was watching her like a hawk. Kitty nodded subtly toward the door as she felt for the knife behind her. Dinah's eyes widened.

"You don't want to hurt us, Mr. Muley." Kitty's fingers touched the blade, thankful it was so dull. She grasped the knife handle and held it behind her. *Dear Lord, please help us.*

The man exhaled loudly. "No, I don't, but I got no choice—"

"You always have a choice. Didn't anyone teach you about right and wrong?" She stepped closer to his left, hoping to get Dinah out of his periphery. "Did anyone ever take you to church?"

He turned suddenly towards her. "Don't you go talking to me about church. God quit on me a long time ago." He looked down. "What you got there behind your back?"

Kitty let go of the knife and held out her hands. "Nothing." She suddenly grabbed the pan of potatoes and hurled it at him. "Run, Dinah!" She grabbed a hold of him as hard as she could to give Dinah a chance to get away, but Muley cast her aside like a rag doll and lunged at Dinah.

Kitty fell over a chair and hit the wall hard, landing in a crumpled heap on the floor. Dinah was jerking at the door when Muley grabbed her. She started screaming…loudly, and he put his arm across her throat like a vise to shut her up.

Suddenly Winnie came alive. She pounced on Muley's back, slapping at his head. The dust rose in the sunlight as the three moved across the floor, spinning in some kind of grisly dance. Dinah fell to the floor with a bloody nose. The man slammed Winnie into the wall, dislodging her from his back.

Kitty shut her eyes for only a moment, she thought, but the smell of smoke forced her awake. Fire?! The oil lamp lay shattered and burning on the floor as flames tore across the newspaper wall. She started crawling towards the door.

Muley and the girls were gone. Maybe they'd gotten away. No, she could hear them screaming outside. *Lord, please keep them safe.*

She heard someone calling her name and tried to answer, but she couldn't for coughing.

The door hit her as it opened, strong arms lifted her from the floor, and she struggled to breathe again. A sharp pain in her side was the last thing she remembered.

J ack sat beside the bed, holding Kitty's hand. Dr. Gilbert said she probably cracked a rib. He said in spite of the fire, her lungs didn't seem to be too affected by the smoke. The fire had just started when they came upon the house. The girls were screaming in the dog-run that Miss Doc was inside.

Jack cringed at the thought that if he'd been only a few minutes later, he would have lost her. Jack didn't know how badly Kitty was hurt, so he took her immediately to Dr. Gilbert's office.

Justus told him later that a number of the neighbors showed up to fight the fire, but all they could do was to keep the neighboring houses from catching fire since they couldn't save the old tinderbox. Justus said the girls said the man that had attacked Winnie had come to the house, and that in y'all's struggle to get away from him, the lamp overturned. They were able to give the marshal a good description of the man that had attacked them, and officers were already looking for him.

Dr. Gilbert gave Jack the option of taking Kitty to the hospital or remaining at his clinic. He asked him what the hospital would do differently, and the doctor told him that she would be in a ward with other women. Jack chose the clinic, away from prying eyes and ears.

Dr. Gilbert wanted to keep Hokee longer, but once the morphine wore off, and he was able to keep his legs under him, he walked out the back of the office and down the alley. Jack figured the man would probably leave Austin for good, and he didn't blame him.

Dr. Gilbert had given Kitty something for the pain and instructed Jack to make sure she moved as little as possible, so he remained by her bed. Mrs. Gilbert came by with some supper for them both, and promised to be back with breakfast in the morning. Dr. Gilbert went home with instructions for Jack to fetch him if there was any problem.

Jack propped his feet on another chair, and dozed off and on through the night. Kitty stirred several times, asking for water once. Around daybreak, her eyes flew open.

"Girls!?" she called out. She tried to sit up, but Jack put his hand on her shoulder.

"Be still! The girls are fine—Justus took them to Liberty's house."

Her eyes finally focused on his face. "Oh, Jack." She touched his face.

"I'm right here."

She looked around, trying to get her bearings.

"You're at the clinic. Do you remember what happened?"

"I was hoping it was all a bad dream," she said resignedly. "But it wasn't, was it?"

"No, love. I'm sorry."

"Is that awful day past us now?"

"Yes, and everything's set to right."

Kitty shook her head and shut her eyes as the tears came. "It will never be set to right for those girls."

"Their daddy's alive, honey."

"What?"

"Hokee's alive. We got him down in time."

He watched the relief wash over her.

"Thank you, Lord," she said as the tears fell again. "It should've snapped his neck."

"He's a strong man—his neck is thick as a bull's. He can't speak much right now, but Dr. Gilbert said his voice box should heal in time."

"The thought that something I said was responsible for killing a man was a burden I don't think I could've handled."

He grasped her hand. "I could say the same about losing you. The marshal told me what the girls said, but I'd like to hear what happened from you, and I'm sure he will, too, when he comes back this morning."

Kitty tried to take a deep breath, but winced at the pain. She felt the wrapping around her chest. "That must be a cracked rib," she deduced. "One of the last things I remember was trying to distract him so Dinah could go get help. Did they catch him?"

Jack made a gutteral sound. "I think he fled when we showed up. If I'd have known he was so close, I would've gone after him."

"I'm glad you didn't, Jack. He was a desperate man."

"How did he find you?"

"When we got to the bridge, I couldn't bear the sight of Hokee...," she shuddered at the memory, "so I tried to get away from that place. Then I saw Winnie and Dinah watching their father... and realized they were on their own. I didn't know where else to take them but their home. Then a few blocks away, Winnie told me she saw him."

"The man that attacked her?"

Kitty nodded. "I didn't believe her because all I saw were black folks around there. Before I knew it, a crowd had gathered and somebody knew who I was and told everyone that I had lied and caused a black man to be hung. I couldn't believe word had traveled so fast.

"The girls had already left the area, and I thought my life was over with what those people were telling me. But I pushed through the crowd and ran until I found the girls' house. We were waiting for Justus to come pick us up, but that man must've followed me there."

"This was the same man who attacked Winnie in the alley?"

Kitty nodded. "But all that time I thought a white man had attacked her, Jack. The light was dim in the back of Franklin's store, but I was convinced I was looking at a white man. And standing in that intersection, I was still looking for a white man after Winnie told me she saw him."

"Who was he?"

"They called him... Muley." She thought for a moment. "*He* was the one inciting everyone to avenge Hokee, although he never called him by name. I couldn't figure out how this man knew about the hanging so quickly. But Muley must've figured his troubles were over since Hokee was arrested, and I guess he felt safe enough on that side of town. He blended in so well I didn't even recognize him." Kitty looked at Jack. "He told me he was three-quarters white. Maybe that's why they called him Muley... he was a mulatto."

"Well, a mule is half..." Jack didn't finish that sentence. "It's probably a nickname, but that's something for the marshal to go on. Sounds like the people in the neighborhood knew him."

"I made the mistake of opening my mouth to defend myself in that crowd of people, but it's like they didn't want to hear the truth. They believed what they wanted to believe... that I was guilty."

"Like the mob that took Hokee."

"I just wanted to help the girls, and I ended up almost destroying that family."

"You did help them, Kitty. Stop berating yourself about the things that went wrong. Focus on the things that went right. You and Bertie saved that baby's life, and Winnie's, too. You've tried to help those girls every chance you got. And you kept that man from hurting Winnie, and Hokee knows that."

Dr. Gilbert knocked and stepped into the room. "How's my favorite doctor this morning?"

"Shirking my duty. I'm sorry to be such a burden, Dr. Gilbert."

"You're no burden," he said as he leaned over and placed his hand on her forehead, felt the back of her head, and looked into her eyes. "How's the pain?"

"Bearable if I don't breathe."

"You won't be able to do much the next few weeks. Maybe that will give you time to plan your wedding." He straightened up. "I didn't mean to eavesdrop, but helping people's a messy business. It usually doesn't involve the degree of danger you've encountered lately, but there is a cost. I believe that's why you pursued this profession, Miss Doc, and that took a lot of courage on your part. But you have to focus on the good and not the bad, or it will eat you alive."

"That's what I've been trying to tell her, but you worded it much better," said Jack.

"Age and experience have to count for something," the doctor said, grinning.

52

Marshal Davis stopped by mid-morning to get Kitty's statement of the incident, and Kitty insisted that Jack take a break and get away from the office for a while—that she was in good hands with Dr. Gilbert and Mrs. Leigh, who checked on her regularly.

Jack headed to his house for the first time since he'd left town by train several days before to look for a new hometown. He was on his third day wearing the same clothes. He smiled to himself thinking how his mother would have a conniption fit.

The house was chilly, but he didn't bother to make a fire. The weather was mild, so he could stand it the short time he would take to wash up and shave, and change into a clean white shirt and pants. He grabbed his coat and hat and headed out the door.

He paused before he crossed Brazos Street and glanced toward his old office across the street to his right. He hadn't been back since Jarvis revealed his big secret, but he still needed to clean out his desk and shelves at work. He'd put that off, not wanting to face Jarvis, but he also needed to tell him the truth.

But not today.

He walked across the street and shook his old friend's hand before climbing up in the chair.

"How you doin', Justus?"

"I got my health, I got my family, I got my faith," he said, smiling as he wiped the dust off Jack's boots. "And I think we're all doin' much better after yesterday. How's Miss Doc?"

"It'll take some time, but she'll mend. How are the girls?"

"They doin' all right, 'specially since they saw their daddy last night." He started smearing blacking on the boot.

"Hokee went out there?"

"Yep. He told 'em he'd be back for 'em, or that's what we gathered. He didn't talk much or stay long."

"Why can't he just settle down?"

"I told him he could stay with me. It's just me and my youngest, and Bertie sent the boys over to make room for the girls, but Hokee refused my offer. He did accept an old quilt from me. I think he spent the night in the old house they used to live in."

"You think he'll stay?"

"Who knows, but Bertie's gonna move heaven and earth to try to convince him. She feels partly responsible for what happened to him."

Jack nodded. "Same with Kitty." He watched Justus get into the rythym of polishing the boots.

When he was finished, Jack climbed down and gave Justus a dollar. When the old man started to dig around the drawer for change, Jack stopped him.

"Keep it, Justus. You earned it yesterday, and I appreciate your help."

The old man nodded. "Thank you, sir. You did all right yourself."

Something caught his eye across the street at the Driskill. A striking woman stepped out of shadow of the door and looked up and down the street. Jack noticed she wore a hat with a veil covering half of her face. She started walking towards Brazos Street.

"Mother?" he said aloud. Surely he was mistaken. She would've told him if she was coming to Austin.

Then he saw where she was heading… toward the Baldwin

Law Office.

That wasn't good.

He dodged the horses and wagons and hurried diagonally across the intersection, but his mother had already stepped inside the office lobby.

The ever efficient Emery met him with, "Can I help..." until he realized to whom he was speaking.

"Jack! Where have you been? Mr. Baldwin kept saying you were away on business, but we knew something was wrong. And your mother just walked in."

"Yes, and I don't have time to explain now, but I'm relocating to Taylor and need to clean out my office."

"What?!"

"I've just come to get my mother out of here. Could you pack everything up for me, and I'll come back later to get it? I'd really appreciate your help."

"Of course, but—"

"Thanks," he said, ending the conversation and heading down the hall.

Jack paused in front of Jarvis's door. He could hear Jarvis asking about her face. He cringed, knowing how sensitive his mother was about her scars.

"I almost died in a fire..."

"I'm sorry."

"I'm not. I was able to save a little girl, but that's not what I want to talk about. Where have you been all these years?"

"I went back for you, Florine, but you had already left... with that Indian."

"Who has more integrity than you will ever have, Eustace."

"My name is Jarvis Baldwin. I turned my life around and made something of myself; something I could bequeath to our son."

Mercy was quiet.

"I didn't mean to make you cry, Flo."

Jack reached for the door knob, but he stopped when he heard his mother speak again.

"My name is Mercy Taylor now, *Mrs. Jimmy* Taylor. I turned my life around, too. I'm not the same self-centered girl you once knew. My husband and I have raised three wonderful children: Jack and his two sisters."

"He's a fine boy; you raised him right."

"Why now?" she asked. "Why didn't you contact me years ago about your son?"

"I didn't realize how lonely it would be to come to the end of my life and have no one coming behind me... of my blood. I'm sorry I left you in Fort Worth, but I came back for you and our child."

"I've come here to set you straight about Jack."

"I know I could never take the place of his father, but I've made him my heir. You wouldn't deny him that, would you?"

"I appreciate all you've done for him, Jarvis, but you should have talked to me first." She paused. "Jack isn't your son."

Silence.

"But he's your firstborn."

"No, my firstborn is buried in Brownwood."

Jack could hear the pain in her voice.

"He was born too early. But he was beautiful, Jarvis, and he was so loved." Her voice broke. "I would have fought the world to save him. I came here with so much anger in my heart for you causing such distress for Jack, but seeing your face now, all I feel is sadness for you. I hope you find what you're looking for, but it isn't with my boy."

Jack had heard enough, and he wasn't ready to face Jarvis yet, so he walked quickly down the hall and outside to wait for his mother.

After a few minutes, Mercy opened the door, and paused to pull her veil down lower on her face.

"I hope you were planning to see me while you were in town," said Jack.

Startled at first, his mother immediately composed herself. "Of course I was. I just had to take care of some business first." She let him kiss her on the cheek.

"You came to Austin again by yourself, Mother?"

"No, your father is drinking coffee across the street. I told him I needed to face Jarvis alone, so I made him promise to not come with me. I also made him promise to not punch Jarvis if he happened to see him while he was in town."

Jack couldn't help but grin at that.

She held out her arm for Jack to escort her across the street.

"So you told Jarvis the truth."

"Yes, and ever since you told us what he said to you, I've wanted to tear him from limb to limb. But when I actually faced him, I felt more sorrow for him than anger."

"Why, Mother? He's done nothing but hurt you—and…"

Mercy put her gloved hand to his lips. "I'm not going to dwell on that. It's harder for me to forgive him for what he did to you than to forgive him for what he did to me. But it dawned on me that for several years now Jarvis believed he had the most extraordinary son, and I just tore that away from him."

His mother's words moved him deeply.

She paused in front of the Driskill and faced him. He was surprised to see tears in her eyes.

"Do you know how much your father changed my life, Jack? Eustace—Jarvis abandoning me in Fort Worth was the best thing that ever happened to me. I tried to imagine what it would be like to not have you in my life, and it hurt too badly to even think about it. And yet, that is what Jarvis is feeling right now."

"So you've forgiven him?"

She dabbed her eye with her gloved hand and nodded. "It costs too much to hang onto the anger."

53

Twenty-three days after the hanging, Justus told Jack that Hokee finally agreed to see Kitty. Jack knew she had been anxious to talk to him since that "awful day," as she referred to it, anxious to apologize and get on with her life.

So Jack accompanied her to Clarksville, her first visit since the attack. Dr. Gilbert had already hired a new doctor who agreed to visit Clarksville twice a month.

Jack stopped the carriage in front of the house and gathered up several packages. They walked across a yard clear of tall grass and up sturdy porch steps onto a clean porch. A simple wreath of twisted live oak branches hung on the door. Christmas was only four days away, and they were looking forward to heading to Grace the next morning. Jack would get to introduce Kitty to the rest of the Taylor clan.

"You ready?" he whispered before he knocked.

Kitty took a deep breath and nodded.

Jack knocked solidly on the door, and almost before he drew his hand away, Winnie and Dinah opened the door. Jack realized they must've been watching from the window. Kitty embraced each of them, then clucked like a mother hen about how beautiful they were.

Jack took another look and realized that the girls were dressed in clothes that fit them; their hair neatly combed, and faces scrubbed. He could see Liberty and Justus's touch all over the place.

Kitty commented on how nice the house looked, and Jack looked around himself, noticing a large table with four mismatched chairs, and mismatched cups and small plates on the table. A couple of other chairs were placed against a wall.

"Are these for us?" Dinah asked about the gifts.

"Yes, for Christmas and not before," said Jack handed them to Dinah, who hugged them to herself as she walked across and set them in the corner of the room.

"If that's all right with your father," added Kitty, looking around for Hokee.

"It's all right with Daddy," said Winnie, then she hollered, Daddy! They're here!"

Hokee stepped up from the kitchen, and nodded to Jack and Kitty. Jack walked over and shook his hand.

"Would you like some coffee?" he asked, tentatively.

Jack realized that was the most words he'd ever heard coming out of the man's mouth at one time.

"Yes."

"We'd love some," added Kitty.

"Girls?" he said, which seemed to be their cue to get the coffee.

He stood there awkwardly after girls disappeared down the kitchen steps, then walked over to the table, pulled out a chair and sat down. Then he stood up again and motioned for Jack and Kitty to sit.

Kitty wasted no time after sitting. "Mr. Hokee, I've been wanting to apologize for what happened that awful day."

Hokee shook his head. "No need."

"But—"

"Justus told me. And you were hurt trying to help my girls—twice. I don't know what woulda happened to Winnie if you hadna been there." He turned to Jack. "And if you and Justus hadna got to the house when you did…" He couldn't finish the sentence.

"I have to give the good Lord credit for that," said Jack.

Hokee nodded.

Winnie brought the coffee pot, holding the hot handle with a towel. She poured coffee in each cup, and Dinah scooted them in front of Kitty, Jack and Hokee. Then both girls sat down on half of the remaining chair.

"Thank you," said Jack, sipping the hot, bitter coffee. "That sure feels good on a chilly day."

Winnie beamed.

The silence felt awkward until someone knocked on the door.

"We got cake comin'," Winnie explained proudly.

"Well, answer the door, girl," said Hokee.

Winnie jumped up and opened the door.

Ira, Liberty and Justus stepped in. Liberty set a plain cake on the table as she greeted everyone. Dinah brought the other two chairs to the table while Winnie poured coffee for them, running out before the last cup.

"We're out," she said.

"Well, go make some more," said Hokee.

Liberty spoke up. "I'm not much of a coffee drinker," she said. "Don't make any more just for me." She slid her cup of coffee in front of Justus and asked Dinah to get her a knife to cut the cake.

Jack felt much more comfortable with Justus present, and Kitty seemed to be more at ease, too.

Liberty started to cut the cake, then asked Dinah to do it. Jack realized Liberty was still teaching them.

"Have you met the new doctor?" asked Kitty.

Liberty nodded as she passed a plate of cake to Hokee. "He's nice, but he's scared to death of us." She chuckled. "Kinda like you were in the beginning. It'll take us a little while to get used to him, too, but everyone is so thankful that he's coming. Daddy says y'all are moving to Taylor soon."

"Yes, after we get married in Galveston after the first of the year."

"That doesn't give you much time."

Kitty smiled at Jack. "It's not the best time of year to have a wedding, but it'll be very simple with only our immediate families there."

Jack was content to let the women talk, but Justus and Ira decided they didn't need to hear all of that, and suggested the men take their coffee and go to the porch. Hokee didn't waste any time pushing away from the table to follow them. Winnie and Dinah slipped into the empty seats, hanging onto every word Liberty and Kitty said.

Justus carried a chair outside, claiming his age gave him special privileges. Jack sat on the porch floor beside him, and Ira sat on the steps. Hokee stood there for a moment, then sat down and leaned up against the wall.

"How's your health, Hokee?" Jack asked, wanting to find out about his throat, but he didn't want to remind him of the hanging.

"Fine."

He hoped Kitty would be satisfied with that answer. "You still working at the freight yard?" Jack knew the answer to that, too; Justus kept him informed, but he couldn't think of anything else to talk about.

Hokee nodded. "My boss fired me for missing a couple a days, but the marshal put in a good word for me."

"I'm glad to hear that," said Jack.

They sat there in the quiet, until Jack noticed it wasn't quiet at all. Sparrows chirped in an elm tree next to the house. He could hear children playing nearby, a donkey brayed, and then a woman started hollering down the road.

"Lester's gone and messed up again, sounds like," said Ira, chuckling.

"He'll be sleepin' with the chickens tonight," said Justus.

Hokee snickered, and the others turned and looked at him, not quite sure what that sound was that came from his direction. But the man actually had a smile on his face. Then it disappeared.

"What?" he asked, defensively.

"Nuthin'," said Ira. "We just never seen you smile."

"I was wunderin' why my face was hurtin'," he said.

Ira looked at Justus. "Did Hokee just say somethin' funny?"

Justus looked at Jack. "I think he did." The old man threw his head back and guffawed.

That got them all to laughing, even Hokee.

After a little while, Kitty came to the door, saying they needed to get home to finish packing.

"I don't know if I'll get to see you before we move to Taylor," Kitty told Liberty, giving her a hug. "I'm going to miss you, my friend."

"I can't thank you enough for what you done for us, and it all started with you havin' the courage to come out here and take care of my husband. Then, stubborn woman, you kept on a comin'," said Liberty, hugging her again. She looked at Jack. "And thank you for helpin' us. I don't know what woulda happened if you hadn't run those speculators off."

"You're welcome," said Jack, "but I'm afraid more will probably come, as fast as Austin is growing."

Ira stepped up and shook his hand. "Well, we'll keep standing our ground."

Kitty turned to face Hokee. "I won't be around to pester you anymore, Mr. Hokee," she said, offering her gloved hand.

He gingerly took it, like it might break. He started to say something, but couldn't seem to get the words out. But the look in his eyes spoke volumes.

Jack offered his hand, and Hokee took it, but Jack wouldn't let go until the man looked him in the eye. Hokee looked up in alarm. Jack held on until Hokee's expression mirrored his own. He finally smiled, and Jack nodded and let go.

Kitty hugged the girls goodbye, and Justus walked her and Jack to the carriage.

"Do you think they'll ever find Muley?" Jack asked the old man.

"Nah." He shook his head.

"So the man's still walking around free," said Kitty.

"No, ma'am. I debated about telling you this, but I don't

want you to worry none, Miss Doc. A woman walked up to me on the street a few days after the hanging, and she told me, 'You tell the lady doctor we're sorry about Muley, and that we take care of our own,' and those was her exact words."

Kitty frowned. "A woman told me that on the street when they were about to stone me. Does that mean they're protecting that man?"

"No, ma'am," Justus glanced at Jack, "I figure it was just the opposite."

When Kitty started to ask him to explain, Jack stopped her.

"Justus says you have nothing to worry about, so that's good enough for me."

Jack noticed Kitty's eyes widen when she realized what Justus meant.

"But, Justus, he needed to get right with—"

"I'm sure somebody gave him the chance, Miss Doc, like the thief on the cross."

"I hope so," she said, shuddering.

"Good night, Miss Doc."

She composed herself. "Good night, Justus. I'll see you before we move to Taylor."

"And you definitely haven't seen the last of me," said Jack, helping Kitty into the carriage.

"You got some important work in front of you," said Justus. "Don't forget us."

Jack turned and looked at the old man. His eyes carried a lifetime of hurt, but Jack also saw something else there... hope. Jack couldn't help but embrace his old friend, hoping he could change things for the better for Justus. He thought about the man's name, realizing Justus's mother had the same hope for her son.

"What did you tell me a while back, that people don't have to do anything if they don't know anything?"

Justus nodded. "They keep themselves busy and blind to what's going on around them. That way their consciences just keep on sleepin' and they don't have to do nuthin'."

Jack climbed up in the carriage and took the reins. "Help me keep my eyes open, Justus."

"I will, son."

Author's Note

One of the best things about writing historical fiction is researching and learning about actual people and events in our history. Austin has a fascinating history, and like most communities, it has its dark side, too. The capital of Texas made a great backdrop for the fictional characters that are still connected to the original Taylor family from Grace, Texas.

The actual people, things, places or events that were used or mentioned in the story include:

1. The Driskill Hotel in Austin
2. Tillotson College
3. Moonlight towers in Austin
4. William Porter (O. Henry)
5. Servant Girl Murders in Austin
6. Henry Brown and William Robinson aka Ben Wheeler
7. The Black Codes
8. Spindletop oil gusher, January 10, 1901
9. Dr. Joe & Daisy Gilbert
10. John Philip Sousa
11. Edward 'Ned' Green and Mabel
12. Netty Green, the witch of Wall Street
13. The *Black and Tan Faction* of the Republican Party
14. Austin Dam and McDonald Lake
15. Governor Elisha Pease & his Woodlawn Plantation
16. Clarksville, Texas (Freedmen community)
17. The Confederates Home in Austin
18. William 'Bill' McDonald
19. Mirabeau Lamar & Waterloo, Texas
20. The Lily Whites
21. Norris Cuney
22. Pinckney Pinchback, first Black governor of Louisiana
23. Governor Edmund Davis
24. Wheatsville, Texas (Freedman community)
25. Guy Town in Austin
26. Jack Johnson, champion boxer, Galveston
27. Future Texas governor Dan Moody from Taylor, Texas, introduced as a young boy in the story

1

All of the actual people, things, events and places on the list were mentioned as historical references or were used as characters and settings in a fictional way. For the people in history that the fictional characters encountered in this story, I tried to stay true to the real person's character and personality.

Racism is taught, and although laws and attitudes have slowly improved, we must be continually mindful that racism will grow like a cancer if we all don't actively work to extinguish it. We must never assume right will always win out with little effort on everyone's part. We must take the blinders off, and *everyone* must make the effort to learn the whole story, not just hearsay and bits and pieces that can so easily mask or distort the truth.

My original author's note was much longer than this, but I decided to shorten it considerably and just leave you with the following brief thoughts. Black history is not just for Blacks.

Black history is American history is our history.

> *Oh, for the day when Americans are categorized by citizenship, character, compassion and contributions to mankind; when colors refer to our flag instead of labels to brandish as a crutch or a bully stick; when our history is one history, undivided, "and with liberty and justice for all."*
>
> -Donna Van Cleve